Claudia Crawford is the pen name of an American writer and entrepreneur who divides her time between London (where she is a member of the Chelsea Society) and New York. Among the subjects of her previous non-fiction books are the British Royal Family, Marilyn Monroe and Princess Grace of Monaco. Her reason for using a pseudonym is 'to protect the guilty'. *Nice Girls* is her first novel.

Nice Girls

Claudia Crawford

HEADLINE

Copyright © 1993 Claudia Crawford

The right of Claudia Crawford to be identified as the Author of
the Work has been asserted by her in accordance with the
Copyright, Designs and Patents Act 1988.

First published in Great Britain in 1993
by HEADLINE BOOK PUBLISHING PLC

First published in paperback in 1993
by HEADLINE BOOK PUBLISHING PLC

10 9 8 7 6 5 4 3 2 1

All rights reserved. No part of this publication may be
reproduced, stored in a retrieval system, or transmitted,
in any form or by any means without the prior written
permission of the publisher, nor be otherwise circulated
in any form of binding or cover other than that in which
it is published and without a similar condition being
imposed on the subsequent purchaser.

All characters in this publication are fictitious
and any resemblance to real persons, living or dead,
is purely coincidental.

ISBN 0 7472 4170 8

Printed and bound in Great Britain by
HarperCollins Manufacturing, Glasgow

HEADLINE BOOK PUBLISHING PLC
Headline House
79 Great Titchfield Street
London W1P 7FN

For Audrey LaFehr with gratitude

There is a Nick Albert in every woman's life, the kind of man who arouses abberant behaviour in the most sensible and desperate longing in the most cheerful, a man of such lyrical impact that for years afterwards and despite whatever else has happened, there remains the lingering wistful question, 'Would I have been better off if I had never met him?' The answer invariably is no . . .

PROLOGUE

Georgina

London, 1988

In the erotic history of London, Bond Street is not particularly noteworthy for its romantic associations. Its name, though world-famous, provides no clue to its origins. It was not named for a royal personage nor, as some American tourists have assumed, for an ancestor of Agent 007, James Bond. In point of dull fact, it dates back rather prosaically to a certain Sir Thomas Bond, a seventeenth-century property speculator.

For Georgina Crane, however, the narrow shop-lined road that cuts through the heart of Mayfair from Piccadilly to Oxford Street was a metaphor for bliss.

For it was in Bond Street, on the pavement outside Asprey's, that she had first encountered Nick Albert over twenty years ago. Every detail of that chance meeting remained permanently etched in her memory and made her giddy to this day. It was hard to believe that so many years had gone by, almost half her life. So much had happened to her and to Nick, and for that matter to Mona and Amy, the two most intricately and personally involved in their lives during those halcyon early days. Now, incredibly, joyfully – dare she say triumphantly? – she was once again in Bond Street, on the pavement outside Asprey's, smiling at her reflection in its window as she made her way to Smythson's to collect her wedding invitations.

She'd done it. She'd waited. She'd maneuvered. She'd swallowed her anger and her pride and kept her own private counsel, confiding in no one. During those twenty years she had become a hugely successful businesswoman, a 'Chelsea bird tycoon' according to the *Financial Times*, a patron of the arts, a trend-setter and hostess. Coolly impervious to speculation as to why she had never married, she had patiently spun her spider's web and snared her prey. Nick

Albert was hers at last. Yet now, seated comfortably within Smythson's pampered confines, a rush of tears threatened her composure as she examined the heavy cream vellum and ran trembling fingers over the engraved lettering:

****

The Lady Georgina Crane and the
Honourable Nicholas Albert request the pleasure
of the company of

———————————————————————

at their marriage

at twelve noon St. Columba's Church
June tenth next and Pont Street, London
afterwards at
Chelsea Mews.
 RSVP: Four Chelsea
 Mews, off the
 King's Road
 London SW 3

****

'Is everything satisfactory, Madam?'

'Satisfactory' did not begin to describe her elation. 'Satisfactory' was hardly the word for her triumph, but it would do very nicely nonetheless, a silent roar of exultation. *Remember, Georgina dear*, mummy had always cautioned, *it isn't lady-like to gloat*. But gloat she must, if only inwardly. Declare a bank holiday, run up the flags! Georgina and Nick were getting married!

'Quite satisfactory, thank you.'

'Shall I send them 'round by hand?'

'No, thank you. My car is collecting me.' The calligrapher would be arriving at the mews to inscribe the individual guest names and do the envelopes. Neither she nor Nick had parents or family. The wedding guests would be primarily friends, members of the fashion and financial press, magazine editors, television news-readers, cherished customers, and her entire British Junque Ltd. staff, including those at the Chelsea Mews headquarters and the salespeople at the six London-area shops. And of course it wouldn't be a proper wedding without Mona Davidson and Amy Humphries in attendance. The two Americans had been mad for Nick Albert in

Nice Girls

the old days. Who could blame them? Silly young girls in London for the first time, and who was the first Englishman they should meet? By now he was just an adolescent memory, she was sure. Both had returned to America after that chaotic summer, married, and had children. Mona had divorced, but now was sending regular bulletins about a new person called 'Sidney' who sounded rather fun.

Nick was supposed to be waiting for her in Bond Street. There was no sign of him. The man was hopeless when it came to time. The Patek-Phillipe watch had not helped because he no longer had it. 'Someone nicked it,' he had said, apparently when he took it off at some gambling club in the Fulham Road because it cramped his style. He couldn't really remember which club. The insurance would cover the loss, he was sure.

Pacing up and down, straining to contain her annoyance and impatience, Georgina realized it had been a romantic and sentimental bit of nonsense to ask her fiancé to run her home from the stationer's with their wedding invitations on her lap and the two of them holding hands. Sheer shopgirl rubbish. She should never have asked him to collect her. She should never have expected him to show up on time. If at all. If she had wanted that kind of promptness, she should have married Simon Longe. If she had wanted to be sure of finding her car waiting for her at a given place at a given time, she should have asked her regular driver.

After half an hour, and with the image of Smythson's manager peering at her as he opened the door for another client, she set off along Bond Street toward Piccadilly, slowing her pace outside Asprey's on the sacred patch of pavement on which she had first laid eyes on Nick Albert. *The swine!* She tried to be furious but she was too happy. At this hour, taxis were like hen's teeth. Turning into Piccadilly, she strode fiercely through the crowds until she had reached the Green Park Hotel, where a five-pound note to the doorman got her a taxi ahead of the waiting queue.

Back at Chelsea Mews, the calligrapher had arrived. Nick Albert had not. Surely he must have rung to apologize for missing her at Smythson's. He had not. But surely he remembered they were dressing for drinks at the Spanish Embassy, the vernissage at the Hayward, and the supper party at Shelagh and Phil's? This was to be their first night on the town as a couple. Where in *hell* could he be?

The calligrapher was asking, 'Only two invitations to America?'

Inquisitive cow! What business was it of hers? Why didn't she shut up and do what she was being paid to do, without asking stupid questions? 'Why do you ask?' she demanded.

'The postage. I've set these two aside for air mail: Mrs. Davidson, Mrs. Humphries. I can post them on my way home.'

Ashamed of her own rudeness, Georgina smiled warmly at the woman. 'How very kind of you to think of that.'

Mona and Amy. Suddenly it was even more important than she had first realized to have her old friends with her when she married Nick Albert. They could stay with her in the mews house they had once shared, but in comfort and luxury as compared to their student days. The three of them would laugh and cry and reminisce, and drink champagne, and send out for fish and chips, and tell each other they looked better now than they did then and talk about men in general and Nick Albert in particular.

Before sealing their envelopes she scribbled a personal note to each, inviting them to London as her guest, all expenses paid including first-class air fare. 'Please say yes. It will be great fun. Promise! I want you and need you with me.'

By the time Nick showed up, singing and disheveled, they had missed the Spanish Embassy drinks and the Hayward vernissage.

'Shall I beg off Shelagh and Phil?' she asked.

'You mean you're not going to tick me off?'

She smiled at him with a tenderness that surprised them both. 'Why would I do that?'

'I'm late and I'm pissed.'

'The point is you're here.'

Tears filled his eyes. 'You're the only woman who's ever really loved me. I promise to love you with all my heart for ever and ever.'

She believed that he believed every word he was saying, and she was for the moment content with her life, except for the nagging premonition that something would go wrong. In nightmare dreams of the forthcoming wedding, she was Jane Eyre about to marry Mr. Rochester when Richard Mason stops the wedding. If anything, anything at all was to keep her from marrying Nick Albert, she wanted Mona and Amy with her to help soften the blow.

That's what friends were for.

Mona

New York City, 1988

A Streetcar Named Desire, Scene Eleven:

BLANCHE
Whoever you are, I have always depended on the kindness of strangers.

Emphasis on *strangers*? Mona had rehearsed the line so many times it was beginning to sound like gibberish to her. Blanche's final words, her epitaph in effect, had become as difficult to interpret as 'To be or not to be.' Audiences knew it by heart, welcomed it as a familiar last gasp of innocence destroyed, and recited along with it.

At yesterday's run-through Bill Neal had encouraged: 'Try it another way, pet. Switch the emphasis. Lots of time to experiment.' This was to be his New York debut as director, as well as producer. She felt totally comfortable with him, and grateful for the friendship that dated back twenty years to their student days in London. The Australian prided himself on having discovered her unique vocal gifts in his acting class. As her agent, manager, and now producer/director, he had guided her career and held her hand through the personal as well as professional ups and downs.

As her self-appointed best friend, brother, father, and kid-glove Svengali, he had seen her through the obsession with Nick Albert, the marriage to Brent Wilson, the brutality of John Simon, the near fatal plastic surgery, until now at last he had raised the financial backing for this, his own production of *Streetcar*. In so doing, he had perhaps, even produced a new lover for his protégée in the person of his major American 'angel,' Sidney Samuels, a stagestruck retired business tycoon who, as Providence would have it, was also a widower.

'I have always *depended* on the kindness of strangers.' Was that better? Or not Southern enough? Too Brooklyn, maybe? Blanche Dubois was Mona Davidson's big chance to break out of the soaps and voice-overs and finally be taken seriously as an actress.

' "I have always depended on the *kindness* . . ."?' That was the key, *kindness*. She scrutinized herself in the bedroom mirror as she sank to the floor, struggling with the invisible straitjacket of Blanche's final descent into madness. Helpless in captivity, her body contorted, her hair wild, her eyes pleading and panicky, Blanche's face beseeched her from the mirror, a harrowing apparition. Black rivers of mascara furrowed the chalk-white powder she had applied to her cheeks to help establish the character. Harsh purple dime-store lipstick purposefully overshot the natural outline of her mouth in a cupid's bow.

Calling on all her emotional resources, Mona slowly changed the look of animal panic in her eyes to one of grateful surrender and at last to the dark embrace of madness. Tears, real salty, stinging tears, coursed down Mona's face. Sobs stabbed her chest. She had broken through the barricade. She had entered the very soul of Blanche Dubois. There were only two months of rehearsal before opening night. Her entire future depended on this performance. She had to be ready.

A glance at the mirror caught her unawares. Her reflection mocked her. Who was she kidding? She was too damned healthy-looking to be Blanche Dubois, too sleek and firm from jogging and working out. Blanche was a fragile leaf floating in the wind. Mona looked as if she could pick Stanley up and smash him against the wall if he got fresh and mouthed off.

Her sudden crushing insecurity demanded an instant chocolate fix. Of the eight chocolate doughnuts in the Entenmann box she had inhaled three, along with half the quart container of chocolate-chocolate ice cream left over from breakfast, when the ping of her doorbell and an accompanying thud announced the delivery of her morning mail.

Without warning, the thick rubber band that had been stretched taut around the huge bundle snapped and flew like a guided missile directly at her head, missing her eye by a lash. It was God trying to get her attention, God warning her to be a better person, God telling her to reorder her priorities and to decide where exactly Blanche Dubois figured in relation to her children and to the

Nice Girls

increasingly present Sidney. And, mostly, God reminding her how lucky and privileged she was to be alive and healthy and successful, and what a good life she had in the universal scheme of things, and to quit bellyaching because she wasn't Meryl Streep. *Yet*.

Freed of its rubber girdle, the mail spilled out over the hall table. Here we go again, she thought as she eyed the daily assault, its variety and intensity astounding her. Catalogs. Magazines. Free vacations in Florida. Adult films. Sample pet food. Limited-time offers? Nobody had to remind her that her time was limited. She was thirty-nine even if still photographing twenty-nine, still trying to be taken seriously as a woman and an actress and – God help her – a mother. Time was running out for this stage of her life. The Big Forty lay just ahead. She must make the transition to ripe maturity with a new career and a new husband, a more solidly grounded lifestyle for her middle years. She must rise strong and phoenix-like from the ashes of Blanche Dubois, surrounded by producers clamoring for her services. She must marry Sidney, even though he bored her to hyperventilation, because . . . why? Because he loved her and treated her like a star, he loved her children, he was rich, he was sweet, and most important, having led a dull businessman's life he was dazzled by her world and grateful to be allowed in.

Nick Albert he wasn't.

Okay, screw Nick Albert.

Mona had more important things on her mind, such as Brent's monthly support check being a week overdue. Not that she needed it. Her floor-wax commercial alone would support them all in style for the next ten years. Okay, five. It was the principle that counted. To be sure she hadn't somehow missed it, she went through the mail again piece by piece, this time with the wastepaper basket at the ready.

The last piece looked like an invitation, but that didn't fool her, not anymore. She had been gulled too many times by thick white envelopes addressed in fancy penmanship with lots of curlicues that looked like real invitations to real events given by people she knew personally and who were personally inviting her to attend.

Screw that, too, including the fancy Chuck-and-Di merry old England stamp. She tossed it unopened into the basket, on top of all the other environmental landfill.

The house phone buzzed.

Now what? 'Yes?'

'Gentleman on his way up. Said you'd know who it is.'

Nick Albert! The thought flashed through her mind as it often did. What a kick in the head it would be to open the door and find Nick standing there like the last time, with that shit-eating grin and a handful of daisies and a bottle of bubbly.

'Sidney . . .!' Reality strikes back.

In his awkward attempt to embrace her, he stepped on her foot. 'Sorry about that.'

'It's okay.'

'I'm really sorry, Mona. I'm so clumsy . . .'

'It's *okay*. Really. Really okay.'

Why was he here? Didn't he remember she had a rehearsal?

'The car's downstairs. I thought you might like a lift.'

'Oh, *Sidney* . . .' Why was she so gut-churning mad at him for behaving exactly the way she had always wanted a man to behave – kind, thoughtful, considerate, devoted?

'That is . . . unless you've made other arrangements. I just thought . . .'

'You thought exactly right, Sidney darling. Thank you, sweetheart.' So theatrical. Sarah Heartburn. 'Whatever would I do without you? Be ready in half a mo'.'

Deep breath, mental checklist, turn on the machine. Beloved star was on her way to rehearsal: thick tawny brown hair pulled taut in ponytail and side combs that also pulled taut the flesh under her chin and jawline; tinted horn-rims instead of contacts; baggy black oversized L.L. Bean turtleneck, worn high on the throat to hide any possible hint of crepe and cinched tight at the waist to flaunt the results of Dr. Howard's pasta regimen; acid-bleached jeans, the thespian rehearsal uniform, sculpted by body sweat to hug her dancer's thighs, clenched buns, and the blatant crease of her Venus mound. The Capezio ballet slippers of yore had given way to scuffed white Reeboks with plaid laces and tennis socks.

Script, Filofax, makeup bag, lemon drops, Fisherman's Friend, vitamins, caffeine, notebook, pens, and tissues all deposited in her battered old green-vinyl Harrods shopping bag, she applied a final zap of gloss to her pouting, succulent lips and headed breathlessly for the door where Sidney was waiting. She really shouldn't be such a bitch. Wasn't it better to have Sidney and his Lincoln Mercury at her disposal than to be shagging cabs in heavy traffic? She vowed henceforth and forthwith to be adorable. 'Ready, darling.'

Nice Girls

'I think you threw this out by mistake.' It was the thick white envelope with the Chuck-and-Di stamp. 'Looks important. From England. Maybe Queen Elizabeth has invited you to tea.'

Exasperation trampled her ladylike veneer. *Damn it to hell, Sidney, stay out of my trash basket! Stay out of my life!* 'It's good and thoughtful of you, Sidney, but I'm sure it's nothing.'

She took it from him and tossed it back into the basket. He twinkled at her and retrieved it, with the maddening self-confidence of the masterful man of destiny taking care of the little woman. 'Aren't you curious? Maybe it's from your friend Georgina you're always talking about.'

'Sidney!' *I will kill you, Sidney. I will throw you down the elevator shaft. I will get my own taxi. I really don't need this. I have two gorgeous children. I have money in the bank. I really don't need to use up my energy like this. I have a rehearsal, dammit! I can sublimate. I can be celibate.* Stress causes wrinkles. She inhaled deeply and filled her cheeks with air like a blowfish, exhaling in rhythmic grunts. *Uhh, uhh, UHHH*.

'If you're so curious *you* open it, okay?'

He grinned at her, savoring what he perceived to be a precious moment of intimacy. 'And the Tony Award for Best Actress, for her performance in *A Streetcar Named Desire*, goes to . . . Mon-a Da-vid-son!' A pause, and then his shout of glee cracked her eardrum. 'What'd I tell you? I was right! It *is* from Georgina! You see? She's getting married!'

Mona stared at him blankly. 'Wha-at?'

Sidney's grin reminded her of the Cheshire Cat; he only did it to annoy. He patted her arm indulgently. 'Where were you, dear? In Daydream Land?' He pretended to fan her with the invitation. 'I was right. Like I told you, it's from your old friend Georgina and she's getting married.'

'Georgina . . .? Married?'

'That's what it says, and she wants you to go to London as her guest, all expenses paid! Now that's what I call a friend!'

That's what Mona called one cool customer. Only the week before, Mona had called Georgina to say she'd seen Georgina's picture in *Harper's Bazaar* and to tell her about her debut as Blanche. 'So, okay, that's enough about me. What's cooking with you, Georgina?' she had asked.

'Not much, I'm afraid.'

Typical British understatement. That's what she loved about them. Not much to report, just that she was getting married.

'So who's the lucky guy, Sidney?' A cabinet minister, an Oxford don? He would have to be somebody really top-drawer terrific for Georgina. Landed gentry maybe, or an investment banker, or somebody with a title or a hyphen or both.

He handed the invitation to her. 'It's somebody honorable, it says.'

The name of Georgina Crane's bridegroom leapt at her throat like a hangman's noose.

Nicholas Albert.

And not honorable in the least.

Amy

Gainesville, Florida, 1988

Becoming a grandmother at thirty-eight was not exactly what Amy Dean Humphries had had in mind while she and Lou were rearing their daughter Sandi to be bright, affectionate, resourceful, and have a mind of her own. She had learned their lessons well, but contrary to Amy's expectations Sandi had eloped with Dan 'the Man' Grady after her high school prom and delivered herself of a fine baby girl the requisite nine months later in the Humphries' guest bathroom.

Unwed, unrepentant, and unconcerned, Sandi had named the infant 'Dakota.' For two reasons: North Dakota was where she had decided to split from Dan and hitchhike back to Florida, and The Dakota apartment house in New York City was where John Lennon had lived and been murdered.

Now, a year later, Sandi had resumed her education at the university, leaving her child in Amy's care without a word of discussion or apology. She had simply assumed her mother would welcome the responsibility, perhaps even be grateful for it.

Amy had taken a stand at the breakfast table. 'We need to talk.'

'What about, Mom? I'm in a hurry. Dad's dropping me off at class.'

'Dakota is your child, Sandi. Why should I be the one to take care of her?'

Amy remembered how husband and daughter had looked at her with bewilderment.

'What else have you got to do?' Lou asked.

She had faltered, reluctant to divulge her own plan for returning to school. 'Well . . . I wasn't planning on being a full-time baby-sitter.'

'Do you want *me* to stay home and mind the baby?' Lou had asked huffily, bristling as he always did when asked to do the simplest thing like fixing the upstairs bathroom door. She knew that litany. Wasn't he carrying a full schedule at the university, teaching thirty hours a week, taking tutorials, monitoring ten master's candidates, and running weekend seminars in literature and the humanities?

She had felt defensive and selfish. Of course he couldn't stay home with the baby. 'Sandi had the baby. Why shouldn't she take care of the baby? Or is that illogical?'

Sarcasm not being one of Amy's stronger suits, her question had made little impression on her husband and daughter. Sandi had blithely resumed her studies, as if childbirth were a minor inconvenience like a head cold. Her attitude was simple. Dakota was there. Somebody had to take care of her, and it wasn't going to be Sandi. It was the same willful stubbornness with which she refused to straighten her room, do her own laundry, or help with the dishes.

She wasn't going to take care of Dakota and that was that, which left Amy with no choice. What in heaven's name was she supposed to do, leave the baby in her crib all day, refuse to change her and bathe her and feed her? Lou and Sandi were right about one thing: What else *did* she have to do all day?

Yet this morning, Lou smiled at the way the toddler lurched after her. 'See? She follows you everywhere.' Dakota would follow Jack the Ripper if she thought he'd give her some apple juice.

'Dakota?' An inner alarm went off. She had not seen her grandchild for some time.

'Dakota?' The house was ominously quiet. 'Darn it, you little minx. Where are you?' She looked around to see if there was a tiny pixie face grinning at her from behind the vegetable bin or inside the broom closet.

'Dakota!' A knot of panic began to form in her throat. The smiling face on the milk container reminded her that children disappeared. More likely she was playing hide-and-seek, the little devil. Just yesterday she had wriggled out of her harness at the mall and run through the main concourse with grandma in hot pursuit, shouting her name and unable to catch her until a laughing man with silver hair had done it for her.

'What an adorable daughter you have!'

'My *grand*daughter!' she had declared, enjoying his disbelief that a woman as young and pretty as she could actually be a grandmother.

'*Dakota!* No more jokes! Grandma is getting very angry!' Dear God, where was she! A cavalcade of household deaths paraded through her mind. Choking. Electrocution. Poison. Scissors. Plastic bags. Knives. Thank God Lou didn't have a gun.

'*Dakota!*' Panic took over. She ran from room to room, looking under and behind everything that could possibly conceal a year-old child. Downstairs there was nothing. Not a sign. Upstairs, she went through the four bedrooms like a hurricane, behind the doors, under the beds, into the closets.

'*Dakota! When I get my hands on you, I will kill you!*'

The upstairs bathroom. She remembered leaving the door open because it had been sticking and the man was coming to sand it. The door was now closed. She could hear water splashing. Death throes . . . Her precious baby was drowning. God in heaven, no! Please God, no! 'Dakota?' The doorknob turned, but the door itself refused to budge. Darn Lou! She had pleaded with him to fix it. Too busy flexing his muscles for the coeds. And where in heck was the handyman? If anything happened to her precious child, she swore she would kill them both with her bare hands and go to the electric chair with a smile on her face.

'Dakota! Grandma has a cookie for you!' A desperate shove with her entire body weight sent the door flying open. Her grandchild smiled serenely up at her from her position beside the toilet bowl.

'Wash, wash, wash . . .'

Relief, mingled with dismay. With evident expectation of Amy's approval, Dakota had thrown the morning mail into the toilet bowl and was aping Amy's washing technique when she hand-laundered her delicate lingerie in the bathroom sink.

Magazines, circulars, catalogues, and bills dipped and bobbed like boats in a stormy marina. Fortunately, Dakota was not yet strong enough to pull down the flusher, another thing Amy had badgered Lou to fix. Thank God for small favors. Despite herself, Amy had to smile. At Dakota's age, Sandi's favorite trick had been to put up the toilet seat and sit on the edge of the bowl with her feet, including her shoes, splashing merrily in the water. It was a good thing babies were so cute. It was all that saved them from infanticide. Mother Nature's way of protecting the human species from extinction.

Amy scooped up the sodden mess and dumped it into the sink. Quick as a flash Dakota was at her elbow, turning on the faucet. 'Wash . . . wash . . . wash . . .'

'Dakota! I'm going to freeze-dry you until you're ten years old! Make it twenty . . .'

She carried the squealing child to the playpen in the family room and thrust a pacifier in her mouth. 'The prison,' Sandi called it; children should be allowed to run free. Of course, Sandi didn't have to chase her.

'Okay, Dakota. You just stay right here and suck your pacifier like a good little girl and wreck your bite and ruin your chance to grow up and be Miss America and marry Mr. Right.' Sandi disapproved of the pacifier, too. If Sandi cared so much, let Sandi stay home!

The Dakota Kid danced up and down in the playpen and played I-see-you with her eyes. Irresistible. Amy clutched the child to her, inhaling her sweetness. 'I love you, I love you, I love you!'

The pacifier dropped from Dakota's mouth. She struggled to break free. 'Down . . . down . . .'

'Oh no, you don't. You've made enough trouble for one morning. You stay right here and ruin your bite like a good little girl.'

She put her back in the playpen and returned to the bathroom to dry off the mail. *The New Yorker* had shriveled into a free-form blob like some papier-mâché sculpture. Fortunately, her *Glamour* and *Architectural Digest* came wrapped in plastic – giant condoms, Lou called them, knowing it embarrassed her. The ink on the thick white envelope with the English stamp had oozed purple and run like mascara in the rain. She blotted it with a white washcloth. Darn it, now the ink was all over the washcloth. The domino effect. Whatever could it be? The envelope was so thick, the water didn't seem to have penetrated it. With thumb and forefinger, she managed to ease the enclosure out of its damp pocket.

The impact of the invitation was immediate and physical. Her knees turned to apple sauce. Her heart pounded. Her ears rang in a funeral carillon of unbearable loss. The part of her she had thought long dead and buried in memory came back to vivid life and died once more. She was young again and back in her little room in Chelsea Mews – Sandi's age, yes, but lacking Sandi's sophistication. Young and ridiculous and sobbing under the covers so that Mona

Nice Girls

and Georgina wouldn't hear her, unable to eat for days after Nick Albert eloped with The Frog.

Carrying the torch for Nick Albert was a humiliating secret Amy had shared with no one – not the therapist that first year after her return from London, and especially not Mona or Georgina. She had thought the torch extinguished, yet at the sight of his name, shame and longing burned her cheeks as her head reeled with graphic and explicit memories.

'Nice grandma . . . nice . . .' Little Dakota had managed to climb out of the playpen and was back at her side, seeming to sense her distress and patting her thigh to make her feel better. The sweet little face, so serious in its concern, made Amy's heart ache even more.

That Georgina! How had she managed to trap Nick after all these years? Never a word, never a hint. Mona! She would be getting an invitation to the wedding, too. Mona would hit the roof. The thought of Mona's invective made her smile, like hearing something funny at a funeral that eased the tension. She needed to connect with Mona, to share the shock of the situation while trying to figure out what her own attitude should be. She was about to pick up the phone to call her when the phone rang. Mona! It could only be Mona.

'Mona?'

'For God's sake, Amy! What are you, a witch?'

'I knew it was you.'

'Well . . .?'

'Well . . .?'

'Can you believe it?'

'She always was a sneak. Remember the time –' Amy couldn't go on. Her voice collapsed into a moan. 'Oh, Mona – I can't stand it!'

'I know. It was okay when he ditched the three of us, but now? The nerve of her, expecting us to be bridesmaids!'

'Attendants.' Amy, being literal. 'Her note says "attendants." '

'So, okay, *attendants*.' Mona made the word sound obscene. 'Bridesmaids, whatever you want to call it. We're still too old for that. What's she planning to do, dress us up like Little Bo Peep carrying baskets of rosebuds? Forget it, Charlie.'

'And to *stay* with her, Mona, at the mews . . .'

'So she can rub our noses in it. Not me, thank you very much. Count me out. She'll have to marry Nick Albert without me!'

'And the nerve of her, Mona! Offering to send us plane tickets, like we're poor relations or something.'

'What does she think we are, Rent-a-Guests? Just because she got her picture in *Harper's Bazaar*! Who does she think she is, Queen Elizabeth? What is this, the royal summons? Like we had nothing better to do? Forget it.'

Silence at both ends. They had run out of juice, no longer able to fuel the pretense of jocularity.

'Oh, *Mona!*' Amy's pain said it all.

The actress's voice softened to a husky whisper. 'I know, Amy – me too.'

'And they're getting married in church. Some nerve.'

That settled it. They agreed that they would politely send formal regrets and a suitable gift. A Lazy Susan, Amy thought, trying to be witty. A ton of manure, Mona thought, a statement that would send a signal to the connubial pair.

There was plenty of time to think up something original, this being April and the nuptials set for early June.

'So that's that, right?' Mona concluded.

'Absotively! We've wasted enough time on Nick Albert. Let's just change the subject. There are more important things going on in the world.' Yap, yap, yap. Nick Albert this, Nick Albert that. She was tired of hearing his name.

1

London, 1968

It was the kind of golden day in June designed for romantic poets and visitors with cameras. The two young women in miniskirts and vinyl boots waited their turn outside the student housing office at the American Embassy in Grosvenor Square. Though chatting easily and dressed enough alike to make them seem like childhood friends, they had in fact just met. It was the first time abroad for each of them. Both were taking summer courses in London and needed a place to stay.

Mona Davidson of Brooklyn, New York, would be taking classes in acting and film at the Royal Academy of Dramatic Arts. Amy Ann Dean of Providence, Rhode Island, was enrolled in a special seminar on architectural history.

As a special service to the thousands of students coming to Britain each summer, the Embassy invited Londoners to open their homes for two or three months as a gesture of hands-across-the-sea and not incidentally, to earn some lolly.

The student housing staff took their job seriously, but could of course not be responsible for what might eventuate. If they were old enough to study abroad, they were old enough to take care of themselves.

When Mona offered her last stick of Dentyne chewing gum to Amy, and Amy countered with an Oreo cookie wrapped in foil, the die was cast. They would room together for the summer, share and share alike. They were shaking hands on it and congratulating themselves when word came through from California. Bobby Kennedy was dead. After eighteen agonizing hours of rumor and speculation, he had finally succumbed to the assassin's bullet.

The two Americans burst into tears and embraced each other in their grief.

'I can't stand it!' Mona wailed.

'Me neither!'

'I was all signed up! Weren't you?'

Amy was bewildered. 'Signed up?'

'For the campaign, stupid! I was signed up to work on the campaign when I got back in September!' Mona's eyes narrowed. 'Hey, don't tell me you're a *Republican!*' She made an ugly gagging sound in her throat. 'I may barf!'

Amy cringed at the vehemence of the accusation. 'Who, me? Well, gosh, I . . .'

Mona thrust herself nose-to-nose with her trembling companion. 'You mean you weren't going to vote for Bobby for president?'

'Well . . . you see . . . I . . .' She was tongue-tied.

'Forget it!' Mona turned her back in dismissal. 'Find yourself another roommate!'

'Please, Mona . . .'

'Forget it, I said! America's a free country. Vote for whoever you want.'

'I couldn't vote for Bobby even if I wanted to . . . and believe me, I wanted to – honest. I can't vote for anybody.'

'You mean you were too dumb to register?'

'I won't be eighteen until December!' Amy gathered her courage and put her hand on Mona's shoulder. 'Okay?'

With a rush of contrition, Mona turned to embrace her again. 'I'm sorry.' She herself had only turned eighteen in April. She fished a wrinkled paper tissue from her shoulder bag. 'Dry your eyes. You'll wreck your mascara.'

'I'm not wearing mascara.'

Mona was determined to lighten the situation. She affected a teasing, hectoring tone. 'You mean those lashes are real?'

'Well, yes . . .'

'Double lashes, like Elizabeth Taylor?'

Amy had never thought of her eyelashes in that context.

'I'd *kill* for lashes like that!'

Amy could tell she was being teased, but was helpless to respond in kind.

'Do you know how many hours it takes me to put on my mascara? Hours. Hours, I tell you. And sometimes I mess up and I have to start all over again. And your lashes are natural? How dare you do this to me? Aren't I your friend?'

All Amy could say was, 'Yes . . .'

Nice Girls

Mona managed a smile. The game was over. 'Blow your nose.'

Amy did as she was told.

'That's better. You okay?'

Amy nodded.

'So we're friends, right?' Mona extended her pinky finger to seal their agreement. Amy took the cue and raised her own pinky finger in the accepted pledge of trust. They hooked fingers for a silent count of one-two-three. A solemn bond had been formed.

Mona assumed her new responsibility. 'It's like this, Amy. Bobby's dead, but we're alive. Like my old Grandma always says, "Life goes on." Right?'

'Right!'

'We're the lucky ones, you and I, and we shouldn't forget it. Here we are in England for the summer! God, I know kids who would give their eyeteeth to be here. Think how lucky we are, right?'

'Right.' Amy was beginning to feel better already.

'We've got to make the most of it. Live every moment to its fullest. Drink it all in, every drop of it. Because you never know, right? You never know what's going to happen, right? One minute you've won the California primary and you're a sure thing to be the next president of the United States and the next minute, bang! You're dead!' Her voice quavered as tears streamed down her face once again. 'Right?' She pleaded for confirmation.

'Right!' Amy's own grandmother also had a saying: 'Something good always comes out of something bad.' Amy had not especially agreed with this philosophy until today. Out of sudden grief had come a new friend, someone to share the summer that lay ahead, someone to help her if what she feared might happen happened. Never in her life had she felt so alone. Her parents had become strangers. Until the previous weekend she had considered Lou Humphries her best friend and future husband. Now she wasn't so sure she wanted to get engaged on her birthday as planned. He had always accepted her standards of behavior. On her visits to Harvard they had made love carefully just short of penetration, until the Saturday night before her departure when, despite her protests, he had crossed the line.

'It was to prove you love me, Amy.'

'You know I love you.'

'Then why are you going away for three months? What am I supposed to do while you're gone, jerk off?'

He knew she hated that kind of vulgarity. He also knew how much this summer seminar meant to her. 'I trusted you. What if I'm pregnant?'

He smiled the superior, confident smile she had always found so reassuring. 'Then we'll get married. Simple. We're getting married anyway, so what's the difference?'

The difference, as he well knew, was their original plan. They would finish school, get jobs, get married, decide where to live, get in some travel, and then have their children. If she was pregnant everything would change. Mona was worldly. After the summer she was going to share a Greenwich Village apartment with three other NYU students, all would-be actresses. If worse came to worst, she could confide in Mona. Mona would tell her what to do.

Miss Canner, the cultural attaché in charge of student housing, dipped into her card file and came up triumphant. 'Here it is, perfect for the two of you! Two small bedrooms in a charming mews house just off the King's Road in Chelsea.'

Mona gasped and clutched her chest. '*Chelsea!* I'm going to faint!' According to a travel piece she had torn out of the Sunday *Times* on Swinging London, Carnaby Street was the place to shop, Vidal Sassoon in Mayfair the place to get a geometric haircut, and Chelsea, *only* Chelsea, was the place to live. All you had to do, the article said, was walk down the King's Road and you'd run into people like Mary Quant and John Osborne, and Twiggy, and other people like that at the Kenya Coffee Bar or pubs like The Chelsea Potter or getting their groceries at Sainsbury's. She had all but memorized the article, hoping she'd get over to Chelsea one day, and here she was about to spend the summer there!

The summer ahead once more loomed bright with promise. RADA would erase all lingering traces of her Brooklyn accent while she learned to become an actress. Rumor had it that Laurence Olivier himself regularly monitored RADA classes.

'You'll play Ophelia. He'll see you. He'll see you're twenty times better than Jean Simmons!' her mother had predicted.

'Not *Ophelia*, Mom!' It was a subject they had often discussed, and always in the same ritualistic way. 'I may barf.'

'Ophelia was good enough for me; she's good enough for you!' Rachel Davidson had played Ophelia in a Yiddish production of *Hamlet* when she was fourteen, and had the yellowing reviews from the *Forward* to attest to her lyrical beauty and talent.

Nice Girls

'She let Hamlet push her around.'

'She couldn't help herself. She was in love.'

'If love makes you that crazy, I don't want it. I'd rather play Lady Macbeth!'

'You're too young.'

'Portia. I'll play her in modern dress, a miniskirt, right? A contemporary lawyer . . .'

'Eat something. You're thin as a rail!' Her mother was a great kidder, too. Mona's battle of the bulge was a continuing problem. She had shed ten pounds on the grapefruit diet, with another ten to go. By the time she played Portia, she would be lean and mean. Olivier would see her and beg her on bended knee to co-star in his next film. *Larry, darling, if you insist . . . I'll postpone my Broadway debut until next year.*

Miss Canner's voice cut into her fantasy. 'The young woman who owns the house seems very nice indeed. Not much older than the two of you, as a matter of fact. A sad story, really. Parents killed in a head-on crash. No will. Everything, well, almost everything went to the government in death duties. Poor girl, all she managed to keep is this little mews house, so she decided to take in some PGs.'

'What are PGs?' Amy asked.

'Paying Guests. It's a genteel way of saying you're taking in boarders.'

The terms were good, considering the locale. Twenty pounds each per week. 'Includes kitchen privileges and use of the sitting room. You will take care of your own laundry and food and drink of course. Milk is delivered to the mews each morning. You can work out your arrangements for the phone, electricity, and hot water. Oh, and one thing more.'

'A ghost?' Mona asked hopefully.

'No central heating I'm afraid, but then again it is summer.'

'Sounds great to me.' Mona was anxious to get moving. One night in the youth hostel had been more than enough.

Miss Canner telephoned to make sure the rooms were still available. 'It's Number 4, Chelsea Mews. You'll be meeting Lady Georgina Crane.'

'*Lady* . . .?' This time Mona tried to contain her excitement, but it was all too much. 'Wait till my mother finds out! And my Aunt Ruth! They'll tell everyone in Brooklyn! My God, do we have to curtsy or anything?'

Helene Canner's patience with American students was often sorely tested, but this one, this Mona, made her laugh in spite of herself and her dignity as a diplomat. Chelsea was definitely in for an experience. 'No curtsy necessary. You'd embarrass her if you did. Remember one thing: People with titles rarely use them, except for wedding announcements. Or getting a table at a restaurant. She'll probably tell you to call her Georgina right off the bat. Just be your own sweet selves. Remember that you represent the United States of America, so be on your best behavior, pay your bills, and . . . have a good summer!'

Suddenly both young women, even the outgoing Mona, looked touchingly young and vulnerable. Helene Canner walked them out to Grosvenor Square and explained where to get the Number 19 bus in Piccadilly. Impulsively she hugged them both. 'If you have any problems, give me a ring.'

Even with the map Miss Canner had drawn for them, finding Chelsea Mews was a challenge. They had walked by the narrow entryway twice without realizing it. A passerby noticed their bewilderment and took pity.

'It's just behind you.'

The painted street sign was not only faded by weather and time, it was hidden behind a tree.

CHELSEA MEWS
Royal Borough of Kensington and Chelsea, SW 3

Royal Borough? The visitors grinned at each other. The adventure was about to begin. Entering the mews was a step back in time to cobblestones, Sherlock Holmes street lamps, and toy houses with brightly painted wooden doors and matching window boxes overflowing with flowers. Lady Georgina's, their new summer address, Number 4, sported a canary-yellow door with a black knocker shaped like a clam shell.

'Isn't it fabulous?' Mona whispered.

'I'm scared! What if she doesn't like us?'

'Of course she'll like us! We're *Americans*, right?'

'Oh, Mona. I'm so glad we don't have to curtsy!'

It was no butler in impeccable livery or maid in apron and cap who opened the bright yellow door, but Lady Georgina Crane herself. A symphony of pastels, her thick, glistening hair was the color of butterscotch, and lay coiled in a soft knot at the nape of her long and graceful neck. With her smooth brow and porcelain complexion, her blue-green eyes flecked with copper, she seemed to Mona Davidson the fairy tale princess on the palfrey in her favorite childhood book.

But instead of the princess's flowing muslin gown and green velvet cloak, this noble reincarnation wore muted pinks and apple greens of traditional fashion, a sweater set comprised of pullover and cardigan with a coordinated pink-and-green plaid pleated skirt (calf-length, not mini). Her sole adornments, a single strand of pearls and a gold bangle. So understated and aristocratic, Mona realized with a start, feeling a sudden grotesque loathing of her own vivid coloring and style. The over-abundance of color and form, the jungle of black curls that seemed to grow wild and out of control, the full lips she tried unsuccessfully to minimize with beige pancake, the hips and breasts that threatened to break the seams of her blouse and miniskirt. As for the new microskirts, forget it. She was a throwback to Rubens. There was no way she could wear microskirts. Damn Twiggy, anyway.

The sight of Georgina also triggered deeper, more disturbing thoughts. Did Mona really think anyone would let her play Portia looking the way she did? Portia looked like Georgina. She'd be lucky if they let *her* play Falstaff. Radio was her future, where nobody could see her. Georgina's looks were beyond envy. Mona could spend a hundred years dieting, getting plastic surgery, having her hair straightened, and it wouldn't matter. She could never look like Georgina. Or sound like Georgina, for God's sake, with that Julie Christie accent. She should never have come to England. Everyone at RADA was going to laugh at her. Maybe she could pretend to get sick and go home. Her mother would kill her.

'How good of you to come round,' Georgina said, with a slight smile that made them feel they were walking on eggs but also somehow reassured them that the eggs were hard-boiled and would support their clumsy feet if they trod carefully.

'Mind the stair carpet,' she added. 'It's a bit loose, I'm afraid.'

Amy felt equally overwhelmed, though for different reasons. She could appreciate dispassionately Georgina Crane's indisputable English-rose beauty, just as she could accept without prejudice her own long-legged tennis-from-infancy body, the short, chlorine-bleached cap cut of the year-round swimmer, and the pert freckled features of her New England heritage. As long as her body and hair were squeaky-clean and she maintained her weight, which was never a problem, she didn't worry about her looks. She was neither envious of Georgina nor tormented by yearnings for self-improvement.

What *did* arouse her emotions was Georgina's sitting room at the top of the stairs. A paradise of profusion, compared to the minimalism of her parents' home. Prints and paintings covered the walls in no apparent plan. Overstuffed sofa and chairs were grouped around a battered low table facing the fireplace, where a brass-peacock fire screen was festooned with dried flowers. When she wrote to Lou, that is *if* she wrote to Lou, this was what she would describe. She preferred not to think about him and the weekend in Cambridge. She had tried to discuss it with her mother. The right moment had never come. Maybe at some future time, when they got to know each other better, she could discuss it with Mona. If it wasn't too late . . .

'May I offer you some tea?'

Georgina gestured toward the chintz-covered sofa. 'Please make yourselves comfortable while I get the tray.'

As Amy sat down she sank into the sofa's depths, so that her chin was almost resting on her knee. Seeing her predicament, Mona chose one of the chairs, perching herself on the edge, her weight pitched forward for balance.

A framed photograph demanded her attention. It was of a startlingly handsome young man in the style of Leslie Howard or Peter O'Toole in *Lawrence of Arabia*. 'Who do you suppose that is? Her brother, maybe?'

'Remember, it's not polite to ask.'

The tea tray held an enormous teapot covered with a crocheted tea cosy, a jug of boiling water, milk, sugar, and a plate of chocolate cookies.

Georgina poured the first cup with the grace of one to the manor born. 'Sugar?' she asked Amy, her tinkling voice a good example of drawing room manner for Mona's Memory Bank. Noël Coward, watch out.

'Yes, please.' Amy had seen enough English movies to respond in kind.

'White or demerara?'

A quandary. 'Demerara.' Whatever that was.

'One or two?'

'Two, please.'

Brown sugar. Now she knew. If anyone at the seminar offered her demerara, she'd know what it was. Travel was so educational.

'Milk?' Amy had said no. It was Mona's turn.

'Lemon, please.'

'Oh, dear.' Georgina looked around nervously, as if expecting to find a lemon among the clutter. 'I'm most frightfully sorry. I do apologize.'

A goof. 'Oh no, please. I'm the one to apologize.' When Mona was embarrassed she talked too much. This moment was no exception. She tried to shut up but couldn't. 'You see, I come from a Russian background. Polish, really. Well, more Russian. Anyway, we usually just have tea when you don't feel well. Or after a heavy meal. In a glass with lemon.'

'Ah, Russian tea. We do it that way, too.' Georgina was the true aristocrat, putting the peasant at ease. 'Next time I'll remember to have lemon.'

'It's not important, really. I shouldn't have said anything. Milk's fine, really. I love milk. Really.' She could feel the perspiration trickling down her back.

Amy was having troubles of her own, trying to balance the teacup and saucer on her knee. When Georgina next offered her a chocolate biscuit, the teacup tipped over, sending the stream of hot liquid down her leg and into her vinyl boot, while the chocolate biscuit went skidding across the room like a flying saucer.

Mona's instinctive leap to help knocked her own teacup over as well. The comical aspect of it all broke the ice. The three young women laughed so hard in nervous relief that Georgina, who had learned as a child to pour tea without looking at the pot, managed to upset her own cup as well.

Years later, when Mona recalled the incident and asked her friend if it had truly been an accident or simply a courteous gesture, Georgina had pleaded a total loss of memory.

'I suppose you want to see the' – Georgina searched for the right word – 'accommodations? Accommodations. Forgive me. This is all quite new to me. I'm not quite sure how to be a landlady. I've never had PGs.'

Mona raced to her rescue. 'And we've never been PGs, have we, Amy? I'm sure we're going to be very happy here, aren't we, Amy?'

Her euphoria was short-lived. To say the bedrooms were small was to recall various old vaudeville jokes. Each contained a narrow bed, a table and lamp, and a chest of drawers.

Where were the closets?

There were none.

Where were they supposed to hang their clothes?

There were hooks behind the door.

Television?

Only in the sitting room.

Mona liked to watch TV in bed. 'I guess I could rent a TV, right?'

'I'm afraid not. The wiring is a bit fragile. Another telly would blow all the fuses. The whole house needs rewiring, I'm afraid.'

By this time, Mona was wishing Georgina wasn't so damned 'afraid' of everything. Didn't she know Americans needed closets and television?

And a shower. There was only one bathroom, the toilet encased in its own separate nook, the bathtub enormous and prewar, with lion's-paw feet. Amy was impressed. 'Wow! Two people could fit into this!'

Georgina blushed. Not such a cold potato after all, Mona noted, wondering if the reason was the man in the picture frame.

'And the shower?'

'Oh dear,' Georgina sighed yet again. Even she, it appeared, was getting tired of saying she was afraid not.

'Oh dear,' Mona echoed. A shower was one thing she could not do without. She needed one to wake her up in the morning. How else was she going to wash her hair? There was no point kidding themselves.

'I'm afraid . . . That is, I think Amy and I . . .'

Georgina hastened to concur. 'I couldn't agree more. Things are rather primitive here. There's never enough hot water. I know the Americans spend their entire lives taking baths. And watching telly. It's a shame really.'

The two Americans agreed it was a shame.

As if to make them feel better, she added, 'And there's no fridge, either, I'm afraid.' They had not even seen the kitchen.

'No fridge?'

'I'm meant to be getting one. That is, a friend is organizing one, or so he says.' The flush returned to her cheeks.

'Well, if you're really getting a fridge, maybe . . .' Amy looked

Nice Girls

wistfully into one of the small bedrooms, the one that would have been hers. It reminded her of Lou's room at Harvard, with its narrow bed. 'The rooms are small but they're cosy. What do you think, Mona . . .?'

'No, I won't hear of it. I can see you won't be comfortable here. I'm sure the Embassy can find you something more suitable.'

Amy and Mona reluctantly agreed. Where would Amy put her tennis racket? 'And my tape recorder and my hair dryer?' Mona didn't mention that she also had a typewriter and a portable ironing board and iron.

'Thanks for the tea.'

The word 'tea' started them laughing again.

The tranquility of Chelsea Mews exploded with the roar of a heavy automobile racing down the cobblestones with a brain-crushing shriek of brakes. A slammed door, and a man's voice shouting, 'Georgina!' A tattoo of bangs on her door-knocker threatened to splinter the bright yellow door. 'Georg-ina! Open this door at once, or I'll smash it in!'

The two visitors stood motionless as their hostess raced down the narrow stairs. They grinned at each other in delicious awe as the muted sounds of erotic skirmish drifted up to the sitting room. Audible within the whispers and giggles was the word 'Americans.' At last, the ascending sounds of footsteps announced the return of a visibly flustered Georgina, blushing more fiercely than before and patting her disheveled hair into some reassemblance of order. The tall, slender man behind her was clearly the one in the photograph.

'Well, well, well . . .' He looked the visitors over with frank appreciation. 'And what have we here?'

Georgina stepped forward to do the proper introductions. 'Miss Davidson, Miss Dean, allow me to present Mr. Nick Albert.' Jane Austen came to Mona's mind, or a formal introduction reminiscent of *The Importance of Being Earnest*. Back in the States it was no longer cool to introduce anyone to anyone.

'You're Americans!' he rhapsodized, as if this were the most remarkable and wondrous thing that could be. 'Absolute bliss! Welcome to London!'

Nick shook hands with each of them in turn, which caused a moment of confusion. In the States, girls didn't shake hands. 'Wherever did you find them, Georgina? They're utterly delicious!'

'You remember. I registered with the American Embassy.'

'And they sent you these two gorgeous things? I think I'll go and register too. Will they send me some, too?'

'Oh, Nick . . .' The previously cool and collected Georgina could not keep her hands off him. Caressing the lapels of his blazer, she asked demurely, 'And what happened to my new fridge?'

'Not *new,* sweetie. I never said *new.* A good used fridge, rarely used in point of fact, from this chap who has it on his houseboat on the Embankment. Never uses the damned thing.' By way of explanation to the visitors, 'Prefers his whiskey neat. No ice.'

'Then when do we actually get to see it?'

Nick Albert felt in his pocket for his silver cigarette case and took his time about opening it and choosing a small cigar, which he then carefully inserted in a tortoiseshell holder. A further search unearthed his silver lighter, which had to be clicked several times before it agreed to function. Impervious to the rapt attention being paid him, he carefully lit his cigar and slowly inhaled before replying.

'The bastard is holding me up for another ten quid.'

'But that's absurd! I've given you fifteen. Surely that should do for a secondhand fridge?'

'Later, Georgina. We really shouldn't be discussing these mundane things in front of your new PGs. Whatever will they think? Not to worry. The fridge will be here tomorrow, and you'll be able to have all the ice you need for your Coca-Colas.' He patted Georgina approvingly on the cheek. 'Clever girl to get these Americans.'

At that point Mona knew she had to speak up, even though she felt like she was doublecrossing her own mother. 'Well, you see . . . it's like this. We're not exactly moving in.'

A crestfallen Georgina confirmed this with an unhappy nod.

'Not moving in? Nonsense, Georgina! It's the fridge, isn't it? Stupid sod that I am, I've let the side down. But not to worry. The fridge will be here tomorrow. Word of honor.'

'Nick, please. It's not on. The rooms simply aren't suitable. They were just about to leave.'

He was not to be convinced. 'They can't just pick up and go! I won't hear of it!

Mona inched toward the door. 'We'd better get a move on.'

'I *am* sorry,' Georgina assured them. 'It's been so nice chatting.'

'Thanks *awfly* for the cuppa!' Mona's astute imitation of

Georgina's accent sent the three young women into spasms of laughter again.

Nick was adamant. 'You can't possibly leave just yet! It would be too rude! I haven't had my tea!'

By now the teapot was cold. 'Sweetie, be an angel and bring us all up a fresh brew?'

As Georgina obediently disappeared down the stairs, Mona could see they were about to be intimidated. 'We're really sorry. The house is really terrific, but . . .' With Nick's eyes staring quizzically into hers, her brain went dead. She couldn't think of what to say next.

Amy finished her sentence for her. 'It's charming. Georgina's great. But there aren't any closets, and there's no shower.'

'No shower? Is that the problem? But haven't you heard the latest scientific evidence?' Showers, he explained, were the reason American women had so many sexual problems. Baths were much, much better for female parts. 'Standing in the shower is for men. For women, it's absolutely essential to bathe sitting down in warm scented water to achieve the proper benefits.'

Mona laughed. 'Come *on*!'

'True! I assure you!'

With the elaborate movement of a conspirator, he made sure the sitting room door was closed before taking each of them by the hand. He seated them together on the sofa and positioned himself on the floor at their feet, his arms resting on their knees.

It was important that they change their minds. For their own benefit as well as Georgina's. He agreed there were certain discomforts, but would they rather be in some modern block with no charm or history just because it offered a shower? Sharing Georgina's house would be an experience they would cherish all their lives. She was of course too modest to tell them about herself and her background.

'She is the descendant of a titled family dating back to Queen Elizabeth I. What's more' – and here he lowered his voice, though he couldn't possibly have been heard in the kitchen below – 'this very mews is on the site of the old Chelsea Palace, where the first Queen Elizabeth lost her virginity, seduced by Thomas Seymour.'

'I saw the movie *Young Bess*, with Jean Simmons!' Mona was enthralled.

Equally enthralled, Amy hung on his every word, even though

she knew it was all lies. She didn't care. The man was irresistible.

'Georgina's family survived all the political changes all through the centuries, and all was well until a year ago.'

It seemed the accident that had killed her parents had also left Georgina penniless. Her aristocratic friends turned their backs on her. Her fiancé, a guards officer from another old family, broke off their engagement. Mona and Amy were her only hope. They couldn't let her down.

'She can go back to the American Embassy, can't she?' Amy suggested.

'She can't do that. I know her too well. She'd be too humiliated. She was so worried about taking strangers into her home, and you two turned out to be perfect. Just seeing you together, I can tell the three of you will get along fine. Think of the fun, the parties, the King's Road . . .' His brow darkened for his final appeal. 'If you leave now, I don't know what Georgina will do.'

They could hear movement on the stairs. Nick Albert clutched the two Americans to him in a warm embrace. He kissed each of their palms in turn. 'Please, I beg of you, don't let her down!'

He opened the sitting room door and took the tea tray from Georgina. 'Great news, Georgina pet! Mona and Amy have changed their minds. They've decided to stay after all.'

Georgina's tear-filled sigh of relief was proof that they were doing the right thing, the humanitarian thing. Her stiff upper lip had kept them from realizing how desperate she really was. Standing behind her where she couldn't see him, Nick sent air kisses to them, mouthing the words, 'Bless you, my angels!'

Nick took over the tea tray and transformed the simple matter of pouring cups of tea into a joyous ceremony of celebration. With Nick pouring, the tea was somehow stronger, hotter, tastier than before. Georgina's happiness embraced them all. Mona and Amy suddenly felt lucky and privileged to be included.

'Tell you what,' Nick ventured.

'What?' the three chorused.

'I've got the big *voiture* outside. Why don't I run the girls back to collect their gear and then I'll cook us all a meal? Sound good?'

Whatever he said sounded good. Who could resist this man and the promise of fun and excitement and glamour, all the things Mona and Amy had come to London hoping to find? *The worst that can happen is we'll be sorry*, Mona reasoned. *No big deal, right?* For

Amy, Nick Albert's style and wit put Lou Humphries and the other Harvard men to shame. Her misgivings dissolved; she had made the right decision about spending the summer abroad.

The 1923 Lagonda, with its enormous head lamps and natural kid-leather upholstery, added yet another dimension to the romantic aura of the secluded mews. Mona and Amy had effectively stepped through an Alice's looking glass into another continuum, a realm where America was at a far remove, Bobby Kennedy a fading grief, and a summer of wonderment stretched ahead.

It was hard to believe they had met only today, had known each other only for a matter of hours. Yet here they were in Chelsea, about to move in with a titled Englishwoman, and being driven around in a vintage Lagonda by a man unlike any either of them had ever known.

As the enormous old car turned into the King's Road, Mona and Amy clutched each other's hands in delirious anticipation of the summer ahead.

'Isn't he gorgeous?' Mona whispered.

Amy jabbed her with her elbow. 'Quiet! He'll hear you!'

2

Georgina

The swine! How dare Nick go off like that! How dare he leave her on her own to clear away the tea things while he went swanning off with the Americans, all giggles and flushed cheeks, so excited to be with him, so quick to change their tiny little minds about moving in? The shabbiness of her sitting room and the hopelessness of her situation struck her with the orphan pain of loss that had begun with her parents' death. Damn them, damn Nick! The accumulated grief and shame threatened to choke her, and it was all Georgina could do to hold herself rigid until the slam of the downstairs door released her into floods of tears.

It was small consolation that before clattering down the steps Nick had turned, framed in the sitting room doorway, and favored her with his most heart-wrenching grin, the swine. 'Not to worry, darling! Shan't be long! It's all going like a dream!'

In her misery she stumbled against the tea table, snagging a ladder in her pantyhose, her last pair of pantyhose. Bloody hell and damn! Money, it all came down to money! She kicked the tea table with such fury one of its legs snapped off, spilling the tea things on the carpet. She kicked them, too, reminded of yet another humiliation, the forced sale of the Sheffield tea service that had reduced her to this bizarre collection of mismatched mugs and cake plates, the chipped teapot and hot water jug.

She picked up the teapot with a view to hurling it into the fireplace. Caution prevailed. It wouldn't help. Her father had always preached discipline. Discipline was all. She must be calm and rational. It didn't help to be angry. In simple terms, she wanted two things: Nick Albert, and enough lolly to get through the next few months while she figured out a way to earn her living.

Honesty compelled her to face a basic truth. It had been Nick's idea to take in paying guests. Like his tour guide clients, the

Americans would pay her in dollars, cash money, and no need to inform Inland Revenue. 'They'll be gone before you know it, and besides' – he had pulled her close, insinuating his lips into the tender entrance to her ear – 'I'll be here.'

If not for his persistence, she still would have been dithering and whinging. Nothing would have happened, and more than likely she'd have ended up losing the house. Even if she were to take a catering course or learn steno-typing, it would be months before she could qualify for a job. So Nick was absolutely right. But why, oh why, must it be *Americans?* Mummy had loathed the Americans, with their chewing gum and cameras, descending on Britain every summer like locusts. Like Queen Victoria, she would not have been amused to find two of them in her house.

The framed photographs of both parents were on the nightstand in her bedroom, her mother in a formal portrait by court photographer Bassano in 1938, her father on the day he earned his wings and joined the 601 Squadron. The frame that had previously contained the engagement photograph of her and Peter Waring now boasted the image of Nick Albert at the wheel of the Lagonda. Nick had decided it looked better in the sitting room.

'Going like a dream,' Nick had said? Not *her* dream, thank you all the same. Her dream was having him all to herself, by themselves, making love until dawn. Along with everything else, there would no longer be the lovers' privacy of having their own little world. With two Americans larking about there would be no more splashing naked in the bath, no more chasing each other with wet towels like naughty children, no more pillow fights on the sitting room floor.

Vivid images of their hijinks further blurred her vision. In the bull's-eye mirror above the mantle, her nose was red and enlarged, her eyes bulbous and streaming. Not a pretty sight, my dear.

It was Nick Albert she yearned to see in the mirror. Early this morning she had been in the sitting room in her nightdress, tidying up, when Nick had appeared silently and suddenly behind her. 'Nick, you idiot! I thought you were asleep.'

'Don't move!' he had whispered as his hands danced on fingertips up her arms and across the back of her shoulders to her neck, where they veered upward to trace the contours of her ears before finally fanning forward full-palm across her eyes and nose and mouth.

'Nick . . .'

'Don't speak. Don't move. If you speak or move, I'll stop.'

Swine. His fingers had paused at her mouth and stopped. She had not, *dared* not speak. His eyes in the distorted mirror had frightened her. *Should I stop*? he had asked quite coldly. He would stop if that was what she wished. Then it was her own desire that had frightened her and kept her eyes riveted to his through the mirror in an eternity of suspense punctuated by wild agonies of murder, pleading, and surrender until languidly, condescendingly, his fingers had resumed their journey.

'Don't move.'

His fingers vibrated at the corners of her mouth, probing for the open-sesame to its interior, only to shift direction again. Her neck arched to accommodate the explorer's travels down her throat. The thin cotton nightdress offered no resistance, made no sound of protest as it was ripped open.

'Don't move.'

He snapped the spaghetti straps and eased the nightdress down from her breasts and belly and hips until it slithered to the floor and she realized with her back against him that he was as naked as she. His eyes had continued to hold hers prisoner in the mirror, refusing to let her close them or look away. *I want to see into your soul* he had told her the first time they had made love. This time he nodded in satisfaction at her obedience and his hands continued their journey, stopping here, wandering there, as if testing her worthiness until she thought she must faint or scream. When at last death itself would have been preferable to ecstasy, his traveling fingers reached their destination and she felt herself invaded and conquered from two directions.

'Don't move.'

Swoon. Old-fashioned word, 'swoon.' Damsel word, 'swoon.' Knees giving way, heart pounding, spiral shrieks threatening to explode.

'I want your eyes to tell me when, Georgina. It's up to you.' His voice was so polite, as if asking her to pass the cheese and biscuits. What did he mean, up to her?

'Your wish is my command, Georgina. It's up to you. Tell me when.'

Up to her? *Liar*. Her wish his command? Then suddenly, she had understood. He had reduced her to helplessness and now he was demanding that she take charge of her own deliverance. Up to her to tell him when? She'd show him.

'Guess, you bastard.'

He was laughing now, gleeful, pleased with her arrogance. 'Now?'

'Guess!'

'Now?'

The memory of this morning still held her in thrall. She had closed her eyes to relive the final moments of their love scene, and slumped against the mantelpiece in exhaustion. When she was able to look into the mirror again her face had become a death mask, drained of color as if embalmed. Except for the crimson bite mark on her neck. *What if the Americans saw it? she wondered. Then she reminded herself that that was the old Georgina, the Georgina Nick Albert was trying to replace with the new, arrogant Georgina. So what if they had seen it?* It was obvious they were thrilled to be in London and staying with a titled Englishwoman. She must keep on reminding herself of that, take the lolly and be thankful for small blessings.

She must stop being silly. Soon they would be back. The yellow door that Nick himself had painted would crash open and there they'd be, her two Americans with all their American gear, the masses of new clothes all Americans had when all she could afford were some knickers from Marks and Sparks. It was of some comfort to decide that the first thing she would buy with their rent money would be a new nightdress.

She must pull her socks up, finish tidying the sitting room, and then get the tiny bedrooms in order. She could not even begin to guess where they were going to put their cases, or how the one small bathroom was going to accommodate all the expensive creams and lotions and rollers and brushes and combs and tablets and God only knew what American girls were using on their skin and hair. American girls always seemed so sure of themselves. Their hair bounced with health and high spirits. They seemed to be able to apply makeup on moving buses. Perhaps she would learn something from her guests.

Guests. Mummy had always reminded her we must make our guests comfortable, see to the telling detail: scented sachets in drawers, an extra pillow for sleepy heads, morning tea on a tray. But Mona and Amy were not guests; they were boarders. Boarders, Mummy, not guests. If you and Daddy had been more careful, had not had that second carafe of wine, you would not have been smashed to bits and abandoned your only child to cope on her own.

Nice Girls

Just as Nick Albert had abandoned her, left her alone to cope on her own while he went toodling off with the Americans. Not the same thing of course, but she couldn't shake the sense of loss and betrayal. He had left her alone to go off with the blasted simpering, not to mention wealthy, Americans. Who was to say if any of them would come back? She didn't even know where Nick lived. She didn't have a phone number for him. If he did a flit, she would have no way of finding him. He could disappear from her life as suddenly as he'd come into it.

Silly cow. Knowing Nick, they were probably at the Queen's Elm, scoffing Scotch eggs and pink gins. Of course he would be back, why wouldn't he be back? And later they would be together in her bed, alone together in each other's arms, safe. Or would they? The hideous reality struck her once again. The two Americans would be crowded in with them, her happiness sacrificed to economic necessity. No more merry chases through the sitting room and down the stairs to the larder, like the night he'd caught her halfway up the stairs and taken her right there on the steps.

Mummy would not have approved of Nick Albert. She had distinct opinions about layabouts, Americans, and Jews, and here Georgina was involved with all three. Mona was a Jewess, she was certain. One could always tell. Sorry about that, Mummy. If she was to survive at all, it would be because of her chance meeting with Nick Albert on a day of such hopelessness she had stayed in bed with the curtains drawn until noon. It had taken all her will power to get up and dress and make her way to Bond Street for her appointment at Sotheby's.

The view of Green Park from the top of the Number 19 bus had raised her spirits somewhat. Her father's battered old RAF duffle bag held the few pieces of the Sheffield tea service that had survived the blitz, her mother's diamond rings, bracelets, and the tiara she had worn for her presentation at Court before the war, all hopelessly old-fashioned and unlikely to fetch much to satisfy her death-duties debt to Inland Revenue. At the last minute, she had withdrawn Mummy's pearls. If she was caught, she would say she'd thought they were fake.

Her mother's jewelry had been meant for her when she married, and meant to be passed along to her own daughter in the fullness of time. Now some bloody stranger would have them, some bloody American most likely. They were everywhere, buying everything, including chamber pots. The previous Saturday at the Portobello Road a dealer had told her the Americans took chamber pots back to America and used them as punch bowls. Mummy would have smiled her superior smile at that.

Continuing her tasks, she turned for comfort to the memory of that day less than a month ago in Bond Street when she had met Nick Albert. As was her habit, she had turned into Bond Street at the Piccadilly end and strolled up the left side, pausing to admire the amber in Sac Freres and savoring the anticipation of Asprey's before actually reaching it. It was a tiny ritual she clung to, reliving the memory of her first such excursion as a four-year-old walking proudly with her grandmother up Bond Street, then across Berkeley Square and finally to Gunter's in Curzon Street for a cream tea.

Approaching Asprey's on that day, she had become aware of a disturbance on the normally placid pavement. A clutch of clucking hens in facetious hats and far too much jewelry were clustered around a languid young rooster in a splendid blue blazer. A shaft of brilliant afternoon sunlight had chosen that precise moment to wreath Nick Albert in a golden halo. His thatch of fair hair glistened and his blue eyes narrowed in self-protection against the glare, as he lit a small cigar in the tortoiseshell holder clenched jauntily between his teeth.

He might have been standing there alone, for all the attention he was paying to his tormentors. Seeing Georgina, his eyes smiled a baleful conspirator's wink that begged her not to judge him by these monsters who seemed about to swallow him whole.

'Ladies . . .' With a graceful flourish, he manipulated the malacca handle of his furled umbrella in a wide arc to ward them off before pointing it dramatically at the splendid Victorian shop front. 'Asprey's! I'm delighted to inform you we have arrived – intact. We are of course expected, and you may be sure we shall be welcomed with every courtesy.'

Despite his condescending insolence to his twittering charges, he had struck her as touchingly sad, a desperate man sinking in quicksand and needing to be rescued. As she would soon learn, this was his talent. Despite or perhaps because of her own desperate situation, she instinctively felt the traditional roles reverse, he the creature in distress, she the gallant stranger to the rescue.

Although usually hopelessly shy to the point of nausea, she astounded herself by greeting him like a long-lost friend. 'Well

Nice Girls

hello, you wicked old thing! What are you doing in London? The last I heard you were playing net ball in Nepal!'

As startled by her words as she was for having uttered them, he didn't move but simply stared at her in amazement. Her audacity then increased – in for a penny, in for a pound. 'Come here at once and kiss me! I'm sure your friends will excuse you.'

What devilish imp had gotten into her she would never know. But for the first time since her parents' death and her broken engagement, she felt exuberantly glad to be alive.

'Darling girl!' He walked toward her, grinning to beat the band. 'How absolutely marvelous to see you!' His back to his captors, his expression changed to one of naked gratitude. He kissed her theatrically on both cheeks, and while pressing his face into her hair darted his tongue into her ear. 'Angel.' Her knees actually buckled, something that had never happened to her even with Peter Waring, and she felt quite ill as the blood rushed to her head.

Her ear still tingled and her chest palpitated at the memory. 'Erotic arrest' was how Mona Davidson would later describe Nick's impact: Mona, with her New York way with words.

'Thank you for rescuing me from the piranhas. One more nibble and I'd have murdered the lot.'

The piranhas were growing peevish.

'Come on, Nick!'

'You can see your girlfriend later!'

'Please do say you'll see me later,' he had whispered. 'I get twenty quid a head from each of these gorgons. Why don't I pop 'round for a drink and then take us out for a whacking great meal?'

And that, Mummy darling, was how it all began. He had indeed popped 'round for drinkies, but they never had gone out to dinner. They had not left the little house in Chelsea Mews for two days, opening the door only to take in the milk. Fortunately there had been some food of sorts in the larder – tea, digestive biscuits, eggs, macaroni, and some tins of pilchards.

With two tea towels knotted together to form a loincloth of sorts, Nick Albert had proved his talents were not limited to sex. He sang bawdy ballads to make her laugh. He recited Keats and Browning to make her weep. He dressed her in tea towels as well, and set her tasks as *sous chef* while he magically created mysterious and delicious treats they arranged on trays and ate in bed.

'Better than dining out,' she had sighed, and a good thing as it turned out. He had not actually received his fee from the ladies. As he had known all along, he would be paid later by the travel agency that had booked them and hired him as a guide. When at last and reluctantly Georgina had told him he must go, he had blithely borrowed a quid for a taxi. Although it did occur to her to ask how he had planned to take her to dinner, she held her tongue. She was by then besotted with the man, wildly, passionately mad about him. Of course he had never offered to repay the pound, a character flaw Mummy would never have let her forget.

Jealousy was a new emotion for Georgina, one that was utterly foreign to her makeup. She had been taught never to covet other children's toys or resent anyone's good fortune. When the first sickening wave of jealousy had hit her she didn't know what it was, only that she felt horribly ill, heachachy, fretful, and given to inexplicable tears.

It hadn't taken a psychiatrist to fathom the cause of her malaise and its cure. Being of strong principle, she had determined jealousy was unworthy of her. When Nick failed to ring when promised – which was often – when he failed to show up at all – which had happened only once – she had accepted his breezy excuses and swallowed her pain.

In point of fact she hated scenes. She avoided them by ignoring his behavior and how it upset her. Until now. More than three hours had passed since he and his simpering harem had left. She had hoovered the carpet, including the stairs, done up the little bedrooms with fresh linens and towels, washed and put away the tea things, all the while craning her neck to hear the first hint of the Lagonda's return.

When the phone rang, her immediate reaction was disaster. An accident! 'Nick?'

It was the woman from the American Embassy, wanting to know how everything had gone. It was after hours, of course. She was home, of course, but she couldn't help thinking about the two young women she had sent along. 'They look grown-up, with that heavy eye makeup and all, but they're really children away from home for the first time.'

Georgina assured her all had gone well and they were in fact moving in.

'You will take care of them, won't you?'

'Of course,' she said, irritated by the woman's concern.

Nice Girls

She had resigned herself to her situation, even going so far as to wonder what she might find in the larder for supper, when the unmistakable roar of the Lagonda announced the wanderers' return.

'Georgina!' Nick's voice summoned her from below. 'Georgina – darling heart!' His kiss was redolent of several pink gins. 'Give us a hand, love.'

Of course they had come back. How could she have thought otherwise? Nick was clearly in charge. The two girls were clearly dizzy with pleasure.

'We brought you a present!' Mona confided in a whisper. 'Don't say anything, right? Act surprised, right?'

The childlike anticipation of this oversized baby doll made Georgina regret her unkind thought. 'Let me help you girls.'

'It looks like more than it is, honest,' Mona hastened to assure her as they unloaded the boot.

Amy chimed in, 'Don't worry, Georgina. Nick says it'll all work out.'

Did he now? Who was he to say it would all work out? This was her house, not his. Who did he think he was? 'Nick!' What was wrong with her? Why was she carrying on like a fishwife? And then it struck her: Of course, her monthlies were almost due.

'Protect me, girls!' Nick pretended to cringe with fear. 'Georgina's on the warpath because we're so late getting back, aren't you, darling?'

She turned her back on him.

'Aren't you, darling?' he teased. He put his arms around her. She shrugged him off.

He pretended not to notice and instead began to massage her shoulders. 'You see, girls, Georgina's giving me the cold shoulder. I shall try to warm her up. Please, Georgina. Forgive us. It was all my fault. We stopped in Soho for food, all your favorites. That's why we're so late getting back. And then we stopped at the French Pub for –'

'Let me guess: a large pink gin?' She felt the shrewish taste in her mouth and swallowed it as fast as she could. She feared sarcasm as much as jealousy. She turned to face them and tried to indicate 'just teasing' by blowing Nick an exaggerated kiss.

'Wine, darling. A marvelous bottle of Chateau Neuf du Pape 1965, courtesy of Mona and Amy. Now be a good little mouse and help get the girls settled while I do the meal.'

Arranged on platters, the meal was a series of beautiful still lifes. Cooked asparagus served cold in a tart lemon dressing, chicken breasts *en gelée* studded with truffles, paper-thin slices of Scotch beef, dressed crab, smoked salmon cornets sprinkled with dill, rounds of dark Russian bread, a basket of raspberries, a bowl of Devonshire cream, a wedge of Wensleydale, assorted water biscuits, and four bottles of wine.

Nick offered the toast. 'To Mona and Amy. For bringing joy – and delicious nosh – to Chelsea Mews. Mona and Amy.'

'Welcome to London, Mona and Amy.' Georgina clinked glasses with each in turn, adding, 'And our special thanks to the honorable Nicholas Albert. Hear, hear.'

She wondered how she could have felt so bad a mere half hour ago and so good now.

'Well said, my darling.' Without explanation, Nick deftly transferred Georgina's plate and his own to a tray and slipped one of the wine bottles under his arm. 'I think we can disappear and leave the young ladies to settle in. Come along, darling.'

Georgina stared at him, uncomprehending. What on earth was he doing now?

'Come *along*, Georgina.'

The Americans watched, goggle-eyed.

'Goodnight, all!' Nick smiled benignly.

'Goodnight!' they chorused.

'Poor things,' Georgina sighed when they had shut her bedroom door.

'Why "poor things"? Silly sods, they have more money than you and me.'

'I think they expected to sit up chatting. They're probably embarrassed. . . .'

'Embarrassed? At what?'

'You know – *embarrassed*! They're awfully young, you know.'

He began to undress her. 'Embarrassed that we're lovers and can't bear to be apart for another moment?'

'Oh, Nick . . .' Her neck and chest were flushed pink. 'Perhaps it's me that's embarrassed.'

'Georgina, if you're really so embarrassed, I'll go. Simple as that.'

'No, please . . .'

He sat her on his knee and fed her a sip of wine. 'Listen to what I have to say. This is your house. You have rented them two rooms and the use of the sitting room, kitchen, and bath, the run of the entire house except for this bedroom, which is off-limits.'

'I know, darling, but –'

He fed her a morsel of Scotch salmon and another sip of wine. 'Are you worried they might hear us?'

She nodded.

'Think of this, Georgina. Think how educational it will be for them to hear us, and how exciting for us to know they're listening.'

Exciting? Yes, exciting, but no, she couldn't ignore the expressions on Mona and Amy's faces. She knew too well the orphan hurt of those who have been left out. To make love now would be like eating a four-course meal while starving peasants pressed their noses to the windows.

'I'm sorry, Nick. I can't.'

He gazed at her thoughtfully for a moment and then began to dress. Unable to deal with his leaving, she got into bed and pulled the covers over her face.

'Don't be such a fool,' he said, his tone of voice a quiet negation of his words. 'You're coming with me.'

They dressed quickly and in silence.

'Where are we going?'

It was getting late. The pubs would be closed.

He picked up the bottle of wine. 'Do you know what one of those stupid tourists asked me today? She was flirting with me, I know. I'm sure her husband back in Cleveland thinks she's cute as hell. I had just taken them to the Albert Memorial and enthralled them with the love story of Queen Victoria and Prince Albert. And that's when she said she didn't care too much about history but she did like the idea of the Queen lusting for her man!'

'Was she intoxicated?'

'Only with lust for me. When I deposited them back at the Dorchester, she put a note in my hand. She said she wanted to make love with me on the steps of the Albert Memorial.'

No wonder he loathed his job. 'Quite an idea.'

He peered deeply into her eyes, as if considering her remark and framing a reply. 'That's what I thought.'

3

Mona

God was punishing her. She lay rigid on the narrow bed, staring at the ceiling, wishing desperately that she were back in New York. Her head ached, her stomach railed against the unfamiliar food Nick had served them. She didn't want Scotch salmon swimming in olive oil and capers, with junky little pieces of brown bread. If she was going to eat smoked salmon, she wanted nova on a toasted bagel with cream cheese, a slice of Bermuda onion, and a spritz of lemon. That's what she wanted.

She didn't want dressed crab either; the thought of it made her want to puke. She wanted a hamburger. She wanted french fries and plenty of ketchup. She wanted bacon and tomato on toast with extra mayo. She wanted a banana malted with pistachio ice cream. She wanted Ted, the one-eyed bear she'd left behind as her brave farewell to childhood and as a sacrifice on the altar of her new life as an adult and as an actress. She wanted her mother.

God was punishing her for the sin of lying and the sin of envy. A fib was one thing. She had been telling fibs as far back as she could remember, little fibs, cute fibs that made the grown-ups laugh, but nothing like this. Her whole trip to London was a fraud. It had all begun innocently enough just before Spring Break. All the other girls were going somewhere glamorous. Esther to her grandparents in Jamaica – Jamaica the island, not the Jamaica in Queens where Mona's Aunt Ethel had a candy store. Sylvia to Hollywood, where her cousin Joel was an agent and was getting her a screen test. Lois to Vail for spring skiing, and so on and so on, everyone doing something exciting while she . . .? She was spending Passover with relatives in Bradley Beach on the Jersey shore.

It wasn't fair. When classes reconvened and the talk shifted to plans for summer, she casually announced she was going to London to take a summer course at RADA. A fib, of course, a dumb lie born of envy and the terrible need to be special. She had not planned to deceive; the whole thing had simply popped out of her mouth. She had not even written to RADA to find out how to apply or how much it cost. If the girls had not reacted with such goggle-eyed envy of their own, she would have forgotten the whole thing and applied for a summer job in the Catskills.

The problem was, she had given too good a performance. Her classmates had not only believed her, they'd chipped in to buy her a gift, a portable tape recorder. Wasn't it cool? Mona was going to London! To study at RADA! Soon she started to believe it herself, or to believe in her ability to somehow make it happen. Celebrity myth was rife with stories of charming deception. The starlet up for a role in a Western always lied and said of course she could ride a horse. The newcomer who couldn't get past a producer's receptionist disguised herself as a waitress at his next beach party, got his attention, got a part, and won the Academy Award.

Not that she had actually planned on going to London. When classes started up in September, she'd have some dramatic explanation for canceling. That's when God stepped in to teach her a lesson. When one of her classmates phoned her at her mother's place and congratulated Esther on Mona's good fortune, the result was maternal excitement, emotional predictions of stardom, a round-trip plane ticket, and a thousand dollars spending money from her and Mona's grandmother.

That's when she should have confessed. She'd had no business coming to London. She hated to think what was going to happen when the truth came out. Her mother? Her grandmother? The girls who chipped in for the tape recorder, and told her to break a leg and give her regards to Vanessa Redgrave and Julie Christie?

She was going to *try* to get into RADA, of course, but what would they say if she wasn't accepted, and what was she going to do for the next two months? And now, on top of all this, there was Nick Albert. She felt as if she'd been hit by a truck. She had never met anyone like him. All the guys she knew were either nice Jewish boys with names like Seymour or Murray or Ed, or midwesterners named Bud or Sonny or Scott. Not one of them looked or sounded or had an effect on her like Nick Albert.

At the first sight of him, her breasts had come to attention. His mere brushing against her on the stairs and when he'd helped her into his car had aroused her to the point of fearing he would see the

Nice Girls

burning flush on her cheeks. The final shock to her nervous system had come a few minutes ago when he and Georgina said goodnight, wishing her and Amy happy dreams before retiring with their trays to Georgina's bedroom. Nick had reached over and pressed his finger into the corner of her mouth. 'Crumbs,' he'd explained. An electric charge was more like it; she felt like Elsa Lanchester as the bride of Frankenstein, certain her hair must have stood on end.

It was impossible to relax. She tried to plan her strategy for approaching RADA, but she couldn't think straight. It was too quiet in Chelsea Mews. She was not used to so much quiet. She was used to noise, music, television, ambulance and police sirens, garbage trucks, people on the phone, people dropping in, loud talking, arguments, laughter, lots of kidding around. Physically as well as emotionally strung out, she tried to remember whether her body clock was six hours early or six hours late. Was it afternoon in New York, or the middle of the night?

Amy had closed the door on her own room across the hall. Georgina and Nick were also behind closed doors, in their bedroom only a few feet away. She strained to hear them, hoping despite herself for sounds of love-making that could only make her feel more lonely and shut-out. This wasn't what she had expected to happen. Bobby Kennedy's face danced before her eyes. Poor Bobby. That wasn't what he had expected to happen, either.

As if she didn't feel guilty enough about lying, she felt guiltier still about Bobby, about not having had one single solitary thought about him and Ethel and the kids since Nick Albert had walked into Lady Georgina's living room. Envy was her problem. She knew it. She tried to do something about it, but envy was always there. She didn't hate the people she envied. She didn't want them to die of a wasting disease, or to mow them down with a machine gun. She just wanted to have what they had, too. Too, not instead.

Logic reminded her that envy was self-destructive. It didn't help her morale or her ambition to envy Faye Dunaway getting picked by Warren Beatty for *Bonnie & Clyde* or Olivia Hussey for getting picked by Zeffirelli to play Juliet or Katharine Hepburn's niece getting picked to play her daughter in *Guess Who's Coming To Dinner*. You could bet your sweet bippy Katharine Houghton didn't have to audition.

The sound of Georgina's bedroom door creaking open caused Mona to switch off her bed lamp. Her own door was open. She wanted it to seem as if she were asleep. In the darkness, she heard the lovers creep past her door and down the stairs, every sound magnified. The street door slammed. The door of Nick's car opened and shut. The engine sputtered, snorted, and finally hummed. The gears shifted. The car took off. How she envied Georgina, the *Lady* Georgina with her aristocratic bones and porcelain complexion. Why wasn't she in that car with Nick, driving somewhere romantic with Nick in the cool night air?

'Amy . . .' she called out timidly. She needed to be with someone. Amy didn't reply. In New York, this wouldn't have stopped Mona. In New York, she'd have banged on the door and demanded companionship. Instead, she made her way in the dark to the living room – excuse *me*, folks, the *sitting* room! – and the telephone perched on an end table by the fireplace. She was a frightened, homesick little girl. She wanted her mother. It was six hours earlier in New York, the operator said. Perfect. Her mother would be sick with worry and relieved to hear from her. Mona would confess her sins and beg her mother's forgiveness. They would both cry, and Mona would promise to catch the next available plane home.

'Sorry. There's no reply.' No reply? Where the hell was she, anyhow? What kind of a mother was that? Out somewhere, when she should be sitting by the phone anxiously awaiting her only daughter to call her from London, England! Out of sight, out of mind. Nobody cared what happened to her, right? Nobody cared whether she lived or died.

A fuzzy brown sofa pillow reminded her of her abandoned teddy bear. She cradled it in her arms and took it back with her to bed where, without bothering to undress, she fell into a deep sleep.

'Wake up, Cinderella!' She could smell Nick's fragrance before opening her eyes, a pungent, expensive cologne that cleared her head. A bright shaft of sunlight made her squint. 'I've brought you a nice cup of tea.'

Nick Albert stood beside her bed holding a small wooden tray, his smile fading to a look of consternation as she tried to sit up. 'Look here, are you all right?'

'What time is it?'

'It's gone eleven. We were getting a touch worried. Amy tried to wake you before she left. She was worried, too. She said you'd slept in your clothes.'

The mother of all yawns overtook her before she could control it.

Nice Girls

She knew she must look like a hippopotamus. Sure enough she hadn't undressed, hadn't washed her face or brushed her teeth the night before, and here was Nick Albert seeing her in this disgusting condition. More of God's punishment. Yet Nick was not the sexy cavalier of the previous night. He was almost avuncular, and clearly concerned.

'Amy said she thought you were going over to RADA today. I'm heading in that direction, so I can deliver you to the door if you like.'

She had lied so convincingly about RADA that she had almost believed it herself until last night's panic. Thank God her mother hadn't been home. She couldn't confess this latest and worst example of sneakiness to the one person in her life who loved her unconditionally, warts and all. She was feeling more like her old self this morning. Since she had an undeniable talent for deviousness, she would turn it to positive use. She would just show up at RADA with her audition pieces and insist on attending some summer courses. What could they do to her, send her to the Tower, have her head chopped off?

She would say she had phoned from New York and that someone had told her to come right over and she had used her hard-earned money from waitressing and babysitting. That would get them.

'Come along,' Nick persisted.

'If you insist. I wouldn't want to take you out of your way.' All she had needed was a good night's sleep. Today she could handle anything. Nick Albert, RADA, anything! Last night's tears and depression had been the result of mixing wine and jet lag. She was not used to wine. She would have to avoid it, if that was how it affected her. She had a *yiddishe kop*; it was true, Jews couldn't drink. Look what it had done to her, making her morbid, imagining all sorts of things about Nick Albert, turning her into a dumb little crybaby over some jerk in suede shoes.

God had punished her and forgiven her and given her perspective. Nick was not the lecher she had conjured up. No question that he was a dreamboat, but there was also no question that he was Georgina's dreamboat and that he was simply being courteous to her and Amy for Georgina's sake, like an older brother she and Amy could depend on.

'Shall I go in with you?' Nick offered, when the Lagonda had reached Gower Street. What was he, some kind of mind-reader?

Could he sense her rising panic and her sudden feverish plan to walk in, pretend to be lost, and beat a hasty retreat?

'Who are you, my father?'

He kissed his index finger and tapped it on her nose. 'Rude child. Behave yourself. Now go on in, before I sweep you off to some cheap hotel and ravish you!'

The building was not at all what she had expected. No grandiose columns, no towering entrance emblazoned with classical carvings and Shakespearean motifs. The doorway was narrow. Above it a barely noticeable sign said ROYAL ACADEMY OF DRAMATIC ART. To its left and right were equally unremarkable friezes of a man and woman looking bored. *British understatement*, she decided, clutching her portfolio in sweaty hands and wishing she looked like Julie Christie.

Her portfolio contained two audition pieces – Molly Bloom's soliloquy, and Kate's final speech from *The Taming of the Shrew*. She entered smiling confidently. The small entrance hall was deserted except for a woman behind a tall, intimidating desk, who rolled her eyes with exasperation at the sight of Mona and continued an angry conversation on the telephone in a mixture of French and German.

In what appeared to be a challenge to Mona's poise and an expression of doubt as to her acting ability, the woman continued to talk for some minutes without further acknowledgment of the visitor, perhaps hoping she would go away. At last, and without ending the conversation, she sighed elaborately and said, 'Hold on, there seems to be a person here.' She covered the mouthpiece with her hand and looked at Mona as if she were a bumblebee at a picnic. 'Well?'

As it turned out, the situation was far worse than Mona could possibly have imagined it to be. It wouldn't have mattered what she was wearing, how she looked, or whether she was Sarah Bernhardt reincarnate. The facts were these: There was no summer course; if there had been, she as an American would have had to file an application months earlier, and would have then had to have been selected for an audition and interview in New York. Few Americans were even permitted to audition, the woman had assured Mona. Fewer still were accepted for study. She had thrust a RADA brochure and application form across the desk before turning her back and continuing her phone conversation, her hunched shoulders expressing her profound annoyance at the interruption.

Nice Girls

Mona was so rattled she dropped her portfolio.

'Allow *moi*!' A young man had materialized beside her. 'Don't mind her.'

'It's okay.'

'You're an American? I'm from Australia, myself.'

'So what am I supposed to do, cheer?'

'Quit the crap. What we both need is a drink. There's a pub across the road.'

'I don't drink.'

'A Coke then?'

His name was Bill Neal. His grandfather had migrated from Dublin to Queensland before the war. He had gotten the acting bug early, appearing in school productions, memorizing the classics. After reading about the London success of another Australian, Peter Finch, he had worked two years in the canebrakes to earn passage to England.

'It took another two years before I got into RADA. But I finally made it. It's been two wonderful years.'

'I can't wait that long. I told everyone I was going to RADA. They all expect me to come back in September sounding like Glenda Jackson.' She and several classmates had seen Jackson play Charlotte Corday in the Broadway production of *Marat/Sade*. 'What am I going to do?'

He stared at her thoughtfully. 'I may have a solution. The good Lord works in mysterious ways his wonders to perform. Can you be trusted?'

Liar and conniver she might be, but yes, in her snow-white heart of hearts she knew she could be trusted. The question was, who in hell was *he*, and could *he* be trusted? From grim experience she also knew in her snow-white heart of hearts that any man who said 'Trust me' could automatically be counted on to jump on your bones.

On the other hand, this guy didn't look like a mass murderer. He had thin wrists, she could probably slam him against the wall if he got cute. Feeling this surge of belligerence improved her state of mind. 'What do you think?'

It turned out he was conducting a clandestine acting class during the summer hiatus. It was against Academy rules, but he needed the money. In fact, he was running late for his afternoon session. If she liked, she could start today. 'Call it a RADA annex.'

Her mother had warned her never to get into a car with a

51

stranger. Nobody knew where she was. She could disappear and never be seen again. He could be a kidnapper for a white slave ring. She could be drugged and transported to Turkey or Syria, forced to commit unspeakable acts, and condemned to a harem. (Unless some sultan or emir fell passionately in love with her pale white body, until he found out she was Jewish and had her executed in the public square.)

Or he could be just an ordinary man. He could take her to some secluded house, slit her throat, and steal her travelers checks and passport. American passports were worth a fortune on the black market.

There proved to be no cause for concern about getting into a car. Bill Neal had a motorbike. The flat he used as his studio was on the top floor of a building in Battersea that had seen better days. 'High ceilings, but the wrong side of the river!'

The class, grown restless with waiting, acknowledged Bill's apologies and his introduction of Mona with languid disinterest.

'American?' one asked.

'That's right.' A breakthrough.

'I do hope you won't keep bounding in here, shouting "Hi!". Why must all you Americans say "Hi!"? It sounds Japanese.'

Before Mona could think of a snappy retort, another question was addressed to her. 'Do you sing at all?'

'Well, I sing a little. I mean I've had lessons, and as a matter of fact I've appeared in some amateur productions. Nothing major – Ado Annie in *Oklahoma*, stuff like that, more comedy than real singing, if you know what I mean. . . .' She was doing it again, talking too much, running off at the mouth. She stopped herself from breaking into a chorus of 'I'm just a girl who cain't say no!'

'How terribly interesting,' her inquisitor said slyly. 'I thought you might be related to Barbra Streisand. You look rather like her, doesn't she, everyone?' The group nodded sweetly, anticipating the kill. 'The nose and all. I'm sure it's a help. Lucky you. Isn't she awfully lucky, Bill?'

Their host had been in the tiny kitchen and had not heard the warm words of welcome. He returned with a battered tea cart in time to hear only the last remark and to call the class to order.

'Very lucky, Minerva, and we're awfully lucky to have her in the class. She'll help us authenticate our Yank accents when we do Odets and Miller later on.'

Nice Girls

By the time the class had ended and she had made her way back to Chelsea Mews, Mona decided no little anti-Semitic English bitch was going to get her goat. Besides, it was true. She did have a big nose. A big *Jewish* nose. If that washed-out blonde thought she could get in Mona's hair she had another think coming.

To her surprise, the insult had acted on her nervous system like adrenaline. When Bill Neal asked her to favour the class with a reading, she had whipped out the Molly Bloom monologue and held them speechless.

'Extraordinary!' Bill gasped.

That showed them, right? What she should have done was ask Miss Washed-Out Blonde whether she knew Leopold Bloom was Jewish and had a big nose? She found Amy and Georgina in the sitting room, eating leftovers from the previous night. 'Come and join us!' Georgina called out gaily, waving an empty wine glass. 'Nick's off somewhere with his tourist ladies. Let's the three of us have a girls' party. Amy dear, be a pet and pour some wine for Mona.'

The pinkish glow on Amy's cheeks showed that she had already had some wine. With a concentrated effort to hold the wine bottle steady, she filled a glass for Mona and replenished her own. Raising hers, she proposed a toast, 'One for all, all for one – Georgina, Mona, Amy – The Three Musketeers!'

Mona clinked glasses with the other two. 'The Three Muskeeters of Chelsea Mews!'

'To Chelsea Mews!' they chorused.

'Wait!' Mona sprang to her feet. 'We're not The Three *Muske*teers. This is Chelsea Mews, right? So what does that make us? The Three *Mews*keteers! One for all, all for one, let's hear it for The Three *Mews*keteers!'

'The Three *Mews*keteers!'

'Ladies!' Nick Albert stood framed in the sitting room doorway. He doffed an invisible plumed hat and made an elaborate court bow. 'One for all, all for one! What an enchanting idea!'

It didn't take the keen analytical mind of a brain surgeon to figure out that Georgina's plan for a girls' night would have to be postponed. Her reaction to Nick's unexpected arrival was so naked in its passion as to be embarrassing. When Amy and Mona took the hint and retreated toward their respective bedrooms, she made no polite move to stop them.

Mona was tired anyhow. Her momentary exuberance had been

deflated like a pin-pricked balloon. It had been a long, punishing day. While taking classes with Bill Neal might not be the right thing to do, it seemed to be the only thing she *could* do. It was a workable compromise. She would benefit from his RADA training and from working with RADA students. If cracks about her Jewish nose were part of the initiation into the club, so be it. There was comfort in the theory that people who attacked you were insecure about themselves and scared to death of your obvious superiority. Poor Minerva. Mona would not rise to the bait. She would treat Minerva like the pathetic person she was, with patience and forbearance. The Saint Mona approach.

Although the door to her room was open, Nick Albert knocked to announce his presence. 'You looked especially pretty this morning.'

A warning signal went off. 'Thank you.'

'How did it go?'

What business was it of his? 'Fine. Really fine.'

'So you're all settled in, with your courses and all?'

'Everything's ginger-peachy.'

'Ginger-peachy?'

'Ginger-peachy, Don Ameche! It means everything's cool.'

'I'm longing to hear every detail.'

The warning signal buzzed louder in her ears. 'Not tonight, Nick. I'm really pooped. My first day, and stuff.'

'Of course. Forgive me.'

She waited for him to leave. He was making her twitch again. He was Georgina's boyfriend, wasn't he? Why didn't he stop pestering her and go back to Georgina where he belonged? The way he was staring at her only increased her discomfort. He draped himself against the door jamb and thoughtfully inserted one of his small cigars into his tortoiseshell holder, an act of sexual suggestion followed by an excruciatingly slow body search for his lighter. He lit up, inhaled deeply, and held the smoke until it seemed to Mona he must have swallowed it, only to release it in a wispy cloud around his head. 'Actually, I stopped by Tower Street to collect you, thought you might want me to run you home.'

'You did?'

'The gorgon at reception said I was mistaken. She said there *were* no summer classes.'

4

Amy

Didn't it beat all? Just when they were starting to have a good time, just when she and Mona and Lady Georgina were starting to relax and get to know each other, just when the little house in Chelsea Mews was starting to feel like home away from home, wouldn't you know that Nick would waltz in and spoil everything?

The Three Mewsketeers? That was Mona all over, a real card, quick like a bunny. Wait till she told Lou. He'd get a real charge out of that. He was always teasing her about having been a Mouseketeer as a youngster. They'd known each other that long. She had stashed away her old Mouseketeer ears in the attic until Lou said he wanted her to wear them on their wedding night, no frilly nightgown, just the ears. The thought had so embarrassed her she threw the ears away.

Forget Lou, anyhow. This morning she had cabled him the Chelsea address and phone number and said she was sorry she hadn't called him before leaving Providence. Not that she really was sorry. She just wanted him to know she wasn't mad at him for what had happened their last weekend together. Even though she was worried sick.

There was so much she wanted to tell him about teaming up with Mona and moving in with Georgina, and about her first day's experiences with the architectural seminar. It would all go into her diary of course. She had skipped last night but would make up for it tonight, and maybe put it in a letter to Lou too if she wasn't too tired.

She'd really been so thrilled when she'd gotten back to the house and Georgina had suggested tea. It was so civilized. Then Mona came in and suddenly it was a hen party, and they were all three of them beginning to exchange experiences and she was just beginning to enjoy herself, when Nick Albert spoiled it all. Girls' Rules were obviously the same in England as they were at home. When a man shows up, all girls' plans are canceled or postponed. Whenever this happened, she was surprised by the sudden change in the girl involved. The phone call or arrival of a man instantly turned a warm, friendly chum into a ferocious, calculating warrior girding herself for the fray.

Mona and she got the message and excused themselves. Nick apologized for breaking up the party and urged them to stay and have a glass of wine. Georgina purposely didn't join in, while begging them with her eyes to please, for heaven's sake, leave!

Amy was sorely tempted to trill, 'Don't do anything I wouldn't do!' It was what her father had said to her at the airport, trying to be jocular while looking everywhere but at her. But jokiness was not his style. To him, life was real, life was earnest. A deeply responsible and quietly devoted family man, he had always spent considerable quality time with Amy for as far back as she could remember – helping her with her lessons, teaching her to ride her bicycle and to sail and ski and drive safely, expecting her to get good grades and to volunteer her services to the community.

Driving to the airport had turned out to be a really miserable experience. She had never seen her father act that way, switching lanes, leaning on his horn, cursing other drivers, coming close to an accident several times. They had been alone in the car. Her mother had said good-bye at breakfast after giving her her own American Express card with a five-thousand-dollar limit, in exchange for Amy's promise to be prudent, courteous, and to make the most of her opportunities to gain knowledge and to broaden friendships. More demonstrative than her husband, she had hugged her lean and coltish offspring to her and pushed the bangs back from Amy's unlined brow. 'Let them see your pretty face, dear.'

Since her parents were themselves leaving the following day on their own trip, her mother had elected to stay behind to pack. On the drive from Providence to Kennedy Airport, Amy had sensed that her father really wanted to say something personal. The best he could do was go over and over in excruciating detail the plans for her trip and the architectural highlights listed in the seminar catalog. He didn't want her to be short-changed. He insisted she assure him that she knew, she understood, she wouldn't forget, and so on and so on. She wished she could have bid both parents good-bye at the house and taken the airport bus, or that Lou had offered to come down from Boston and drive her. Lou had not even called her to wish her good luck.

Thank goodness her plane had taken off on-time. If there had been a delay, and there generally were delays on trans-Atlantic flights, she didn't know how in the world she could have endured her father's painful attempts at conversation. When the flight was called, he looked so sweaty she thought he might be sick. His usual good-bye to her was a stiff hug and a pat on the head. This time he stepped back and formally shook hands. An attempted smile punctuated his parting benediction, a piece of advice totally out of character, 'Don't do anything I wouldn't do!'

The trouble was she already had, two weekends ago with Lou Humphries. She had known before it happened that it was going to happen and that it was the wrong thing to do, wrong for her anyway, against her ingrained principles and sense of self-respect. It didn't matter to her what all the books and magazines were saying about sexual freedom for women. She had been raised to believe a woman's body was a temple to be guarded against defilement. She personally believed it was vulgar and cheap to 'go all the way' before marriage, even with a boy who said he loved you and to whom you were unofficially engaged.

She truly believed a girl who went all the way would automatically forfeit a boy's respect. If she cheapened herself he had every right to break their engagement, or if he did the gentlemanly thing and married her he would never respect her in quite the same way. She was angry with herself for what had happened. She had known when she'd agreed to spend the weekend with Lou that this was *it*. This was not going to be a 'Harvard weekend' in the traditional sense; there was no special event as camouflage. His roommate would be away. They could be alone. What could be clearer than that?

She was in love with Lou Humphries. Or *thought* she was in love with Lou Humphries. Or thought she *should* be in love with Lou Humphries, because they'd grown up together and because he said he was in love with her and because they had always said they would marry when they finished school. Their parents knew each other. Her mother approved of the fact that he was still 'clean-cut' when so many of the boys had let their hair grow long and greasy, and that he didn't seem interested in burning down the university.

She had tried, truly tried, to get her mother alone to discuss things both before and after the fateful weekend. Contraception, for one thing. What did the older woman think about the Pill, or what about the diaphragm? The right moment had never come, and to be candid, her mother probably didn't know any more than she knew. The only gynecologist she could think of was her mother's. Her one and only professional visit to him had convinced her he would not respect her privacy. He had joked with her mother about what a ripe peach she was and about how she had blushed during the examination. 'I envy the lucky fellow who gets her.'

On an impulse, she had made an excuse to go to New York to visit an architectural exhibit, and gone instead to the Margaret Sanger clinic, where she had been fitted with a diaphragm. Out again on the busy Manhattan streets, shame had overwhelmed her. Sex before marriage was totally against her values. Shaking with nerves, she had stopped in an empty doorway to pull herself together. It was no use. She didn't want to be liberated. She let the small package drop from her hand and took off down the crowded street.

'Lady . . . lady! You dropped something!'

Good Samaritan rushes to the aid of Scarlet Woman. She had sneaked it into the house and locked herself in the bathroom to try inserting the diaphragm herself. It had seemed so easy at the clinic. Now the so-called 'odorless lubricant' filled the bathroom with its telltale aroma. The word 'vaginal' made her queasy. Her hand trembled. The diaphragm itself had a life of its own. Several times it flew into the air like a flying saucer, mocking her for her evil intentions.

Lying on her narrow bed in Georgina's house reminded her of Lou's room. The memory of the rubber cap and the tube of slippery gunk still made her shudder. The whole experience made her shudder. She wasn't sure what had gone wrong. She wasn't sure if she had got the cap in right. It was so sticky, and it refused to bend in half the way they had demonstrated. The lubricant squirted out of the tube all over the bathroom floor. She must have put too much in the applicator, because it began to run down her thighs.

If she had thought Lou would be happy and excited after all the months of pleading, she was mistaken about that, too. Now he kept asking her if she was sure. After a lot of fumbling and heavy breathing he was on top of her, crushing her ribs so she couldn't breathe. His bed was lumpy and bruised her back. She couldn't feel anything except his weight bouncing up and down against her thighs, rubbing her raw. Straining to hear what he was saying, she realized he was cursing. The ultimate ecstasy she had expected after all the months of petting had failed to materialize.

Was that all there was?

'You all right?' he had gasped. She had nodded and shut her eyes, hoping that indicated passion spent. He had rolled off and rolled over, his back to her. Her stomach wet and sticky, she wondered if it was her stuff or his stuff. If this was going all the way, she much preferred the hours of kissing and hugging and touching they had previously experienced.

Back in Providence, she had felt bewildered and alone. She wasn't sure if she had lost her virginity. She wasn't sure if she had inserted the diaphragm correctly. Lou didn't seem to know either, although from the way he behaved afterwards he seemed to think everything was fine. He didn't hate her in the morning or behave coldly. Rather, he seemed to think that her sexual surrender meant that she would cancel her plans for London and spend the summer with him.

'The seminar is important to me, Lou.'

'More important than me?'

'Important in a different way.' She had again tried to explain about this unique opportunity to examine living examples of architectural history like Sir John Soane's house in Lincoln's Inn Fields and the Queen's House at Greenwich designed by Inigo Jones.

'You're a selfish bitch!'

He knew she hated that kind of language.

'You're selfish, too! This is important to me and my career!'

'*What* career? I thought we were getting married! Besides, you don't need to work. You've got all those trust funds.'

He had refused to discuss it further. If she was intent on going to London, that was her decision. He warned her that hot weather made him horny, and he might meet someone else during the summer months ahead. In one respect she hoped he would. Alone now on her narrow bed in Chelsea Mews, she focused her thoughts on what Lou called her 'honey pot,' even though he knew she hated that expression, too. She conjured up sexy thoughts but felt nothing, just as she had felt nothing with him on top of her.

Frigid. Other girls were hot; she was cold. She had listened to all the talk and managed to nod knowingly and brag about how great Lou was. Because he was big and handsome and acted possessively, everyone said how lucky she was and to hang on to him.

She remembered hearing a bunch of girls say that when they thought about boys they got hot. 'And wet!' Rachel Sanderson had sniggered, causing an explosion of giggles and red faces.

Wanting to feel hot, she concentrated on Lou, trying to conjure up his presence, trying to feel how nice it would be to have him lying there beside her, to snuggle in his arms, and tell him about her first day at the seminar and how she had learned that the name London came from the Saxon words 'Lynn Din.' 'Isn't that fascinating?'

'What's fascinating?'

Nick Albert was smiling down at her. The sight of him did what the image of Lou Humphries had not done. She felt hot. She felt wet. She felt terrified by the unknown.

Caught in the act! *What* act, she wasn't exactly sure, except that it was somehow shameful. Her seventeen years' conditioning of showing courteous good manners in any situation deserted her. She scrambled to her feet, pushed him into the corridor, and slammed the door shut.

'Amy!' He tapped gently on the door. 'Good Lord, Amy! Sorry if I startled you! Please let me apologize. It's Nick.'

Nick. Another name for the Devil? She really had to laugh at that. Or was it that she had to force herself to laugh and remind herself that all this was a new experience? For the first time in her life, she was away from home. Nick was Georgina's boyfriend. The house was small. She had left her door open. He had heard her say 'Isn't that fascinating?' and stopped by to chat.

'Amy?' Georgina. 'Amy, dear, may I have a word?' A murmur of voices ceased abruptly with the slamming of a door – Georgina's from the sound of it.

'Come on in.'

A frazzled Georgina stood timidly in the doorway. 'Was Nick being rude?'

'Well, no . . .'

'I will not have any rudeness in my house. Did he say anything to offend you, Amy?'

'No, of course not. I was just startled to see him. I should have closed my door.'

Georgina's face softened. 'He was startled, too. He couldn't imagine why you slammed the door like that.'

It was a good thing he couldn't imagine the reason for her upset.

'I must have dozed off and I was surprised to see him there, that's all.'

'He asked me to give you his apologies.'

'Accepted.'

'We're going out.'

'Have a good time.'

'You and Mona, if you haven't any plans, may I suggest you explore the King's Road? There are hundreds of little shops, coffee houses, boutiques . . .'

'And pubs! Tell them to call in on one of the pubs – The Chelsea Potter!' Nick's voice came from somewhere behind her. 'Two pretty birds, someone's sure to stand them a drink.'

Mona seemed even more depressed than Amy was. 'What do you think? Should we get some stuff and make our own dinner? We do have kitchen privileges, you know.'

'We should eat something.'

Mona's eyes filled with tears. 'I'm never going to eat anything ever again. Ever!'

'Mona! What's wrong? Are you sick?'

'Sick is right. Sick of being fat as a pig!'

Amy was genuinely bewildered. 'But you're not fat. You're . . . voluptuous.'

Mona's nose had turned red as the tears spilled down her cheeks. 'What do you know? You're a skinny *merink*. You were born with those bones. You and Twiggy. You've never had to diet in your entire life, right?'

'Gee, Mona . . . I'm sorry!' It wasn't her fault that she was skinny, so why was she apologizing? She had been raised to be courteous and attentive to other people, to try to be tactful and not hurt their feelings. Apologizing was not the same thing. Apologizing meant you'd done something wrong and the other person had to forgive you. She had apologized to Lou for the trip to London. She had apologized to Nick for shutting the door in his face when he had intruded on her. Now here she was practically begging Mona to forgive her for being thin. If she wasn't careful, it could become a habit. She would apologize her way through the rest of her life.

'I'm sorry, too, Amy. I didn't mean what I said.'

'Well, I *did* mean what I said. You're *not* fat! You're voluptuous, like a Renaissance painting. Georgina's right. We should explore the King's Road and find ourselves a little restaurant. My treat.' Waving away Mona's attempted protest, she added, 'It's okay. I've got a trust fund.'

'Okay – but you can't go looking like that.'

'Like what?'

'Your face. It's naked. Come with me.'

Docile as a lamb, Amy sat on the rim of the lion's-paw tub and surrendered her face to Mona's expert ministrations. An ivory base, lavender lips and cheeks, charcoal eyeliner smudged above and below, more lavender on the lids, and feathery pencil marks to define the natural arch of her brows. 'Have you ever worn false eyelashes?'

Amy swallowed the impulse to say they looked like bugs. Mona was being the older, more sophisticated sister. Mona knew so much more about the world. Maybe she could confide in Mona, tell her about Lou, ask her advice about things. 'No . . .'

'Well, tonight's the night, kiddo! Close your eyes and don't blink.'

'We look like something out of a magazine!' Mona declared, in approval of a job well done. In their vinyl boots, patterned pantyhose, mini-dresses, and bangle bracelets worn above the elbow, they set out for their first taste of Chelsea night life, the fabled Chelsea of the Swinging Singles.

When they had reached the King's Road, Amy stood paralyzed with uncertainty, looking to Mona to take the lead. The sidewalk was crowded with milling groups of people who seemed to know each other. All were about the same age as Mona and herself, but it was in some instances hard to tell the difference between the boys and the girls. They all had long hair, wore earrings and bizarre makeup, and for the most part sported second-hand Army uniforms or blue jeans with cowboy boots. Traffic was heavy. The red double-decker buses wove in and out of herds of raffish jalopies, their occupants standing up and demanding to be seen.

Amy felt totally intimidated, as if she were back at the freshman mixer where she didn't know a soul. What did they do now? *Mona, what do we do now?*

'Isn't this great?' Mona whispered. 'Come on! There's a pub.'

The Chelsea Potter was a belly-to-belly babble of bodies, each clutching a precariously full glass which miraculously did not

Nice Girls

splatter or fall. 'Isn't this great?' Mona repeated. 'Reminds me of the subway during rush hour.'

The bartender smiled benignly, his face florid above a green turtleneck sweater inside a tattersall shirt. 'And what can I offer you, my darlin's?'

A man beside Mona ordered a half-pint of bitter. 'I'll have a half-pint of bitter. Amy? What about you?'

A Coke was what she really wanted, a cherry Coke with lots of ice. 'I'll have the same.'

'Bitter' was the word, all right. 'Very interesting flavor,' Amy commented to no one in particular.

Mona had shifted her attention to the man crushed against them. 'Hi!'

He sipped at his drink before acknowledging her. 'Ah, the American invasion.'

Mona jumped at the opportunity. 'My name's Mona. This is my friend Amy. We just arrived in London yesterday.'

'How very brave of you.' He turned to a woman half-hidden behind him. 'This is my wife. Love, come and meet two brave Americans who just arrived in London yesterday.'

'Married, dammit,' Mona whispered. 'I thought I'd find somebody to buy us dinner.'

Amy whispered back, 'Forget it. I'm buying dinner. Remember?'

Unlike movies about beautiful young American girls abroad, neither prince nor peasant detached himself from the crowd and offered to show them around. The dark ale, after only a few tentative sips, had settled in Amy's legs. Mona's glass, she noted, also had barely been touched. 'Please, Mona, let's go.'

'If you insist.'

If only Lou were there! They wouldn't be standing like two lost souls, wondering which way to go to find a restaurant. Not that Mona wasn't terrific. Without Mona, she would have gone straight back to the house. But Lou would have taken them each by the arm and marched them down the street until they'd found a restaurant – a man's job. It made her angry to admit it, but it was true.

'Here we go, luv!' Mona trying out her English accent.

After the pub hubbub, the Royal Kitchen was a quiet cavern of plaster walls and wooden tables lit with red candles.

'You know what I'd really like? A toasted bagel with Nova Scotia and cream cheese.'

'Me for tuna salad on whole wheat toast.'

The menu offered eggs and chips, sausages and mash, steak-and-kidney pie, and American hamburgers. 'But I wouldn't have the American hamburgers if I were you,' the waitress cautioned.

'Why not?' Mona wanted to know.

'Because you're Americans, that's why. I had an American here yesterday. Shouted the place down. Said if that was an American hamburger he'd eat his hat. Between you and me, the eggs and chips is safest.'

Hot food, soft candlelight, and the relief inherent in being together in a foreign environment soothed their nerves and encouraged the sharing of confidences. Because she wanted to talk about Lou, Amy started the conversation by asking Mona if she was in love.

'Only with my career. But you are, aren't you? Have you heard from your boyfriend?'

That simple question opened the floodgates. Everything that had happened that weekend in Boston, and everything since, came pouring out. 'Oh, Mona! What if I'm pregnant? What'll I do?'

'Are you in love with him?'

'I . . .' She had to admit she wasn't sure. 'Of course I'm in love with him. We're engaged to be engaged.'

'Are you *sure* you're in love with him?'

'Of course I'm in love with him!' How dare Mona question her? Mona didn't know the first thing about it!

'Then why did you leave him alone?'

That's what Lou had said. 'Well, what about my career?'

'I don't know. If I had a boyfriend I was crazy about, I wouldn't leave him alone for five minutes!'

Amy had been enjoying the thick fried potatoes. Now she pushed them aside, unable to chew or swallow. Mona was right, Lou was right. She should never have left. Lou would find another girl. She would be too scared to have an abortion. He would refuse to marry her. She would have the baby and give it up for adoption and become a nun or join the Peace Corps.

'What should I do?'

'Frankly?'

'Frankly.'

'Forget Lou. At least for the summer. It's like we said yesterday. This is a chance for both of us to broaden our experience. Get it while you can. Tomorrow we could be dead like Bobby Kennedy, right?'

'But what if I'm pregnant?'

'When are you due?'

'July 4th!'

'Independence Day! It's a crap shoot. If you get your period, you're a free and independent woman!'

'And if I don't?'

Mona paused to consider her answer. 'We'll figure it out, okay? So let's change the subject, okay? What do you think of Nick Albert?'

The question caught Amy completely off-guard. Fortunately the restaurant was too dark for Mona to notice the sudden surge of color to her cheeks.

'Georgina's really crazy about him, isn't she? What do you think?' Dare she tell Mona how sexy Nick made her feel?

'Well . . .' Mona leaned toward her with the bright-eyed excitement of confession. 'I think he's got a crush on me! It's very embarrassing on account of who he is . . . Like you say, he's Georgina's boyfriend. But the way he looks at me . . . And this morning he insisted on driving me to school. I don't know, I just have this crazy feeling he's going to make a pass – and then what do I do?'

'Gosh, I don't know either.' Thank goodness she hadn't taken Mona into her confidence. A good example of why you must never succumb to the pleasures of confession! It never failed; you'd *always* be sorry.

'It's not that I've led him on or anything.'

'Of course not.'

'I mean we've only been here since yesterday, right?'

'Right . . .'

'Still . . . I've just got this feeling that something may happen, and I certainly don't want to make Georgina unhappy.'

'Of course not.'

Returning to Chelsea Mews, they found Nick's Lagonda parked outside and the house dark. 'They're back.'

The two young women let themselves in and crept up the narrow stairs as quietly as possible. Amy was, on balance, feeling much better about things. Being with Mona had put everything into perspective. She might be in love with Lou, but not as much in love as she had thought or she would never have left him for a summer abroad. If she was in fact pregnant she would know it by July 4th, and if that was the case she'd decide what to do then; meantime, there was no point worrying. As for Nick Albert, he certainly made her hot and bothered, a fact that frightened her enough to make her vow she would avoid him henceforth and spend the next couple of weeks at least concentrating on the history of British architecture.

A whispered good night. Mona disappeared into her room. Amy into hers, where a lovely surprise awaited her. A note from Georgina said Lou had phoned. He was, according to Georgina, desperately sad that he had missed her. He said she was not to phone him back because he was going sailing and that he would try again in a few days. The note concluded: 'He misses you and sends you much love!'

Amy kissed the note and fell rapturously on her bed, clutching the piece of paper to her breast. Lou loved her! She had stuck to her guns and won! Absence *did* make the heart grow fonder! Everything was going to be all right! The sound of a door opening, and muffled voices, brought her back to her feet. Georgina and Nick. Straining to hear, all she could make out was Nick's 'Night night, angel. Ring you first thing.'

She shut her door and turned the key. Mona might think Nick Albert had a crush on her. But the look in his eyes earlier this evening when he'd stood over Amy's bed continued to make her feel uneasy, and somehow guilty of inviting his attentions. She would avoid any further chance of misunderstanding. Holding her breath, she listened to his footsteps. Was it her imagination? Had he stopped at her door? The doorknob turned. 'Amy? You asleep? We heard you come in. Just want to be sure you got the message.' The doorknob turned again. 'Ah, well.'

At the sound of his retreating footsteps she could breathe again, her heart thumping as if she'd run a mile without a warm-up. Sound traveled in the quiet of night. She could hear the downstairs door, the yellow door Nick had painted for Georgina, open and then close.

She shut off her bed light to avoid being seen, and moved to the window. The mews looked like a chocolate-box painting, the nineteenth-century buildings and even older cobblestones bathed in the glow of a Victorian street lamp. She watched mesmerized as Nick checked out the Lagonda and leaned against its side to light

Nice Girls

one of his small cigars. The ritual of inserting the slender cigarillo into the slender holder completed, he lit up, took a long, sensuous drag, and inexplicably looked up at her window.

Panicked, she jumped back, her chest pounding once again. What if he had seen her? She listened for the sound of the Lagonda starting up and taking him away.

'Don't turn on the light!'

He was in her room, smiling at her. With the grace and agility of a snake, he had used the hood of his car as a stepping stone and slithered through the window. His hands cupped her face. 'Georgina wanted me to apologize.'

'Apologize?' Her head was spinning. The bitter. That's what it was, that bitter had been much stronger than she'd thought.

'Apologize for entering your room uninvited and upsetting you.' His lips caressed her eyelids. 'Baby bird. I would not upset you for the world.'

5

Georgina

Absolute bliss! She was alone in the house. Mona and Amy had gone off to their respective classes. Nick was away on an overnight excursion to Stratford-upon-Avon with a party of blue-haired ladies. From Wichita, Kansas, he said, or was it somewhere like Idaho or Iowa, one of those odd places that all sound alike? Much as she longed for him and missed him madly, it was sheer heaven to be on her own and still in her dressing gown though it had gone noon, sipping her second cup of coffee in the deserted sitting room, smiling to herself.

In the fortnight since the Americans had arrived, Mona's facetious little idea about 'The Three Mewsketeers' had caught on. Nick was so enchanted he had mentioned it to a chum on the *Evening Standard* and Bob's-your-uncle there they were, a jolly good photograph of the three of them under a head YOUNG CHELSEA BEAUTIES JOIN TOGETHER AS 'THREE MEWSKETEERS.'

Great fun, really, old friends ringing to say they'd been meaning to ring since her parents' accident and were furious with themselves for not ringing sooner, poor darling Georgina, but now, after seeing her and her Americans in the *Evening Standard Diary*, they were relieved to see her in such a good form. And why didn't she and the Americans come 'round for tea?

Then some of the fashion girls picked up on it and wanted to do stories on them for *Cosmopolitan* and *The Tatler*. Were the Mewsketeers planning some outrageous social do? an editor asked. Leave it to Mona. Quick as a flash she announced that The Three Mewsketeers were about to give their first annual Fourth of July Picnic and Square Dance, with hot dogs and sweet corn, all in the name of Anglo-American friendship.

'A smashing idea!' Nick had exclaimed. 'Clever girl, Mona. Isn't that so, Georgina?'

Jealousy choked her. 'Nobody asked what I think! After all, it's my house, isn't it?' Mona might have discussed the idea with her before announcing it to the world.

'Georgina! Don't spoil the fun!' Nick had scolded, his tone unusually stern.

The Americans looked stricken with the embarrassment of being trapped in a lovers' quarrel.

'It was just an idea,' Mona apologized.

'Not at all,' Georgina had capitulated. 'It's a splendid idea. A Fourth of July Picnic! Splendid.'

'You won't have to do a thing,' Mona assured her.

'I'll make the Boston Baked Beans and the cole slaw,' Amy chimed in. 'And we'll get that woman at the Embassy to get us into the commissary for some real hot dog buns.'

'And relish.'

'And mustard.'

'And sauerkraut.'

'And whipped cream, lashings of whipped cream!' Georgina had cried.

'Whipped cream on hot dogs?' Mona protested.

They all laughed at that, and Georgina breathed a sigh of relief that she'd skirted an unpleasant disagreement with Nick. Whenever Nick took on that imperious, commanding tone, she felt a *frisson* of fear larded with a rush of sexual excitement. It didn't matter to her whether his fierce tone had been a playful tease or a harsh demand. She had shut her mouth and done what she was told. The fact was that, although for reasons she could not define, she trusted Nick completely. Put another way, she was happy having his advice and judgment.

It had been his idea to take in American students as paying guests, and now she had money in her pocket. It had been his idea that she spend some of that money on herself – a new hair style at Vidal Sassoon's, a badly overdue manicure, and at Nick's insistence, her toenails varnished a particularly vulgar shade of crimson because he rather enjoyed kissing her toes.

'How beautiful are thy feet in shoes, O Prince's daughter!' he had crooned in that reverential tone he adopted when paying homage to the separate and varied parts of her body. She was only passingly familiar with 'The Song of Solomon.' Once again, as in previous situations, he had astonished her with his erudition by reciting it all from memory.

His mere presence still caused her cheeks to blaze. It was clear he had that effect on the two Americans as well, poor lambs. Not that she blamed them. Mona especially could be seen going all over peculiar at the very sight of him. He knew, and could be very naughty, too, running his finger down her backbone while urging, 'Stand up straight, Mona! One can't be a great actress if one slumps over.'

The other night, he had asked Mona about her acting course and what roles she was playing.

She had squirmed a bit before replying. 'Don't laugh – Juliet.'

Juliet! Poor darling Mona! Of course she was all wrong for Juliet. What on earth were they doing giving that tender, fragile role to a brash New York Jewess who would as soon spit in your eye as look at you?

Nick Albert did not agree. 'Americans are insecure; all of them, from the president in the White House to the lowliest shorthand typist. All Americans are insecure. It's because we let them go in 1776. Americans still wish they were English. But Americans *can't* be English no matter how they try. They can wear Jean Muir. They can take lessons in British at Berlitz. They can marry a title and live in Gloucestershire with dogs, horses, and the braying gentry, and it *still* won't matter a sausage. They can't be English whatever they do. So all we can do is to let them mingle with us and of course pay handsomely for the privilege, all the while making things as nice for them as we can.'

By way of illustration he had persuaded Mona to let him play Romeo in the balcony scene with her as Juliet, again reciting the lines from memory. So hypnotic was his presence that for one incandescent moment the Mona who had more closely resembled the captain of a girl's basketball team had turned into the tremulous, yearning maiden on the brink of womanhood.

'Wow!' Amy had sighed, as Mona/Juliet burst into tears of emotion.

'Wow, indeed! Well done, you!' Nick congratulated Mona when the scene was through. 'What we need now is some wine.' Soon after their arrival, Amy had elected quietly to stock the larder with masses of food and drink as what she called her 'small contribution' to the household. As she filled their glasses and offered water biscuits and great wodges of brie to all, Georgina was glad to see her looking more like her old self. For several days past she had been pale and withdrawn, missing her beau more than likely, and working far into the night on her architectural course. Still waters ran deep. She had said little about her personal life. To Georgina, at any rate. Perhaps she had received an ardent letter from America, or better yet, Georgina preferred to think of the transforming powers of a new love. Even better yet, perhaps she had met someone here in England who was bringing the sparkle back to her eyes.

Midday sun flooded Georgina's sitting room. She knew she must dress and get on with her life but found it impossible to stir, impossible to break out of the bubble of happiness that encased her, impossible not to keep returning again and again to the memory of Nick's embraces and to count again and again her blessings. Never again would she take anything for granted. She savored the exquisite flavors of the strong coffee made from freshly ground beans, the rich double cream, the crusty toast in its silver rack, the Danish butter and raspberry preserves, the *Daily Telegraph* and the morning post scattered on the floor, and the flowers, flowers, flowers everywhere. Bowls of them, vases, pots of flowers on every surface.

During the desperate weeks after the accident she had cut her expenses to the minimum. Doing without flowers had been the worst deprivation. Not having flowers had made her feel more poverty-stricken than not having new clothes. Or food for that matter. There had been days of such black depression that she had lived on boiled eggs and tinned soup in order to have a few pennies for a handful of flowers.

Nick! She had read an article about emergency resuscitation of accident victims with the 'kiss of life.' She was the victim of an accident, and Nick had assuredly kissed her back to life! The thought amused her, though his influence went beyond sex. His bullying was so clearly for her own benefit. He himself had supervised the restyling of her hair, discussing the various possibilities with the Sassoon stylist as if she weren't there, pulling and pushing her thick burnished copper tresses into various configurations until 'Yes! By George, you've got it!' Professor Higgins congratulating the stylist, the decision made without consulting her.

'We're getting rid of that old maid aunt look,' was all he had said.

The result was short, full, bouncy, and so glorious she found herself sneaking looks at herself in mirrors and in the reflections of shop windows, touching her hair to make sure it was still there.

He had made other changes, too, particularly in the matter of her underwear. He had thrown away her underpants and bought her a suspender belt to hold up her hose. Underpants were an invention of the Devil, he said. Throughout history women had never worn underpants until the nineteenth century, and what had that led to? War, revolution, and utter chaos. It was his theory that a woman's parts had to breathe free, that covering them tightly with fabric bred bacteria and disease. He further explained, in the same matter-of-fact tone in which one might discuss cricket, that it pleased him during the dreariness of amusing his blue-haired ladies to think of her in her suspender belt, and what heaven it would be to reach up under her skirt and fondle her.

Nick! She lay back spread-eagled as she had that night at the Albert Memorial, reliving every detail. Little had been said in the short time it took to get them from Chelsea to Kensington. When he'd parked the Lagonda in a shadowy cul-de-sac behind the Royal Albert Hall, she remembered thinking, *He's done this before.* He didn't waffle about looking for a space, he turned directly into the narrow passage obscured by trees with the evident knowledge of its being there.

When he took her in his arms she further remembered thinking that this was what he'd had in mind, that this secluded bower in the heart of Kensington, protected from view but with the pulsating hum of traffic as background, was where they would make love and be happy.

Her fear of discovery quickly vanished in the cloak of intimacy he wrapped around them. She blushed to remember that it was *she*, not he, who had yanked off her knickers and then dimly understood why, when they were getting ready to leave the house, he had insisted she wear a skirt instead of trousers. In retrospect the wisdom of wearing a suspender belt was apparent.

Just as she was settling into the soft leather seat, Nick opened the car door. 'On your feet, miss.'

'Where are we going?'

'Be quiet, Georgina. Do as you're told.'

He took an old tartan rug from the boot.

'Nick . . .?' She stood beside him on the pavement.

'Be *quiet!*' This said, he pushed her hard against the car door, stooped before her and ran his hands up the inner sides of her legs, stopping abruptly at the tops of her thighs. 'Shall I stop right here?'

Bastard.

'Do you want me, Georgina?'

She could only gasp.

'Then stop being a bore and do as I say!'

Like thieves in the night, they crept silently around the darkened Royal Albert Hall and waited for a break in the traffic to cross the Kensington Road. Rising murkily above them was the Albert Memorial, Queen Victoria's overwrought tribute to her beloved consort, whose death at the age of forty-two had left her a grim, grief-stricken recluse in permanent mourning for the remaining forty years of her reign. A bit much, Georgina had always thought, but with Nick Albert in her life she could understand the Queen's pain.

'When I was a child, my mother's lover amused himself by telling me the Albert Memorial was named for me. I was two or three at the time and I believed him. It came as a rude shock to find out he was having me on and that it was named for him.'

He pointed to the fourteen-foot statue of Prince Albert looming high above them. 'Come.'

On each of the four sides of the memorial, marble steps were set into grassy hillocks. Choosing the side furthest from Kensington Road, he led the way to the top of the steps, where he spread the tartan rug. Memory of this first of many subsequent visits to the monument activated the stinging ache of the bruises on her back acquired from being crushed against the marble steps.

'Darling heart. What is it?'

So enraptured of the moment she had not wanted to break the spell, hoping her tears of pain would be perceived as tears of joy.

'The steps . . .'

He rolled them like a snowball into the grassy slope. 'Why didn't you tell me?'

Triumph and obeisance merged as she giddily retorted. 'You told me to be quiet! To do as I was told!'

It was then that she quite suddenly saw there was power in submission, power in allowing Nick to think he was her lord and master while learning slowly but surely to manipulate his ego.

He had treated her like porcelain ever since, utterly devoted and caring. Last night, for example, he had taken the time to ring her from Stratford-upon-Avon. To touch hands, he said. To enlist her compassion for the horrors of his situation. 'Imagine, darling,' he had said, 'imagine having to spend a fine summer evening with eight screeching old harridans demanding one's attention!'

'Poor you,' she had commiserated. 'It's best that you face it. All the Americans fancy you. Amy goes all crimson and fidgety when you come into the room, and Mona tosses her hair like a zebra in heat, pretending not to notice you.'

'Stop pulling my leg, Georgina.'

'They're really rather sweet – very young and inexperienced, I would say. So behave yourself, darling. Promise?'

'If you promise to be waiting for me when I get back to London.'

Of course she would be waiting for him. Never had she been so happy, so optimistic about the future and their eventual marriage. Having finished her coffee she wanted more than anything to hear his voice, but foolishly he had forgotten to say where he and the tour group were staying. Not that she could expect to find them hanging about the hotel. They were doubtless peering at Anne Hathaway's herb garden and buying tons of grotty little Shakespeare souvenirs. Still, it would have been fun to leave a telephone message with the hall porter to give him courage for the return journey.

Meantime there were other things to think about. The Three Mewsketeers First Annual July Fourth Anglo-American Picnic was little more than a week hence. Her mission today was to buy sheets of red, white, and blue poster board so that tonight Amy could make the invitations. Mona was in charge of assembling the guest list. The three of them planned to get everything finished and ready to post tomorrow. She was thankful for tonight's activity. It would keep her mind off missing Nick.

Dressed in one of the new summer chiffons from Biba, and with the Harrods charge card she had not used since her parents' death, she was about to go off on her round of errands when the sound of the downstairs door-knocker vibrated through the house. Odd, she thought. The doorbell was in working order. The clamshell knocker was really for decoration. Only one person preferred using it and that person was Nick Albert, and then only when he was being naughty.

Could he have returned earlier than expected from Stratford and

come round to surprise her? She clambered down the narrow stairs.
'Nick, darling? Is it you?'

'It's Roxanne!' A woman's voice with a slight French accent.

Georgina opened the door. 'Who did you say?'

'Nick's cousin, of course. Roxanne D'Orsainville.'

Cousin? Nick had never mentioned a cousin.

'I'm Georgina Crane. How may I help you?'

The shock of finding her on the doorstep was exacerbated by her startling resemblance to Nick Albert. His face smiled merrily from the short, tousled frame of thick flaxen hair, his blue eyes and fine-boned facial structure were further enhanced by the small cigar poised jauntily in a tortoiseshell holder. Dressed in jonquil silk, with a Hermès scarf knotted on one shoulder and a Hermès pouch slung insolently over one wrist, she thrust a parcel at Georgina.

'I'm rather glad you're home. I was wondering how on earth I was going to push this through the slot. Nice meeting you! Must dash!'

Georgina stood dumbfounded. 'But what is it?'

'Nick's dressing gown, of course. Some boring nonsense about a pot of orange marmalade. Too sticky to pack. Asked me to take it back with me.'

'Back . . .?'

'From Stratford, of course. Poor Shakespeare must be spinning in his grave. You wouldn't believe the sort of people!'

Georgina managed to find her voice – good breeding and all that. 'How rude you must think me. Do come in for a glass of wine or a coffee.'

'Good of you to ask, but I'm on my way to the airport. My father is waiting for me in Cannes.'

Her superbly manicured fingers combed through her thicket of hair in a gesture of elegant haste. Turning briskly away, she started up the mews to where a driver stood ready to open the door of a Rolls-Royce. After only a few steps, she stopped abruptly as if she had forgotten something.

'Georgina . . . one more thing.'

Whereas mere moments before Georgina had felt smartly turned out, she now clutched the dreadful parcel awkwardly to her bosom, crushingly certain she looked dowdy and stupid.

'Yes, Roxanne?'

'Nick's told me so much about you.'

'Really? How excruciatingly boring for you!' A vain attempt at one-upmanship.

'And you know what I think, Georgina?'

'I couldn't begin to imagine.'

Roxanne D'Orsainville smiled magnanimously, as if delivering a food basket to the deserving poor. 'I agree wholeheartedly with Nick. You're absolutely super!' A regal wave and she was gone.

6

Mona

It was hard to concentrate with Nick watching her. Instead of dropping her off at Bill Neal's flat as had become his custom, this time he insisted on going upstairs with her.

'He's going to kill me. Nobody's supposed to know about this.'

'Not to worry.'

'Please, Nick. I shouldn't have told you. I promised not to tell anybody. Bill will get thrown out of RADA.'

'Not to worry, pet. I'll say I'm a West End producer.'

Bill and the members of his illegal class reacted to Nick's appearance as if it were a police raid. Scripts disappeared into book bags and behind backs as if they were contraband. A gay couple locked arms bravely, ready to face the firing squad. Only the formidable Minerva, sitting cross-legged on the floor ceremoniously peeling an orange, seemed unperturbed.

'Mona . . .' Bill Neal greeted her with his ritual embrace. 'And this is . . .'

'Nicholas Albert, Bill. Delighted to meet you. Please don't be cross with Mona. She didn't invite me along. I insisted on coming. Be assured your secret's safe with me.'

'And what secret is that?' Minerva's throaty voice reminded Mona of Joan Greenwood in *Kind Hearts and Coronets* and *The Man in the White Suit*. She had peeled back the orange skin in several neat sections, so that the orange looked like a sunburst. Gazing coolly up at Nick, her knowing fingers deftly plucked free one of the orange sections and bit it in half, allowing the juice to gush over her lower lip for a tantalizing moment before halting its flow with lip-smacking enjoyment.

Minerva had toned down the venom since Mona and the Mewsketeers had appeared in the *Evening Standard*. In fact the entire class including Bill was treating her with more respect, but Mona still was wary of her lacerating tongue.

Clearly Nick was amused by the attack. 'My dear. If I were to tell the secret it would no longer be a secret, now would it?'

Turning his attention to Bill Neal he said, 'Mona Davidson is my interest. I believe she has the makings of a major star. There's something about her that's intangible, that transcends beauty . . .'

Minerva groaned disparagingly and blew a mouthful of orange pips into the air. Nick's response was to take her gently by the hand and raise her to her feet. Turning her slowly in place as if she were his partner in a dance routine, he commented. 'Lovely. Beautiful from every angle. A classic English beauty.'

Minerva's mask of cynicism remained intact, though her eyes showed signs of welcoming his praise.

'Mona . . .'

My God, what was he going to do? She could tell he was up to something. There was that look of the mad inventive genius that came over him when he was about to do something crazy.

'The two of you stand together, if you please.'

How could he do this to her, humiliate her before the others? She had confided in him, told him how ugly she felt as compared to the English beauties, especially this Minerva.

'Now, I am part of a consortium that will be producing a play in the West End next spring.'

Every muscle in every body in the entire room swelled to attention.

'We will not be casting for a while, but my job will be to do something fresh and creative. To bring a contemporary excitement to the classics. As, for example, we are considering a futuristic *Hamlet*, a twenty-first century projection of a timeless play. Fifty years from now what will we look like, how will we dress? Look at these two young women. Which of them should play Ophelia?'

The class stirred uneasily. No one spoke.

'Come on, all of you! It's Minerva, of course. She looks the part, her face and form the perfect representation of the classic Ophelia, the doomed maiden we love to feel sorry for. But by the time the next century rolls around, Ophelia will be . . .' He took his agonized protégée's hand. 'Mona Davidson!'

The dirty double-crosser! She had told him in confidence about her mother playing Ophelia in a Yiddish production, and how much her mother – and grandmother, and the whole damned *mishpuggah* – believed in her talent and were expecting her to co-star with Olivier, if not right away this summer then sometime soon.

She girded herself for a Bronx cheer, but the class members were mesmerized. Nick Albert had hypnotized them as he hypnotized everybody. All of them, including Minerva and especially Bill the Australian, were nodding agreement as Nick continued.

'We are talking about producing *Hamlet* intact. We won't touch a word. It will be the interpretation, the nuances of the play and the casting that will project the future. And Mona Davidson will be an Ophelia no one has ever seen.'

You can say that again, Mona thought. In another minute they would see that he was putting them on and they would tear him limb from limb.

'Mona Davidson will recite Ophelia's lines, but as a tough and belligerent woman who chooses to put up with Hamlet's sadistic treatment of her because he's the only man who can make her come.' There was a slight gasp at that, but Nick showed no sign of acknowledging it. 'Then, when he kills her father and screws his mother, she decides the only way to wreak revenge is to kill herself – to kill herself boldly, an aggressive act not a weak, simpering one – knowing that her brother will kill Hamlet for her.

'When Mona's Ophelia does her final scene, she snarls and bellows her lines, a warrior queen sacrificing her life for brutal cause, not out of soppiness.'

The circle of earnest faces made it clear. They were his, utterly captivated by the picture he was painting and wanting to be part of it.

'Think what you could do with *The Merchant of Venice*!' Bill was aglow with possibility.

Less so Minerva. 'Quite. Mona would be quite marvelous, wouldn't she?'

Mona fell for it. 'You really think so, Minerva? I've always wanted to play Portia.'

With the poise for which she was known and feared, Minerva plucked Nick's tortoiseshell holder from between his lips and took an exaggerated drag. 'No, I meant Shylock. I think Mona would be riveting as the Jew in drag.'

Nick's eyes on her gave Mona strength. She braced herself for the stabbing pain in the pit of her stomach. It did not come. A few sarcastic remarks occurred to her, such as that Leslie Howard and Claire Bloom were Jews and that her Aunt Becky the Card Shark looked exactly like Queen Elizabeth.

Instead she laughed, a convincingly genuine belly laugh that shook her entire body with a contagious glee that infected them all. 'Oh, Minerva! You're a regular laugh riot! Isn't she, Nick?'

'She is indeed, Mona.' He grinned benignly, as if she had passed with honors some test based on his teaching. With an all-encompassing salute to the class, he made as if to leave. 'Bill, my apologies. I've held up the class far too long. Mona tells me you're brilliant. We must lunch at my club.'

It didn't take much for Bill to convince him to stay. While it was hard for Mona to concentrate with Nick watching her, she knew within herself and from the class's response that her improvisation that day was the best she had ever done.

As the class ended, Nick once more invited their attention. 'I'm sure you've heard that Mona is one of The Three Mewsketeers?'

He knew they had all seen the piece in *The Evening Standard*. She had told him they'd mentioned it, and had been a little more respectful of her and not quite as nasty as the first day Bill had brought her into the class.

'Well, The Three Mewsketeers are giving a bash, a Fourth of July Picnic, and Mona wanted me to tell you you're all invited!'

How to make friends with colorful theater folk? Invite them to a party with plenty of food and drink. And a charming producer, of course. Why hadn't she thought of it?

Once outside, the group slowly dispersed except for Minerva. Mona had settled herself into the front seat of the Lagonda, while Nick fiddled with something in the boot.

'I daresay I know this little buggy.' Minerva stood on the pavement with the accusing stance of a kindergarten teacher.

'It is rather fun, isn't it?' Nick replied in the chummy voice he always used with Georgina, a kind of clench-jawed baby talk, a superior language for the in-group. *What is that slug Minerva up to?* Mona wondered. *Can't she see Nick isn't interested and is only being polite?*

'I thought it belonged to Roxanne D'Orsainville. She gave me a lift back to London after a particularly boring house party in Wiltshire. I'd know this buggy anywhere.'

Nick was not the least bit perturbed. 'Full marks, Minerva. How very observant of you. It is Roxanne's, of course. She's lent it me for the summer while she's swanning around the south of France.'

Minerva's triumph was evident. 'How very convenient for you.'

She was flirting with him, that's what she was doing, flirting the stiff-upper-lip British way, using small talk to make sex talk in a way that left Mona feeling helpless to intervene and nauseated with jealousy.

Nick made things worse by offering Minerva a lift.

'Can we drop you off somewhere?' *How about dropping her off London Bridge? In a fog*, Mona thought, shifting her body closer to the driver's seat as a means of placing herself between Nick and the intruder.

Minerva made things worse still by declining Nick's invitation. 'Thanks awfully. I've got my own baby buggy around the corner.' She blew a passing ta-ta-for-now kiss at Mona, but her farewell was a blatant provocation to Nick. 'The Fourth of July, you said?'

'That's what I said.'

The skunk. So, that's why he invited the entire class. To get Minerva.

Minerva handed Nick her card. 'Do ring me with the details. I'm hopeless at remembering things.'

As Nick maneuvered the Lagonda into the busy afternoon traffic, he smiled to himself. It was as if Mona weren't there and he was alone with his lascivious thoughts. She didn't understand. Only this morning he had said he had arranged to show her a friend's houseboat on the Chelsea Embankment. 'We can be alone there, just the two of us, looking out on the river. There's so much I want to say to you. Privately.'

She knew a forward pass when she saw one. He wasn't inviting her aboard his friend's houseboat to discuss Einstein's theory of relativity, or her grandma Davidson's recipe for chopped liver (which she had made the past weekend). He had the hots for her – she had known it since the night she and Amy arrived at Chelsea Mews – and now they were going to make love.

He was absolutely mad for her, he had said just before they'd arrived at Bill's. 'Besotted!' And she was head-over-heels bananas for him, which was why she couldn't understand his making a play for Minerva right in front of her.

Lacking the nerve to mention Minerva, much less blow her stack, she instead asked. 'So who's this Roxanne? She must like you a lot to lend you her car.'

'Mona, pet. If you want to know something, ask me. Don't go beating around the mulberry bush. Roxanne D'Orsainville is my cousin. We grew up together. In fact, friends say we look so much alike we could be twins. A remarkable girl really. You'll see for yourself.'

'I will?'

'Of course. July Fourth.'

Who did he think he was, anyway? Who gave him the right to invite people? The Three Mewsketeers were giving the party. In fact Amy had offered to pay for everything, she being the rich kid on the block. She wondered if there was a British word for chutzpah.

'Almost there, darling.' His hand on her thigh banished all petty annoyance. Roaring along the Chelsea Embankment reminded her in a crazy way of being on the Staten Island ferry, the wind off the water battering her face and whipping her hair across her eyes. The names of the bridges excited her in a way she could not explain. Like the bridges across the East River at home that never lost their appeal: the Manhattan Bridge, the Williamsburg Bridge, the Brooklyn Bridge, the Hellgate, the Verrazano, the Throg's Neck, Triboro, Whitestone.

By comparison, the London bridges were like toys from F.A.O. Schwarz. They weren't falling down like the nursery rhyme, but the Thames was narrow and the bridges didn't arch high above the water.

Streaking past Chelsea Bridge, the next one was the Albert Bridge. 'I know, I know, you don't have to tell me. It was named for you, just like the Albert Memorial.' She was teasing. She could hear the gentleness in her voice, the lovingness. God, she was crazy about this guy.

In another moment they had passed the Battersea Bridge and reached the cluster of houseboats bobbing in the tiny basin abutting Cheyne Walk.

Leaving the car. Nick led the way along the sagging gangways to what looked to Mona like an illustration in a children's book, a pink-and-white candy cottage sitting on an oversized rowboat. Once inside, she expected him to crush her in his arms. Instead he sat her down and took her hands, raising each in turn to his lips for a gentle kiss.

Nice Girls

'I'm in love with you, you know.'

It wasn't what she'd expected. She wasn't sure exactly what she *had* expected, but this simple declaration was not it. She had known he was going to jump on her bones. No guy went to all the trouble of making arrangements to be alone, and on a houseboat yet! How romantic could you be?

He kissed her hair and her eyelids. Her eyes closed, she waited euphorically to feel his mouth on hers.

Instead he whispered, 'Open your eyes, Mona.'

Nick's face was transformed. This was not the same man who had so brashly lied to her class about being a producer, not the same man who had so blatantly flirted with Minerva. This Nick looked touchingly shy and boyish, his expression yearning and vulnerable.

'I meant what I said, Mona. I'm in love with you, and if I'm not mistaken you're in love with me. *Are* you in love with me? Tell me. Tell me now.'

Was it a trick? Was the Candid Camera crew going to jump out of the woodwork shrieking, 'Smile!' How could this gorgeous hunk of man be in love with a plump Jewish girl with a big nose, when there were people like Georgina and Minerva around?

'Tell me, Mona. I insist you tell me.'

'Yes. I'm in love with you, Nick.'

'For God's sake, don't cry!' She was crying. The salt tasted great when he finally kissed her.

'Like anchovies,' she said.

'Anchovies? Did you say anchovies?'

'You know. Salty. Like anchovies. Salty kisses.'

He gathered her close, laughing exultantly. 'We shall never be bored! Anchovies.' Whirling her around in the cramped space, he managed to undress them both before careening onto the canvas-covered bunk, pulling a crocheted shawl over them.

After a time he asked, 'Am I the first, Mona?'

'Are you kidding?' He was the first in certain respects, in getting her to do some of the things she'd never before tried, but certainly not her first lover. Although to call the guys she knew in New York 'lovers' was a joke, like comparing liverwurst with French pâté. A virgin she was not; a sexpot she would become, under Nick's expert tutelage.

He took away the shawl and knelt at her feet, holding up his hands as if to frame her naked body. 'You're not fat. Never let me hear the word "fat." You are voluptuous. Glorious. What a woman should look like. Not an ironing board.'

'Like Twiggy?'

'Twiggy!' He growled with disgust. 'An aberration. Nothing to hold on to. Nothing to cushion a man when he's making violent love to the girl he adores.' He fell on her with a joyful cry. 'You don't belong in those dreadful miniskirts, those vinyl boots. These breasts. These hips. My darling, you belong in a sultan's harem. Chiffons. Velvets. Satin pillows. Perfumed baths . . .'

The body so warm against hers suddenly stiffened. Simultaneously, she understood why. The unmistakable voice of Lady Georgina Crane was calling his name.

'Nick? Nick Albert! Are you there?'

Nick pushed the curtain just far enough aside to peer through.

'Bloody hell! It's Georgina!'

The rat. 'You mean you've brought her here, too?' Men were shits. She scrambled for her clothes. What was she going to say? How could she get the hell out of there? Over the side? Maybe she could slide into the river and cling to the side of the houseboat until after dark, like in one of those movies about the Old West.

He turned on her with a fury that frightened her. 'I have *not* brought Georgina here! It is *not* a doss house! She probably saw the car.' That was it. Peering again through the window Mona could see the telltale Lagonda clearly in view on the Embankment. No need to paint a sign saying NICK ALBERT IS HERE. The presence of the Lagonda said it all.

He could see Georgina standing near the gangway, uncertain as to what to do next. There were at least fifty or sixty houseboats moored. She couldn't very well approach all of them, could she? What's more, the wind clearly had gone out of her sails. Whatever wild impulse the sight of the Lagonda had generated had run out of steam. From his vantage point beside the window Nick watched her hesitate, make as if to shout once more, gaze around her as if embarrassed, and then walk to the Lagonda, where she scribbled a note. After one more visual scan of the houseboats, she disappeared in the direction of Old Church Street.

'Of course! I should have remembered! How stupid of me!' Nick sighed in relief. 'Georgina said she was going to see about taking a stall at the Antiques Market. It's just up the road. She must have decided to have a walk.'

Mona was nonetheless deeply shaken. 'What if she'd found us?'

'She didn't.'

'I know, but what *if*?'

'I told you, I've never taken her here.'

How could she have accused him of such a thing? Her and her big mouth, always putting her foot in it.

'I'm sorry, Nick. I just thought –'

'You just thought nonsense.'

'I feel so guilty.'

'God in heaven, what for?'

'For lying. I feel guilty about lying.'

'Silly child. I lie all the time. It's the only way to make life bearable. If you lie enough, it becomes the truth.'

'That sounds like Adolf Hitler.'

'Stop being a bore. Guilt, guilt, guilt. The Jewish disease. I had another Jewish girlfriend. Worse than you. Guilty about everything. You must get rid of that guilt, Mona.'

'But I feel so . . . awful. Not guilty, awful. I lied to my mother about RADA. I've even lied to Georgina and Amy. They think I'm at RADA every day. And now I feel . . . *awful*, really awful about you. About what Georgina will say when she finds out about us.'

'I do not belong to Georgina.'

'Well . . .'

'Well, what? I can hear the wheels going round.'

'Do you belong to me?'

'No – not yet, at any rate. But let me tell you something. You're an American, and America is the future. Britain is the past. Britain is finished. It's inbred. These English girls you envy, these English beauties – Georgina, Minerva – think about it, they all look alike. Cut from the same cloth, and the cloth is fragile, unraveling. You don't recognize your own strength. Mona. Those girls – all the girls you see in the magazines, *The Tatler*, the society pages, Lady this, the Honorable that – their blood is thin, they're like inbred poodles. You? You're a magnificent mongrel, a street-fighter. You're the next wave, don't you see? Stop wasting your time worshiping the Oliviers and that ilk. The future is the Beatles, the working-class energy that doesn't give a damn about manners – and guilt! When I look to the future I see Mona Davidson, and that's where I want to be.'

There was more. As they made love again it was in a more

leisurely fashion, comfortable and intuitive. They would be good together, he said. In point of fact he did have an ambition to produce plays, and he did feel convinced of her talents as an actress.

They would keep their relationship secret; there was no need to hurt Georgina now. He adored Georgina, no question about it. She was starting to pull up her socks and organize her life. Antiques, for example. The girl knew her stuff, for she'd grown up with it. The idea of having a stall at the antiques markets was a good way for her to begin. Her idea was to cover small country fairs in out-of-the-way places, buy cheap and sell dear.

'But . . .'

'But what?'

Mona couldn't help blurting out, 'Isn't she expecting to marry you?'

Nick pursed his lips, the disapproving schoolmaster. 'If that is her expectation, I shall have to disabuse her of it – in the fullness of time.'

'And when exactly will that be?'

His shout of laughter startled her. 'What happened to your guilt? You want us to go right back to Chelsea Mews this very minute and tell her we're engaged?'

Shame replaced guilt. She could not be that callous. 'Of course not.' In her growing delirium of happiness, she could not be cruel. Georgina, as he'd said, was growing more independent every day. Since the piece about The Three Mewsketeers had appeared, various fair-weather friends had phoned and sent notes, including the creep, Peter something, who had dumped her. She was putting her life back together. Nick was right. Soon she wouldn't need him to prop her up.

'Well, then, what shall we do now?' He advanced on her with clear erotic purpose. Slipping out of his grip, she began to dress.

'I've got a great idea. My grandmother just sent me a check. Let's go to Harrods and buy something!'

It was hard to believe, almost too good to be true, but he seemed to be honestly captivated by her.

'Here. Wear this.' He took a cotton paisley handkerchief from his pocket and tied it around her hair. 'Gypsy-style. You're my wild, untamed gypsy.'

The intoxication she felt was something she would later recognize as akin to the ecstasy of being onstage before a clamorous audience.

For now, she was the cherished star of their love scene. Happiness fueled her. She was a runaway freight train. She could not slow down. God help anybody who got in her way.

7

Amy

> Nine seconds of pleasure
> Nine months of pain
> Nine days in the hospital
> And out comes Mary Jane.

Amy dolefully remembered how she and her little friends had giggled at their own audacity as they'd recited the 'dirty' quatrain, five-year-olds bouncing a hard rubber ball in the schoolyard. At that age and in that time (could it only be little more than ten years ago?) they didn't even know where babies came from.

Today she knew where babies came from. She was pregnant. She was sure of it. The date for expecting her 'friend,' marked on her calendar as always, had come and gone. Her breasts felt full and heavy, threatening to overflow her A-cup bra. Her stomach was distended. Her legs felt heavy and achy. For the past few days she had been queasy. No question about it. Pregnant.

Perhaps it ran in the family. Her mother had been just nineteen when she'd had Amy. Once, as a little pitcher with big ears, she had overheard a visiting relative joking about a shotgun wedding before being shushed. Although her parents had known each other since childhood, and snapshots in the family album showed them hand-in-hand at birthday parties and picnics from earliest days, Amy was in fact born seven months after the wedding, a healthy if somewhat premature baby (if anyone cared to mention it, which nobody ever did).

She had told no one of her predicament, apart from Mona. She knew that air travel could upset the menstrual cycle. She also knew that if she was pregnant she and Lou could simply move up their wedding plans. Abortion was out. Not for religious or political reasons but because abortion was illegal. In America, not Britain.

There was still time to consider it of course, time to discuss the problem with Mona and Georgina.

The little mews house was in a frenzy of activity as the July Fourth picnic drew near. She wasn't sure how Mona and Georgina would react to her developing friendship with Nick. She was sure they wouldn't understand the special bond between them that had begun the night he'd climbed in her window.

'Baby bird' is what he had called her. 'Too soon out of the nest,' he had observed. 'Too young to stave off the hawks and vultures waiting to *pounce*.' It was with mixed emotions that she had soon realized he was not going to pounce. Instead, he'd arranged himself cross-legged on the narrow patch of floor in the tiny room and invited her to join him. They had sat face-to-face as if in an American Indian powwow, whispering like naughty children.

He had been wanting to talk with her, he said. Americans fascinated him, he said. There were so many kinds of Americans that it was impossible to point a finger and say 'that's an American.' But his blue-haired ladies were utterly hateful – so demanding, so greedy.

'Maybe they're making up for their lost youth. Maybe they weren't as lucky as Mona and me to be going abroad when they were young.'

'They drive me mad with their questions.'

'Oh, come now, Nick. If they were cute college girls in their twenties, would their questions be driving you mad?'

She had surprised herself with her astuteness. There was something about Nick Albert, something ineffable that made her think with a strange new clarity.

'Perhaps you're right, baby bird. One should not condemn starving people for getting what they can. Myself included.'

'You? Starving?' She had been amazed.

'Perhaps not starving. *Hungry* is more like it. Hungry for a life of richness, a table laden with goodies.'

'You mean a rich wife?' Again she had been amazed, this time at her own candor. As a matter of fact *she* was rich, and would be richer still on her fortieth birthday.

'Or a rich patron,' he had laughed, going on to tell her how one of his blue-haired ladies had teasingly offered to adopt him. 'Should I accept the offer, baby bird?'

'Are you serious?' Her protest a spontaneous reproach.

'Of course I'm not serious. How could I be serious about such a thing?' He stroked her cheek and gazed thoughtfully into her eyes. 'You are an *ethical* baby bird, aren't you? You'd keep me on the straight and narrow, wouldn't you? You might even save my life.'

At that he had seemed to drift away in his thoughts before he suddenly stood up to leave. 'I think you know I have a special fondness for you. It may be one of the few honest things in my life. Promise you will think of me as your friend. I *am* your friend. If you need me you must come to me. Promise?'

'Promise.'

As he prepared to leave the way he had arrived, through the window, he said, 'I can tell something is troubling you, something serious. Am I right?'

She nodded.

'You can trust me, Amy. Will you let me help?'

Unsure of how to respond, she nodded again.

'You're a cool one, much cooler than you seem.' With one leg over the windowsill he crooned, 'Three cheers for the red, white, and blue!'

It was only after he'd gone that she had realized he hadn't crushed her in his hot embrace, as she had envisioned when he'd appeared in the window. It wasn't often that she had dreams, but that night she did. Image on top of image, like an amateur eight-millimeter home movie of the kinds of events immortalized in home movies: their wedding, honeymoon, birth of their child, dream house, dinner with her family, washing the car together, Amy polishing the chrome. Nick kissing her.

'Amy! Amy Dean!' From deep in the circle of Nick Albert's embrace, she could hear her name being called as if from a great and echoing distance. *Who could be calling her? Didn't they know she was asleep with her husband and was not to be disturbed?*

'Amy! For God's sake, unlock the door!' The rattling doorknob and furious pounding on the door itself finally penetrated her dream haze and awakened her to the fact that it was morning and late morning from the look of the sunlight pouring through the window. She was alone in her narrow bed at Number Four Chelsea Mews and what's more she was supposed to be meeting her seminar group at Westminster Pier for the day's visit to Hampton Court Palace.

Georgina and Mona greeted her with evident relief. She might have been ill, Georgina said. Or *dead*, Mona added; they were worried sick! Another minute and they'd have broken down the door! 'I – I'm – sorry!' was all Amy could manage to say. Being worried about was something of a new experience for her. It would take some getting used to.

Meantime, she had exactly forty minutes to shower, dress, bolt down some OJ, and get herself from Chelsea to Westminster. By now she knew her way around the Underground. She was not one of those loathsome tourists with a telltale map in hand; she knew the Sloane Square station was a mere three stops away from Westminster. On the Circle Line! She allowed herself to gloat over her newly acquired knowledge.

Despite her forebodings about pregnancy, her talk with Nick Albert had somehow strengthened her sense of herself. If she was pregnant, and she would soon know if she was, she was now not so sure about marrying Lou Humphries. In fact, she had to peer at his picture in her wallet to remind herself what he looked like.

She wished he were more interested in what interested her, and that she could share her newly acquired knowledge with him. She had written him one longish letter all about Sir William Bayne, who was running the seminar, and enclosing the syllabus listing all the historic places she and the others were going to see and the architectural aspects Sir William was going to discuss. The letter ran three typewritten pages, single-spaced. After mailing it she realized Lou would only skim over it. She could have saved her energy. She hadn't written any more letters, limiting herself to picture postcards. So far he had written exactly once, from the Cape, a postcard from a bar with the simple message, 'Having a drunken time, wish you were here to show me the way to go home!'

Yet despite everything, she had to admit she wished he were with her on today's excursion to Hampton Court Palace. He would see that architectural history was not dull. Like so many of Britain's famous houses, the joint was jumping with scandals and intrigue. Lou might be bored with the dates and architectural styles, but he would like the way King Henry VIII had conned Cardinal Wolsey into giving him the palace, with all its rich furnishings, in order to keep in good with him. It would be as if somebody today who worked for a powerful boss turned over a country mansion to him in order to keep his job.

A modern comparison was feeble. It didn't stand up to scrutiny.

Today's mansion might have fifteen rooms, maybe twenty if it was one of the Newport 'cottages' built by the Vanderbilts and such. In Henry VIII's day, Hampton Court Palace boasted over a thousand rooms and three hundred silken beds! That fact alone would make Lou wiggle his ears. The fact that this and the Tower of London were living records of English kings and queens held no interest for him whatsoever. She must stop kidding herself about Lou Humphries. He was a good, intelligent man. He would be a perfect husband for her in the broader scheme of things. But if he was in England, sitting beside her on this lovely riverboat gliding up the Thames to Hampton Court, she knew he would ruin everything. He would be bored and impatient. He would find things to joke about. If there were gargoyles, he would say they looked like his father. If Sir William invited questions, she shuddered to think what kind of stupid question Lou would ask, pretending to be serious.

It was something he would outgrow, she felt sure. What's more, most couples had separate interests which they pursued independently. Separate careers, too, although she was still not certain she wanted to pursue a serious career. Her secret ambition to be an architectural historian was another thing she had kept to herself. Like the possibility of being pregnant. If she were pregnant, of course, her career would go out the window.

Even a home and baby would not stop her from reading, of course, especially the work of Sir Nikolaus Pevsner. He said architecture was the result when design and personal aspirations merged. Thomas Jefferson's Monticello proved Pevsner's point.

These were things she wanted to talk about with Lou. Perhaps after this trip they could have more serious conversations. Unless she really was pregnant, in which case their talk would revolve around wedding plans and a house. Compared to the English queens and mistresses who had lived and loved and died at Hampton Court Palace, her dilemma was pretty tame. It cheered her to think that Lou Humphries might *want* to chop off her head like Anne Boleyn's but he couldn't, could he? The rules had changed somewhat.

Since schoolgirl myth asserted that liberal doses of gin could disrupt a pregnancy, Amy knocked back three double gins-and-tonic at lunchtime, and was sick to her stomach all the way back to Westminster Pier.

But, if it worked, it would be worth it. In her imagination she felt it happening. Several visits to the ladies room proved, alas, that it had not.

With the Fourth of July party just a few days away, she had a lot to do – decorations to make, all-American dishes to plan. One day at a time. By July 4th she would be less than two weeks late. Time enough to have The Three Mewsketeers meet in closed session. In the meantime she would put Lou, the baby, and Nick Albert out of her thoughts.

Mona and Georgina had left the menu planning up to her. In addition to the frankfurters and beans, the corn on the cob and deviled eggs, the hamburgers and fried chicken, she planned to make her famous tuna noodle casserole with the potato chips on top. Harrods had packages of ice cream cones in its import department. Tops on her To Do list was finding out where she could order some tubs of chocolate, vanilla, and strawberry ice cream.

There would be prizes for anyone who could name the thirteen original colonies, and party favors. Since 'God Save The Queen' and 'My Country 'Tis of Thee' had the same tune, she was going to suggest they start things off with a hearty rendition of both. To make sure she wouldn't forget, she added to her list of chores a notation to type out both sets of lyrics and have them mimeographed.

Nick Albert would find out that she was more grown-up than he had thought. She wondered what her parents would think if she invited him to visit Rhode Island. Of two things she could be sure: He would charm the socks off them, and he would genuinely enjoy seeing the millionaire mansions in Newport. Her mind was racing. Maybe it was the gin, maybe it was being away from home. If there was a baby, she might ask Nick Albert to make an honest woman of her.

Informed of her marriage and motherhood, Lou Humphries would wither and die of grief, like something out of an early American folk song. And she would dance on his grave.

8

The Fourth of July

They had gambled on the weather – and won. It was high summer, warm and dry. It surprised the two Americans to discover how very far north the British Isles were, on a line with Newfoundland if you looked at a map. On a fine July night such as this, daylight persisted until after ten o'clock.

Mona and Amy skipped classes. Nick turned the day's batch of blue-haired ladies over to another guide, with the proviso that he bring them to the picnic as the surprise climax of the day's outing at an additional five pounds a head.

'You are incorrigible!' Georgina laughed.

'So stop incorriging him!' There was a hard edge to Mona's voice, a tinge of impatience she did her best to hide. Was Georgina blind? Couldn't she see Nick wasn't in love with her?

By six o'clock the four of them had transformed the cobblestoned area in front of Georgina's house into an all-American refreshment stand of the kind found at any beach or lakefront resort. A long trestle table covered with red, white, and blue stood ready and waiting with piles of red, white, and blue paper plates, cups, and plastic cutlery. At one end stood an old-fashioned tin bathtub Georgina had found at the antiques market, filled with blocks of ice and assorted soft drinks. At the other end, a King's Road pub had supplied a barrel of lager. There were enormous bowls of American potato chips, pretzels, and peanuts in their shells, plus an enormous tray of American condiments: Hellman's mayonnaise, French's hot dog mustard, Heinz's ketchup, four kinds of pickle relish, and sauerkraut.

Waiting to go in the kitchen under Amy's supervision were platters of deviled eggs, fried chicken, cole slaw, and partly cooked frankfurters and hamburgers, poised for final grilling in the inadequate stove when enough guests had arrived.

The numbers expected varied from minute to minute. They had invited in a haphazard manner everyone they could think of, including some of Georgina's erstwhile closest friends, Amy and Mona's fellow students, people from the American Embassy, and the chums Nick Albert thought might be amusing.

On a whim, Mona had sent an invitation to Queen Elizabeth and Prince Philip. 'What the hell. They're pretty sharp cookies. It would be good publicity to attend a July Fourth picnic. Great for tourism, right?' she explained to a dumbfounded Georgina. 'You can't know until you ask. They might have a free evening. Right?'

Her Majesty and consort did in fact respond, or more precisely an equerry replied on embossed Buckingham Palace note paper. Her Majesty and the Duke of Edinburgh wished to thank Miss Davidson for her kind invitation.

'How do you like that, kids?' Mona exulted. 'The palace!'

'You mean they're coming to the picnic?' Amy was sipping a glass of milk. Ever practical, she reasoned that if she was pregnant, milk was important.

'Don't be a twit.' Georgina's exasperation was more due to Nick than Mona's hijinks. Nick hadn't stayed with her last night, and she had lacked the nerve to demand an explanation.

'Come on, Mona. Don't keep us in suspense! Will we have to get a throne, so the Queen will have something to sit on while she eats her hot dog?'

Mona tried to prolong the suspense, although her mind was on Nick Albert. A note left under her door this morning had said he had something important to tell her. Tonight. After the picnic.

'Well, now. Let's see. Ah, yes. Where were we. Okay. Blah blah blah. Thanks me for kind invitation, but, ah yes, here we are . . .' She smiled angelically. 'You really want to hear the rest?' Dodging the spoon flung at her by Amy, Mona continued to read. 'But' – she drooped the corners of her mouth to convey deep disappointment, as Bill Neal had taught her – 'Her Majesty and His Royal Highness deeply regret that previous engagements prevent their acceptance.'

'*Quel surprise!*' Georgina sniffed. Nick had promised to come along early, ten-ish he had said, to go over arrangements and see what last-minute things were needed. She had lacked the nerve to ask him more about his cousin Roxanne D'Orsainville. When he got back from Stratford, she had mentioned the return of his dressing gown. 'Terribly kind of Roxanne, wasn't it?' was his sole retort. She had lacked the courage to ask what his cousin was doing in Stratford.

Mona ignored the sarcasm. 'And get this. Her Majesty wishes to convey her best wishes for a happy occasion. The Royal Family recognizes the strong links of cultural heritage and affection that exist between our two countries, which events like your Fourth of July Picnic will strengthen and enhance. Signed sincerely – can't read the handwriting – Equerry to Her Majesty, Queen Elizabeth II. Can't read his signature, dammit.'

'They do it on purpose. Clear handwriting is not done.'

'What's not done?' Nick Albert, as usual, had entered the sitting room silently, wreaking varying degrees of havoc in each of the young women.

'You're looking very grand!' Georgina observed, pouring coffee into the extra mug she had brought upstairs from the kitchen in preparation for his arrival. At the sight of him she wished desperately that she could wave a magic wand and make the two Americans disappear.

Mona showed him the letter from Buckingham Palace and tried to signal a private message with her eyes. See you later, alligator; in a while, crocodile. Only one gray cloud threatened tonight's picnic. Bill Neal, Minerva, and the rest of the class really believed Nick was producing a play. They would be here in force. She was sure Nick could handle them. She hoped that by the time they found out the truth, the summer would be over and she would be back home in New York.

As for Amy, she peered solemnly up at him over the rim of her glass of milk. When she put it down, Nick said, 'You've got a white mustache.'

'It's my new look.'

'The baby bird is older than she says. Or else she's had a fright and her hair turned white. Has anything happened to you, Amy?'

Cunning. The man was so cunning. He was able to ask her if her period had started right in front of Mona and Georgina without either one of them catching on. 'No. Nothing.'

The little house and the mews itself soon wore a magical air of feverish complicity. The four of them together were a well-oiled wheel – Nick the hub, the three women the spokes connected to him and moving evenly spaced between each other.

By late afternoon they were ready. At Mona's suggestion,

Georgina had invited the other residents of Chelsea Mews. 'That way, they can't complain about the noise!' she reasoned.

'Clever girl!'

Mona's unspoken motive became clear when she knocked on the nearby doors and asked to borrow chairs, bowls, trays, and space in their refrigerators, if they had one. A mortified Georgina, who had been trained never to ask people she didn't know for *anything*, not even the right time of day, watched in astonishment as the usually po-faced neighbors almost killed themselves in their haste to be part of the occasion.

When Amy returned from a foray to Peter Jones with one hundred and ninety-two red, white, and blue balloons to denote that many years of American independence, they formed their own 'hot air' squad and blew up all of them. Each was then attached to a string and passed along to Georgina and Nick, who tied the balloons over the doorway, from the windows, the roof, on the refreshment stand, and even the door handles of the Lagonda.

The American Stars and Stripes and the British Union Jack comprised the centerpiece on the buffet table. Nick had strung a long extension cord from the sitting room, so that the gramophone could be set up in the mews. Georgina remembered some old gramophone records in a box under the stairs. 'My father liked marching bands,' she said, cheerful despite the sad reminder.

The Three Mewsketeers had passingly toyed with the notion of dressing like sexy female versions of Athos, Porthos, and Aramis, but decided it was beside the point. They settled on red, white, and blue. Amy's idea of their dressing as The Spirit of '76 was dismissed out of hand. Neither Georgina nor Nick knew the famous American poster, and Mona wanted to know who would play the drummer boy.

Amy's feelings were hurt. 'Nobody pays any attention to what I have to say! I'm the only *real* American here!' The New England Yankee defending her heritage.

'So what does that make me, chopped liver?' The immigrant's grandchild, feeling the cold wind of prejudice.

'My family was in America in 1776. I should know how to celebrate July 4th!'

'Well, my family arrived at Ellis Island on July 4th, so don't tell *me* how to celebrate July 4th!' That this was patently a lie was clear to everyone, so much so that Mona began to laugh at her own audacity. She put her arms around Amy. 'I'm sorry. Don't be mad.' She could feel Amy tremble. Was she catching a cold? Something must be wrong. Amy never flew off the handle like that.

'I'm sorry, too.'

'You feeling okay?'

Amy could see Nick watching her. 'I'll be fine. It's just been so hectic. I think maybe I'll take a little walk.'

'I'll come along,' Nick offered. 'Everything's organized. The guests won't be arriving for an hour.'

'No, I . . .' She looked to Georgina, as if for permission.

'Run along, you two. After all of Amy's hard work, we want her to enjoy the party.'

They walked silently through the quiet side streets of Chelsea. It was the ideal opportunity to outline her proposition. She was pregnant. There was no longer any doubt. Nick had talked about wanting a wealthy patron, wanting to live in America. She was rich, and would be richer still in the years to come. How would he feel about making an honest woman of her while she made him a happy man?

She could not bring herself to say it, any of it.

'I gather that nothing has happened.'

She could only shake her head miserably.

He reached into his pocket. 'I thought that might be the case.' He opened a small silver box and extracted two white pills. 'Can you take pills without water?'

She nodded.

'These will do the trick, I promise.'

She clamped her mouth shut and shook her head no.

'Amy?'

She glared at him defiantly, at the same time wondering why she was angry at him. The pregnancy wasn't his fault.

'Do you trust me?'

She nodded reluctantly.

'Close your eyes and open your mouth.'

He fed her the pills one at a time. 'I guarantee these will solve the problem.' He embraced her briefly. 'Sweet baby bird. You left the nest just a little too soon.'

They got back to the mews just as the BBC television crew arrived to set up their cameras. A few of Nick's Fleet Street chums were already hoisting a few. The music was loud and stirring – 'Yankee

Doodle' and 'Rule, Britannia,' ricocheting off the walls of the small houses lining the mews. As if on cue from an invisible Cecil B. DeMille, a feverish horde descended on them through the iron gate at the top of the mews and danced across the cobblestones as if part of some Hollywood spectacular.

The party was on. The spirit of the event infused its three hostesses. All problems forgotten, they glowed with the pleasure of their accomplishment. Each looked beautiful and knew she looked beautiful, each was in perfect harmony with the other two as she greeted the guests and worked the press as if cameras had been a regular part of her daily life.

Nick's experience as a tour guide only served to heighten his natural magnetic charm. 'Nick! Nick, old boy!' Hearty shouts from men. 'Nick! Nick, darling!' Flirty, pouty cries from women demanding their kiss-kiss, hug-hug.

Mona was glad to see Bill Neal and the other members of the acting class – except for Minerva. She was not glad to see Minerva at all, and even less glad to see Minerva seek out and find Nick. She did her level best to ignore her rising gorge of fury. Mingling with the others, friends from the American Embassy, people from Amy's seminar, Georgina's crowd (who looked like they'd stepped out of the social pages of *The Tatler*), she was compelled to search out Nick with her eyes.

Minerva had attached herself to Nick like a barnacle, and it didn't look as if he minded. Mona couldn't stand it. Minerva was whispering in Nick's ear. Minerva was giving Nick a sip of her drink and wiping his mouth with her fingers. Mona had to do *something* or bust.

'Have a frankfurter, Minerva?' Mona offered a paper plate to the other young woman. The frankfurter roll was too small for its contents. The frankfurter itself, red and greasy, protruded from the end that Mona thrust into Minerva's mouth.

Minerva batted it away. 'Don't be obscene.'

'Obscene? The word suits you, Minerva. I was only being friendly.'

'What's going on here?' Georgina appeared at Nick's side, a press photographer behind her, his face sensing news.

'It's nothing, Georgina.' Nick assured her. 'Minerva dropped her plate. Mona was worried someone would slip and fall.'

'Minerva? Minerva who? I don't believe we've met.'

Nice Girls

Mona could see that Georgina had gotten the message all right, and was staking out her claim. She assured herself that Georgina had no claim on Nick. Nick had told her so. But it was obvious he had not told Georgina. Not yet. She felt sorry for Georgina. She could identify with how she felt.

Minerva was not the least bit intimidated. She regarded Georgina with a look of disdain Mona realized she should memorize for her future career as an actress. Nobody did contempt and disdain as well as the Brits. 'Sorry, dearie. We have most certainly *not* met, and we are not about to meet now!' Minerva brushed Georgina aside. Before disappearing into the crowd, she said to Nick, 'Where did you find these unspeakably vulgar yobbos? Ring me if you can bear to tear yourself away. I'm in the book.'

Nick's reaction was to shrug. 'Silly bitch.'

Uh-oh, Mona thought, here it comes. She wished Georgina would go away before Nick said what she knew he was going to say. 'As for you, Mona – you'll have to admit that was a bit awkward.'

Georgina was raptly awaiting Mona's reply. 'What?' Mona knew she couldn't get away with the innocence routine, but tried it anyway. 'What'd I do?'

'Nick?' Saved by the gong. Amy looked flustered. 'Some girl said to find you, Nick. *Très important*, she said. Your cousin, Roxanne.'

'Oh, yes – good that she could make it.' He opened his arms wide as if to embrace all three of them. 'I want you all to meet her.'

Georgina looked about to keel over, the color draining from her face. 'You forget, Nick. I *have* met her. The dressing gown?'

'Of course. Wait right here.'

Mona and Amy closed ranks with their friend as Nick disappeared into the crowd, the private passions of each for the moment forgotten.

'What is it?'
'What's wrong?'
'Roxanne!'
'His cousin?'
'She was in Stratford-on-Avon when he was in Stratford-on-Avon. He spilled something on his dressing gown. She brought it to the mews. She told me she'd been with him.'
'But he said she's his cousin!' Amy persisted.
'I know, and *she* told me she's his cousin.'
'But you don't think they're cousins, right?'

Georgina looked from one to the other, helpless in her misery. 'I can't bear to think about it at all.'

'Think about what?' With his customary ability to appear suddenly, Nick Albert confronted Georgina.

Seeing that she was too frazzled to reply, Mona groped for an answer. 'The contest. We've got to announce the winners, and we haven't had a chance to read the entries!'

Amy had passed out entry forms and pencils earlier in the evening. The idea was to name the thirteen original colonies, the winners to receive a bottle of champagne.

Georgina's jealousy was so painful, she could not meet Nick's eyes. Instead, she motioned the two Americans to follow her into the house. The box of entries was in the kitchen. 'See that everyone's happy, Nick. We'll only be a moment.'

Going over the entries relieved them from further discussion of Nick's cousin.

'Listen to this one. *Chicago* as one of the thirteen colonies?' Mona's laugh was hollow. She remembered Minerva's crack about the Lagonda. She could have killed Minerva and the cousin, Roxanne whatever her name was.

'This one's perfect! All thirteen colonies.' The contest was Amy's idea, and she was glad to find a winner. Most of the other contestants had treated the contest as a joke, writing absurd names like 'Niagara Falls' and 'Hollywood.'

'Just in time!' Nick was waiting for them at the refreshment table. 'Shall I make the announcement?' Without waiting for their agreement, he leapt onto the now nearly bare buffet table. 'Hear ye, hear ye! Beautiful ladies and gallant gentlemen! On this the one hundred and ninety-second anniversary of the act of treason committed against Mother England by the ungrateful North American colonies – otherwise known as the Declaration of Independence – I am pleased to announce on behalf of the Three Mewsketeers –'

Cheers and catcalls from the guests.

'– the name of the one person – and there was *only* one – who could name the thirteen original colonies. And that person is . . . Bill Neal! An *Australian*, mind you!'

While Georgina and Mona presented Bill with a bottle of champagne, Nick Albert took advantage of the diversion to whisper a brief message in Amy Dean's ear: 'Meet me at midnight at the Albert Memorial.'

Nice Girls

Helping Georgina to disconnect the gramophone and carry it up the stairs to the sitting room, he whispered to her, 'Meet me at midnight at the Albert Memorial.'

Finding Mona by herself collecting the empty trays in the mews, he repeated the message for the third time: 'Meet me at midnight at the Albert Memorial.'

By ten o'clock, summer light had finally given way to summer night. The members of the press had long since packed up and left for the next event. The last guests lingered until the last crumb of food, the last drop of drink had been consumed. Finally, the last merry group was seen capering out of the mews under a canopy of red, white, and blue balloons.

The Three Mewsketeers went about their cleanup chores in a mood of quiet contemplation. The party had been a huge success, they assured each other. By unspoken agreement each kept to herself, while yet working in harmony to finish the job as quickly and efficiently as possible. What they would not know until later was that they shared a secret. In seeming to concentrate on restoring the mews to its normal condition, each was trying to figure out how to slip out of the house in order to meet Nick Albert.

'I'm ready to drop. Let's call it a night and finish up in the morning, right?' Mona simulated a yawn that would have made Bill Neal proud. She was afraid the other two might want to sit up and rehash the evening. By now it was after eleven, not much time to feign sleep and somehow sneak out.

There were no arguments, however. Amy and Georgina dropped what they were doing – like schoolgirls hearing the dismissal bell, Mona thought – and hastily bade each other good night. Soon the house lay in darkness. Behind each of the three bedroom doors, a wildly impatient young woman prepared for her secret rendezvous.

9

Midnight

Hot anticipation rode the soft summer night in three separate taxicabs, destination the Albert Memorial. Although the hour was late, the fine weather had brought out a goodly number of people walking their dogs or just walking arm-in-arm for the pleasure of it before retiring.

An inbred diffidence caused Georgina to instruct the driver to let her out in front of a nearby block of flats. She worried that she would appear too conspicuous leaping out of a cab directly in front of the Albert Memorial. The driver might want to know what she was doing there in the middle of the night, not that it was any of his business.

What on earth was she rattling on about? She must control her emotions. Nick Albert wanted to see her. Alone. At a place important to them both. A place of sweet memory, and of privacy they could not have at Chelsea Mews with the two Americans underfoot. All sorts of possible reasons for this meeting coursed through her brain. What if he wanted them to run away together? Tonight? To Gretna Green? To get married? In her quiet frenzy to slip out of the house without being seen, she had thought to find her passport and have it with her just in case.

It was a few minutes before twelve. She made her way to the far side of the Memorial, shielded by its very design from casual view. 'Nick?' The eager hope that he would spring from the shadows and embrace her was quickly dashed. She was alone, waiting. For no particular reason, she remembered a line from Alfred Noyes' 'The Highwayman': 'I'll come to thee by moonlight, though hell should bar the way.' The real hell was the waiting.

Mona's approach to sneaking out had been based on a lecture she had once attended in New York concerning stagecraft and the art of visual deception. Comparable to the techniques used by magicians, the idea was to divert attention from what was actually going on. In this spirit, after all three of them had shut their respective doors Mona had noisily opened hers, pretended to stumble, and called out to nobody in particular, 'Don't mind me! I'm thirsty as hell! Just going downstairs for something to drink!'

Her clumping footsteps down the stairs were loud enough to wake the dead. More noise, the clanking of glasses and bottles, and she clumped back up the stairs and into her room with a final slam of the door. 'Sorry about that!'

As it turned out, her performance was entirely unnecessary. When, seconds later, she silently eased open her door and padded barefoot, boots in hand, through the sitting room and down the steps, what she didn't know was that Georgina and Amy had already left, Amy by way of the window that Nick had proved so easy to use.

Remembering how Nick had stood on the Lagonda to reach the window, before 'retiring' she had casually placed one of the borrowed tables in the same position. It would be an easy drop, she was sure, ten feet at the most, and the jolt might bring on her period. Nick's pills had not yet worked.

A passing cab, hailed at the top of the Mews, now sped through the elegant streets and squares. 'You're sure you want the Albert Memorial?' the driver asked. 'This time of night?'

'I'm meeting someone.'

'Right you are, madam.'

Madam. She liked the way the Brits called women 'Madam.' *Madam Albert, if you please*. Nick was the most exciting man she'd ever met, and what's more he cared about what happened to her, didn't he? If not, why had he gone to all the trouble to get those pills?

Amy's watch said five after twelve. She was five minutes late. Could he have left, convinced she wasn't coming? *Nick?* She couldn't just stand there like a ninny. Two sets of steps led up to the monument itself, the huge, ornate, cage-like affair with an enormous statue of Prince Albert in the middle. Below the central statue were blurred figures that were hard to make out. *Nick?* Was he there, concealed among the statuary?

She sprinted up the stairs, and had reached the marble base when a figure emerged from the shadows. 'Nick? Oh, Nick, I'm here!'

Nice Girls

Mona Davidson stepped into view. 'What the hell are *you* doing here?'

Stunned, Amy jumped back, and would have fallen backward down the granite steps if Mona had not grabbed her.

'Who told you I'd be here?' Mona demanded. 'Were you eavesdropping on me and Nick? Tell me, you little momzer, or I'll shake you till your teeth fall out!' True to her intent, her hands squeezed Amy's upper arms tight against her slender torso, rocking her body back and forth with such violence Amy thought her neck would snap.

'Please . . . Mona . . . don't! You're hurting me! Mona! Stop! You're *hurting* me, Mona! For God's sake, Mona, stop!'

The clatter of hurried footsteps on granite, shouts, and a hurtling body trying to pry them apart. The impact tumbled the three of them onto a grassy hillock beside the steps, rolling them in a human snowball of arms and legs clawing and kicking to prevail, until Georgina extricated herself and fell back on the grass with a moan of rage.

'He couldn't do this! He wouldn't!'

Breathing hard from her emotions, all Mona could say was, 'He did.'

Amy lay facedown, inhaling the sweet smell of the grass in an attempt to restore her equilibrium.

'Oh my God, are you okay?' To Mona, Amy looked like a rag doll, her limbs twisted and broken. 'Did I hurt you? My God.'

'I'm fine.' The younger girl sat up and gathered her knees to her chest. With a bewildered look at each of the others, she said, 'You mean he told all of us to meet him here? But why?'

'Maybe he's robbing the house,' Mona ventured.

A dry laugh from Georgina. 'Not much to steal.'

'Then heavens to Betsy, why?'

At that precise moment the answer became evident. The familiar sound of the Lagonda screeched to a halt on the roadway below, followed by an insistent rat-a-tat of the horn. With a flamboyant wave, Nick Albert vaulted from the driver's seat with a package, which he deftly placed on the lowest step. He was back at the wheel and on his way before anyone could react.

'Watch out! It might be a bomb!' Mona shouted as they scrambled down the slope.

The package contained a magnum of champagne, three Water-ford flutes, and a note addressed to the three of them. 'Forgive the melodrama. Roxanne and I are flying to France to be married. Since I am sure you will all agree that I am a greedy fellow with a bizarre sense of the absurd, I ask you most humbly to drink a toast to my new enterprise as a special memorial to the companionship we found in Chelsea Mews. I shall think of each of you with love, and wish you all your hearts' desires. As ever and forever, Nick Albert.'

'Bullshit!' Mona shouted.

'Please, Mona!' Amy hated that kind of language.

'It's *our* champagne!' Georgina protested. 'Or Amy's, really.' Amy had ordered two magnums of Moët Chandon from the wine merchants at the bottom of the road. This was one of them, as proved by the merchant's stamp.

'Son of a bitch!' Amy exploded.

'*Please*, Amy!' Mona fanned herself as if about to faint dead away. 'Your language!'

Georgina likewise fanned herself in mock shock. 'We're *ladies*! You know we can't bear that kind of talk!'

Amy would not be humored out of her distress. 'But *why*? I don't understand!'

How naive can you be? Mona thought. 'You want me to draw you a map?'

Her remark brought sobs from Amy and a furious glare from Georgina. 'How dare you speak to her like that! The poor girl's heartbroken! She had a crush on Nick! Anyone could see that!'

'Oh, yeah? Well I'm heartbroken, too. Nick and I . . . well, we should have told you and he promised to tell you . . . Nick and I were going to be married.'

Fire flashed from the Englishwoman's normally lake-blue eyes. 'Liar!' She slapped Mona hard across the face and pushed her down on the ground. 'Nick Albert loved me! He was going to marry me! He –' Her tantrum was cut short by a savage tackle around the knees by Mona that sent the two women into a no-holds-barred brawl, kicking, scratching, pulling each other's hair.

Their shrieks and curses showed off a ripe vocabulary that neither would have previously admitted to possessing. Amy watched for a moment in stunned disbelief before finally trying to pry them apart. 'Stop it! Stop it, I said!' To no avail. Her entire body aching, her legs leaden, her stomach wrenched by cramps, Amy used her well-conditioned upper body to separate them and hold them apart.

Nice Girls

'So help me God, I'll tear you limb from limb, you scuzzy little bint!' Georgina flayed the air in a vain attempt to reach her opponent.

'You and what army? You and that fakey-poo accent! Marbles in the mouth! I'll give you marbles in the mouth! I'm going to knock out all your teeth!'

Amy Dean, of proud New England stock and trained from infancy to behave courteously and with decorum, tried to be firm. 'The two of you! Enough is enough!' Again to no avail. The two women were breathing hard, gathering their strength for the next round.

'Bitch!'

'Slut!'

That's when Amy lost her temper. 'Stop fucking around!'

She was as stunned as they by what had come out of her mouth.

'Amy! Did you hear what she said, Georgina?' A broad smile wiped the fury from Mona's face.

Georgina, too, reared back and beheld the younger woman. 'Amy! How could you? I'm shocked! I'll have to report you to the authorities!'

All at once the fisticuffs and fury turned to hugs, laughter, and awkward apologies. In the taxi home to Chelsea Mews, Mona said, 'If we had known, we could have saved money and shared a cab here in the first place.'

Female friendships start out in a wide variety of ways. They develop and flourish for an even wider variety of reasons, mainly having to do with convenience, serendipity, and the more self-serving aspects of need and survival in a world run by men. Aggression, envy, sneakiness, and sexual desire play their roles. Circumstances plus private, often shameful, goals fill out the equation.

Small girls who smash each other's toys in the playground often wind up being bosom pals and, as the old saying goes, buy their bras together. Hormone-juiced Lolitas fighting over the same pimply boy later become college roommates working in tandem for their doctorates. Women fighting each other tooth-and-nail for professional or social advantage will yoke themselves together with oxen strength when threatened by spoilers.

For Georgina Crane, Mona Davidson, and Amy Dean, their friendship really began that night at the Albert Memorial, and further evolved in mutual anger at Nick and support for each other during the early hours of the following morning. Too emotionally charged to consider sleep, they huddled together in Georgina's sitting room.

'What on earth am I going to do now?' Georgina moaned, wringing her hands.

Mona went swiftly to Georgina's bedroom and returned with the framed photograph of Nick Albert. 'Forget him. Tear this up. Throw it in the garbage where it belongs.'

Georgina put the photograph face down in her lap. 'It's my *life* I'm talking about! It's earning my living! The two of you know what you're going to do. You've got family behind you. You're studying for your careers. I have nothing. No training. No prospects. I had always thought I would marry and live in the country somewhere and raise children and roses. All I have is this house. It's wonderful having the two of you as paying guests. It's given me a few pennies in my pocket. But the house is too small. It would be hopeless to have boarders the year round. They could never be as sweet and as dear to me as you two.'

She confessed that her plans for the future had revolved around Nick Albert. 'He was going to start his own tour-guide agency, specialized guided tours for people with particular interests like painting or agriculture or history, and I was going to work with him. He said all the Americans, not just the dreaded blue-haired ladies, all Americans were bonkers for things British. We were going to make a bloody fortune.'

'You're giving me an idea!' Mona sprang to her feet. 'Georgina, stay where you are! Amy, come with me!'

Left alone with the photograph of Nick Albert, Georgina caressed the image behind the glass with trembling fingers. That he loved her, she was certain. That he had left her to marry Roxanne did not mean he had stopped loving her. There must be a reason. This was not the end of Nick Albert in her life, only a temporary hiatus. He could not stay away from her, anymore than she could stop loving him. They belonged together. Hearing Mona and Amy on the steps, she thrust the framed photograph behind some books in the bookcase.

With Mona pulling and Amy pushing from below, they had managed to move the old wooden box from under the stairs and into the sitting room. The day before, when Amy had said they really

Nice Girls

should have some patriotic music, Georgina had remembered her father's collection of old 78 RPM gramophone records.

Now, Mona smiled delightedly at Georgina, indicating the large box.

'There's a lot of stuff in here, Georgina. Stuff you can sell, right, Amy? Like that feather boa?'

Digging into the debris, Amy found a wispy pink boa and wrapped it around her neck. 'Tra-la!'

'You're mad, both of you,' Georgina said. 'It's all worthless, only good for dress-up parties, just a lot of junk.'

'Not *junk*, Georgina. *Junque!* J-U-N-Q-U-E! Look at this stuff! Feathers. Laces. Fans. Look at these!' Opera-length kid gloves. Lizard handbags with claw clasps. A box camera. A Fortnum & Mason shoe box full of pipes and cigarette holders.

'Those were my father's and grandfather's. The assessors said they're worthless.'

'*Vintage* is what they are!' Mona upturned the box, dumping its entire contents on the floor. Binoculars, lorgnettes, enameled and painted pill boxes, an embroidered handkerchief case, and a lady's travel vanity fitted with bottles and flasks for all manner of toiletries.

'And a manicure set, too!' Amy uncovered the delicately honed instruments.

'Ivory. From Mummy's trousseau. She never used it. Couldn't bear fiddling with cuticles or nail varnish.'

Last of all to emerge was a mauve cardboard box labeled HOUSE OF WORTH, PARIS. Opened, its crushed tissue paper released a fragrance redolent of a honeymoon in France. Originally it had held the going-away suit worn by Georgina's mother, who in turn had used the box to store dance cards from country balls, menus from the Savoy Grille and the Ritz, a family collection of picture postcards of Europe and the Holy Land dating back to before the First War, and a set of Baedekers in a folder marked GRAND TOUR, 1913.

Georgina could not see the reason for their enthusiasm. 'I couldn't get more than a couple of quid at a church jumble sale.'

'That's right,' Mona agreed. 'But you're not going to sell it at a church sale. You're going to sell it at your friend's stand at the Chelsea antiques market. Or better yet, the Portobello Road! *Everybody* goes to the Portobello Road. Tourists. Movie stars.

Models. The chic place to be on a Saturday morning, right?'

Georgina rose angrily to her feet. 'You must be mad!'

'It's a *great* idea, Georgina!' Amy was as thrilled as Mona at the possibilities. 'It'll be loads of fun, honest! I've been to Portobello! It's neat!'

Neither of the Americans understood the depth of Georgina's revulsion. '*Me?* Hawk my wares from a barrow, like some cockney yoick? What if my friends see me? What will I say?'

Mona assumed her best Barbra Streisand accent: 'What will you say, dollink?' Then added with a know-it-all shrug, 'You'll say, "For you, sweetheart, I make a special price." '

Georgina had to laugh, in spite of herself. Mona and Amy were mad. She could just see the condescending faces of her erstwhile chums. Sara. Perdita. Cornelia. Annabel. Where were they when she needed them? Why should she care what they thought? Nick called them The Young Constipateds, insisted they all looked like they had sour stomachs.

'But I can't just go to Portobello Road and say "Here I am!" One needs a license. I'm sure. A stall. One can't just set up shop and start shouting, "I say, I say, I say! Step right up and buy Bonnie Prince Charlie's christening gown." '

She explained it was a hoary old myth at country fairs that someone was sure to show up with an embroidered infant's cap and robe that had been hidden away for three hundred years and was whispered to be the very garment worn by the exiled prince at his christening.

But Mona wasn't listening. She was making a list. 'We'll need tags for marking the prices. A receipt book to keep records. Bags to wrap stuff in. Money to make change, plenty of coins and single pound notes.' She licked the point of her pencil and simultaneously remembered her grandmother Davitsky, who had worked in a stationery store when Mona was a baby, and Professor Benson (formerly Bernstein) who had advised aspiring performers to find a single gesture that would reveal a character's entire life.

In one improvisation, Mona had been exploring a nouveau riche socialite ashamed of her ghetto past. Licking a pencil point had proved to be the dead giveaway that pinpointed her assumed pretensions, and it also earned her a rare compliment from Professor Benson.

'Use what you have,' he said repeatedly to the class. She said it now to Georgina. 'And we'll need a sign, too. "Lady Georgina's Junque Shop"! Right?'

Georgina considered Mona's suggestion carefully before replying. 'It would be more suitable to say "The Best of British Junque; The Lady Georgina Crane, Proprietor"!'

Amy's stomach cramps were getting worse by the minute. She tried to ignore them, her fingers mentally crossed with the hope that the pills Nick had given her were working. *Please God, forgive me for sleeping with Lou Humphries! Forgive me for lusting after Nick Albert, and for even thinking of marrying him!* She could tell herself that all she'd wanted was a father for her unborn child. But she couldn't fool God. God knew she wanted Nick Albert for herself, for the way he made her feel, for the certainty that she would never feel that way with any other man.

Several times she had left the sitting room in the forlorn hope that her friend had come. Nothing. Just the same aching sensation in the groin. It couldn't be labor, could it? From what little she knew, a five-week fetus was the size of a raisin.

'So what do you say, Georgina? We'll be right there with you. You'll be a smash, right?' Mona needed the diversion, a project to keep her mind off Nick Albert and the end to all her plans. At least his elopement would get Bill Neal and the class off her back. The man was on his honeymoon, right? Any plans to produce a play would naturally be postponed until after he had returned, *if* he returned. Whatever the case, by then Mona would be long gone back to New York.

The illegality of Bill's class aside, she was learning a lot about her craft and about her ability to cope in a alien milieu. What's more, Bill said her voice had a peculiar quality, a timbre that was memorable. An ad-agency chum of his would be holding auditions next week for a series of animated commercials. Bill had recommended her for one of the voice-overs – an American coffeepot searching through a British supermarket for the right brand of coffee.

Minerva could take a flying leap. Mona was the one for the job. She bloody well had an American accent, right?

'We'll talk about it tomorrow.' Georgina pointed to the pier clock on the mantelpiece. 'Half-past four. I'm knackered.' 'The Best of British Junque' was a splendid idea. Bless Mona. And darling Amy, of course. Exhausted as she was, she made a mental note of the market towns within a few hours' drive from London. If the idea caught on, the contents of the box would sell at once. The English countryside would provide sustenance and maybe riches for her future, just as it had provided the produce that had enriched her family's past.

Alone in the room she had so passionately shared with Nick Albert, she found that, as usual, she could not express her feelings in her own terms. Like so many Englishwomen of her class, she turned to literature to help her. 'In bed we laugh, in bed we cry.' Samuel Johnson had written that, in the eighteenth century. 'And born in bed, in bed we die.' Not her. Not yet. She punched the pillow on Nick's side of her bed so hard the seam burst, releasing a choking storm of feathers.

She was *not* going to die. Not of love for Nick Albert. She was going to live and prosper, and get him back no matter what she had to do and no matter how long it took. In the meantime, the first thing she must do tomorrow was change the lock on the downstairs door. The bastard had walked off with her latchkey.

The house lay silent. For each of the three exhausted women, the Nick Albert wound would fester and throb for days and weeks to come. It would take a long time to heal, if ever. Each would have to find her own means of recovery.

While Georgina fell into a restless sleep with Nick's pillow in her arms, Mona took out the script for the coffee commercial Bill Neal had given her to memorize. Screw Nick Albert. The most important thing was her career.

Amy Dean folded her lean and lanky frame into the prenatal position, trying to ease her cramps and get some much needed rest. As the pains subsided and her body at last relaxed, she allowed herself to think of Nick Albert. She had heard of men who drove women wild, men like Porfirio Ruberosa and Aly Khan, but she had never met one until Nick Albert. The idea of such ecstasy frightened her.

Her eyes closed, she further allowed herself to wonder what it would be like to have Nick Albert with her in the narrow bed that was like Lou Humphries's narrow bed, but making love to her with a passion Lou did not nor ever would have. Nick's gaze alone was more caressing than both of Lou's clumsy, grasping hands.

In the final moment of surrender to sleep she gave in to the fantasy of Nick's arms around her, as he rocked her like the child she still was and called her his baby bird. A warm moist sensation crept slowly down her thighs. Without looking, she knew it was the right warm moisture at last. Unwilling to stir yet knowing she must, she snuggled for one last moment in Nick's phantom embrace before getting up and resuming her life.

She would complete the seminar. She would return to college. She would get engaged to Lou Humphries. All as planned for an orderly, productive life.

10

A Fine English Summer

Nick Albert was gone, but not easily forgotten. The next day's papers covered two stories: the amusing July Fourth picnic given by Lady Georgina Crane and her two American house guests, and the elopement of jet-set heiress Roxanne D'Orsainville and ex-guards officer Nicholas Albert.

The newspaper accounts of both varied, in accordance with their publishers' politics and the readership they served. Fact had little to do with social reportage. It being a slow news time, Fleet Street fell on the elopement with a frenzy normally reserved for royal escapades, rock stars, and members of Parliament.

When William Hickey of the *Daily Express* noticed that a staff photographer had captured Nick Albert early the previous evening munching a frankfurter in the adoring company of Georgina, Mona, and Amy, and later had caught him and Roxanne boarding her Piper Cub two-seater at Gatwick airport, he had run the photos side by side with the copy line, IN THE NICK OF TIME.

The Daily Mail ran comparable shots with the headline CAUGHT OUT!, gleefully revealing that on the day of his elopement with Roxanne he had been caught playing up to the tragic Lady Georgina, whose parents had so recently been killed in an auto crash, and her ravishing American house guests.

The afternoon papers further revealed Nick Albert's rumored role in at least three instances of debutante betrayal, one of whose mothers said he was no longer welcome at dances or at-homes. A city banker anonymously branded Nick 'a cad and a home-wrecker,' and said it was a pity dueling was outlawed or he'd have run Nick through.

Unwilling to let the story die, correspondents in Paris, Cannes, and Monte Carlo crawled through laundry chutes, dressed as waiters, and trained telescopic lenses wherever rumor hinted the runaway couple might be. There were reports that Roxanne's outraged father, the Baron D'Orsainville, had disinherited her and stopped her hundred-thousand-pound-a-year allowance, while another source said that Roxanne's English-born barmaid mother, now married to an Arab prince, had given the couple a flat on the Île St Louis, a schooner she wasn't using, and a hundred thousand pounds to make up for the Baron's cruelty.

The inhabitants of the little house in Chelsea Mews read every word of every report. In the days that followed, they themselves became peripherally famous. Reporters desperate for anything at all returned again and again to the house, photographing whichever of them was there and writing insinuating non-stories suggesting they knew what was going on but had vowed secrecy.

The benefits of press exposure turned out to be positive for all three. Georgina politely announced plans for her Best of British Junque stall at the Portobello Road, and was quoted as saying that all of her friends were ransacking cupboards and old trunks for bits and pieces. Mona described herself as one of the new breed of American actresses. Dedicated to the classics, yet eager for contemporary meanings. Her dream? To play Portia in a miniskirt, with Beatles and Stones music as background. Inspired by her own wit, she said, 'Take Shylock. In a rock version of *Merchant*, he could sing "Can't Get No Satisfaction"!'

Amy contented herself with saying how much she admired English history and architecture, and why it was important to Americans. One frustrated reporter decided that was dull, and had her tearfully reproaching the British for 'letting America go' in 1776.

The following Sunday the Nick and Roxanne story reached a dizzying height with nude sun-bathing shots of them on the deck of their schooner, and its zenith the following day with wedding photographs of the lovers wearing matching white tuxedos as they exchanged vows before the mayor of Cap Ferrat.

'Enough, already! I'm late for class.' Mona accidentally-on-purpose dropped a slice of toast jam-side-down on the newspaper. 'Sorry about that.' It was getting to be her favorite British phrase – so clever of them, the phrase for all occasions. *Sorry about that.* It would come in handy in New York.

'Not to worry,' Georgina assured her. 'I think we've all just about had it.' To prove her point, she removed the silver spoon from the

Nice Girls

pot of orange marmalade and wiped it across the grinning, self-satisfied faces of the newly married couple. 'Matching white tuxedos, indeed!'

Amy piped up. 'One of the kids in the seminar said he'd heard they're brother and sister.'

'Maybe Roxanne's his brother in drag!' Mona picked up on the idea. 'Does that make it incest, Georgina?'

'Go to hell, both of you! Can't you see I'm trying to get ready for an engagement with my bank manager? Shall we try to have one single conversation without Nick Albert?'

Earlier, pouring the coffee, she had said she had been thinking about Nick and all the newspaper reports. 'In a way, I guess I should thank Nick. If not for him, I wouldn't have the two of you as friends. If not for him, my bank manager wouldn't be seeing me this morning.' The press reports of Georgina's Best of British Junque concept had blown it all out of proportion. Women's magazines had asked to do layouts. A woman in Cirencester had rung up to say she made inexpensive copies of Victorian jewelry and needed a London outlet. A marketing person from Harrods had suggested meeting, with a view to developing a Junque Shop in the gift department.

It was taking all of Georgina's energy and poise to prepare for the bank meeting. In asking for a loan and a large overdraft, her collateral was a combination of her name, her idea, and the press exposure since Nick Albert's defection. Mona and Amy had supervised her executive image: the magnificent hair that Nick liked to see hanging loose once more tightly coiled in a burnished knot, the chalk-white silk dress, the matching T-strap shoes, her mother's pearls and gold button earrings. She was ready to present the red-white-and-blue folder, handsomely stenciled by Amy in a Union Jack design and with a bold black logo, BEST OF BRITISH JUNQUE, LADY GEORGINA CRANE, PROP. Inside, a simple statement of intent outlined her plans, modest to start, for selling vintage merchandise. 'Not "secondhand"!' Mona had cautioned. 'Vintage!'

The bank manager needed little convincing. When she was announced, he came out personally to escort her into his office. Newspaper cuttings about her were ostentatiously arranged on his desk so that she would see them. ' "Best of British Junque," eh? Very amusing. Now what can I do for you?'

It seemed that he had met her parents years before, and was indeed dreadfully saddened by their tragedy. With a compassionate hand on her knee, he confessed with a stutter that he had been frightfully keen on her mother.

That evening, when Mona and Amy returned from their respective studies, Georgina was waiting for them with the happy news. 'A straight-out loan of two thousand quid, cash on the barrel-head! And another thousand overdraft!'

What she did not disclose was a further cause for astonishment. When the bank manager had sent for Georgina's pathetic file, she knew her account had at most forty or fifty pounds, a circumstance that had kept her from using it. 'Mmmm, I see. How very interesting.'

Wondering what it could be, certain she had not overdrawn the account, she held her breath and waited for the ax to fall.

'A person called Nicholas Albert . . .'

Good God, Nick! What could have happened? Had he found her cheque book and forged her name? The bastard! Doing a midnight flit was one thing, but if he had queered her reputation with the bank she would personally track him down and kill him.

Au contraire, mon cher. According to the record, an international bank draft for five hundred pounds had been transferred to her account from this Nicholas Albert care of American Express, Monte Carlo.

'Isn't that' – the bank manager riffled through the cuttings on his desk – 'the elopement chap?'

Groping for an explanation, Georgina said, 'How kind of him. In all the excitement, I didn't think he'd remember his promise to help me get started on my new enterprise.'

The five hundred quid, not to mention the American Express address where she could write to him, was information she would keep to herself.

Mona and Amy congratulated her and settled down over cups and cups of strong coffee and chocolate biscuits to organize her debut as a Junque dealer the following Saturday at the Portobello Road.

Each of the two Americans had her own secret as well. On Mona's arrival at Bill Neal's, he gave her a letter addressed to her in care of him. Skimming it quickly as if it were only of passing interest, she was waiting to be alone in bed to devour every word. The gist of it was that Nick missed her madly, and that she was to work hard and become a famous actress. Bill Neal had told him she had the makings. His last sentence jumped right off the page:

Nice Girls

'Please don't cut me out of your life; send me your New York address!' To be sure the letter didn't get lost or fall into alien hands by mistake, she tucked it into the top of her panty-hose, where she could feel it against her bare skin.

Amy, too, had received a communication, by way of a phone call from the American Embassy in Grosvenor Square. A letter addressed to her had arrived in the diplomatic pouch from Paris, with instructions to ask Miss Dean to collect it in person. Nick felt guilty as hell, he said, but thought it important to tell her the pills he had given her were aspirin. He hoped the power of his suggestion had worked, and that she would keep in touch.

'New house rule,' Georgina announced. 'The name Nick Albert is herewith and henceforth banned from this establishment! Agreed?'

She extended her right hand. Mona covered it with her own. 'Agreed!' Amy, her hand placed topmost, echoed, 'Agreed!' Mona added the exuberant postscript: 'One for all, all for one. *None* for Nicholas Albert!'

True to their vow, Nick Albert's name was never mentioned during the remaining weeks of their summer together. Yet his impact on their lives continued. The publicity generated by his elopement had not only launched Georgina's new career, it shone a spotlight on Mona and Amy as well.

Bill Neal had been apprehensive that his clandestine acting class would be exposed and he would be thrown out of RADA. But after a conversation with Nick, he decided to no longer be a hostage to the establishment. He was young, he was talented. He had come all this way from Australia. Now it was time to move on to New York. Acting as such had lost its appeal. From working with actors these many weeks, he saw his future as an agent or manager and, in time, a producer. He could spot talent, develop talent – Mona Davidson, for example. The girl had a certain something that was inborn, something that could not be learned but could be trained.

Through a contact with an Australian friend at a London advertising agency, he arranged for the audition that led to the coffee commercial. Now his friend was being reassigned to the agency's New York office. He suggested Bill get off his Pommy ass and come along, too.

Between Mona and himself a special intimacy developed, based on mutual admiration and emotional need. They could let their hair down with each other and have confession time – he about his homosexual adventures in the netherworld of the Piccadilly Circus tube station, she about her longings for Nick Albert's body and the various hideous accidents she would love to see befall Roxanne.

'Never mind Roxanne. He married her for her money. You're going to be a star. Nick will be sorry. He'll dump her and beg you on his hands and knees to take him back.'

The vision of Nick Albert begging on his hands and knees comforted her. She found she could talk endlessly about him to Bill, bore him silly, discuss things she didn't feel comfortable discussing with other women, and certainly not with Georgina and Amy. She assumed they both knew of her affair with Nick. To save Georgina's feelings she went along with the idea that she as well as Amy merely had crushes on him, and that's why they had gone to meet him at the Albert Memorial.

She couldn't tell for sure whether Georgina knew the truth. Nick had betrayed all three of them. It was not the time for recriminations. It was the time for unity, closing ranks and retrenching. For Mona, any discussion of Nick in the house in Chelsea Mews was risky. She worried that she might slip and say something self-incriminating.

Talking with Bill Neal was her only outlet, her only way of keeping the touch and taste and smell of Nick Albert in the foreground of her thoughts until the day at the end of August when she boarded the plane to New York.

The man in the seat beside her was a marked physical contrast to Nick Albert. Sprawled against the window, he was already asleep when she arrived. His thick dark hair curled into a shaggy frame around his deeply tanned face. As compared to Nick's sculpted elegance, his features were almost primitive – thick brows, beak nose, generous lips. He needed a shave. He smelled salty. Not sexy salty. Ocean salty. Astringent. Like anchovies or clam broth.

A sailing vacation, she speculated. He was on his way home from the Greek Islands or someplace and had changed planes at Heathrow. The sleeves of his faded denim shirt were rolled up to reveal muscular mahogany forearms and surprisingly slender, well-shaped hands. A concert pianist, or brain surgeon at least – her mother would love that. His white duck pants looked as if he had jumped in the water and let them dry on his body, throwing his thighs into prominence. His ankles were bare, the laces of his sneakers loosened.

Nice Girls

She settled into her seat, her arm pressed tentatively against his on the shared armrest. Without waking, he shifted restlessly and kicked off the confining sneakers. His feet were as long and tanned and beautifully slender as his hands. In another spasmic shift, he crossed one leg over the knee nearest her. Confronted with the sole of his foot, she felt a sudden overwhelming urge to tickle his instep with her tongue.

The impulse startled her. Was she nuts or something? That's all she had to do, right, start running around licking the soles of men's feet! Nick Albert liked it. He had told her to do it. But he was her lover, right? He could ask her to do whatever he wanted. This man was a stranger. With his eyes closed she didn't even know what color they were, though she guessed brown from his other coloring. Or what nationality. Just because it was an American plane didn't mean he was an American, right? That was all she had to do, lick the foot of some foreigner. Send for the guy with the butterfly net!

To divert herself, she looked at the heavy gold identity bracelet on his wrist. B-R-E-N-T, it said. Was that a first name or a last name? If it was a last name, and with that nose, he could be a Jew whose family had changed its name at Ellis Island. If it was a first name, he could be anything. Men who had last names for first names were trouble, and if they had a Junior or a number attached to their name, they were sheer menace.

When the takeoff failed to awaken him, her curiosity got the better of her. The corner of his canvas duffle was sticking out from the seat in front of him. Bending over in an elaborate pretense of finding something in her own carry-on bag, she pulled the duffle out far enough to see the baggage tag.

'Brent Wilson's the name. Okay?'

Son of a bitch! She tried to brazen it out. 'I . . . I was just looking for something. Sorry I woke you.'

'I wasn't asleep. I always pretend to be asleep until I see who's sitting next to me. I've been watching you since you arrived.'

Some people had all the luck. 'And . . .?'

He rolled toward her and smiled, his eyes a startling hazel flecked with amber. 'And it's going to be a long trip across the Atlantic.'

'So . . .?'

'So we might as well get acquainted.'

Before leaving Chelsea Mews, Mona had done her best to cheer

Amy up. Her moodiness was attributed by Georgina and Mona to an adolescent crush on Nick. Though not much younger than they, she seemed to them more a kid sister than a contemporary. Poor baby! At seventeen, carrying a torch was serious.

With Nick gone, Georgina and Mona especially nagged at her to stop moping and to try to have some fun. 'Isn't there someone interesting in the seminar? That guy William? I saw him at the picnic. I think he has hot eyes for you!'

Come to think of it, Sir William did seem to pay her an awful lot of attention. Just the other day, in fact, he had asked her if she'd care to look at an architectural ruin.

'Where?'

'My flat, actually.' Groan.

Everyone knew he was married and lived with his wife and children in the country. He talked about it often enough. She brushed aside the invitation, if invitation it was. The English sense of humor eluded her. He was probably just being nice. He was at least twice her age, maybe more, maybe forty-five.

'I'm not interested in other men. I'm engaged, or at least engaged to be engaged, to Lou Humphries.'

Mona would not be put off. 'When did you hear from him last? I haven't seen any letters from Lou. No phone calls, right?'

'It's none of your business, Mona! Lou and I have an understanding. We're getting officially engaged at Christmas, and that is that!'

'Then why doesn't he write or call? Something's not kosher, right?'

Georgina interceded. 'Leave her alone, Mona. What she does is really up to her.'

'I think she should have an affair with William. It will be a good experience to have an affair with an Englishman.'

He was the wrong Englishman. It was Nick she wanted. 'I'm not interested, do you hear? I'm in love with Lou. We're getting married. In fact I think I'll call him right now. You two nosy-bodies can listen in if you want to.'

Lou Humphries' phone rang several times before it was picked up. A girl's voice said. 'Lou Humphries' Hideaway! This is the secretary speaking. May I ask who's calling?'

With Georgina and Mona looking on, Amy played it cool. 'It's Amy Dean calling from London.'

Nice Girls

A burst of giggles was followed by 'I'll give him the message – as soon as he zips up his pants!'

The phone went dead. Amy steeled her composure and continued to talk. 'Away till next week? What a shame. Please tell him I called.'

A few days later she took Sir William up on his invitation. His flat reflected nothing about his tastes in architecture and design. It was a square white concrete cubicle, furnished to the minimum with a battered sofa and two chairs covered with patterned Indian prints. There was a dark shade on the single window, a floor lamp that tilted dangerously, and a shelf holding an electric kettle. An open door revealed a toilet bowl and sink in a duet of gushing water.

'Welcome to the passion pit, my dear.'

Good manners prevented her from leaving right away. After all the man was a famous expert, or at least that's what the brochure said. It was late afternoon. She was a grown woman. She had accepted an invitation to have a friendly drink. She should be able to handle such a situation, or else she should have stayed home in Providence. *Passion pit?* How corny could you get? All he needed was a waxed mustache to twirl.

It had been a mistake to come. She felt very uncomfortable. The flat was ugly in the extreme. She had a hunch conversation was going to be difficult. She would have one drink and leave.

'Apple cider?'

The jug had a color photograph of a shiny red apple on it.

'Is it strong? I prefer something non-alcoholic.'

He assured her it was fresh from the countryside, just ripe apples pressed for their juice.

It was delicious. She was thirsty. In less time than she would have thought possible, her host was on top of her on the sofa, which even in her sudden state of intoxication she could tell smelled rotten. Like a garbage can that hadn't been properly washed. Or a dead cat.

'I want you! I want you!'

'Well, I don't want you!' She wanted to get out of there. She wanted someone to save her. Nick Albert? He was on his honeymoon. Lou Humphries? It was all Lou's fault. The nerve of him letting some girl answer his phone, when he was almost engaged to her!

'I know you want me! I can tell! I can feel you wanting me! I'm going to do all kinds of unspeakable things to you! Tell me you want me! Tell me!'

With the strength of the natural athlete she managed to push him away and stagger to her feet. The cider sent her reeling. He was coming at her with his necktie in hand. 'I'm going to tie you down and force you to do my bidding! It's what women want, what women deserve, the nasty little creatures!'

He somehow managed to get the tie wrapped around her wrists, but then, with a deep breath that cleared her head, Amy rammed her knee into his groin and slammed him across the head with her bound wrists.

In the taxi, she wondered how quickly she could get a flight to Boston. Nick Albert was right. She *was* a baby bird. She was not equipped to fly alone. She needed the safety and security of a nest and the orderly progression of courting, mating, and being part of a family unit.

She mustn't blame Lou for his behavior. It was her own fault. She had left him to pursue some romantic dream of a career in British history and architecture. She had expected everyone, including Sir William, to be devoted to the subject and eager to welcome her into their merry band. What she had to show for it was some visits to historic houses she could have seen better on her own, some lectures that covered ground she already knew, and a stained old school tie that she would have preferred using to choke its owner senseless.

She belonged with Lou. Her future was at his side. She would tell him so, as fast as the plane would take her to him. And if the girl answered the door, she would take care of that, too.

Georgina truly missed her Americans. The house in Chelsea Mews felt so empty and quiet without them. With money coming in from her Junque stall and her prospects for the future improving, she was discovering that she possessed an inherent talent for commerce. She would have enjoyed having Mona and Amy there not only for companionship, but also to discuss what items might appeal to American tourists.

Still, as she remarked one afternoon in September when Nick Albert stopped in for a drink, having the house to herself had certain compensations.

11

Mona

New York, 1973

Decisions, decisions . . .

Bill Neal said if she wanted to make the transition from voice-overs to on-camera stardom, she would have to get her nose fixed. In the five years since they'd met in London, he had more than proved his belief in the unique qualities of her voice. It turned out she was a natural for the specialized field of radio and television commercials. She had an uncanny ability to sound like anything from a toddler to an octogenarian, from a nagging housewife to an orgasmic prune, and to give voice to other inanimate objects like vitamins, toilet bowls, frozen dinners, and in one particularly lucrative case, a polar bear inviting folks to Alaska.

As her repertoire grew, so did the demand for her services. Her knack for dialects earned her healthy contracts for regional accounts. Not only did she have an ear for American accents, she was a quick study and could do French, German, and Spanish dubs for such international products as soft drinks and electronic equipment.

It was a real kick in the head that her British accents won out over genuine transplanted English accents. Her Liverpudlian out-Beatled the Beatles. Her 'plummy clenchjaw uptight strangle,' based on Georgina and Nick, was greeted with howls of approval for its Monty Python humor.

The money was rolling in, the residuals were bordering on the obscene. Her thoughts often turned to James Dean in *Giant* when his oil well came in: 'I'm a rich boy!' Well, she was almost a rich girl, and trying to act sensible and grateful, which she was. She'd have to be a jerk not to be happy about that part. And an ingrate maybe, to be unhappy about the other parts.

Whenever she tried to discuss her yearning for a real acting part, her mother always cut her short with the 'starving children' reminder. 'Thousands of actresses are walking the streets. Starving to death. Working as waitresses. Car hops. Worse!' (They both knew what that meant.) 'Thank God for what you've got!'

She did thank God, but she still wanted to play Portia or Blanche or any of the film roles played by Shirley MacLaine and, okay, Barbra Streisand.

'Barbra Streisand didn't need a nose job, right?'

It was a continuing argument with Bill. 'The camera loves Barbra Streisand. It's not something you can negotiate, Mona. The camera does not love you. It likes you but it doesn't love you. There are no guarantees. You might wind up photographing like Mona Davidson with a nose job.'

She had heard there was another reason Barbra Streisand hadn't had a nose job. She'd been afraid it might do something terrible to her voice. Mona's voice might not be Streisand, but it *was* her meal ticket, right? Her golden goose that she did not want to kill.

Decisions, decisions . . . There was another decision she had to make. As her manager, agent, sounding board, and best friend in the whole world, Bill Neal was the one person she could confide in, the strong shoulder, the crying towel. Since her father was dead, and although her mother had silently disapproved, she had even asked Bill to give her away when she married Brent Wilson.

It was to Bill she had run in the middle of the night that time Brent had punched her in the nose, shouting 'Stop bugging me about a nose job! You want a nose job? Here's a nose job!'

Three months ago, when she'd found lipstick on Brent's jock-strap, Bill had patiently led her through the pros and cons of a divorce, and then had even gone so far as to act as mediator when Brent begged him to convince Mona he was sorry.

She had all but decided to go ahead with the divorce when she'd discovered she was pregnant. As it happened, Amy Humphries had called her from Providence moments after she'd gotten the gynie report, inviting her and Brent to Sandi's first birthday party.

Decisions, decisions . . . To have an abortion? There was still time, she was in the first trimester. Abortion was now legal. But no, how could she have an abortion? No. Divorce Brent and raise the baby herself? Brent was behaving himself to the point of nausea. The picture-book husband – handsome, tanned, all those white teeth. Dumb. It had taken her a long time to realize what an oaf he was, a world-class lout.

He had lucked into a job with a family-owned insurance company. The accounts he serviced were handed to him. His main responsibility was to have lunch and smile a lot. His interests were limited to sports (doing and watching), hanging out at sports-oriented bars and restaurants, and collecting pornography.

Had it not been for the timing of Amy's phone call, she might not have mentioned her pregnancy. As it was, she blurted out the news to her one friend who was a mother. Amy's delight was contagious. Having a baby was the most wonderful thing in the world! In the midst of their giggles, Mona realized that this quite ordinary news about the most ordinary accomplishment that the most ordinary woman could achieve generated more approval from friends and family than all her fancy contracts or the duplex she had bought on Central Park West.

Decisions, decisions . . .

Why was everything left to her? She was only twenty-four years old! Why did *she* have to decide whether to get divorced, have a baby, get a nose job, and which wallpaper to choose for the guest bedroom that was probably going to be the nursery if she decided to go ahead and have the baby? *If* . . .

'Kiss Auntie Mona! There's a good girl. Auntie Mona's going to have a sweet little girl just like you!' Amy had brought Sandi down from Providence for the day. Lou had driven down earlier in the week for what he called 'the meat market.' 'He says he's in the catbird seat. Very few men are going into education these days. Wall Street, Advertising, Communications. That's where the big bucks are. Lou's getting his master's in education. The big universities have been sending their scouts around to snap up the graduates. A number of them told Lou he could teach and work on his doctorate at the same time.'

The meat market was a series of hospitality suites at the Roosevelt Hotel, where representatives of the various schools of higher education conducted interviews with preselected prospects. For Lou Humphries, the lure of a career in education offered the good life – full of perks, minimal responsibility, and the company of young people, especially girls, in a cloistered situation away from the stress of competitive business. Money was not the incentive, so long as the offer wasn't insulting. He had a modest income from an inheritance, and Amy was rich in her own right. Her parents' wedding gift had been a hefty check, to be used when they bought their first home. Her major inheritance would come due on her fortieth birthday. He had her, he had Sandi, he had a choice of easy jobs up for grabs. Let the other guys break their balls on Wall Street or Madison Avenue. He had it made.

'Oh, Amy! She's gorgeous!' The miniature Amy snuggled against her, the tiny arms around her neck. 'But how can you guarantee I'll have a girl? That's what I want, a little girl!'

Saying it, Mona knew it was true.

'If it's a boy, you can give him to me!'

'Oh no, you don't. "Nine seconds of plea-sure" . . .'

' "Nine months of pain"!'

Together they chorused, ' "Nine days in the hospi-tal, and out comes Mary Jane"!'

'*Two* days in the hospital!' Amy laughed. She clutched her daughter to her. 'And out came my little Sandi. My beautiful Sandi!'

'Okay, okay. You sold me.'

Amy's relief was evident. Now the real reason for her visit to New York became clear. Mona's talk about abortion had horrified her. 'I brought you a big bunch of baby clothes.'

'Ah, Amy . . . ?'

Her visitor had just dumped the contents of a large canvas bag on Mona's bed, a pastel antipasto of yellow, blue, pink, and white morsels of infant wear, miniature rompers, sleep suits, bibs, booties, caps, rattles, coverlets, and a menagerie of squishy whales, lambs, kittens, pups, and teddy bears. 'Don't worry about the teddy bear. Sandi's got her own teddy bear. One is enough.'

'But Amy . . .!'

'But Amy what?'

'I can afford to buy my own baby clothes!' No hand-me-downs for her kid.

Amy's New England frugality stood firm. ' "Use it up. Wear it out. Make it do. Or do without!" '

'It's so sweet of you! But . . . why not give it to some worthy charity?'

Amy was highly offended. 'Sandi's baby clothes on strangers? Are you kidding? Baby clothes are precious. You don't give them to strangers. You pass them down through family and friends.'

Mona picked up a pink terrycloth sleep suit embroidered with tiny rosebuds. 'What if it's a boy? A boy can't wear this!'

'How will he know?'

'Oh, Amy! Can't you see? I want to go wild! I want to buy out the baby department at Saks!'

'If the Queen of England's grandchildren can wear hand-me-downs, so can you. And I have a cradle and a car cart all ready to bring down.'

The mention of England brought them up short. Their summer in Chelsea was the glue of their friendship. By silent agreement, Nick Albert was never mentioned. If ever they reminisced it was about the house in Chelsea Mews, the discomfort of their bedrooms, the weirdness of the English food, and the fun the three young women had had.

'Have you told Georgina about the baby?'

'Not yet.' She hadn't even told her mother. She kept telling herself there was time, still time to make a decision.

A week later, when she was describing the situation to Nick Albert, she said, 'That's when I decided to have the baby. Sandi was sitting in the middle of the bed draping the baby clothes on her head. "That's what I want," I thought. A baby. A baby to make me whole.'

As for the nose job decision, it was one only she could make. Nick Albert thought the whole idea obscene. She was a glorious, sensual Mediterranean woman. Didn't these idiots know that Cleopatra had had a bump on her nose, Nefertiti a long pointed one? No sense talking to him. Or Amy, for that matter. As much as Amy loved her, there was no way Amy, with her itsy-bitsy schnozz, could imagine the humiliation Mona felt when Bill Neal put her up for a Faye Dunaway part or an Ali McGraw part or a Sally Field or Natalie Wood part and the casting people were respectful of her credits and cloyingly polite in their abject sorrow that she was 'not quite right.'

It wasn't for lack of training, either. Since returning from England she had maintained a strict regimen of classes in voice, body movement, fencing, ballet, and jazz. She had slimmed down to a voluptuous size eight and undergone painful electrolysis to improve her hairline. She had tried every trick in the makeup artist's repertoire, including the dark shading on the sides of the nose, the lighter stripe down the center. It worked to a degree, in photographs. With the right compensatory lighting, and a good retoucher.

On camera, the shading looked obvious and pathetic.

Decisions, decisions . . .

How boring can you get! She was ignoring her guest. Amy was six months younger than she. Amy still looked like the baby of the house in Chelsea, and yet here she was, the first of them to marry and have a child. 'Enough about me and my problems. Tell me, Amy, what's with you? Do you regret giving up your career?'

Amy wrapped her arms around Sandi and rested her head atop the child's. 'Not with this little rascal running me ragged! I keep up on things, though. I have subscriptions to *Architectural Digest* and *Historic Preservation*. I'll get back to it one of these days.' She laughed. 'When Sandi's in college.'

'And Lou? He's still behaving himself. I hope?'

Amy ran loving fingers through the strands of her daughter's silky hair. 'We're fine, Mona, honest. An old married couple. When he decides which job he wants to take we can move into our own house, just the three of us. Everything will be fine.'

The two friends gazed into each other's eyes with sweet and compassionate affection. It struck Mona that the tender, unfulfilled yearning that now smiled at her so reassuringly was exactly the needful expression she saw in her own eyes when they were caught unaware in the mirror.

'Hang in there, kiddo,' she said, when it was time for Amy and Sandi to leave.

'You too.' Amy hugged her friend. Good manners compelled her to add, 'I wish you every happiness.'

Decisions, decisions . . . They never ended. Solve one problem, and another popped up to take its place.

Her musing was interrupted by the telephone. Bill Neal, calling about a commercial for African safaris. 'How'd you like to be a mother giraffe, with her baby giraffes inviting American mothers to bring their kids to the Serengeti?'

With a Yiddish accent? Mother to mother? *Oy vey!* But Bill Neal did not appreciate her yenta moods. 'I thought giraffes had no vocal chords.'

'That will make it that much easier for you, dear, now won't it?'

She knew all too well what 'it' was. If she hated playing giraffes and melting ice cream so much, she had no choice but to have the nose job.

'What kind of accent do they want? French? Italian? Russian?

Sounds like a choice of salad dressing, right?'

'They know your range of accents. They haven't decided yet.'

'I think Russian. I'll play her as a Russian spy disguised as a giraffe. You likee?'

His voice softened. 'I likee you, Mona, and I would likee to get you the roles you want and deserve. But until you get your nose fixed, I'll get you giraffes and you can take the money and run! I love you, darling. Think about it.'

Playing a giraffe. Was this *it*? A Clio award for the best performance as a giraffe? She looked around her at her duplex apartment, and down at her barely swollen belly. 'Ars gratia artis' was all well and good. But for the time being she would laugh discreetly all the way to the bank, clutter her mantelpiece with Clios and continue to work at her craft as an actress.

12

Amy

Providence, Rhode Island, 1974

It was her fourth wedding anniversary. Lou remembered, because Amy's mother had reminded him. Early this morning, he had left the 'Happy Anniversary, Darling' card she had bought for him in Amy's sleeping hand before leaving for his tennis game.

Soon, too soon for Eleanor Dean, her daughter would be leaving the little guest house behind the garage, where the newlyweds had lived and where baby Mellisande had been born. Lou had been recruited by the Education Department at Fordham University in New York City. In a few weeks the little family would be leaving the comfort and security of the peaceful Providence neighborhood for the squalor and crime of Manhattan.

'What about the house your father and I are buying you?'

Amy explained that the academic life was like the military – you moved around. Lou guessed they'd be in New York for two or three years, then move on to another university. 'Then we can buy our own house.'

'But New York! The rats! The roaches! The street crime!'

'Don't worry, Mother. Mona's there. I've been to her place. No rats. No roaches. A view like a helicopter overlooking Central Park. Sandi will love it. Swings. Sandboxes. A children's zoo. Sea lions. The Museum of Natural History right there.'

'Well . . . as long as it's what *Lou* wants to do.'

Yes, Mother. It is what Lou wants to do. For the four years of their marriage, everything they had done was what Lou wanted to do. Her mother's words of wisdom to her on her wedding night had been plain and succinct: 'Remember, to make your marriage work, your husband comes first.' It might not be the fashion, but Amy had taken her mother's teachings to heart. Unlike a lot of the girls she knew who hated their mothers, she genuinely admired hers. It was a family tradition at holiday get-togethers for Eleanor to recall how, even as a toddler sitting on telephone books at the dinner table, little Amy had always said that when she grew up she wanted to be a mommy.

There had never been a cross word between them. Amy had always obeyed and behaved. Such a good little girl! In a recent nostalgia trip through the family album, Amy had noticed that she always seemed to be looking to her mother for approval, and getting it. Until recently.

The first real instance had come on a quiet weekday morning. Lou had no classes until the afternoon. He lay stretched out on the couch reading the sports section, with a bag of potato chips on the floor beside him. Eleanor had dropped in for coffee.

Amy plunked a squirming Sandi onto her father's stomach. 'Give Daddy a kiss. Ask him to take care of you while I run to the library.'

Lou rose up like an angry hippopotamus. 'Can't you see I'm reading?'

'I'll only be gone a few minutes, a half-hour at most. I'm going to the library.'

'Not that article again?'

They had met the editor of the *Rhode Island History Review* at a university party. When he had asked Amy about her interests and she'd mentioned architecture and history, he'd said he was looking for someone to write a piece about The Breakers, the Vanderbilt mansion in Newport.

'Not that article *again,* Lou. This is the first chance I've had to do anything about it. I thought as long as you're home you can keep an eye on Sandi.'

'That's your job. Isn't that so, Eleanor?'

Amy's mother took his side against her. 'Lou's right, darling. If I didn't have a beauty parlor appointment, I'd babysit for you. The library will be there. You can go some other time.'

Lou pushed aside the newspaper with the martyred sigh of saintly forbearance that had become habitual in Eleanor's presence. 'I think I'll take my shower.' Pausing to pick up the potato chip bag, he escaped the room.

Turning to her mother for an exchange of wifely commiseration, she was stunned to find her mother's face contorted in disapproval. 'Do you want to lose your husband?'

Nice Girls

Amy stood dumbfounded.

'How do you think I've kept your father all these years?'

Amy had never considered her parents as anything other than a happily married, compatible couple.

'Which brings me to something I've been meaning to talk to you about.'

'Yes, Mother.'

'That summer in London? Remember?'

'Of course I remember. What about it?'

Had Nick Albert called her mother about the false pregnancy? Or Sir William – had *he* written her mother the real reason why she had left before the seminar ended?

'Just this, young lady. Your husband tells me he begged you not to go to London for the summer. He pleaded with you to spend the summer with him. His fiancée. The man you were engaged to marry!'

'We weren't engaged then.'

'But you were going to be! You *knew* you were going to be! You could have lost him then, and the way you've been acting you could lose him now.'

By leaving Sandi with him and going to the library? Still, the idea of losing him did frighten her. Being settled was the important thing. Mona's talk about divorcing Brent had frightened her. Fighting with her mother frightened her most of all, because it marked the end of the mother-daughter relationship she had always known. From now on it was clear Eleanor would see her only in the roles she had purposely chosen for herself. As the women's liberation movement accelerated, she was clinging to values and responsibilities she felt absolutely certain were the best.

And the safest. One day two years ago Nick Albert had called the Providence number she had sent him, along with the Providence address, in reply to a note he had sent from Monte Carlo expressing regrets and wishing her well.

'Sorry Roxanne and I couldn't make your wedding.' Amy had sent him an invitation, just to let him know she was getting married. 'Was it bliss?'

Roxanne was staying with friends on the Cape. He was motoring up through New England to join her, and would adore stopping off at Providence to have a cup of tea with Amy.

'I see you've brought your bodyguard!' Nick looked more dazzling than ever, particularly in contrast to the others at tables around them. 'Are you still worried I'll seduce you?'

'This is Mellisande Humphries – known as Sandi.'

'Same father?'

'Yes, as a matter of fact.'

'Didn't need the aspirin this time?'

'Was it really aspirin?'

He regarded her with seriousness. 'You've grown up, baby bird.'

'Was it?'

He took his time lighting the small cigar in the familiar tortoiseshell holder. 'Does it matter?'

She had taken Sandi with her that day.

She would take her along to the library this day. She had started to teach Sandi to read. It was time to introduce her to the pleasures of the children's reading room.

When Lou returned home at the end of the day he asked her how she had made out.

'Where?'

'You damn well know where! The library. You took Sandi with you. Did she scream the place down?'

'She read *Babar*.'

'So, how'd you make out with the Vanderbilts?'

'Fine.'

'Get what you wanted about The Breakers?'

'More or less.'

'Well . . . too bad we won't have time to drive over to Newport before we move to New York.'

'It's okay. We don't have to.'

'But what about your article?'

'I've been to The Breakers lots of times as a child and in high school. I really just needed to read up on the architectural details.'

Lou Humphries knew he'd been wrong, that he should have been gracious about minding Sandi while Amy went to the library. But he couldn't bring himself to admit it, much less discuss it. Evidently it was still on his mind a few months after they had moved into their apartment on Riverside Drive, overlooking the Hudson River.

Amy had been invited to a baby shower for Mona. She was dressed and ready to go, the white-ribboned blue gift box from Tiffany's in its matching carrier bag, when the phone rang. 'Manuela sick, Señora Humphries.' It was the mother of Sandi's babysitter. Her daughter would not be able to come this afternoon. She was sorry.

'Not as sorry as I am!' Amy hissed, stifling the impulse to slam down the receiver or rip the entire phone off the wall.

'Problem?' Lou called from the den, where he was playing with his stereo components. Getting no reply, he found her in their bedroom slumped on the bed.

'What is it, your mother?'

'Manuela – she's sick.' Amy kicked off her shoes.

'You mean she's not taking Sandi this afternoon?'

The way he said it made it sound like an accusation, like it was something Amy had done.

'It's okay. I won't go to the shower. Mona will understand. I'll take Sandi to the park. Go back to what you were doing.'

Before she knew it her husband was sprawled on the floor before her, putting her shoes back on her feet like some demented Prince Charming. 'What *I* am doing is taking my little girl to the park, and what *you* are doing is going to Mona's and getting smashed on champagne.'

'Oh, darling!' She was as excited as a teenager going to her first prom. 'Thank you, darling! Sandi'll be thrilled to pieces! Going out with her big handsome Daddy!'

'Shut up and get going. Or I may change my mind.'

'Oh, Lou!' She felt herself blush. Maybe things really *were* getting better now that they had their own place.

He walked her to the elevator. 'Promise me one thing?'

'What?'

'When you girls start to dish, promise you'll tell them what a great lover I am!'

The blush flared again. Her face hot, she fought to maintain her cool. 'I promise. They'll never believe me, but I promise. But *you* have to promise *me* something.'

'Okay. That I'll hump you till your eyeballs fall out?'

He knew that kind of talk upset her. 'I'm serious. I want you to promise to hang on to Sandi for dear life. She moves with the speed of light. Take your eye off her for one second, and she's gone!'

'Don't worry about a thing. Have a good time. My best to Mona.'

Amy's job at the shower was to keep a log of all the gifts, listing each one alongside the name of the giver. Her gift of a traditional sterling silver cup and baby spoon was applauded along with the rest. But she soon saw that it was the zany presents – the rubber mat made of breasts 'for walking the floor and breast-feeding at the same time,' the panties stenciled CLOSED FOR REPAIRS – that got the howls. She comforted herself that her gift was forever, an heirloom in the making that would stay in Mona's family and be handed down to the next generation.

She was glad she had come. It was good to be sitting on the floor in the company of women, with a buzz on and a run in her pantyhose that she hadn't had when she'd left home. The hell with it! She hooked her fingernail into the run and made it worse, which made her feel even better.

When one of Mona's actress friends called for attention, Amy leaned forward with the others. All eyes were riveted to the tape recorder held above their heads.

'I have here, for your delectation, an exclusive preview of the first time our mother-to-be indulges in sex after she has the baby!'

Amid the cheers and catcalls, Amy asked, 'How can you tape something that hasn't happened?'

Mona patted her head. 'It's okay, ladies. She ain't as lame-brained as all that. It's the champagne.' Crashing down beside her friend, Mona whispered, 'It's a gag. Just listen.'

'Let me set the scene before I turn on the tape,' the actress continued. 'It's a dark and stormy night. Mona is back in shape – in *all* ways – and back in her bedroom with a new, handsome, demanding, and *built* lover! And this is what it sounds like!'

With a lascivious flourish she turned on the tape recorder. Mona's voice issued forth in a monologue of ecstatic disbelief and gratitude. 'Oh, God! Look at this . . . I don't believe it . . . Just what I wanted, how did you know . . .? Holy shit, I can't get this damn thing open . . . Get it open! I can't wait . . . Break the knots . . . Don't fuck around, for God's sake! What a color!'

It took Amy a few minutes to catch on. The actress had taped Mona's reactions to her baby gifts. She was laughing with the others, enjoying herself to the hilt, when Lou stumbled into the room.

'It's Sandi! I lost her. At the playground!'

13

Georgina

London, 1983

Self-mockery sells. The world had enormous fun taking the mickey out of the British, but no more than the British enjoyed taking the mickey out of themselves – as witness the success of Monty Python and the *Fawlty Towers* and *Yes, Minister* series. Plummy-voiced twits played by John Cleese were regular pitchmen in American telly commercials. American tourists often made a point of telling Georgina how much they loved the British sense of humor, stiff-upper-lip and all that.

Nearly fifteen years had gone by in what seemed like the twinkling of an eye. In line with the new tax laws, her accountants were advising her to set up separate companies for each of her new endeavors, all under the umbrella of British Junque Ltd. Her earlier idea of manufacturing blatantly fake reproductions of the Crown Jewels under the label Clown Jools had skyrocketed beyond all expectation. Its success encouraged her to diversify into equally farcical send-ups. Waterfraud Crystal in breakproof plastic, and a *Horrids* shopping bag identical to the green Harrods original, were selling like the proverbial hotcakes.

She retained her original stall in the Portobello Road as a talisman, and because visitors from abroad came clutching old travel books that listed it. Impressed by Richard Branson and his Virgin record shops, she opened Worst of British Junque shops in three London locations and in Manchester, Liverpool, Edinburgh, and Bath. Next on her agenda were the airports – Gatwick for starters, in plenty of time for 1992 and the influx of European as well as other international travelers.

Amy Humphries was due in later in the day on the first leg of a five-country escorted tour. Lou was using his sabbatical to take

Amy and Sandi abroad before they moved to Washington. Amy loved living in New York. She and Mona had become close friends. From her letters, Georgina could sense Amy's reluctance to pull up stakes and move to a place where she knew no one and would have to start all over again.

Selfish lout! Georgina had met Lou Humphries only once and that was five years ago, shortly after that ghastly experience with Sandi and the playground. Amy was such a loyal little thing. The sole hint of her unhappiness at leaving New York was a wistful little remark about missing Mona and the fun she and Sandi had with Mona's two kids.

Georgina had offered to put them up in Chelsea Mews. 'You wouldn't recognize the place.' Although she long could have afforded something larger and smarter elsewhere, she had been unable to cut the one tangible link with her roots. At first she had bought the equally rundown houses on either side of her own, and converted the three into a comfortable single unit with all the modern conveniences. More recently, as other property had become available, she'd enlarged her living quarters on one side of the mews and converted most of the opposite side into state-of-the-art offices, computerized with telephone link-ups to her warehouse in Welwyn Garden City. To encourage what the Americans called 'the work ethic,' she had installed a health club with sauna, shower bath, and exercise horse to keep them all fit, herself included. As a result, her employee turnover was virtually nil.

Her private renovations included two separate guest suites, self-contained with every comfort. Amy, poor darling, accepted the invitation and then had to ring back. Lou had made other arrangements and preferred to stick to them. She hadn't the heart to tell Amy their hotel was in some ghastly side street near Paddington Station.

She'd find out soon enough, poor baby. Instead of sending the Rolls to collect them at the airport, Georgina decided to go along personally. Amy sounded as if she needed a friend, and this was her first visit to London since *that* summer. Georgina was proud of her accomplishments. In press interviews and in her acceptance speech at the recent Women in Commerce awards, she always credited the suggestions and encouragement of her two American friends. She thought Amy would enjoy the vintage Sedanca-de-Ville Rolls, with its cabriolet chauffeur's seat and the flower vases on each side of the passenger seat.

Truth to tell, Georgina felt very protective of Amy. Truth to tell, she wanted to impress that grotty husband of hers. Amy might not remember but Georgina did remember Amy's letter from Boston a few weeks after her return to America. In translation, this Lou person was making Amy eat shit. He was punishing her for having had the temerity to spend the summer in England when his lordship had wanted her with him. Even more distressing was Amy's ultimate announcement that Lou had forgiven her and they were getting engaged.

From then on, according to Amy, everything had been absolute bliss. Not according to Mona. The whole sorry business of Sandi's disappearing in the park was more than Mona could stand. Calling London to thank Georgina for the baby gift, she had exploded in fury over Lou's irresponsibility. 'The kid could have been butchered! Or raped! Or forced into some porn film! And the bastard managed to shift the blame to *Amy!* Can you imagine?'

Georgina's plan was simple. She would collect them from the airport, drop them at their dreary hotel, and charm the socks off Herr Doktor Professor Humphries into letting Amy have one afternoon alone with Georgina for old times' sake.

In the meantime she would take care of the extraordinary order that had arrived in the morning post from Texas. It was from a woman she dimly recalled meeting at the King's Road shop. Georgina's instinct said Texas Millionaire. Sure enough, she ordered enough goods to stock a good-sized shop.

Was she in retailing?

'Sell these things to strangers? Not on your ding dong!' They were to be party favors when friends came by for barbecue. Texas hospitality.

As an afterthought she had also purchased a restored red telephone box that Georgina had bought from a building site, where it lay on its side covered with dirt. As the venerable object stood tagged for shipment to the States, at least a half-dozen other American tourists demanded to have one just like it. 'Perfect for the pool area or the patio!'

Some inspired detective work led to a small factory that actually manufactured new red telephone boxes in reasonable quantity. Again obeying her instincts, she ordered fifty of them, cash on the barrelhead to enjoy the best discount, crated for shipment, just in case. The gamble paid off, bigger and better than she could ever have anticipated.

The woman in Dallas had written to say everyone thought her telephone booth was as cute as a bug's ear. She wanted Georgina to wrassle up a dozen or three more so she could give them to folks for Christmas. To expedite matters, she enclosed a signed blank cheque from the London branch of a Texas bank. 'Just fill in the amount, darlin'. I trust you. You come see us now, y'hear?'

If this was what happened when Texas came to the British Junque Shop, she wondered what might happen if British Junque went to Texas. From what she could see, Texans left hundred-dollar-bills as tips. When she expanded her operation to America she might just skip over New York and go straight to Dallas. There was a bloody fortune waiting for her. All she had to do was put on her Lady Georgina la-de-da and Texas was hers for the taking.

'Are you sure you didn't poison him, Georgina?' Amy tried to look concerned about the sudden attack of gastritis that kept Lou moaning and retching in their hotel room. In his misery he was relieved to be left alone, and grateful that Amy had somewhere to take Sandi. At the sight of the yellow door with its clam-shell knocker, Amy felt a wild sense of release. Lou treated her like a lame-brain, like she was incapable of getting around London without him. Darn it, didn't he realize she had lived in London for an entire summer? This was his first trip, and what did he do? He threw up. She did her best to keep a straight face.

'Sandi . . . this is where your Mummy and Aunt Mona lived before you were born! Hurry up the stairs, love. There's a lovely surprise waiting for you.'

'Oh, Georgina, you shouldn't have!'

'Of course I should have. You're one of my oldest and dearest friends.' From what Georgina could see Amy looked the same, tall and angular with the same natural grace, her blonde hair the same short bouncy style, her skin flawless as ever. Yet there was something terribly wrong. While Sandi opened her prezzies Georgina poured the coffee, nattering on and on about all she had gone through in the monumental task of redoing the house even as she tried to work out what was amiss.

That Amy looked the same was what was wrong. Here was this thirty-two-year-old woman, a wife and a mother, looking like an old

Nice Girls

photograph that had been left out in the sun. She looked faded. On closer inspection, there was gray in the blonde. The slender frame seemed somehow hollow. What had been a dignified New England reserve now seemed apologetic, a little too anxious to please.

'Well, Amy love, tell me all about married life. Mona's divorced. I've been too busy. You're the only one of us to be happily married. Tell me what it's like to be a faculty wife.'

At first Amy told her how happy she was. How lucky she was to have a husband like Lou, how bright his future looked, how proud she was of his success. How thrilled she was to be moving to Washington.

'Oh, but I thought you were so mad about New York?'

'I am. That is, I love New York. But Washington is going to be a real challenge.'

'Mona's going to miss you.'

'Mona . . .?' Amy seemed surprised.

'Mona! I rang her the other day to say hello. She said she was heartbroken that you were leaving. It was like losing a sister, she said.'

'She said that?' Amy's bewilderment dissolved into tears.

'What's wrong? What did I say?'

The unhappiness poured out of her like a river of pain. Lou had said that Mona wasn't a good friend, that Mona was only using her and was a bad influence now that she was divorced and screwing everything in pants. 'He said he was only telling me these things for my own good. He said he hated to see me flimflammed like that, and that one of the main reasons he took the new job was to get us away from New York. It's no place for families. There's too much sex and violence. No place to raise Sandi.'

The penny dropped. 'Are you sure he's not still embarrassed in front of Mona?'

'Embarrassed?'

Georgina wanted to shake her. 'Yes, embarrassed, dammit! About the Sandi thing! You know full well what I'm talking about! Mona told me everything!'

'It was all my fault!'

Georgina could not believe her ears. 'You mean to tell me Lou took your child to the playground, and let her out of his sight, and that was all *your* fault? Explain that to me before I go mad!'

Amy sat slumped, her chin on her chest, her voice barely audible.

'I should have sewn name tapes in her clothes. If I had been a good mother I'd have done that, and they'd have known who she was and we wouldn't have had to spend half the night looking for her.'

Brainwashed. Georgina had read about the brainwashing of prisoners. The bastard had brainwashed her into thinking she was an incompetent ninny! Mona had told her how Lou had thundered in on the baby shower, frantic with fear, not having a clue what to do. He hadn't even had the sense to ring the police, which Mona did at once. She and Amy returned with him to the playground, where a few children were still playing. They were older children. The younger ones had long since gone home. Amy showed them the photograph of Sandi she carried in her wallet. Nobody had seen her.

The police fanned out through the trees and bushes, probing the underbrush with flashlights and shouting the child's name. A police car equipped with a loudspeaker rolled slowly up and down the adjacent streets, asking if anyone had seen a three-year-old girl named Sandi.

Lou was no help at all, Mona said. All he did was get in the way, telling the police what to do and threatening to kill whoever laid a hand on his little girl. When darkness fell, a searchlight crew set up their equipment. The officer in charge told them to go back to their apartment. He would let them know the minute he had any news. What he really wanted was to get Lou out of his hair.

And of course just as they reached the entrance to their apartment house, there was little Sandi running toward them from the opposite direction, a young woman close behind her. The young woman was a games mistress at a private kindergarten. She had taken her tiny charges to the playground and when it was time to return, she hadn't noticed the extra little girl who was tagging along. In fact it wasn't until all the other children had been collected by their parents that they realized Sandi was not one of theirs.

Sandi knew her name, but she couldn't pronounce 'Humphries.' When cajolery proved fruitless, the games mistress asked her where she lived. While she couldn't give the address, she tucked her hand into the woman's and was skipping down the street toward her house when she spotted her parents and ran toward them.

Georgina took her friend's hand. 'You've always made excuses for Lou. Can't you understand what really happened? Mona said Lou blamed her. He said it was her fault. That if she hadn't invited you to her baby shower, you wouldn't have shirked your responsibility as a mother!'

Amy defended her husband. 'He was upset! He didn't know what he was saying!'

'Maybe not then, Amy. But later he did. Later he tried to blame Mona and you for his own stupidity.'

Amy drew herself up. 'I can't let you talk that way about my husband! I'm a happy woman! I have everything I want! A husband! A child! A home!'

'Fair enough. Let's not spoil things. We'll change the subject. Thanks for sending me the article you wrote. It was excellent.' She refrained from asking what Lou had thought. *If* he thought. Amy had written a charming piece about the architectural history of Riverside Drive from the early days of Manhattan's northward development along the Hudson River to the present – its mansions, churches, and grand apartment houses.

'Thank you.'

Stalemate. For once in her life, Georgina could not think of another thing to say. When Nick Albert had rung from Paris earlier in the day, she had told him about Amy's visit. 'The baby bird? Give her my love.'

Amy Humphries would not approve of her being on speaking terms with Nick Albert, much less having an affair. It was best that not a hint of their relationship be allowed to seep out. They had been careful, extremely careful. So far as she knew, nobody had a clue.

What had begun as an all-too-short day of happy reminiscence had come to a dull standstill. If Amy had been anyone else, Georgina would have blithely manufactured a sudden crisis and made a graceful exit. But this was Amy. She could not abandon her in her misery.

'I have another surprise!' she announced brightly. 'I'm taking us all to Vidal Sassoon's for a makeover. And that includes my precious Mellisande!'

Ignoring Amy's protests, she buzzed her secretary to send the car around. Then, adroitly excusing herself to collect her things, she rang the salon from her bedroom to make the arrangements. The new Lemon Blond would be perfect for Amy. The more she thought about it, the more determined she was to give Amy a new lease on life.

Her good deed done, she could go off to Paris for a few days with Nick with a clear conscience. So far as her staff was concerned, she would be making one of her frequent raids on the Marché Aux Puces. On her last visit, she had found a packing case of pristine Noël Coward seventy-eight RPM discs in their original paper sleeves. Rather than sell them to vintage gramophone collectors, she had had each disc set in a double frame opposite a gorgeous photograph of Coward at his most elegantly decadent.

Nick? Paris? All in the line of business!

14

Mona

New York, 1986

A brutal attack by John Simon, the Butcher of Broadway, convinced Mona that she had no choice. If she wanted to play starring roles, she would have to undergo plastic surgery. She must resist her mother's insistence that she was beautiful just as she was, and her own superstitious fear that God would get even with her for having tampered with nature. The surgeon would sneeze, the knife would slip, and her next role would be the Hunchback of Notre Dame.

After fifteen years in New York, Bill Neal had turned producer, his first production being an off-Broadway revival of Noël Coward's *Private Lives*. Despite his misgivings about having an American actress play the brittle, outrageous Amanda, Mona's uncannily superb rendering of an upper-class Mayfair accent convinced him to cast her in the role.

'Enchanting! Gertie Lawrence could not have done better!' he told her most sincerely after the final dress rehearsal. She moved well, like a sensuous panther on the prowl. Her figure was glorious, lean yet voluptuous in 1920s costumes inspired by *The Great Gatsby*. What's more, her voice and comedic sense had preview audiences roaring their approval in a standing ovation.

But not John Simon. As bad luck would have it, the regular off-Broadway critic had eaten a polluted oyster. A Noël Coward aficionado, Simon had agreed to fill in for his indisposed colleague.

The following day, theatergoers were told the play had stood the test of time. The sets, direction, and ensemble performances were superb. Mona Davidson's accent and overall performance were equally superb, except for one fatal flaw. 'There is something horrible about a plain woman carrying on as if she were a raving beauty; it is so utterly unconvincing, presumptuous, and dishonest, that, in a sensitive spectator, it produces not only aesthetic revulsion but also moral indignation.'

'Vermin!' Bill Neal cried, trying to console her. 'Everyone knows he's an assassin!'

Mona recalled how another outraged actress had tracked John Simon down to a restaurant and dumped a bowl of spaghetti over his head. Mona would have preferred thrusting Grandma Davitsky's stiletto hat pin through his heart. Instead, she called the plastic surgeon and arranged for her nose job.

Having made the commitment, she kicked herself for having waited so long. She was thirty-five years old, long in the tooth for ingenue roles. She hated California, it's cold and it's damp, and Hollywood was out of the question anyway. She was a New York actress, one of the tight-knit group who did guest shots on the soaps, did commercials, and tried to do quality productions on Broadway and off, in workshops, and for public service television.

The sympathy generated by the Simon attack was gratifying. Letters and calls poured in. Brent called from his new offices in Philadelphia. The kids had called him.

'You want me to hire a hit man. Mona?'

'No, Brent. I want you to send me the child-support money you've owed me for the last two years.'

'Oh, that. Here I am calling to commiserate and you have to bring that up!'

'That' being about all she could take, she turned him over to the children. 'Tell him you're barefoot and starving.'

The plastic surgeon turned out to be booked ahead for the next eight months. He was rumored to do ten procedures a day. All those double chins, all those lumps and bumps and sagging flesh.

So began the grueling task of going to see various personally recommended surgeons, auditioning them as to their credentials and general attitude. It occurred to her that her life was an endless series of auditions. Friends, husbands, lovers, housekeepers, lawyers, hairdressers, always looking for the right person. In all categories of life, she looked for good value and honorable interchange. With few exceptions – her mother, Georgina, Amy, and of course her two children – the only consistently reliable person in her life was Bill Neal, and she knew she was damned lucky to have him.

As the date for the rhinoplasty procedure drew nearer, Mona affected a gallows gaiety. 'Bill, why don't you ask John Simon to pick

Nice Girls

me up in his limo? Then we can say he drove me to plastic surgery!'

It was nothing, everyone assured her. Like having your teeth cleaned. Nothing. She thought of Mary Queen of Scots preparing for her execution. Having your head chopped off was a rather extreme form of plastic surgery, right? Cutting off more than your nose to spite your face. A total change in appearance. Shorter, of course, without a head.

The night before she was due to check in at the private hospital, she sent the children to stay over with friends in the building. 'I vant to be alone!' she said in her best Garbo groan. She would wash her hair, moisturize her face, and quietly compose herself for the ordeal that lay ahead.

Only Bill Neal was allowed to come by. 'Break a leg, darlin'! I'll be right there when you wake up. What do you want me to bring you? Chicken soup? Chocolate ice cream?'

' "These are a few of my favorite *theengs*!" ' she trilled, mimicking Julie Andrews in *The Sound of Music*.

'Be serious. What do you want me to bring you?'

Tears filled her eyes. 'A real part in a real play. That's the only thing I want, Bill.'

After he'd gone, she stretched out on the double king-size bed. Her most recent lover had compared it to the flight deck of an aircraft carrier. She had lied to Bill and to herself. There was one other thing she wanted – Nick Albert. If only he were here with her, holding her close, getting her to laugh, and making her shriek with pleasure.

From her lips to God's ears – the phone rang. It was Nick, saying he and Roxanne had just flown in and were at her family's apartment at the Plaza. Roxanne had just gone to the health club for a massage and a workout.

'Thank God I found you in, Mona! Must see you, sweetie! Jump into your knickers, and meet me for an hour at the Sherry.'

The man certainly enjoyed living dangerously. The Plaza Hotel was just across the way from the Sherry Netherland. What if The Frog and some chums from the health club decided to have a drink at the Sherry, too?

She was in for the evening, didn't feel like getting dressed, didn't tell him why. 'But tell you what. How's about you jumping in a cab and coming to me?'

'Five minutes too soon?'

She remembered his visit with mixed emotions during the painful weeks that followed. It was as if the blissful hour in his arms, and the deep, refreshing sleep that followed, had been preordained to give her the strength and will to survive her ordeal.

As the anesthesia wore off, the smiling nurse asked, 'How do you feel?'

'Like I've been hit by a truck.' The tight bandage across her face obscured her vision. Everything from her chest up to the top of her head felt battered and bruised. It was not the least bit like going to the dentist. It was like childbirth. Nobody ever told you the truth. You had to experience it firsthand.

The nurse continued to smile knowingly. Of course she was uncomfortable. That would pass. For now, she could have liquids and watch television. Tomorrow, the bandages would come off. 'But remember, you'll still be swollen for a while, and you'll probably have black eyes for another day or two.'

During the night, she woke up screaming with pain and delirious with fever. In an evident panic, the night nurse telephoned the doctor. When he arrived in his pajamas and overcoat, he was not smiling. Within minutes she was in an ambulance rushing her to Mt. Sinai Hospital and the Intensive Care Unit.

For a week it was touch-and-go, a contest predicated on who was stronger, Mona Davidson or the massive infection that was running rampant through her bloodstream, attacking her vital organs with deadly intent. Emerging from the dark at last, the first thing she heard was the disembodied voice of Bill Neal.

'Never you fear, love. We're going to sue that bloody quack for ten million dollars.'

She slowly became aware of something on her face. A bandage? A mask to cover her hideousness? She didn't want ten million dollars. She wanted to be pretty. It wasn't fair, all those women born with perfect noses who never gave it a second thought. Georgina and Amy, to name two. And the girls she saw every day who she wanted to kick in the slats because they didn't know what they had. The waitresses and receptionists and counter girls at McDonald's. Doing stupid, menial jobs. Didn't they ever look in the mirror? Didn't they know what they had?

The fog began to dissipate, as if it were morning in San Francisco. Flowers, fruit baskets, get-well cards and a giant HUG bear with outstretched arms came into focus. At least she could see and hear.

So much for playing Helen Keller. Blobs at the end of the bed materialized as Bill Neal and her mother. He had spoken; her mother had not.

Grim-faced, cross-armed, the person who had given her life and had always said she wanted more than anything on God's earth for Mona to be a Broadway star glared at her with matriarchal fury. When Mona saw something she wanted to file in her memory bank for future use she memorized it, and so she gazed long and hard at her mother's expression – a combination of grief, fear, worry, pain, anger, and naked reproach.

Mona had lied to her mother. She hadn't told her about the nose job. She had said she was going away to a health farm in Montauk for a few days' rest. She had so looked forward to showing her mother her brand-new nose.

Her mother didn't have to say a single word. Mona knew what she was thinking. God was punishing Mona for trying to be something she wasn't, for trying to look like something she wasn't.

'Hey, Mom. It's me. Don't you recognize me?' Tears poured down the older woman's face. As she rushed to her daughter's side and covered her hands with kisses, it struck Mona that her mother's delicate, small-boned, heart-shaped face was blessed with a short, straight, perky nose that even had the audacity to crinkle when she laughed. Yet another one who couldn't know what it was like for Mona even if she wanted to know, which she didn't.

'Mom? What do you think? Will I ever be able to go out in public without a bag over my head?'

There was some pleasure in feeling her mother's body convulse in spasms of sobs until she realized that nobody, not Bill Neal, not her mother, had answered her question.

15

Amy

Europe, 1983

For the first time in her life, Amy felt really and truly blonde. Ordinarily, the women in the Dean family did not dye their hair. In summer they used lemon juice or vinegar as a final rinse, ostensibly to remove all traces of shampoo, and then sat in the yard with wet heads until the hot sun had done its work. While Amy was still in high school there was a vogue for using beer or mayonnaise as a conditioner for flyaway hair, and this also conferred a golden luster to drab, dirty blonde.

'Smashing!' Georgina said, when Amy and Sandi met her for tea at Brown's. 'You, too, Sandi pet!' At thirteen, the girl was Lolita incarnate. The young stylist assigned to shape her wayward snarl of curls into something sleek and bouncy had clearly been unnerved by Sandi's aura of emerging sexuality. He had dropped his comb and scissors several times before retiring in confusion. Mr. Erik, Georgina's man, had finished the job, once he was satisfied with what he had wrought for Amy.

'How old is she now, Amy? I can't keep track.'

'Thirteen going on thirty,' Amy said, with the mingled pride and fear of the mother who is just starting to realize how helpless she is.

'Wait till Lou sees you, Amy. He'll be mad about it.'

The deed was done. Two men had murmured at her when she and Sandi had entered Brown's. People at nearby tables craned their necks ever so casually to have a better look.

Georgina was amused. 'They think you're Princess Diana.'

'Oh, Georgina, please!'

'Yes, Mom, you *do* look like her, you do!' Amy's blush and lowered lashes only heightened the comparison.

'Nick Albert should see you now!'

'Nick Albert? Gosh almighty, Georgina. That's a name from the past. Whatever happened to him? Is he still married to the heiress?'
'The Frog?'
Sandi's eyes gleamed. 'He married a frog?'
'It's a naughty word for someone who's French. Not to be repeated, Sandi love. It's a terrible insult.'
Whether to be contrary or because she meant it, Sandi said, 'I want to be a frog.'
Nick Albert's name was forgotten as quickly as it had been mentioned. Soon it was time for Amy and Sandi to go back to the hotel.
'You look a bit odd, Amy. Don't tell me you're coming down with a gyppy tummy, too?'
Amy's stomach was in fact in an uproar, but not from anything she'd eaten or from jet lag. She was dreading Lou's reaction to her hair. Faculty wives were not supposed to look fashionable. Most of those she met looked like throwbacks to the 1950s, dressed in drab, shapeless blouses and wrap-around skirts, with no makeup and hair that most of them had cut themselves.
She could have spared herself the anxiety. Lou Humphries was so involved with himself that he didn't notice the change until three days later in the South of France. They were staying at the Hotel Negresco, and their first day included a visit to Vallauris and the Picasso villa, followed by lunch at the fabled Colombe D'Or at St. Paul de Vence. There, on the broad terrace overlooking the panoramic sweep of the Alpes Maritimes descending toward the sea, Lou was ordering for all three of them, without consulting anyone else, when he became aware of the change in her appearance.
'Why are you wearing your sunglasses on your head?' Sandi had copied her mother. Her sunglasses were on top of her head, too. 'Either you need sunglasses for the glare, or put them away, Amy. You mustn't be so conspicuous. It's as if you're trying to look like a movie star.'
Amy meekly removed the sunglasses. Sandi curried her father's approval by doing the same.
'Not you, sweetheart. It looks cute on a little girl.'
'I'm not a little girl.'
'To me you're a little girl, and you look cute as a button with those sunglasses on your head. Now your mother . . .' He patted

Nice Girls

Amy's hand, as if to assure her she was back in his good graces. 'Your mother looks fine just the way she is.' He turned his full attention on his wife, as if to further reassure her. 'See how blonde she looks in the sun? Isn't it wonderful how the sun brings out the color?'

'Oh, but –'

Amy could see her daughter was about to spill the beans. 'Sandi!' They had agreed not to mention the visit to Vidal Sassoon's. It was to be their little secret. A female secret shared with Aunt Georgina. Daddy wouldn't like it if he knew Aunt Georgina had treated them. He liked to okay all family expenses.

'Moth-er!'

'What's going on, you two? Let Daddy in on it, Sandi.'

Amy's only child rolled her eyes at her mother as if to say she was sorry, but she had to answer Daddy's question. As she blinked in artful innocence and opened her mouth to speak, an unmistakably English voice crashed down on them.

'Baby bird! Is it really you?'

Nick Albert tousled Amy's blonde hair as if she were a child, looking miraculously younger than the last time she had seen him more than fifteen years before. His white shorts and striped scivvy punctuated a lean body toasted brown and crusted with salt from a life in the sun and the sea. The person with him in matching shorts and top was his twin image – lean, tanned, and as firm of form as he. The sole indication that Nick's companion was a woman was her jewelry, a ruby-and-emerald ring on one hand, counterbalanced by a diamond bracelet she had made famous from having it welded closed on her wrist so that it would not come off when she dove off the deck of the yacht.

'This is my husband, Lou Humphries, and my daughter Mellisande, also known as Sandi. Darling, this is Nick Albert.'

'Delighted to meet you. This is my wife, Roxanne.'

Roxanne deflected the introduction. 'They're waiting for us.'

Maybe it was the blonde hair. Or Nick Albert's encouraging presence. But whatever the reason, the usually shy Amy Dean Humphries ignored being ignored and boldly put out her hand. 'So nice to see you again, Roxanne.'

'Again?' Such impertinence was not to be tolerated.

'In Chelsea Mews. The summer of '68. Our July Fourth picnic. Remember?'

'This is simply too boring.'

Her rude departure did not bother Nick in the least. 'Whatever are you doing here? Never mind. No time now. Come sailing with us tomorrow. Monte Carlo harbor at noon? Can't miss us. *The Roxanne*! White with black trim. Be there!'

Amy's husband sat there dumbstruck, with an artichoke leaf dripping vinaigrette suspended halfway to his mouth. At last he found his voice. 'Some nerve! Giving us orders! Who does he think he is?'

'He's cool, Mom. How did you meet him?'

'Oh, he was just one of the people Aunt Mona and I met that summer.'

'Boy . . .' Sandi closed her eyes dreamily. 'When I'm eighteen, can I go to London by myself?'

Lou glared pointedly at Amy. 'Nice girls from good families don't go to London, or anywhere else, by themselves.'

'Oh, Daddy, please!'

'It's five years from now. We'll talk about it then.'

Sandi was not to be deterred. 'We can talk about it tomorrow on the yacht.'

'What yacht? We're not going on any yacht!'

'But, Daddy! He *invited* us!'

'Just because someone invites you doesn't mean you have to accept.'

'But, Daddy, *please*!' Sandi could usually wrap her father around her little finger. To make certain this did not happen, Amy joined the pleading chorus. Even after all these years, there were still things she did not know about her husband. Of one thing she was sure, however. She could count on his controlling nature always to oppose what she wanted to do.

The thought of sailing with Nick and Roxanne and heaven knows who else filled her with dread. Who knew what Nick might say about Chelsea Mews and the pills he had given her – whether they were or were not aspirin. She had never told Lou how she had thought she'd gotten pregnant from their first sexual encounter in Cambridge before she left for London.

These days marriages fell apart for much less cause. Everyone she knew was either separating or getting a divorce. She did not intend to let that happen to her. She needed the stability of a home, husband, and family life. Soon Sandi would be going to college, and eventually she would meet a nice young man and marry him. Family and continuity were the most important things in Amy's life.

Seeing Nick Albert like this in his natural surroundings – the South of France, yachts, Roxanne and her jewelry – erased forever any lingering regrets Amy sometimes had had about rushing back to the States after the experience with Sir William rather than staying in London and maybe spending some time in Paris or Rome. She could see she would always be a tourist. She would never fit in or feel at home with people like Nick and Roxanne, or even with Georgina.

'Did you see the way that woman looked at me?' Lou said when they were driving back to the Negresco. 'She looked at me as if she was going to have me for dinner with a nice cream sauce!'

Roxanne making a pass at *Lou?* It was laughable, pure vanity, but Amy tried to keep a straight face.

'That's really why I didn't want to accept your friend's invitation, honey. It's awfully close quarters on a yacht. I didn't want her coming on to me. I hope you don't mind.'

She said she thought it would only be polite to stop by the yacht basin in Monte Carlo the next morning before they toured the Palace and visited Princess Grace's tomb. When they got back home, she wanted to have a good story to tell Mona and Georgina about the man none of them had seen since the night he'd left the three of them at the Albert Memorial.

The Roxanne was not in the Monte Carlo boat basin. When queried, the harbor master said it had sailed on the early tide.

'Well, I guess that Roxanne was afraid to be on a boat with me. Afraid of what might happen,' Lou said jovially. His ego bolstered, he embraced his wife and daughter. 'Hey, I've got the two prettiest women in the entire world!'

Lou Humphries was never one to show affection in public. The free love of the flower children and hippies had disgusted him. Blame it on the Mediterranean sun, blame it on the riot of color and the mingled scents of flowers and chicory and garlic, blame it on primal jealousy triggered by Nick Albert's blatant attention to his wife. Whatever the cause, Lou startled Amy by pulling her so close she could feel him getting hard. His face buried in her hair, his lips found their way to her ear.

'I forgot how blonde you are. My beautiful blonde wife.'

So intense was his ardor that when his mouth found hers in a voluptuous kiss, Sandi felt drawn to throw her arms around both parents while several onlookers applauded.

Amy had not thought about Nick Albert in years. The mere mention of him in conversation with Georgina always reminded her of his erotic impact on her. That afternoon, alone with Lou in their room with the shutters down, the door locked, and Sandi off at the beach in her bikini, Amy wondered whether it was yesterday's brief encounter that was making her so hot. And if that was so, how long the feeling would last.

When they got back home to Georgetown, she intended to follow a double secret agenda. She would color her hair, and think sexy thoughts about Nick as often as necessary to keep her marriage alive and well.

Among the picture postcards she sent from Portofino were two bearing an identical message to Georgina and Mona: 'Guess who I ran into on the Riviera?' Writing them made her feel like a member of the jet set, if only en passant.

16

Georgina

London, 1986

A MATCH MADE IN HEAVEN, according to the press. When the first photographs and stories began to appear in the dailies, Georgina thought, 'Are they out of their tiny minds?' Her 'No comment's, 'absolute nonsense,' and 'just friends,' only served to give credence to the rumors. She began to understand how Lady Diana Spencer must have felt when word spread that Prince Charles had popped the question and an engagement would soon be officially announced.

For Georgina, the first 'exclusive report' from 'reliable sources' that she was about to marry the new Prime Minister was too idiotic for words. Yet, being wary of the pitfalls of public relations, she played the rumor game with charm and finesse. To do otherwise, to say that Simon Longe was a third-rate wet and a pompous twit and that the idea of marriage was nauseating, would be to insult the head of government. It could even be misconstrued by imaginative reporters as an allusion to his potentially awkward sexual orientation.

The whole brouhaha had begun innocently enough at a small British trade association luncheon party. Successful young entrepreneurs such as herself had been invited to meet the new PM in an informal setting to give him some of their ideas for improving Britain's economy. It was natural that they should be photographed together. The *Financial Times* had recently named Georgina Woman of the Year, and predicted bigger things ahead as she expanded into world markets. The Princess of Wales had paid an 'unscheduled' visit to the British Junque Shoppe in the King's Road, where Georgina, alerted by the Palace, personally gave Her Highness a huge biodegradable sack of prezzies for her next AIDS benefit.

Simon Longe was nobody's fool. As yet unmarried at age forty-six, his party line was that he had up until now devoted his life to politics and making Britain great again. As Prime Minister his next priority was to prove his commitment to traditional values and the future of the country by finding himself a wife and helpmate and joining the rank and file of Britain's often neglected, hardworking married men.

It was hard to figure out what if anything was going on between them. The courtship that had begun as rumor had become fact, or at least media fact, and very exhilarating indeed. A quiet dinner at an out-of-the-way country restaurant became front-page tabloid news. Whether the restaurant or the PM's press officer had tipped the papers was anyone's guess. All fun and games, Georgina thought. Both of them were single. They photographed well together. Watching the royal family in action had taught her one invaluable lesson: Let the media think they're using you, while in reality you're using them!

Soon, 'Simon and the Junque Lady' were being asked everywhere together. Protocol was such that no one would presume to invite them as a couple without the approval if not the contrivance of the PM's engagements secretary. Banquets, dedications, concerts, and diplomatic receptions soon led the couple to the more rarefied and privileged environs of Buckingham Palace.

In point of romantic fact, they spent little time alone during the first halcyon weeks. It reminded Georgina of stories she'd read about film stars in the old days going out on 'dates' as the Americans called them, and giving interviews on how ecstatically blissful they were together. Yet she had to admit that the more time she spent with Simon Longe, the more she liked him. He had the old-fashioned virtue of good manners. He appeared to know something about business and economics. He was not, so far as she could tell, condescending toward women. He believed fervently in the parliamentary system and in trying to stimulate the now moribund spirit of excellence that had once made British goods and services the envy of the world.

What had been at first a plus was beginning to worry her. As Mona would say, he never tried to 'jump on her bones.' At first she had been relieved. There were no sparks between them, at least none coming from her. It would have been extremely awkward if he had tried to seduce her. On several occasions when he ran her back

Nice Girls

to Chelsea Mews in his vintage XKE-120 Jag, his own security people and the press were, as usual, in attendance. She had assumed he would bid her a formal good night and return alone later in a taxi or on foot.

That's what she would have done if she had been in his boots, but then women were always more resourceful than men. But ego aside, the situation was fine just as it was. As she had said to one features writer demanding to know if she was secretly engaged, she was married to her job. Success was the ultimate gratification.

'Better than sex?'

'No comment.'

She didn't need a man in her life – or at least that's what she told Nick Albert, about a month after her friendship with Simon had begun. Nick's jealous rage pleased her at first. Nick had never expressed any reaction to other men in her life, and he was hardly in a position to demand fidelity. But Simon Longe was another kettle of fish.

The last time she saw Nick was when he had appeared unannounced at Chelsea Mews in a drunken fury. 'I know the bastard's in there!' he bellowed, driving the front of his Mini Metro into the yellow door until the hinges snapped and the burglar alarm went off.

'I will not have this, Nick!' she commanded, standing barefoot in a filmy robe.

'Where is he?'

'You're lucky he's not here! I would have to ring the police and have you charged.'

'I love you, Georgina! I won't let you marry him!'

'What I do or don't do is none of your concern.' Having said it, she believed it.

'But we love each other, Georgina. We belong to each other. I want to marry you.'

She could suddenly look at him and sincerely believe she was tired of the whole bloody thing. 'You have a *wife*, Nick.'

'I'll get the divorce, I promise! In fact there may be a way to get an annulment.'

'Good. Then we can invite the Pope to our wedding!'

'Please, darling. I implore you. Promise you won't do anything rash. You *can't* marry that prig. I won't let you!'

'Piss off, Nick! I never want to see you again.'

'But Georgina! Darling!'

'Piss off! This time I mean it.' She watched him drive the crippled motor up the mews. Having said this, she found she really did mean it. *You bore me, Nick Albert*. If Simon Longe asked her to marry him, that's exactly what she would do.

The next news of Nick came in the form of press photographs of Nick and Roxanne taken at the international polo matches in Argentina, and through cryptic postcards sent from various other points in South America. An envelope from a luxury hotel in Rio contained wadded-up cuttings torn from Portuguese, Spanish, and French newspapers showing Georgina with Simon. No note enclosed. How childish could one be?

No photographer was present Christmas Eve when Simon Longe asked her to marry him. The ring he presented was an exact duplicate of the one Charles had given Diana, an enormous oval sapphire surrounded by fourteen diamonds and set in eighteen-carat white gold. Made by Garrard's, the royal jeweler, it cost over thirty thousand pounds. Georgina knew this not so much because she was interested in the royal family but because a consistent best-seller at her British Junque shops was a remarkable copy of the Princess Di engagement ring, selling for a brisk fifty quid each.

The cliché applied: 'This is so sudden. Simon. I really don't know what to say.'

' "Yes"! A simple "yes" would do nicely!'

His proposal *was* sudden, and she *didn't* know what to say. The possibilities boggled her mind. She was a one-woman band, and a damned successful one. For so many years the target of her single-minded pursuit of a husband had been Nick Albert. For so many years he had been a hunger that could be temporarily appeased when they met but never totally satisfied.

Her realization that she could live without Nick, and in fact would be well rid of him, had come to her at the same time that Simon came into her life. Looked at in realistic terms, she had spent her entire adult life, nearly twenty years, on her own, an independent woman with no one to answer to but herself. Success gave her permission to do exactly as she pleased, when and how she pleased.

To marry now would mean a complete change – sharing a bedroom full-time, and not just for romantic interludes. Accommodating *his* schedule, *his* habits, *his* needs. Thinking of herself as part of a 'we' rather than just 'me'. Taking on the duties of the Prime Minister's wife and hostess in addition to her own. Moving into

Nice Girls

Number Ten Downing Street, for God's sake, and being blown up by terrorists!

On the other hand, there was much to be gained. Marrying Simon would place her solidly, visibly on the highest level of the Establishment, with instant access to the inner workings of government, commerce, banking, and all aspects of communications. She had often thought of doing her own television show called *The Junque Lady*. A kind of send-up of stuffy programs about antiques, it would invite people to bring in family heirlooms and odd bits and pieces found in trunks like the one that had launched her own enterprise. A panel of 'Junque' experts would evaluate the goods. She would interview the guests about their lives and how they had come to be in possession of their treasures. The finale would be a loud raucous auction, the very antithesis of Sotheby's, with members of the studio audience as bidders.

The wife of the Prime Minister would surely have no problem getting air time. She had learned in the past twenty years exactly how to manipulate the media. Since the July Fourth picnic put on by The Three Mewsketeers, she had created endless amusement for the press up to and including her current friendship with Simon. She was sure his handlers knew as well as she that there would only be the mildest media attention if Simon Longe were seen out and about with a woman less prominent than herself.

'I'm terribly honored, of course.'

Why didn't the idiot kiss her? Why did he just stand there shaking? How could she think of marrying someone she hadn't been to bed with?

'I adore you, Georgina!' His ardor broke through his reserve in a clumsy, passionate embrace. His sincerity of purpose touched Georgina's heart. But if she was to make a decision, it would have to be made in her bedroom. There would never be anyone who aroused her like Nick Albert, nor did she expect anything comparable from Simon.

She was pleasantly surprised and not at all displeased. He was affectionate and considerate, his performance adequate. He followed her guidance without a hint of embarrassment or inhibition. What's more he felt good, smelled good, and when at last they fell asleep he fitted himself companionably to her contours and did not snore.

Over breakfast he repeated his proposal. As she knew, he had been asked to spend the New Year's weekend with the Royal Family at Sandringham. If Georgina were to agree to be engaged he could then properly inform Her Majesty of his happy news, and ask if his affianced might accompany him.

'Think of it, Georgina! What a way to start off the new year! Say you'll marry me, dear!'

The temptation was nearly overwhelming, but she resisted it. What made her good at business was her inborn ability to see beyond decisions. She could not make a snap judgment on something that would change her life forever. Perhaps ruin it.

'You've swept me off my feet, Simon. I need a little time to think about it.'

'How much time?'

'When do you return to London? The day after New Year's? I'll have my answer ready for you then.'

'Promise?'

'Promise.'

He pressed the Garrard's jewel box into her hand. 'Will you wear it while I'm gone?'

If she did accept him, this was not the ring she wanted. Didn't he see that it was bad form for the Prime Minister's wife to wear an engagement ring exactly like the future queen of England's? She slipped it into his pocket. 'Take care of it for me. I'm such a silly goose I'm liable to mislay it.'

Shutting the door after him, she slumped against it. 'Silly goose'? Why on earth was she calling herself a silly goose? Was this a foretaste of her life as a wife, talking baby talk? Her instinct had been dead right. She needed time to think.

London was deserted during the week between Christmas and New Year's. She herself had closed her offices and given everyone the entire week off. A light sugar coating of snow gave Chelsea Mews the pearlescent glow of a Victorian print. Looking down from her bedroom window at the cobblestones and the Windsor lanterns standing straight and dignified as if guarding her tiny kingdom, she wondered if this was the last Christmas she would spend in Chelsea Mews, whether this Christmas marked the end of one chapter in her life and the New Year would be the start of another.

Apart from the personal upheaval, there were financial considerations to evaluate. One thing was certain: She was richer than Simon by half. She phoned her solicitor at home in the country.

Without saying who her prospective husband might be, she asked him to come up with a pre-nuptial agreement. She was shaky on British laws about property rights in marriage. What was hers was hers and she had no intention of jeopardizing what had taken all these years to build.

So far as she could tell, Simon's sole income was the fifty thousand pounds a year he received as prime minister. There were perks, of course, but they didn't amount to much. What if the party was defeated at the next election? Then what? Would she then have to create a job for him, and spend hours and hours soothing his ego?

Selfish bitch? Of course. She had spent years learning to be exactly that. Fame was merely the icing on the cake. She was a heroine because she was successful. Let things go wrong, let the cake start to crumble, and the smiling jackals would tear her to pieces and eat her alive.

By December 31st she was feeling relaxed and refreshed from several aimless days of quiet self-indulgence – reading old fashion magazines she usually never had time for, watching the telly, eating lovely cold food on trays and letting the dishes pile up in the dishwasher.

Simon rang at teatime. From Sandringham. 'Her Majesty just asked how is that delightful young woman I presented to her at the last garden party? So I thought I'd ring you and see if there's anything you'd like me to tell her.'

'Ah, Simon . . . we agreed . . . after the New Year.'

'Whatever you say, dearest. I'll ring back at midnight. Next year, we'll toast the New Year together.'

His call stirred her out of her delicious torpor, upsetting her plan to stay cosy and content in her favorite old flannel dressing gown and the fox-fur slippers Mona had sent from Bergdorf's. Restless now, her energies back in high gear, she slipped into her American blue jeans, her Texas cowboy boots, and one of the new British Junque Lady sweatshirts that were selling like a bomb. With her old leather mac pulled tight at the waist and her old Liberty scarf tied Sloane Ranger–style over her hastily brushed hair, she set out through the winter dusk.

Unexpected tears stung her eyes. *Lucky girl*. The snow had stopped falling but it was still in the air, an icy spray of exhilaration that sent her running and skipping toward the river. It was only a bit past five, yet darkness had descended. A grayish mist tinged with pink made the Thames and the buildings on the opposite bank look strangely unreal.

This was her tiny part of the world, of her London. Dick Whittington had come to London a penniless boy and become Lord Mayor. She, too, had started with almost nothing. Surely, it would be in the best British tradition if she were to marry the Prime Minister.

She walked swiftly back to Chelsea Mews, her mind a jumble of plans for the wedding and where it would be held. Westminster Abbey? St. Paul's? Trafalgar Square? Chelsea Registery? Piccadilly tube station? A small country church? Giddy with possibilities, she turned into Chelsea Mews in a high state of excitement. She had made up her mind.

She didn't see the huddled figure of the man on her doorstep until he stood up, bleary-eyed, unshaven, and reeking of sick.

'Happy New Year, darling heart!' Nick Albert tripped over his boot lace and collapsed against her. 'I've left her! Will you marry me?'

His foul breath did not stop her kissing him full on the mouth and taking him in. She undressed him and washed him like a baby. He was asleep before she'd finished plumping the pillows and tucking him up.

She herself was deep in sleep on the chaise longue, with a magazine on her lap, when the telephone shocked her awake. What bloody fool was ringing her in the middle of the night? In her groggy state she tried to focus on her watch. Midnight. The penny dropped: Simon, ringing to wish her a Happy New Year and a happy new life with him.

The leaden figure of Nick Albert stirred, flailed, but did not wake up. Georgina stayed rigidly still, as if Simon could hear her move through the telephone lines. At last the ringing stopped, only to start up again. He could not accept her being out. He must have assumed the Sandringham telephonist had dialed the wrong number.

Feeling guilty at first at the thought of his impatiently waiting for her pick up, her remorse turned to anger when he persisted in letting the rings go on and on and *on*! How thick could a person be? Why ring the house down? Couldn't he see there could only be two reasons for the phone to go unanswered? Either she was out and therefore could not answer, or she was home and did not care to answer.

At long last he gave up. He would try again in the morning, she was sure. That didn't give her much time to think of a tactful way to let him down.

17

Mona

New York, 1986

Bed.

Always her favorite place, her most reliable place, her hiding place. Her sanctuary. Her library. Her experimental sex lab, her athletic field, her children's playroom, her movie theater, her rehearsal hall, her sushi bar, her ice cream parlor, her beauty salon, her synagogue for private prayer.

Now it was her prison. From being a Dumas 'mewsketeer' she had become a Dumas spinoff of *The Man in the Iron Mask*. It was hard to believe that a tiny nylon suture could cause such havoc. The infection that careened through her blood-stream with such malicious speed gave every sign of victory. The nose operation was a success but the patient died; at least she would look good in an open coffin.

In true soap opera fashion, this patient had the will to live. She might be hideously deformed, but she still had the will to hunt down her plastic surgeon and feed his face to a rabid pit bull.

That image nourished her during the weeks in the hospital and the transfer home after the final reconstructive surgery. Her 'iron' mask of splints and gauze allowed her to eat and talk, within limitations. But because her reading glasses would not fit over the bandages, it was hard to read. Talking on the telephone was also a problem. The first time she tried it she accidentally brushed the phone against her nose and panicked, convinced she had ruined everything.

She wanted to walk but was afraid to, afraid she might fall or bump into something and be back in the nightmare all over again. But things were looking up. Tomorrow she would be returning to Mt. Sinai to have the mask removed, perhaps for the final time.

'I'm not promising,' Dr. Minkow had said at her last checkup.

'But it's healing nicely, better and faster than I expected.'

'Strong peasant blood,' she said in her best Maria Ouspenskaya accent, her first attempt at humor since the operation, a good sign of recovery.

Rest, everyone urged, plenty of rest. It wasn't difficult to comply. Her day was spent dozing and watching TV until the kids returned from school. At first she had thought they were angry at her for what had happened, selfish little brats, until it dawned on her they were frightened out of their wits.

Her first day home she awoke from a nap to find Melissa massaging her hands. 'They're so dry, Mom. Should I rub some cream on them?'

'How's about giving your poor old mom a manicure?' It was by way of a peace offering from mother to daughter. Mona had often scolded the girl for spending so much time on her nails, time better spent practicing her music or cleaning up her room. 'If you do a good job, I'll let you do my toes.'

Her head bent in concentration on her mother's cuticles, Melissa asked casually, 'Hey, Mom. Who's Nick?'

'Nick?' Had he called or dropped in?

Pretending to be jealous, Melissa pouted, 'You kept calling for Nick. "Nick, darling . . . Nick, I need you!" How come you didn't call for me or Greg – we're your children, aren't we? We were very insulted!'

Bill Neal sat silent in the corner of the bedroom, there on his regular daily visit. He grinned past Melissa as if to say, *Talk your way out of that one, Mona love*. 'I was insulted, too. How come you didn't call "*Bill*, darling . . . *Bill*, I need you!"?'

'You two are impossible!'

'Answer the question. Who is this Nick?' Melissa demanded.

She could feel a trace of her old combative spirit, another good sign. 'It must have been that hot dream I was having about Mick Jagger. "Mick . . . I need you! Mi-i-c-k!" '

'Oh, *Mom* . . .'

'Cause I can't get no –'

'Sat-is-fac-tion!' Melissa joined in.

For Bill, Mona affected a Margaret Thatcher accent, 'And I *tried* and I *tried* and I actually really and truly *tried* . . .' She rotated her pelvis suggestively and threw an exaggerated Mick Jagger smirk to her old friend.

Nice Girls

'Mom! You're embarrassing Bill!'

Her younger child chose that moment to saunter into the bedroom, swinging a baseball bat and finishing off a dripping slice of pizza.

'Hi, Mom.'

She chose to ignore the rising maternal gorge that wanted to shriek at her ten-year-old to watch out for stains on her satin comforter. 'Hi, kiddo. Have fun in the park?'

'Dad says hi.'

Dad? Brent's child-support payments were over six months in arrears. According to the divorce agreement, he had the right to see the children one night a week, one weekend a month, and on either Christmas or Easter, this to be amicably agreed to by both parents. In the five years since the divorce, he had remarried and moved to Philadelphia. His visits with Melissa and Greg were as erratic as his child-support checks.

Her lawyer had strongly advised her to seek alimony as a bargaining chip. She had refused, on the grounds of her own considerable income. Child support was another matter. Melissa and Greg were his children, too. She had insisted on Brent's paying a reasonable share of their living expenses, school fees, and summer camp fees, as well as contributing to a trust fund for their higher education.

But Mona's former husband had been a dead-beat from the word go. Her lawyer's fees to keep him in line were enough to support a third-world country. Of two things she was sure. She was not going to let him get away with it, and she was never going to disparage him to his children. Divorce was rough enough on kids. She wanted them to have as much fathering as Brent could give, with no dividing of their loyalties.

'Did you tell him what happened?' As much as possible, for professional as well as personal reasons, Mona wanted to keep the botched nose job a secret. Rumors could spread like wildfire. The woods were full of voice-over hopefuls just waiting to hear that Mona Davidson was sick, that she had lost her voice, that she had throat cancer, that she'd choked on a chicken bone and scarred her larynx! God knows what stories would get around. True, the ad agencies loved her. They knew they could count on her to bring a unique and memorable quality to their commercials, but they had to protect themselves. They had six- and seven-figure budgets to justify. If rumors proliferated, they might not want to jeopardize their high-end accounts by signing an actress who couldn't deliver the goods.

So far Bill had dealt with the problem. Her major contractual obligations had been met before the plastic surgery, had in fact been planned that way so she would have time to recuperate before getting back to work. But now more than three months had elapsed, and her accounts were getting restless. It was here that Bill Neal proved his brilliance as a manager. Since Mona's distinctive voice behind live action or animation was what provided emotional continuity for the consumer, why didn't the agencies change the visuals and re-edit Mona's previously recorded voices to fit? And none the wiser?

The point being to keep the emergency operation a secret; the fewer people who knew about it, the better. 'So did you tell Daddy?' Mona repeated. Greg had turned on the television and seated himself cross-legged on the floor, his face all but touching the screen.

'Tell him what?'

What did he think she was doing with this bandage on her head, auditioning for *Phantom of the Opera*? But at a warning glance from Bill, she let the matter drop. Better to not make a big deal of it.

'So how is he, Greg?'

Her son turned when he heard his name, the TV blaring behind him. 'How is who?'

'Your father!'

Melissa laughed. 'Don't mind him. He's a space cadet.'

'He's okay. He gave me a hundred dollars.'

Melissa stopped laughing. 'What about me!'

Her brother dipped into his pocket and pulled out two hundred-dollar bills. 'Oh, yeah. Here's yours.'

Bill saw Mona's face tighten. 'Scoot, kids. Mona's got to rest.' Grudgingly, the two complied. As they soon they'd gone, Mona exploded.

'Son of a bitch! He stiffs them on child support. I'm a gent. I don't say anything. I pay all the bills. Then he comes along and showers them with money. Their hero! Dammit! I'm going to haul him into court. Call the lawyers.'

'Not now, sweetie. You have more important fish to fry.' He moved his chair close beside her.

'You mean the case?' The lawyers for the plastic surgeon were offering a substantial out-of-court settlement.

'I think you should take the money and run.'

Her lawyers wanted her to hold out for more.

'Why prolong the agony, Mona?'

'I want the bastard to suffer.'

'*You'll* be the one to suffer. The bastard knows what he did. He's told the insurance company to settle. If you don't accept, you'll have to go through depositions and medical examinations and God knows what. And after months, maybe years in court, you're liable to wind up with less.'

'Who cares? I want that pig thrown out of the AMA. I don't want what happened to me to happen to anyone else. I don't give a damn about the money.'

Bill Neal took her hand. 'Don't make that mistake.'

She looked at him with alarm.

'There's nothing to worry about. And there may not be anything to worry about, but –'

'But what?'

'But I had to pass on two new accounts. They wanted you. They're shooting over the next few weeks. They have schedules to make, marketing plans and print ads coordinating the campaign. They were disappointed; intensely, deeply disappointed, but –'

'That's show biz, right?'

He squeezed her hand. 'Take the money and forget what happened. Listen to me. Your voice is fine, better than ever.' They had amused themselves by making a bedside tape the previous day. She had to agree. The magic quality was still there.

Tomorrow, the bandages would come off. In the wake of disaster, it had been her good luck that Dr. Jerome Minkow, one of New York's leading experts in reconstructive facial surgery, was actually at the hospital when she was rushed into the emergency room. She had been haunted by stories of bungled breast surgery where the breast had to be cut off. Would her nose have to be amputated? Would she walk around with a hole in her face, like some pictures she'd seen of war casualties?

Dr. Minkow's bedside manner was forthright. Cosmetic surgery for vanity's sake did not especially interest him. He left that to other competent surgeons. His particular interest was congenital malformations and also victims of accidents, car crashes, fires, muggings.

'Frankly, I would not have taken your case if I hadn't seen you when you came in.' He chose his words carefully. 'From the look of you, you were mugged. It's not ethical to question another surgeon's skill, but I'm curious to know how you chose this particular surgeon – if in fact he is a licensed surgeon.'

She was ashamed to say, 'I read about him in a magazine.'

His silent incredulity caused her to defend herself. 'You don't understand. I'm an actress. I have to be photogenic. I have to have a face!'

Mona had purposely avoided telling her mother when the bandages would come off. Doubtless Esther Davitsky wasn't to blame that her anger, controlled as she may have thought it was, created unbearable tension. The minute she entered her daughter's prison, Mona's nervous system blew a fuse. Coffee cups fell over, medication was spilled, Mona's throat contracted in coughs that threatened her bandages.

Why didn't you listen to me? was etched into every line in Esther's still handsome face. She was a superb actress, a disciplined, focused performer in every sense of the word, and a model for Mona. Esther never relaxed. Esther was always 'on.' Contemptuous of the traditional role of the *oy-vey* Jewish mother, she did not nag in the accepted or expected way. Her weapon was reproach, a sad and patient reminder of the decisions Mona had taken despite her mother's opposition.

Shortly after her return from London Mona had left NYU Drama School. Bill Neal was getting her so much work she didn't see much point in training for a career that had already begun. 'Voice-overs? Who are you, Edgar Bergen? What kind of acting is that?' When Esther was Mona's age, she was playing Hedda Gabler.

Three years later, Mona had married Brent Wilson. Nice girls didn't live with men they weren't married to. She wondered what Esther would say if she told her about Nick and the time they'd made it in the backseat of a taxi? To Esther, her living with Brent was a sin. To actually marry a goy was an outrage answerable only to heaven and the memory of Mona's father. And yes, her mother did beat her breast, did thank God that he had not lived to see such a thing.

With the perversity of the perpetually aggrieved, Esther did not hail the divorce as a triumph of right over earlier wrong. For her it marked yet another failure on Mona's part. As for the children, she

Nice Girls

for the most part kept her opinions to herself. When she said, 'Things were different in my day!' her daughter agreed wholeheartedly and changed the subject.

Mona had managed to establish certain rules. Esther was not to drop in without phoning first. Esther was not to buy clothes for the children unless she was prepared to return those the children didn't want. Esther was not to pry into Mona's financial or romantic arrangements. Mona made it clear that she respected her mother's opinions and would ask for them when needed. But her calling Bill Neal 'a pansy' had only strengthened Mona's resolve to keep Esther from butting in.

The ground rules established, the two women had enjoyed a long period of mutual affection and companionship, speaking most days on the phone, meeting for lunch, taking the kids to concerts and movies. All was well until Mona decided to have her nose fixed without discussing it with Esther.

'Keep her out of here!' she had begged Dr. Minkow after Esther's first hospital visit. 'She's making me crazy!'

Robbed of opportunities for confrontation, Esther wrote letters scolding her daughter and telephoned every five minutes, despite the fact that she was told Mona couldn't take calls because she wasn't supposed to move.

When Dr. Minkow allowed Mona to return home, Esther announced that she was moving in. At Mona's plea, the doctor once more came to the rescue. Hospital rules were still in effect, he told her. Absolute quiet, no talking, brief visits, just rest and relaxation. 'You do understand, Mrs. Davitsky?' Esther was a woman who obeyed doctors. After meeting Dr. Minkow, she wondered aloud why Mona couldn't have married someone like that.

Mona knew her mother would be upset when she found out her daughter had gone to have the bandages removed without her. For Mona it was a question of whose feelings were better served. If she didn't tell her mother, her mother would be upset. If she did tell her mother, *she* would be upset. The choice was obvious.

Bill Neal had a limousine waiting for the short drive to Mt. Sinai Hospital.

'Oh, Bill. You shouldn't have. We could have hopped a cab.'

'Nonsense. You're a star. A star travels in style.'

Dr. Minkow had the kind of phlegmatic personality that could make a moon walk seem anticlimactic. Mona could almost hear drum rolls and trumpets and violin music swelling in the background as the brilliant surgeon snipped away the last layers of tape and gauze. With a crescendo in her heart, she watched his face for a hint, an inkling of good news to break the suspense.

'There.' Joan Crawford in *A Woman's Face* flashed through her mind. She had seen it at a Joan Crawford Film Festival at the Film Forum. Conrad Veidt was supposed to be the rat and Melvyn Douglas the good guy, but in her heart of hearts she would have gone with Conrad Veidt. Dr. Minkow was a good guy. He had saved her face and probably her life. So why was she thinking of Nick Albert, and wondering how long it would be before she could quite literally face him?

'Care to look in the mirror?'

Was it her imagination or did she detect a faint gleam of a smile on the doctor's face? Bill Neal was smiling broadly. She took a deep breath and looked at herself.

It was Mona Davidson all right. 'Can I touch?'

'Go ahead.'

She touched her nose tentatively. 'It feels real.'

'It is real. It may be sensitive for a while.'

Her relief instantly gave way to critical appraisal. *Picky, picky, picky*. Her nose looked like a blintz. It had no shape. No definition. The texture of the skin was different from the rest of her face. It looked like wet clay slapped on and left to dry. She could not of course bring herself to say these things. 'Will it . . . How long will it be before it looks like a nose?'

'Mona, darling! Dr. Minkow saved your life!' Bill Neal was embarrassed by her lack of gratitude.

'I know. I'm sorry. I'm an ingrate. Forgive me. But please, Dr. Minkow, tell me. Will I ever be photogenic?'

'Your nose will look better than it does now. Maybe not a movie-star nose. But a human nose.'

Bill Neal interrupted. 'And remember, darling, your voice is divine. I'll have you working again in no time!'

'She can start tomorrow morning, if she likes.'

'But not in front of the camera, right? I went through all this, and I still won't be able to work in front of a camera, right?'

Dr. Minkow's patience was wearing thin. 'In a few months, the swelling will be totally gone. The shape of the nose will certainly improve. I assure you people will not flinch at the sight of you. Then if you like I can send you to a cosmetic surgeon, a colleague of mine, who may be able to improve the contours of your nose. Frankly, I think you've had a very lucky escape.' He opened the examining room door.

Bill Neal stepped into the breach. 'Forgive her, doctor. She's been through a lot. We're both grateful to you for what you've done. I can assure you we'll bless you for years to come.'

Mona was not to be mollified. 'Sure, we'll invite him to our wedding!'

'What wedding? Don't tell me you're marrying *him*?' From the waiting room, Esther Davitsky's maternal radar had picked up a signal. When she had phoned the apartment, Greg told her Mona was at the doctor's, having the bandages removed.

Her stress was such that it took another moment for her to realize her daughter's face was free of bandages. 'Oh, Mona, my *schoene maidele*! My beautiful little girl! Thank God! Thank God!'

18

Amy

Washington, 1986

Her daughter's room looked like the wreck of the Hesperus. It broke Amy's heart to see such little appreciation of all her work. When Lou had accepted the professorship at George Washington University, she'd decided to furnish the Georgetown house from the ground up. This was going to be their home for a long, long time. Although the rooms were small, their proportions were superb in the federalist tradition. In choosing the furniture and fabrics, her aim was not to copy the past, not to make their home into a Colonial Williamsburg clone, but rather to reflect the past in a modern interpretation.

'Cool, Mom,' was Sandi's sole reaction to the pink floral wallpaper, white shutters, and muslin-draped four-poster bed. Not yet fifteen, her manner was that of a world-weary courtesan, her habits those of a deliberately infantile slob. The thick cream carpet, chosen to receive the delicate bare feet of a princess, was stained with spilled makeup, food, and the detritus of school projects requiring rubber cement, masking tape, marking pens, staples, and other materials which were supposed to be used on her desk. Sandi preferred working on the floor.

For Amy, the final insult was the *Mad* magazine poster Sandi had taped to the wallpaper, as if her bedroom was a locker-room or something. It displayed Alfred E. Neuman's famous gap-toothed grin, along with the seminal eighties message, 'What, me worry?'

Yes, she worry! She had worried with sickening apprehension of what might happen from the moment she took Sandi to Union Station and put her on the New York train. Aunt Mona and the kids were meeting her at Penn Station with a weekend of plans. To Melissa, twelve, and Greg, nine, Sandi was a heroine, rock star, sage, and witch combined.

Sandi's trip to New York had its genesis a month or so back when Amy received a frantic phone call from Mona. 'I hate to bother you, Amy, but my kids are at some motel somewhere in Washington. They're not exactly sure where. That son of a bitch ex-husband of mine dumped them! He was taking them to Washington, just Daddy and the kids, the first time he's invited them anywhere since the divorce. They were so excited, so thrilled, all week long "Daddy this, Daddy that," you could puke! So what happens, he brings a new girlfriend along, the asshole! It's nine o'clock at night, right. Thank God I'm home. The phone rings and it's Melissa. They're sitting alone in a fucking motel room . . . I'm sorry, Amy.'

Mona knew Amy hated dirty language. 'It's okay – what's the number?' Sandi went with her when she went to pick up the kids and bring them back to the house. Sandi more than rose to the occasion, fussing over them, microwaving frozen pizzas, making ice cream sundaes with mountains of Cool Whip, playing her tapes, and arranging pillows and blankets on her bedroom floor so the three of them could sleep together.

No wonder they adored her. Watching them. Amy had wondered if she'd deprived her only child of siblings. But Lou had laid down the law: One child was enough. Amy would have liked more, but as usual had deferred to her husband's wishes.

No wonder then, when a grateful Aunt Mona phoned to thank the Humphries and asked Sandi what she wanted for her birthday, that Sandi's prompt request was a trip to New York. Amy protested that it would be an imposition. Mona insisted it would be a pleasure. Melissa and Greg were delirious with anticipation. Lou said Amy should quit treating Sandi like a baby. She was fifteen. A hundred years ago she would have been married and a mother. *And dead at thirty*, Amy thought but did not say.

Treating Sandi like a baby was not the point. Amy was simply terrified of her own inadequacies in the face of Sandi's increasingly precocious behavior. She had not told Lou about finding their daughter with a college boy, both of them naked as jaybirds, in Sandi's four-poster bed, the music so loud they had not heard her come home. Sandi swore the boy had given her a joint and she hadn't known what she was doing and she would never do it again, and got Amy to promise on the Bible not to snitch on her to her father.

'What, me worry?' prompted a smile, as Amy straightened out some of Sandi's mess and gathered up the worn tights and bras and sweatsuits from the closet floor and under the bed for the washing machine.

Always a morning person, Amy enjoyed doing household chores before Lou woke up. Sandi's photo album sat on her small white rocker with her teddy bear. Amy paused as usual to flip through, watching her daughter grow from the squinting blob to the playground rascal and up through the stages of missing teeth, bony knees, first bike, school play costumes, and the recent visit of Melissa and Greg.

Tears formed. Lou was right. She was treating Sandi like a baby. She missed her. Less than twenty-four hours had passed, yet the house was unbearably empty. And quiet. What was that old saying, 'It only hurts when I stop'? At that particular moment she'd have given anything to hear Sandi's tapes and find her lip prints on the orange juice container.

Mona had considerately phoned to say that Sandi had arrived safely. They were going to Radio City, followed by a raid on the new Tower Record store in Greenwich Village.

'Amy – I'm up!'

Her master's voice. 'Master' was a word that made women like Mona spit nails. Men were not the master race. Amy knew it, but it didn't matter. She liked the sound of it, if only to herself. After sixteen years of marriage, she still liked the small excitements of waiting for her lord and master to awaken and then listening for his shower to slow and stop – a signal to start his bacon, crack his eggs into a bowl, put the English muffins in the toaster ready to press down, and hot up his coffee cup with boiling water.

She clung to these daily affirmations of her happiness. She chose to ignore his unexplained latenesses, such as last night's, when he had known Sandi was gone and she was alone in the house, waiting. His contrition when he finally got home salved her bruised feelings, and his ardor made up for his inebriated state.

Lou was sipping his second cup of coffee when the phone rang. 'Sandi!' They grappled for the receiver. Lou won.

'Sandi? You behaving yourself, sweetheart?'

Amy could hear Mona's voice. 'It's Mona, Lou. How the hell are you?'

'Missing my little girl. Put her on.'

'I . . . don't want to wake her. The kids were up all night. I just peeked in. They're out cold.'

'You're sure? Not just one little hello for Daddy-O?'

'You don't want me to interrupt her beauty sleep, do you?'

'It's just that I'm leaving in a few minutes.' He realized this was news to Amy. 'No rest for the weary. Saturday or no Saturday, when the head of the department calls a meeting, you go! Anyway, give my little girl a great big kiss when she wakes up. Here's Amy.'

He seemed relieved at not having to explain further about the Saturday morning conference. Amy was glad Mona was on the phone. Mona was much more sophisticated than she. Maybe Mona could give her some advice. There was nobody else to ask. Her mother only seemed to want to hear that everything was fine and to ask her how she was managing her money.

'Mona?' She could see Lou pick up his briefcase as he headed out the door – perfect timing for a confidential chat.

'Can Lou overhear us?'

'Can Lou . . .?' Why in the world did she ask that?

'Answer me, dammit! Is Lou still there?'

'Well, no – he just left.' The alarm bell finally went off. Where was her brain? 'What happened? Is it Sandi? Tell me, Mona! Is Sandi okay?' What didn't she want Lou to know?

'I don't know!' Amy had never before heard Mona cry. 'I don't know what to do!' Sometime during the night, Sandi had sneaked out of Mona's apartment.

'Where did she go?'

'If I knew I'd go and get her!' Mona snapped, then instantly apologized. 'I'm sorry, Amy. It's not your fault.'

'That's what you think. Wait till Lou finds out.'

'Well, he's not going to find out. I just thought you might have an inkling. Some boyfriend. Is there anyone who writes to her? Calls her?'

Two years had passed since they'd moved to Washington. Sandi never mentioned anyone in particular. 'I think I'd better fly up right away.'

'No, Amy. Give me a few hours. I feel so responsible.'

'It's not your fault.'

'She was in my care.'

'I'll catch the next shuttle.'

'No, Amy. I shouldn't have told you.'

Nice Girls

'You mean like you shouldn't have told me about the nose job and how you nearly died?' It slipped out. She hadn't meant to bring it up. She had found out when Mona's children inadvertently let the cat out of the bag. They had obviously thought Amy knew all about it, including the fact that the next operation would be in about six months.

Fortunately, Amy had been alone with Melissa and Greg, getting them settled in her house after their rescue from the motel, when Amy bemoaned the fact that it was nearly two years since she and Mona had seen each other, time passing so quickly and all. That was when Melissa had said that her mother was putting the duplex up for sale because of all the doctor's bills. Melissa also vowed never to see or speak to her father ever again. Not just for leaving her and Greg to fend for themselves at the motel, but because he owed Mona thousands of dollars in child support.

'We've got to cut down,' she had gravely informed Amy.

'Your mother is extremely talented, naturally talented. You'll see. One of these days she's going to be a big star!'

'When she gets her new nose,' Greg had said solemnly.

Now there was a gasp at Mona's end of the phone. 'I know I should have told you.'

'I'm sorry, Mona. I'm sorry I said that. I respect your privacy. Look, we'll discuss it when I get there.'

'No. Amy – please!' Sound of voices at the other end. Sound of the phone knocked to the floor by what Amy later found out was Mona's elbow. The sound of Mona raising the receiver to her ear. 'Relax, Amy. She's back!'

'Let me speak to her.'

'She ran to the bathroom. I think she's being sick.'

'I'll make her sick!' It was Amy's turn to cry.

'Take it easy. Look, I'll call you back, okay?'

'Maybe I should come and get her. Maybe we shouldn't trust her to get back here by herself.'

'Relax. You don't want Lou to know about this, do you? It'll be our little secret. And believe me, when she gets out of that bathroom, I'm going to read her the riot act. I'm going to tell her a thing or three a mother can't tell her.'

The danger having passed, Amy was becoming very defensive about her child. 'Exactly what do you mean by that? Just because you've got two children and I only have one doesn't mean you know more than I do.'

'I know more about one child named Mellisande Humphries than her mother does.'

'Meaning what?'

'Okay, you asked for it. I just happened to overhear a conversation your daughter was having with my daughter. The two of them alone in my dressing room trying on my jewelry, and you know what your charming daughter told mine?'

Amy tried to laugh it off. 'Oh, you mean about the time I caught her with a boy?'

'No-o, she's probably saving that for another time. No, Amy. This is going to shock the socks off you. I heard Sandi tell my daughter about oral sex.'

'What?'

'Do I have to explain it?'

'Of course not. Listen, it's in all the magazines. She was showing off.'

'Yeah? Well she was even telling my little girl about the caloric content of sperm!'

'She *what*?'

Suddenly the humor of it sent both women into peals of hysterical laughter.

'It's true, Amy! I swear! I couldn't believe my ears!'

'I'll have to talk to her when she gets back.'

'You might learn something.'

'And what's *that* supposed to mean?'

'Get real, Amy!'

'I know you think I've only slept with one man. Well let me tell *you* a thing or three. I'm much more experienced than you think. I've had a few lovers.' It was a lie, but perhaps not for long. She knew about the seven-year itch. After sixteen years of marriage to a husband who thought he was fooling her with his Saturday morning conferences, and with a fifteen-year old daughter who knew more about oral sex than she did, a seven-year itch sounded mild. Scratching the sixteen-year itch would require someone very special.

'Just don't jeopardize your marriage, kiddo!' Going all the way back to the start of their friendship in London. Mona had always assumed the role of the older, wiser sister.

Amy's long-simmering resentment of Lou's behaviour boiled over. 'If you can get a divorce, I can get a divorce!'

'Look here, Amy. Your daughter's just come out of the bathroom. The kids are up. I'd better fix breakfast. Just don't do anything rash – at least not until I speak to you later, okay? Divorce is no fun. You're thirty-six years old, right? You've never really dated, right? It's a jungle out there. You'll spend all your time and energy suing for child support.'

'I have money. I won't need child support. You're divorced. Georgina's never been married. You both have careers. Why can't I have a career, too?'

Mona changed the subject. 'Have you heard from Georgina lately?'

As a matter of fact, Amy had been feeling neglected. She hadn't heard a word from Georgina in ages. 'No, have you?'

'Not a word. Ah, well. Maybe she's in love.'

Each voiced the fervent hope that Georgina had found a man worthy of her at long last.

Neither mentioned the name of indelible Proustian memory, the man they each of them had loved and lost during that long ago summer in Chelsea.

19

Georgina

London, 1987

'A woman to see you, Georgina.' The usually unflappable Dierdre looked as if she were choking on an invisible bone. It crossed Georgina's mind that Dierdre rarely if ever came into her office to announce visitors; she buzzed through on the intercom. These days, of course, anything could happen. A daring daylight break-in? There was her jewelry, what she had on, but not much else. They didn't keep much cash on hand. The computer setup and other equipment was much too cumbersome to carry into a van. According to the insurance lads the mews, having only one way in and out, was its own protection, a trap when the alarm system signaled trouble.

Or could it be kidnappers? The IRA come to take her hostage? After the recent spate of articles about her growing empire, she had been bombarded with hate mail, the kind she'd been told was routinely received by rock stars, politicos, and the royals. Several, from women, referred to her much-reported romance with Simon Longe. One accused her of screwing the Prime Minister as a shortcut to success.

Another, written in pencil on lined paper by an elderly widow living on an old-age pension, said it was Georgina's fault that the government had fallen. Her reasoning? A woman's job was to support her man. When the rumors of an impending engagement were officially and charmingly denied by both Simon and herself, the gutter press had had a field day accusing her of breaking Simon's heart and ultimately breaking his will to govern. The letter concluded with the dire prophesy that Britain was going down the drain – the Communists and Jews were taking over, and it was all Georgina's fault.

She idly wondered if she should bump up her personal security, hire a bodyguard. Everyone knew how to find her. Here in Chelsea Mews, she was a sitting duck.

'Dierdre, you know I don't see people in the morning. I'd never get anything done. Ask her to make an appointment.'

The usually efficient and articulate Dierdre stammered. 'I t-told her we had a rule against smoking and asked her to p-put out her cigarette and –' She stopped short.

'And . . .?'

'Well, it wasn't actually a cigarette, a small cigar really . . .'

'And . . .?' Something told Georgina it could be only one person. Six months had passed since Nick Albert had appeared on her doorstep. She wondered what had taken The Frog so long.

'And she ground it out on my desk and knocked over my coffee mug, coffee all over the new carpet.'

Nobody knew about Nick. Georgina intended to keep it that way. 'A dissatisfied customer, perhaps?'

The door to her office flew open.

'I have come to collect my husband.' The Frog. It was inevitable, she supposed.

'Shall I gift-wrap him, or do you prefer to eat him here?'

A mistake; a poor joke, and a bad mistake. If she had taken a good look, she'd have realized Roxanne was halfway around the bend. The gun she pulled out of her quilted Chanel clutch could not prudently be ignored. 'Where is he?'

'Put the gun away, Roxanne. Nick is not here. I haven't a clue where he is.'

'Liar! Bloody liar! He's mine! I'll kill you before I'll let you have him!' The gun drooped in her hand, as if her wrist were weak.

Behind her, Dierdre moved silently toward the door with the obvious intention of getting help, the last thing Georgina wanted. Police, reporters, a madwoman waving a gun and accusing her of stealing her husband? Not quite her image, thanks all the same.

'It's all right, Dierdre. Everything's under control. Not to worry.'

'But Georgina . . .'

'I think what's needed is a nice cup of tea.'

Roxanne spat contemptuously. 'Tea? A nice cup of tea? Pig piss! That's what's wrong with the English! Bring me a cognac!'

'Good thought. Make it two cognacs, Dierdre dear, if you wouldn't mind. And remember –'

Dierdre stood poised at the door.

'– not a word, Dierdre. To anyone. Understood?'

'Understood.'

Roxanne sat herself down in the visitor's chair, holding the gun before her with two hands, its silver nose pointed at Georgina's chest. 'I'll give you five seconds to tell me where he is.'

At this particular hour of the morning, Nick would be finishing his morning swim before joining the others for group therapy. The small private clinic on the south coast near Brighton was modeled in miniature on the Betty Ford Center in California. According to the medical team that had examined him, it was a miracle he was alive. His liver was shriveled and black as a walnut, his kidneys were about to seize up. That his lungs functioned at all defied logic.

Too weak and ill to fight her, he had clung to a modicum of self-respect by joking again and again that he had returned to Chelsea Mews 'in the Nick of time.' Before anyone really noticed that she had a house guest, Georgina quietly organized his admittance under an assumed name to the seaside retreat and managed to visit him every week. Progress was nonexistent at first. They couldn't understand why, until he collapsed with kidney failure. That's when they discovered the drugs and drink being smuggled in to him by a mousy little man pretending to be his cousin.

The combination of the near collapse of his vital organs plus Georgina's threat to abandon him was enough to make him pull up his socks. After six months, the doctors and therapists agreed that his health was restored and he would soon be fit and able to leave. Visiting him the previous weekend, Georgina's heart had sung as she'd realized he was once again his former self. Tall and once again elegantly self-assured, he was still boyishly slim enough to wrap a paisley scarf twice around his middle in place of a belt. The puffiness gone, the delicate bones of his face emphasized the poetic quality of his blue eyes and the shaggy unruliness of his hair.

As Georgina's grandfather had once taught her, the best way to stop a snake from striking is to keep calm and look it squarely in the eyes. Now that she was eyeball-to-eyeball with Roxanne, she could see that the Frenchwoman's resemblance to Nick was truly uncanny, like one of those bad dreams where people turn into other people. Somehow the gun did not frighten her. Most probably it wasn't loaded, although one never could tell.

Why was she taking the risk that it wasn't loaded? What was the appeal of looking down the barrel of a gun in the hands of a mentally deranged person? Danger, perhaps. Control. Mona Davidson had sent her a magazine article about successful women. Its theme was that successful women were not seeking money so much as they were seeking control, control over their own lives and control over the lives of others, including their lovers.

'I warned you, Georgina. I'm giving you five seconds to tell me where Nick is!'

Dierdre chose that moment to return with two balloons of Georgina's best brandy.

'Thank you. Dierdre. You may go.'

Roxanne accepted the brandy with one hand while using the other to keep the gun aimed at her hostess. Without deflecting her gaze, she swallowed the brandy in one gulp. 'Not bad. Not good, but not bad.'

'Kind of you to say.'

'Enough chitchat. I said five seconds. One . . . two . . . three . . .'

Georgina's private telephone interrupted the countdown. Only a very few people had the number, Nick Albert being one. Fearful that it might be Nick, that he had chosen exactly the wrong moment to ring, she did not pick up.

'Why don't you answer your phone? Are you deaf?'

'I did not wish to be rude, Roxanne. Dierdre will pick up.'

Dierdre of course would not pick up on Georgina's private line. *Make whoever it is ring off*, Georgina prayed, quite forgetting that the answering machine would click on after six rings.

'Darling?' The unmistakably exaggerated, insinuating drawl of Nick Albert oozed from the speaker. 'Why the hell aren't you there when I ring? Naughty you. But never mind. Good news, love. I've just signed myself out. Catching the choo-choo at Brighton. See you lunchtime. Take warning, I'm randy as hell!'

At the sound of Nick's voice the two women had leapt up and stood paralyzed like creatures frozen in a museum's Ice Age tableau, until Roxanne took aim at a life-size teddy bear Georgina had dressed in a Junque Shoppe sweatsuit and shot it right between the eyes. She glanced at her watch. 'Lunchtime, Georgina?' She resumed her seat, leaning back and crossing her long legs as if settling in for a nice social call. 'Sit down, Georgina darling. You might as well be comfy while we wait. What shall we talk about? Clothes? Have you been to this year's collections?'

Clothes? The bloody woman was holding a gun on her, and any doubt about there being bullets, or about Roxanne's ability to shoot straight, had been thoroughly dispelled by the hole in the teddy bear's head. But things had gone too far for her to summon the police; in fact it was impossible, since she had banished Dierdre and ordered her silence. Calculating the time it would take Nick to reach the Brighton station, the hour or so run to Victoria, and the taxi to Chelsea, Georgina reckoned a good two-hour wait. Clothes? That was as good a topic as any. She wondered if this was how those Beirut hostages had felt during the first minutes of captivity. Humor the terrorist with the gun. Make small talk.

'No. I didn't quite make it to Paris this year.'

Roxanne cast a critical eye at her captive. 'I can see that.'

Georgina chose not to take umbrage. What she called her 'work uniform' consisted of silk shirts, trousers, and suede boots, hundreds of them in multitudes of colors, with an assortment of coordinating jackets and cashmere cardigans to tie at the shoulders. Comfort was the determining factor. If she was lunching out or had a meeting or function to attend, all she had to do was walk across the mews to her private quarters and change into something more impressive.

Flattery, she decided, might get her somewhere. 'I envy you, Roxanne. You look divine. Unquestionably French couture. But you see, I have another problem. Now that I'm on the board of the Buy British Trade Association, I've got to dress British. Jean Muir, Belinda Bellville, Jasper Conran.' She shrugged apologetically. 'Not really fair, of course.' That was it, make her feel superior.

'*Pauvre petite!*' Roxanne sympathized.

'You know . . .' Georgina shamelessly swallowed her pride. 'I've always envied you your sense of style. A natural chic. You were born with it, I think. You probably wore designer nappies.' Her winning smile was met with blank incomprehension. The Frog might speak English perfectly, but irony and wit clearly were beyond her.

'Nappies were Nanny Patterson's department. I had a Scottish nanny, of course.'

'Of course.'

The conversation dragged. Barely a quarter of an hour had passed. How was she going to keep this woman calm, perhaps lull her into dropping her guard, before Nick arrived and walked into the trap?

'Roxanne!'

'Georgina!' The mockery in her voice was intentional.

Once more Georgina chose to ignore the provocation. 'This is hardly the time or the place, but –'

'But what?'

If time and experience had taught Georgina one clarion truth it was this: One could never be too blatant with admiration, or too shameless with compliments. The bigger the ego of one's adversary, the bigger their appetite for praise and approval. 'But . . . As a matter of fact, I was thinking. As long as we're sitting here, waiting . . .' She trailed off. This was not going to work. Nobody could be that thick.

'Stupid bitch. Say what you mean!'

'Well, I wonder if you could give me some advice. About my hair, for example. I loathe wearing it scraped back in a knot. It makes me look a hundred years old.' That was Roxanne's cue to assure her she looked utterly marvelous.

'It does make you look years older.'

Thank you, Roxanne. How very kind. Try another tack. The cognac? She raised her empty glass and turned it upside down. '*Quel dommage!*'

'Good God! Must you show off your schoolgirl French? Your accent is atrocious. People have been hanged for less.'

'I was only thinking we might give ourselves another brandy.'

It was obvious Roxanne was tempted. 'Where do you hide it?' What a charmer.

'The drinks cupboard is in reception. Shall I ask Dierdre to bring in the decanter?'

Point scored. Now the question was, would Roxanne allow her desire for brandy to jeopardize her situation? Georgina was her prisoner. Nick Albert was en route. All she had to do was keep Georgina at bay until her wayward husband presented himself. And then what? Shoot them both? It was a new and terrifying thought. 'Wife murders husband and lover' was boringly common. She had been stupid not to tell Dierdre to get the police.

'Protecting one's reputation' was all very well. It would look divine on her designer tombstone.

'Shall I ring through? I could really use a nip.'

Nice Girls

Roxanne leapt to her feet, waving the gun.

'Touch that buzzer and I'll blow your head off!'

'I can ask her to bring it to the door. You can open the door and take it.'

'She'll ring the police!'

'Why would she do that?'

'You'd send her a signal. She'd see the gun. You've stolen my husband, damn you! In France, I could kill you and any court would acquit me!'

'She has no reason to get the police.'

'She's not stupid! She knows something is going on!'

'That's still no reason to get the cops.'

Roxanne wavered. 'I need a drink before I face that bastard. *Alors, chérie*, don't try anything foolish. Tell her to bring the decanter. You will go to the door. I shall be behind the door where she can't see me. With the gun pointed at your head.'

Dierdre responded at once – she must have been poised over the buzzer. 'The brandy decanter?'

'The brandy decanter,' Georgina repeated, wishing she could figure out some brilliant way to tell Dierdre to send Nick away, across the street to the house, anywhere away from The Frog.

'Is everything all right?' she asked a few moments later, as she tried to look past Georgina into the office while she handed her the silver tray holding the decanter.

The muzzle of the gun was pressed against the back of Georgina's head. 'Of course.' Not much joy in that exercise. At least the doomed woman would have a large brandy. Her faint hope now lay in the possibility that Roxanne could not hold her drink. By some trick of fate, Georgina had found that she herself had a hollow leg. A useful talent in business, she could drink everyone under the table, an idiotic act of camaraderie that impressed factory owners who produced merchandise for her, the bank manager who had advanced that first two thousand quid, and myriad money men and insurers. Ridiculous but true, if she had not had a head for drink she might not have had her business.

'Shall I pour?'

'What are you trying to do, get me drunk?'

'I could pour some back.'

'Stupid bitch! You English are so literal.'

The brandy felt good going down.

Roxanne tried to sip but that was not her style – too slow. She emptied the snifter in one long voluptuous intake. An ominous silence descended between them. Georgina poured another round. In films, there were always poison pellets at hand for slipping adroitly into drinks. She must remember to get some to keep in the tiny ormolu patchbox that normally lived in the shadow of Nick's framed photograph. Fortunately, the leather frame had cracked and she had returned it to Smythson's for repair. The photograph itself was in the desk drawer, a fact of fate to which she might very well owe her life. The sight of it on her desk might well have pushed Roxanne over the edge. Instead of the teddy bear's forehead, the bullet hole might have been in hers.

The waiting was beginning to get to her. She was generally hyperactive, but the brandy had only served to heighten her need for activity. She felt best doing several things at once. It was often hard for her to sit still. On the phone or dictating correspondence into a tape deck she paced up and down her office, did knee bends, or rode the exercycle in the adjoining room.

As she sat silent and rigid, the suspense was becoming unbearable. Was it her imagination, or were Roxanne's eyelids starting to droop, the gun hanging limp? Her desk stood between them. She could slide off her chair and under the desk, to make a lunge at Roxanne's gun from below. Or she could casually stand and stretch her arms, as if stiff from sitting. If that didn't arouse Roxanne's suspicions, she could yawn and casually move around the desk to stretch her legs. If there was still no hostile reaction, she would sidle closer to her prey and pounce.

'Georg-ina!' Nick's voice bellowed from the mews. How could it be? The train could not possibly have arrived so soon!

'Nick? It's Nick!' Her face contorted in renewed fury, Roxanne resumed her fierce grip on the gun and scurried to her earlier position behind the door, her body arched in a feline posture of attack.

'Georg-ina!' Dierdre's attempt to stop him could be heard. 'Georgina, darling!' The door opened. 'I couldn't wait for the bloody choo-choo. I hired a car. Damn sight quicker.' He burst into the office, arms outstretched. 'Darling, I –'

Roxanne stepped from behind the door and blocked his path. 'Yes, my dear. Your darling is right here, waiting for you.'

For once, Nick Albert was speechless.

Tears streamed down Roxanne's face. The gun in her hand trembled. 'I love you! I won't let you go! We belong to each other! From childhood! Remember? Twins. They all said we looked like twins. We *are* each other!' She swung the gun toward Georgina. 'I won't let this English whore take you away! I'll kill you both!'

'Roxy! *Chérie!*' Nick's face radiated loving concern. Disbelief mingled with hope. Roxanne hesitated and, as in the proverb, was lost. Nick grabbed her wrist, forcing her to drop the weapon. Georgina kicked it aside and tried to help Nick subdue the biting, scratching, screaming woman.

'Make her stop screaming, Nick! We'll have the police on our hands!'

'Roxanne, please! You're exciting yourself!' His attempt to reason with her only caused her to scream louder and more hysterically.

Dierdre pounded on the door. 'Georgina . . .?'

'For God's sake, Nick! Do something!'

'Sorry, *chérie!*' A crisp, immaculate whack on the chin, and the screaming stopped. Roxanne slumped against him.

'Help me, darling.' Together they lifted her onto the sofa, Georgina thinking, *Why did this dreadful woman have to spoil everything?* She retrieved the gun from under the desk where she had kicked it. 'Maybe we can fake a suicide. Maybe we can shoot her in the head and put the gun in her hand! Get her out of our lives once and for all!' With Nick standing so close, she felt once more as she had through all the years since their first encounter in Bond Street – an overwhelming giddiness, and a desperate need for him.

Nick took the gun. 'Why not?' He placed the muzzle at his wife's left temple. 'Mistake. She's right-handed.'

Could he possibly mean it? 'Are you mad?' Georgina protested. He allowed her to take the gun and lock it in her desk.

'Mad for you, my angel! I can't wait another minute!' So saying, he opened the office door a crack in order to tell Dierdre, 'Lady Georgina asks not to be disturbed!' A turn of the lock and they were at each other, clawing at the ties and zips and snaps that bound them, crashing finally in a heap on the floor, their passion fueled by long absence from each other and the presence of their enemy.

'You'd best go,' Georgina said reluctantly.

'What about her?' A half hour had passed. Roxanne was still out cold.

'I'll take care of it. Do you know where I can ring her father?'

He gave her the Paris number. 'Be careful. He loathes me. He says I ruined his sweet innocent daughter's life. He can be monstrous.'

All passion quite literally spent, Georgina could once more think clearly. Scrubbing her hair back into a knot seemed to restore her managerial logic and acumen. 'I shall tell him she forced her way into my office waving a gun, that she shot at me and missed.'

'She's a crack shot. He won't buy that.'

'That in her highly excited state she missed, and the bullet struck my bear, proof of her murderous attack. I shall say I struggled with her for the gun and accidentally knocked her out.'

'Darling, you're truly tremendous! But what about me? What will you say about me?'

'I won't say a word about you. I shall simply advise him to send someone to collect his daughter and take her back to France. I shall explain that I've decided not to report this sorry episode to the authorities – to protect my good name as well as his.'

'Brilliant! But she's sure to tell him I was here.'

'I shall deny it utterly. I shall suggest she is slightly 'round the bend. Imagining things. Accusing me of stealing her husband. I shall suggest that for her sake and that of his family's reputation, he send her to a psychiatrist.'

'Brilliant,' he repeated. 'Let me have the key.'

'What key?'

'To the house, of course. I'll wait for you, all bathed and powdered, until you get rid of her. Knowing Papa, he'll come himself in his personal jet.'

'You must be jesting.' Did he really think he could hang about across the mews while she attended to this delicate situation? More than likely, after she made contact with the Baron, Roxanne would come to and Georgina would have to find a way to keep her occupied until she could turn her over to her family. Given all the options, it seemed best to take Roxanne across the mews to the house, prove to her there was no sign of her missing husband, and convince her she had experienced an aberration. 'Possibly drug-induced?' she asked.

'Pills and booze – the more the murkier. The Baron won't need convincing. Last year, she ran naked and shrieking through the Hotel de Paris in Monte Carlo. Papa paid off everyone – hotel staff, guests, even a freelance photographer who was about to make a deal with *Paris-Match* and the *News of the World*.'

The figure on the sofa stirred as if to waken, then fell back with a snore. 'Please leave, Nick. I don't want you here when I ring Paris.'

'Where shall I go?'

Her nerves were stretched to the breaking point. What was wrong with him? Did she have to do *everything*? 'Suss it out for yourself. Go to the Tate. The cinema. The Food Hall at Harrods! Have you got your passport?'

'I always carry my passport, on the chance that some lovely girl will invite me abroad.'

She was in no mood for raillery. 'That's exactly what *we're* going to do. As far as anyone knows, you haven't been here. You can't be traced through the clinic, because you were there under an assumed name.'

'And what about Dierdre?'

'Dierdre does not know you, did not see you, period. Now, go!'

'I'll need some money.'

'Of course.'

'What time shall I ring you?'

'Might be best not to ring. I'll meet you later.'

'Where?'

She considered. Simpson's? Yes, Simpson's. 'Be in front of Simpson's at eight o'clock sharp. I'll swing by for you and we'll drive to the coast. Dover, I think. There's a late-night ferry and a marvelous little hotel near Calais. You'll cross first and I'll join you in a day or two. Then we can work out what to do next.'

'Whatever would I do without you, Georgina?'

'Fool!'

'Eight o'clock sharp, at Simpson's.'

As he had predicted, the Baron dropped everything and was in Chelsea Mews by mid-afternoon. By then Roxanne had fully recovered consciousness. What Georgina had not predicted was her rival's adamant refusal to move. Georgina patiently explained that her father was on his way to collect her, and courteously suggested they cross the mews to Georgina's private quarters, where Roxanne might want to freshen up.

'Where is Nick?'

'Nick isn't here, Roxanne. It's something you've made up.'

'He hit me and knocked me out.'

'You fell, Roxanne, and hit your chin on my desk.'

'Where is my gun?'

'What gun?'

'My gun!' She pointed to the giant teddy bear. 'How else did he get that hole in his head?'

Treat her like the spoiled child she was. 'Come, Roxanne. We both had a touch too much brandy. You were cross with me. You thought Nick was here. You lost your balance and knocked yourself out. Now why don't we go across the street, where we can be comfortable and have a nice cup of tea?'

Contempt covered Roxanne's face. 'Go fuck yourself!' Arms belligerently crossed, she sat rigidly upright, her eyes daring Georgina to make her move. For nearly three hours she sat there motionless and staring – surely a symptom of madness, Georgina thought. No normal human being could stand the strain. In fact the strain was beginning to penetrate her own defenses, when the rumble of a Rolls-Royce on the cobblestones heralded the arrival of the Baron D'Orsainville.

Although Georgina had never met him, she had come across his photograph in the social columns. Now she could see he was divinely attractive, far better than his photographs – lean, aristocratic, and with that aura of inherited power that could never be bought or learned. She remembered that at the time of the elopement, a fledgling journalist had reported the rumor that Nick Albert was actually the Baron's illegitimate son through a liaison with a titled Englishwoman. Later, through Fleet Street chums, she had learned that the Baron had threatened a libel suit, whereupon the reporter was transferred to Australia and the rumor effectively quashed.

Georgina rose to greet him. 'I trust your journey was pleasant.'

He chose to ignore her existence.

'Roxanne?'

Like father, like daughter – Roxanne behaved as if he weren't there.

'Roxanne? I'm speaking to you!' An imperious snap of his fingers summoned two men from the reception area, who unceremoniously raised Roxanne to her feet and carried her by the elbows between them.

Only then did he bow dismissively to Georgina, as if she were a peasant on his demesne. *'Merci, Madame.'*

'Attendez, Monsieur.' She gave him Roxanne's gun. 'A dangerous

toy. You might want to put it somewhere out of reach.'

By half-seven she had made all the necessary arrangements for Nick's trip to France – the booking on the late-night ferry from Dover, French francs, clothes, and the latest magazines. Driving out of the mews, she had the uncomfortable feeling she was being watched. Ridiculous, but when she reached Piccadilly she kept on going, straight past Simpson's and up Shaftesbury Avenue to Oxford Circus, before wending her way back through narrow Soho streets to the arranged meeting place in front of the famous London shop.

Simpson's had shut for the day. Quite a few people, tourists from the look of them, browsed at the windows and in animated clusters under the art deco canopy. Nick Albert was not among them. Eight o'clock swiftly became nine o'clock. No Nick. Where could he be, asleep in some cinema? Holding court at some pub, and ruining all those months of drying out at the clinic?

The familiar sick feeling rolled over her in waves. Stupid. For a smart woman, she was bloody stupid to allow this cancer in her life, eating her innards, killing her. Enough. Nick Albert had swanned off somewhere. God knows where or with whom. He had done her a favor, thank you very much. She was finished with him. Forever.

Suddenly she was mad with hunger. What with all the uproar, she hadn't eaten a thing all day. Now she could eat a horse: Damn Nick! If he were here, they would go to his favorite restaurant in all the world, Simpson's in the Strand, for roast beef and Yorkshire pudding. *The Strand!* Panic gripped her. Nick was waiting for her at Simpson's in the Strand, while she, bloody pratt that she was, had been waiting for him in Piccadilly.

She kicked herself for not having a phone in the car, an idea she had dismissed as too bourgeois. *Please!* she beseeched the Gods of all known religions. *Please let him be there!* Daggers of anxiety stabbed her chest. Traffic conspired against her as she inched around Trafalgar Square and into the Strand.

'Georgina! Thank God! I thought something had happened!'

Miraculously, it had. The Nick Albert waiting for her on the pavement had shed his usual carefree manner. He made no effort to hide his joy and relief at seeing her.

'Darling. You won't believe it. I was waiting at Simpson's *Piccadilly*.'

'Just like *Far From the Madding Crowd*, when Fanny Robin waits for Sergeant Troy at the wrong church and loses him forever!'

'But we found each other, Nick, and we're going to live happily ever after.' She was only half joking.

Though tempted to stop at Simpson's for a meal, they bought fish and chips and jam rolls to sustain them on the journey to Dover. Never had food been so delicious.

With his kisses warm on her lips and the sharp salt air of the English Channel making her wish she had boarded the ferry with him, she watched it slowly recede into the darkness. It was only then that she experienced the fleeting sensation of having seen two men on the upper deck, two men who, in retrospect, resembled the ones who had accompanied Roxanne's father to Chelsea Mews.

20

Mona

New York, 1987

Sunday at the Frick.

Earlier in the day, Bill Neal had taken Mona and Greg and Melissa to the Plaza for brunch. Afterwards they had strolled up Fifth Avenue, browsed at the outdoor book stalls, and dropped the children at the zoo before continuing on to the Louis XVI mansion steel magnate Henry Clay Frick had built – as a place to live, but more importantly a place to house his collection of furniture, sculpture, and paintings. A precise man, his will had stipulated that the mansion continue as a private domicile for his beloved wife. At her death, his gift to future generations was to open the house and all its treasures as a museum for the public.

Mona knew what Bill Neal was up to. He had planned this Sunday excursion as an elegant and inspiring way to prepare her for tomorrow's audition. The Plaza Hotel, the splendor of Central Park, the grandeur of the Fifth Avenue apartment houses with their doormen dressed like Ruritanian generals, and finally into the Frick, where as usual Mona made a beeline for the Romney portrait of Lady Hamilton.

'No wonder Lord Nelson flipped for her. Wasn't she gorgeous?'

'Depends.'

'What do you mean? I'd give my eyeteeth to look like her.'

Bill groaned. It was an old story. Mona's obsession with her looks. He was a patient man, and he loved her. This was a rough period for her, so he chose not to argue the point. 'It depends on whose point of view you take. Vivien Leigh's Emma was breathtakingly beautiful – slender, exquisite, unparalleled. Glenda Jackson's Emma was more historically accurate – a blowsy, loudmouthed vulgarian who could drink Nelson under the table and belch without blushing!'

Staring up at the pale, romantic tones of the Romney portrait, Mona sighed. 'I'll take the Vivien Leigh version. Why wasn't I born looking like Vivien Leigh instead of . . .' She turned to Bill. He had stood by her patiently all these months of recuperation, his assurances constant and unequivocal. She looked fine. Her nose looked fine. It might not be the nose she had wanted, but it looked fine. Tomorrow's audition was for one of the biggest, costliest, and longest-running TV campaigns in the history of advertising. It was a voice-over, with Mona playing six different characters who wind up singing a sextet, meaning she would record all six parts which would then be computer-blended in harmony. 'I know you hate it when I talk this way, but I can't help it. Am I crazy for wanting to look like Vivien Leigh instead of' – she searched wildly for a comparison – 'instead of Charles Laughton in *The Hunchback of Notre Dame*?'

Even she had to laugh when Bill broke into an imitation of the deformed Laughton with one shoulder raised, squinting at her from his hideously twisted face. 'You're absolutely right. This is absolutely how you look: "Sanctuary! Sanctuary!" '

'Okay, okay. I'll stop! You're right. I'm working. That's more than most actresses can say. I'm one lucky kid.'

That's what she had to keep reminding herself. Lucky to have the money to pay the doctor and hospital bills. She had known cosmetic surgery was elective surgery and not covered by her health insurance. Fair enough, she had thought. She could understand that. What she could not handle was the subsequent cost of repairing the error. Starting with the outrageous charge for the ambulance that had rushed her to the hospital and accelerating into thousands upon thousands of dollars for the emergency surgery, the stay in the hospital, and all the attendant bills for tests and medication and follow-up.

As if that weren't enough, Brent had stopped sending child support entirely, using the Washington incident as his excuse. He threatened to haul her and Amy Humphries into court for abducting Melissa and Greg from the motel and charge them with conspiracy to cause him emotional distress by means of his children's disappearance and to deprive him of his parental rights.

Bullshit, her lawyer had agreed at his hourly rate. The man was a conniving turd. But that wouldn't prevent his demand for reduced child support from dragging through family court for months. At one point, while Mona was lying in bed under orders to keep her

Nice Girls

face still and talk as little as possible, she had made the mistake of answering the phone. The father of her children had informed her that he preferred giving his money to his lawyers rather than to her.

Determined to protect the children's feelings, she had told them Daddy had money problems. 'Is that why he dumped us in Washington?' Melissa asked.

'Will we have to go to public school?' Greg panicked.

There was no need to worry, she assured them. Her financial reserves, her investments might be gone, but her residuals continued to pour in. The ad people were howling for her services. Things would be back to normal soon. The only thing she decided to sell was the apartment. Between the mortgage and the maintenance, it was a luxury she felt unable to support.

Her acting career could end tomorrow, quite literally tomorrow, if the audition didn't pan out. The real-estate broker had promised her the apartment would go for seven hundred and fifty thousand, nearly twice what she had paid. She would get a tax break by buying a smaller apartment that she would rent out, and then take a rental apartment for herself and the children.

That way, whatever happened, she would have money plus income. Rather than fight Brent, it might be easier to cut him out of their lives. She was tired of glossing things over to protect the kids. The fact was their father was a shit. Not all men were shits, but it was time they learned the truth about this one. Then it was up to them to decide whether a father who was a shit was better than no father at all, or if they were better off without him entirely.

Bill Neal was more of a father to them than Brent had ever been. Not to mention more caring and devoted to her. Without him she didn't know how she could have survived her ordeal. The past months had brought them even closer together than before. He had always kept his private life private. He had never invited her to his apartment. Though she had heard others refer to his roommate, Bill always appeared solo at industry affairs and social events.

With the AIDS crisis spreading, she worried about his lifestyle, wondering if he cruised gay bars or public baths or God knows what. Their affectionate habit of kissing each other on the mouth worried her. Could he have it? Could he give it to her? Or the kids? But never by word or deed did she indicate her fear.

A week ago he had said, 'I think I should tell you something that you've probably guessed. I live with somebody. We've been together five years. Faithful lovers. At least I've been faithful. I don't think we're infected, but to be safe, no more wet kisses.'

'Oh, Bill. I trust you completely.'

'I know you do. That's not the point. We don't know what the hell's going on. All this chat about body fluids. What does it mean? Spit? Snot?' He laughed harshly. 'I love you, Mona. I know you love me. I don't want you to be afraid to have me in your home.'

'I love you, too. You're the only one I can really talk to.' She could level with him about how she'd married Brent on the rebound from Nick Albert after that summer in London. She could discuss Nick with him, and how she couldn't get him out of her system even all these years later. Bill remembered him from the London days, confessing, 'I rather fancied him myself, that day he showed up with you!'

Monday morning, the real-estate agent called. She had shown the apartment yesterday afternoon while they were out. The couple had called first thing with a firm offer. Mona knocked wood. Good luck came in threes. Charlie Gordon, currently the town's numero uno makeup man, arrived to do her face and hair. It was not that she would be on-camera, the job was a voice-over. It was just that she felt leery about her blintz nose. Although she was reasonably skilled at doing her own makeup, Charlie had a genius for making eyes seem twice their size and skin look, as he said, as if she had been kissed all over.

When she and Bill walked into the studio she wanted to knock 'em dead, and leave no doubt that she was back in stride looking and sounding fabulous.

'What can you do with my nose, Charlie?'

What he did was the second piece of good luck.

Bill's beaming face assured her he meant it when he said she looked glorious. 'For God's sake, don't cry! You'll wreck your mascara!'

The third piece of good luck was the audition itself. 'You're sure I shouldn't be wearing a yashmak?' she whispered to Bill as they were ushered in.

'Shut up. Think naughty thoughts. Remember what I've always told you: Fuck them with your voice.'

The good news was she got the job; Bill would negotiate the small print the following day.

The bad news was the evaluation of her nose by the cosmetic

surgeon recommended by Dr. Minkow. He had read Dr. Minkow's report and reviewed the post-operative X rays at every stage of the healing process before examining her himself. 'I'm sorry to disappoint you. The septicemia corroded the inner structure severely. Dr. Minkow has given you a perfectly serviceable result. My advice is to leave well enough alone. I cannot recommend that you risk further surgery.'

Mona was furious. 'Minkow sent me to him on purpose! He thinks all women are narcissists! Don't they understand? Look at me, Bill!' They were outside the medical building waiting for the lights to change.

A truck driver leaned out of his cab. 'Hey, Bill! Do what the lady says! Look at her! She's gorgeous!'

'You see, Mona? You're gorgeous.'

'We'll find another doctor.'

'We'll find a cab.'

'Where are we going?' she asked when they'd settled in.

'Downtown.'

They rode in silence for a while.

'Bill?'

'That's me. Just your Bill.'

'You mad at me?'

'Frankly?' No teasing tone; he was serious.

'Frankly.'

'I want you to forget this nonsense with your nose. I spoke with Dr. Minkow. He only sent you to Dr. Lee because you were such a pest. He is absolutely against any further surgery. Your face could cave in! Dr. Lee just confirmed it. What do you want to do, keep seeing doctors till you find some quack like the first one? Your nose is fine. Serviceable.' He attempted a grin. 'Nothing to sneeze at!'

'Okay. I hear you.'

Looking past the driver's shoulder, she found her image in his rearview mirror. *I feel pretty, oh, so pretty!* She was too old to play Maria. Not only that, she couldn't sing. But hey, that had never stopped Lauren Bacall from doing a musical. Bill was right. The nose wasn't great, but she was getting used to it. She caught the driver watching her. He winked and gave her the high sign.

'Promise? No sneaking off to some butcher?'

'I promise. Besides, you just saved me a fortune. Now tell me, where are we going?'

'It's a surprise.'
'Is it Nick? Are we going to meet Nick?' Shortly after she had been rushed to the hospital. Nick had phoned the apartment to say hello and had been told what happened. In the following weeks he had phoned Bill at intervals from various places – Marbella, Hydra, Sri Lanka – until she was out of danger.

'We're going to my place. I think it's time you met Richard.'

Mona felt a stab of disappointment. But it was just as well. If she was really smart, she would never see Nick Albert again. She would find a nice new man.

They had reached the West Village. Arm-in-arm they climbed the carpeted stairs of the well-kept Victorian townhouse. At the first landing, she threw her arms around him. 'Thank you, Billy! Thank you for being such a good friend! For giving me a life. If it weren't for you I wouldn't have a career – or a nose! I promise to stop kvetching and work my little tush off!'

'And a nice little tush it is!' He patted her affectionately and they continued the ascent. 'It's worth the climb. We have the whole top floor, what used to be the servants' quarters. We built on a terrace overlooking the back garden.'

She wondered what Richard did for a living, but decided not to ask. Patience. She'd find out soon enough.

'Richard? I'm ho-ome!'

The aroma of cut flowers which mingled with the scent of lemon furniture polish, the heavy woods and marble tabletops, the fringed shawls and dark wallpaper, all were redolent of Henry James, reminding Mona of *The Heiress*. That was an idea. She didn't have to be gorgeous to play Catherine Sloper. She would mention it to Bill, maybe do a revival off-Broadway – like Downtown Beirut, some place where John Simon couldn't make it.

'Richard?'

She was trailing behind Bill, slowed down by the myriad objects that competed for her attention.

'Oh, my God! Richard!'

She found Bill on the terrace. The word *Sorry!* was scrawled on the tiled floor. Bill was slumped over the wrought-iron railing, reaching helplessly toward the body Mona could see sprawled face-down, like an exhausted swimmer, in the garden below.

21

Amy

Washington, 1987

She had insisted on taking their picture before they left for the tennis courts. Dressed in matching outfits, they looked more like brother and sister than father and daughter. Good-looking, everyone said, a good-looking all-American family. Lou prided himself on his flat-gut ability to wear the same size shorts he'd worn in college. Sandi attributed her powerhouse service and natural co-ordination to her father, ignoring Amy's intercollegiate medals for track and swimming.

Amy tried not to let it bother her. Teenage girls and their mothers were supposed to be enemies. Sandi's behavior at Mona's house had broadened the rift, despite Amy's promise to keep the incident a secret between mother and daughter and not to tell Lou. That she had kept her word did not change Sandi's attitude as she had hoped. To the contrary, this glowing sixteen-year-old who looked as if butter wouldn't melt in her mouth was an accomplished tease. She sat on Lou's lap, hurled her arms around him, called him the handsomest, smartest father in the world, and declared herself forevermore to be Daddy's Girl.

Amy had to laugh as she remembered Mona Davidson's oft-repeated, 'So what am I supposed to be, chopped liver?' Being taken for granted was something you read about in magazines, and here it was happening to her. Chief cook and bottle-washer, chauffeur until Sandi got her own wheels. She had chosen the role of homemaker, helpmeet and mother. *Her career*, she reminded herself. It would have been more than enough if she'd been appreciated.

Amy's profession was showering her husband and daughter with interest and emotional support for everything in their lives without receiving reciprocal support for her doings. This particular Saturday morning was a perfect example. Lou and Sandi were competing in the annual Father-Daughter Tennis Tournament. Amy had tried to share in the experience. She had laid out their matching outfits the night before, prepared a high-protein breakfast, and packed a cooler with orange juice and Gatorade.

As a good-luck gift, she had bought an extra-strong barrette for Sandi's ponytail and had put it on her plate with a Smile sticker. After her daughter and husband had condescended to pose for a couple of Polaroids and then piled into the car, she returned to the kitchen and found the barrette on the floor. Careless child. She tried to make light of it. No, she corrected herself. Rude, ungrateful young woman, and no longer a child.

She was reaching the point where she could no longer ignore their behavior. Perhaps it was her own fault for having allowed it for so long. For too long she had chosen to pass off her hurt feelings as the result of thin skin. The *Father Knows Best* family was not real life. This morning for instance, she had not been invited to the tennis tournament. Other mothers would be there, cheering for their loved ones. She supposed she could have assumed she was going, and simply have gone with them. What were they going to do, throw her out of the car? But she had sensed their desire to be a twosome without old mom around. Hovering over them, anticipating their every need, she had waited for the invitation that never came.

Making the best of it, she told herself she was glad to have the morning to herself. She hadn't mentioned the paper she was writing for The Georgetown Walking Tour. Only a week away, it was a fund-raiser for the homeless organized by some local women. Asked to join the committee, she had volunteered to put together a brief history of Georgetown and its architecture. The highlights of the tour were to be the three houses where Jackie Kennedy had lived before and after her three years in the White House.

Scrupulous in her research, Amy had personally visited the small townhouse in Dent Place that the Jack Kennedys had rented for six months in 1960 before moving into the White House, and the eleven-room mansion on N Street lent to Jackie and the children by Averell Harriman after the assassination. The third 'Jackie stop' on the tour would be directly across the street from the Harriman house, a fourteen-room red-brick colonial where the young widow and her children had lived until the relentless crowds of sightseers

Nice Girls

and reporters forced them to move to New York.

At least the committee appreciated her. The tour was oversubscribed because of her Jackie idea. Everyone wanted to see where Jackie had lived. Flushed with this success, plans were being made to take a busload of people to Jefferson's home in Virginia. They would need her to do the historic research and to write the architectural commentary on Monticello and its environs.

When she told Lou about the Georgetown tour, he had asked who were the beneficiaries and laughed uproariously when she told him.

'The homeless? You must be kidding!'

'What's wrong with helping the homeless?'

'Taking a bunch of overfed matrons to gawk at a bunch of millionaires' mansions, in order to buy peanut butter and jelly for the homeless! And you don't think that's a barrel of laughs?'

With husband and child out of the house, she settled down at the kitchen table and wrote the commentary for The Georgetown Walking Tour. After reading it into Sandi's tape recorder, she sighed with pleasure when she played it back. Not bad.

When Lou and Sandi returned, she had planned not to ask them whether they'd won – give them a dose of their own medicine, show she had other things on her mind besides them.

'So what happened? How'd you make out?' How could she not ask? This was her family.

'Great. You should have been there. The wives were asking where were you. Weren't you interested in seeing us play?' Lou untied his sweater from around his shoulders and threw it on the kitchen chair. 'Can you do something about the elbows? They're grimy. Maybe you can get me a new sweater.'

She could hear Sandi in her room, the sound of her sneakers being kicked into a corner. Her daughter had rushed past her without saying hello.

'Soooo . . .?' she asked her husband.

'Sooooo? What soooooo?'

'Did you win?'

'Of course we won. Why would you doubt it? We're in the quarter-finals. Next week-end.'

Why chew her out? Or was he trying to pick a fight?

'What would you guys like for lunch? There's cold roast beef, tuna salad. I can whip up some pancakes, and there's the maple syrup my mother sent from Vermont.'

He had his back to her. 'Just make us some sandwiches and maybe a thermos of soup. We'll eat them on the road.'

On the road? What road? 'Where are you going?'

'Oh, didn't I tell you? I thought I'd take Sandi for a little trip down to Gainesville.'

'Gainesville? *Georgia?* That's hundreds of miles!'

'No. Gainesville, Florida.'

'That's even farther!'

'I hear it's a great university town. Just want to look it over. There's some talk about a new chair in education. Tailor-made for me.'

'How long will it take to get there?'

'Eight, maybe ten hours. But it's okay, I don't have any classes Monday and Sandi can skip a day of school.'

'Why didn't you let me know sooner? I could have been packed and ready to go.'

He fished in the refrigerator, his back again turned to her. 'Well, as a matter of fact, Amy . . .'

Now she understood, she wasn't invited.

'As a matter of fact *what*, Lou?'

'Well, as a matter of fact, Sandi and I thought it would be fun for just the two of us to take a little trip together. You know, father and daughter getting to know each other.'

He had of course forgotten that earlier in the week they had talked about going to the Smithsonian, or driving out to the Maryland shore for a fish dinner.

'Besides . . .' Her husband had turned from his exploration of the fridge and was looking at her with that winning half-smile of personal sincerity that made his female undergraduates feel special. 'We know how important this walking tour is to you. We thought you would like to work on your commentary without having to bother with us.'

Swallowing her pride, refusing to express anger, she had started to make sandwiches when Sandi barged into the kitchen with a show of impatience. 'Don't bother, Mom. Dad's got the names of some great places to eat.'

As Sandi's car pulled away with Lou at the wheel, Amy idly wondered how they'd feel if they returned to find the house burned down and her missing. Annoyed, no doubt. It would serve them

Nice Girls

right if she did take a powder. She kept reading about how the Eighties were the Me Decade. She was probably the only person in the entire United States who was not putting 'me' first.

At least she was taking care of her hair. Georgina had made sure of that. When they got back from their trip abroad, a letter was waiting for her. Georgina had got the Sassoon colorist to write down the formula. 'Take this to your hairdresser. Have them ring Sassoon's if any question. I shall be extremely cross if you let the side down.'

Amy had not let the side down. Her hair did look terrific if she did say so herself, which she did, since she could have stood on her head and whistled till she was blue in the face before she ever got any compliments at home.

She wished she could be more like Georgina. So poised. So assured. The Englishwoman wrote to her with some regularity. Not letters, exactly. Nothing long, just short, chatty notes dashed off on that blue onion-skin paper she liked in that indecipherable handwriting that took Amy hours to decode. When Amy had studied penmanship as a child, the idea was to write clearly. Once, in discussing Georgina's handwriting with Mona, Mona had said the English aristocracy took special penmanship courses – with the highest grades given for the least legible.

As chatty and frequent as Georgina's letters were, she never said anything personal. When she failed to acknowledge Amy's postcard from the South of France, Amy wondered if she was still carrying a torch for Nick Albert after all this time. She hoped her mention of running into Nick hadn't upset Georgina. Could she have decided never to marry, because she couldn't risk being hurt again?

Was marriage becoming obsolete, like the magazines said? After nearly seventeen years, she was wondering more and more often if she had made a mistake. In marrying in general, and in marrying Lou Humphries in particular. These thoughts upset her. There was nobody she could discuss them with. Was this the mid-life crisis she read so much about? For an educated, well-read woman, it was ironic that she had to turn to popular magazines for answers.

She was only thirty-six years old. Yet looking to the future made her feel old, used-up, and defeated. A few weeks ago, she had toyed with the idea of having a baby. Her biological clock was still clicking. She had enjoyed her pregnancy with Sandi, but had deferred to Lou's conviction that one child was quite sufficient. That was sixteen years ago, when they were moving around. Now was now. She had mustered her courage and broached the subject.

'Are you nuts? Before we know it, you'll be forty!'

'Plenty of women give birth at thirty-seven or forty. I'm in great shape. It'll be a snap.'

It wasn't her ability to bear a child that was upsetting him. It was her trust fund, the legacy that was to be hers on her fortieth birthday. 'Then we'll be free to do whatever we want.'

We! The word still stuck in her throat. It was *her* money, wasn't it? And the way she felt this minute, on this beautiful Saturday morning sitting alone in the house she had paid for, with the weekend stretching ahead of her while her husband and child danced off hand in hand without so much as a backward glance, she had half a mind to pack a bag and take off. Without burning the place down, of course.

But it was no good. Where would she go? She liked the house. She liked Georgetown. If she was being honest, she had to admit she liked being a wife and mother. If only her husband and child felt the same way about her! Lou had been right about one thing: Now was her chance to rework her commentary for the Jackie Tour. She was reading her final draft into the tape when the telephone rang.

'Amy love?' A voice like none other. 'It's Nick.'

Nick Albert?

Good manners – once learned never forgotten, like riding a bicycle – prevailed. 'How nice to hear from you! How are you?'

'Absolutely tremendous! And you?'

'Fine.' She could have been dying of the plague, her hair could have been coming out in handfuls, she still would have said 'fine,' followed by the next polite question. 'And how is your wife?'

'Splendid as ever. And your husband? Lou, isn't it, and that ravishing child?'

'They're splendid, too.'

'Well, then . . . I thought I might come around with a bottle of bubbly. An apology for running out on you all in Monte Carlo. You must have been rather put out when you got to the harbor and found us gone.'

She decided to lie. 'As a matter of fact I thought *we* owed *you* an apology. Something came up and we never did get to the harbor. So there's no need to apologize.'

His laugh told her he didn't believe her. 'Well then, what am I to

Nice Girls

do with this bottle of champagne? Why don't we drink it anyway?'

Manners again. 'It would be very nice to meet your wife again.'

His disbelieving laugh caused her to laugh as well. Roxanne had made no bones about her contempt for the visiting Americans. It would not be the least bit nice to meet her again.

'As a matter of fact, I'm on my own. Roxanne and her father have gone off to stay with friends in Virginia. Fox-hunting, in this day and age!'

' "The unspeakable in full pursuit of the uneatable." Oscar Wilde.'

'Brava. The lady is well read. When shall I come 'round?'

For the first time in how long – years? since before her marriage? since London? – she felt reckless and utterly free of responsibility. No chores to do. No meals to plan. No nagging desire to straighten up Sandi's room or clean out the refrigerator. 'How about right now?'

She would wait until he got here to tell him her husband and daughter were away for the weekend. Then again, she might not tell him at all. She might be smart for a change and try to figure out what was best for *numera una*. Two thoughts were paramount as she opened the macadamia nuts and arranged the smoked oysters and black olives in the compartments of her favorite hors d'oeuvres tray. The magazines were right about one thing: A good hostess always kept a supply of gourmet goodies on hand for unexpected guests.

In honor of the occasion she changed her clothes from the skin out, suddenly wishing she owned black garter belts and push-up bras. Why didn't magazines advise the hostess to keep a supply of sexy underwear on hand for unexpected guests? Maybe they did; she hadn't noticed. Because she never wore perfume, she rummaged through the mess on Sandi's dressing table and found the bottle of musk oil her daughter had described as 'decadent.' 'Turns guys on, Mom.'

When the doorbell rang, she peered out the upstairs window to look at Nick unobserved. She was glad about two things, that she had just yesterday been to the beauty parlor and had her hair tinted with Georgina's formula, and that she had never considered betraying her husband until now.

'Baby bird,' Nick had called her. Baby bird was ready to fly the nest.

22

Georgina

London, 1987

Desolate and sick of an old passion! The words of her favorite poet throbbed in her head all the way back to London from Dover. Forced at school to memorize Ernest Dowson, she remembered dismissing him as disgustingly maudlin and self-pitying in the extreme. Why on earth did he have to go on and on and *on*, wallowing in misery and obviously enjoying every boring, relentless moment of it?

She looked at herself in the car mirror. 'And that's exactly what *you* are doing, miss!' she upbraided herself in schoolmistress tones, as she sped toward London along the deserted A-20, alone and distraught. There was no question in her mind: D'Orsainville's bully boys had by now cornered Nick on the channel steamer. Like a prized pedigreed pet who had run away from home, he had been tracked down and now would be returned to his owners.

She was certain now, but she wouldn't be absolutely certain of what happened for hours and hours, until mid-morning at the very earliest when, according to the rough timetable she had worked out, Nick would be arriving at the inn. The way she had figured things out, the ferry would deposit Nick in Calais at dawn. The next stage of his escape would depend on how early the car hire garages opened. From Calais, it was an hour's run to the inn. She had suggested he ring her from Calais to say he'd arrived. 'Don't be silly, darling. I'll ring the moment I get to the inn.'

Back in Chelsea Mews, alone in the bed she should have been sharing with Nick, she lay rigid with exhaustion. She could not sleep. The large whiskey that could always be counted on to put her out like a light had no effect whatsoever. Her eyelids felt as if they had been glued open by some sadistic torturer. Nick was her self-appointed sadistic torturer. She couldn't shake off the sense of doom. If this episode was to teach her anything, it was what she had already known for years but refused to acknowledge: Nick Albert was a blight on her life, a bad apple she must get rid of before her obsession with him destroyed her.

His addiction to alcohol and drugs was child's play compared to Georgina's addiction to him. Where could she go to dry out? Was there a clinic that could treat a sexual and emotional obsession that had been going on for all these years and was as strong if not stronger than the day she had met him in Bond Street?

Having fallen at last into a chaotic sleep, she awoke with a start with sun in her eyes. She had forgotten to draw the curtains. What time was it? Nearly ten o'clock. Although Nick could not by any stretch of the imagination have reached the inn, she nevertheless rang through. *Non*, Madame. Monsieur had not yet arrived. Compelled to do something, anything, she rang the Calais ferry terminal and got the numbers of the car hire firms adjoining it.

Non, Madam, there was no record of Monsieur Al-*bare*. My God, from the sound of their voice they were protecting him! She sounded like a wife hunting down her errant husband. France traditionally protected the man. Trying a more businesslike approach, she explained she was Monsieur's secretary and that she had something *très important* to tell him.

Rien. Bloody frogs, all of them!

By noon she had accepted the inevitable. A third call to the inn confirmed her suspicions. The D'Orsainvilles had recovered their property. By now he was home with Roxanne with a new leash around his neck, unless they had thrown him off the steamer in the dark of night. She wished they had. Then it would at last be over and done with.

She had no way of knowing what had happened. She couldn't ring the French police, could she? What would she say? That her lover's wife, of the formidable D'Orsainvilles, had kidnapped him? Nor could she risk hiring a private detective. Fleet Street paid well for tips. She and Nick and the D'Orsainvilles were fair game for the gossip writers. Wouldn't they just love a story about the Chelsea Junque Lady and the playboy son-in-law of the French billionaire?

Since no body of a man had been found floating in the English Channel, she would have to assume Nick was back in the bosom of the D'Orsainvilles. In their mansion in the Bois de Boulogne? The farmhouse in Provence? The villa overlooking the harbor in Monte Carlo? The yacht, the ski lodge, the private island in the Aegean? Not that it mattered. What difference did it make? She had deluded herself long enough. He had the morals of a tart. He could be bought. She of all people knew that. She had been willing to buy him, but The Frog was infinitely wealthier than she.

She was a businesswoman. It was time to cut her losses. She would forget him and get on with her life. She had no regrets about Simon Longe. At least she'd been right about him. No longer the Prime Minister, the story was he'd been corraled by a Texas cattle heiress. Another one of those Texas women; where did they all come from? Like others who regularly descended on Britain, this one could afford to buy anything she liked.

The thought sobered her. She had been behaving exactly the same way when it came to Nick Albert, trying to lure him away from The Frog with promises of a cushy life with her. And yet she was sure of one thing: Nick Albert did adore her. They had a genuine connection – not strong enough to take him from Roxanne, but a connection nonetheless. She had to break the connection or be forever left waiting for the phone to ring. To do so, she would have to go cold turkey.

She tore up his photographs and letters, bundled up his dressing gown, toiletries, and other personal items for the church bazaar, and took herself to Enton Hall for a few days of health-farm self-indulgence. She'd been working too hard, she told Dierdre. She needed this break to prepare her for the challenges ahead.

An international consortium wanted to franchise her in America and Japan.

A television packager wanted her to compere a panel of Top Women for a syndicated series on women and success.

An associate of Simon Longe's had asked if she had ever thought of standing for Parliament, and suggested discussing it over dinner. If Maggie Thatcher could do it, why not she?

'And don't forget that Beverly Hills boutique that wants a hundred toast racks!' Deirdre tried to cheer her up. The Americans loved toast racks. They used them for filing bills and letters and God knows what.

'We'll deal with that when I get back.'

Being busy helped. Her daytime hours crammed with meetings, her mantelpiece overflowing with invitations to social and cultural events, she had little or no time to brood about Nick Albert. By the time she crept into bed she had neither the energy nor the desire for love, before sinking like a rock into a deep embracing sleep.

At thirty-eight her beauty had ripened to its utmost – her skin a glowing alabaster, her hair a coppery radiance with a slight assist from Sassoon, her figure kept trim and flexible through the ministrations both of the personal trainer who worked with her every morning at seven and the chef who catered healthful lunches for the staff.

One morning about six months after the mad dash to Dover, she closed her eyes and tried to visualize Nick's face. It was blurred. Later in the day, sipping coffee while flipping through the new *Vogue*, she looked at a photograph of a handsome young Parisian at a ball until she realized it was Nick. Feeling as if she'd been told she no longer had cancer, she attended a vernissage at a trendy new gallery dressed to kill, like Diana the Huntress on the prowl.

The young men were a gorgeous international antipasto of colors, shapes, and flavors in tempting display. She chose a Madrileno with the arrogant stance of the corrida and the shadowed eyes of a Modigliani portrait. They had arrived at Chelsea Mews and were just making themselves comfortable when the phone rang.

Jean-Pierre was ringing from Paris on her private line. He sounded extremely odd, as if someone were breathing down his neck. What was wrong? Had he been caught pilfering an abandoned warehouse? Her most valued purchasing representative on the Continent, Jean-Pierre worked on commission and had an absolute genius for finding unique vintage goods. There was the dusty crate of 1930s Bakelite jewelry from the basement of a dead and long-forgotten costume designer, and the boxes of peacock feathers from the dressing room of a provincial theater about to be torn down.

She had met him on her first buying foray to the Marché aux Puces fifteen years ago. Such was their relationship that she had given him leave to ring at any hour of the night or day if he came across something extraordinary that required instant cash.

'*Oui*, Jean-Pierre?' What treasure had he found this time?

A friend who worked at the Hotel Ritz was clearing out a storeroom in a subbasement and was just about to throw away a water-logged, mildewed footlocker when he noticed a barely discernible U.S.G.I. tag at one end. 'United States Government Issue,' he explained.

What was inside? Gold bullion? Eleanor Roosevelt's knickers? Anything they could get arrested for?

'Flags. Hundreds of American flags.'

'A bit disappointing. Why would people flock to buy them?'

Her soon-to-be new lover was trying to hurry her up by slowly stripping off his clothes. For the moment an air kiss would have to mollify. This was business.

Jean-Pierre lowered his voice, as if fearful of spies. 'Because they are vintage World War II, authentic government issue. They have only forty-eight stars. Remember? The current flag has fifty. And they're exactly the right size for your band of seamstresses to sew them on jackets.'

'How much do you need? I'll have it transferred to you first thing in the morning.'

There was a problem. His friend was an expatriate American married to a French woman. He was fearful of the authorities, the French and the American. Selling something that wasn't his was one thing. Sending it across national boundaries, he feared, could send him to prison or get him deported.

The only deal the American would accept was this. She must come personally with five hundred dollars American and give it to him at a place he would designate, in an immediate exchange for the footlocker.

Jean-Pierre had set up stranger deals, and Georgina was glad to consent. 'Will tomorrow afternoon suit?' It would be great fun. It was simply ages since her last trip to Paris. In the meantime, there was this person in her bedroom patiently admiring himself in her full-length mirror.

Jean-Pierre was waiting for her at the airport in his prized vintage Citroën, the black getaway car of René Clair films.

'Are you going to blindfold me?'

Beads of perspiration pocked his face. His bear-like hands clutched the steering wheel as if the two of them were making a getaway. What was she walking into? How could a trunkful of possibly contraband World War II American flags, abandoned and forgotten over forty years ago, have him in such a state of nerves? If she hadn't dealt with him for more than fifteen years she'd have stopped the car then and there.

The building looked ordinary enough.

'*Deuxième étage. Numéro dix.*'

'You're not coming with me?'

'If no one witnesses the sale, no one can ever testify against him, *oui*?'

'Jean-Pierre, I trust you.'

'I wait for you here.'

'I'm too old for the white slave trade.'

'Georgina . . .' He raised his palms and his shoulders, in the familiar Gallic protest of innocence challenged.

She had reached the second floor and rapped on the door of Number 10 when the thought struck her that this might be a kidnapping by terrorists. Arabs, Israelis, IRA? Stranger things had happened. If British businessmen could disappear off the street, why not a British businesswoman? She turned and was racing toward the stairwell when an unmistakably plummy English voice sang out, 'Georgina! Darling! Where on earth are you going?'

Standing in the doorway, with his arms extended in welcome, was Nick Albert. The sight of him stopped her in mid-flight. Before she could protest he had gathered her in his arms, his tanned face exaggerating the whiteness of his smile and the blueness of his eyes. 'Dearest heart. Let me explain.'

From the depths of her soul she summoned the strength to pull away from his tempting embrace. 'Sod off, and go to hell!' she spat. While he struggled to keep her from escaping, she kneed him in the groin and fled down the steps to the street, where Jean-Pierre was visibly surprised to see her so soon.

'*Chérie* . . .?'

He jumped from the car and moved toward her. 'What is it? What has happened?'

She sent him flying with the back of her hand. 'Sod you, too!'

'Georgina. please! He said it was urgent! Life and death!'

By now Nick had caught up with them. 'Please, Georgina! I beg of you! Let me explain!'

Such was her fury, her nose began to run, which made her angrier still.

Nick offered his handkerchief. It was one of those printed cotton squares one bought at the tobacconist's, which had originally been manufactured for those who used snuff. 'The original snot rag, don't you know!'

Naughty and irresistible as ever, he was. Yet as her anger evaporated she could honestly say she was cured. She was no longer desolate and sick of an old passion. There was something rather touching and pathetic about his attempts at charm.

'Why this cock-and-bull story about American flags? And why did I have to fly over from London? If you have something to say, why don't you write me a postcard? Perhaps one with the Eiffel Tower, in glorious color.'

'Please come upstairs and let me explain.'

She feigned exaggerated excitement at the prospect. 'Be still, my beating heart. Is this your *maison d'amour* where you bring your girlfriends? Not terribly chic, is it?'

His entire manner turned somber. 'Jean-Pierre has kindly lent us his flat so that we may talk privately away from prying eyes.'

Jean-Pierre's flat. Of course. How could she be so rude. 'Jean-Pierre . . .' She must apologize.

He bowed gallantly. They were *copains*, weren't they, the three of them going all the way back to a stolen weekend she and Nick had spent prowling the stalls at the Marché aux Puces for things to resell at the Chelsea Antiques Market.

With Jean-Pierre once more installed in the Citroën, Georgina and Nick returned to the second floor.

'But there *are* American flags!' Georgina exclaimed, as she opened the footlocker. Even after all the years of water damage it had remained airtight, its contents preserved in perfect condition. She thrust her arms into them up to her elbows. 'What bliss! What fun! Perfectly marvelous! I'll make a bloody fortune!'

But why all the cloak-and-dagger? Why couldn't she have simply sent the money and had Jean-Pierre ship the goods as usual?

'It was my idea, I'm afraid,' Nick said. 'I ran into Jean-Pierre just after his friend found them, and suddenly it all clicked. Jean-Pierre is a shameless romantic and agreed to go along. The fact is, I need to talk to you.'

'Really. I can't imagine why. It's only six months since I left you at the Dover ferry.'

'Long enough, I assure you. I've been virtually a prisoner of the D'Orsainvilles. Two of their goon squad cornered me on the ferry and took me back to Paris. Then Roxanne did her famous suicide number – she's done it a thousand times, only this time it nearly worked. The Baron warned me that if she died he would have me tortured and killed and my body fed to his dogs in little pieces.'

Georgina was aware of a new sensation. She was bored. Nick's tales of woe no longer roused her.

'What's it got to do with me?'

'I'm asking you to help me. I can see you don't want me back, and I can't say as I blame you. But in the name of what we had, or out of ordinary sympathy, I'm begging you to help me. You're the only person on God's earth I can trust.'

'Why can't you simply pick up and leave?'

'They've got something on me. I took some money. Some of Roxanne's jewelry. I haven't a bean of my own, Georgina. I made a bad deal. I don't have a job. The only thing I was good at was those blue-haired-lady tours. Some gigolo I've turned out to be! I don't even get an allowance!

'They caught me, of course. Made me sign a confession. Roxanne still wants me. I can't think why. If I do a flit, they'll have the gendarmes on me. Have you ever seen the inside of a French prison?'

'What can I do? You know what happened the last time you ran away from home. I got you all dried out and healthy again and they stole you away.'

Embedded in the American flags was a brown paper parcel. 'I want you to keep this for me.'

'Oh no, you don't. Not bloody likely, Professor Higgins.'

'What are you talking about?'

'Now you want me to smuggle – what? Drugs? Diamonds? Do you know what the inside of a British prison looks like?'

'Nothing like that. How could you think such a thing?'

His plan was as simple as it was devious, a means of blackmail to free him from the blackmail that kept him a prisoner. The lovely Roxanne had become increasingly involved in the subterranean world of sexual experimentation. With the introduction of the video recorder, her exhibitionism had come into full flower.

'A set of the tapes is in the parcel. I want you to keep them in a safe place until I'm ready to negotiate my freedom. These tapes, in exchange for my confession and an annulment. That's why I had to see you. I couldn't risk writing to you or ringing you and having you slam down the phone. Besides, I think they monitor my calls. Will you do this for me?'

Back in Chelsea Mews several hours later, she realized how

harebrained she'd been. Customs had merely glanced at the American flags and waved her through. Had they found the brown paper parcel and examined its contents she could have been had up for bringing pornography into the country.

Her Madrileno would be arriving any minute. She had bought him a gorgeous Hermès cravat before boarding her flight. She rather enjoyed buying gifts for men. It gave her a sense of power. She found that she preferred giving gifts to receiving them, except for things like flowers and champagne. She preferred choosing her own clothes and her own furnishings.

Hearing the Madrileno's taxi on the cobblestones, she thrust Nick's parcel into the linen cupboard behind some towels. Although she could honestly say she was no longer in love with Nick Albert and mean it, the fact remained that he could still wrap her around his little finger.

23

Mona

New York, 1987

Now it was her turn. Bill Neal had been there for her throughout the long and frightening months of her ordeal, patient with her tantrums, generous with his time, affectionate in his refusal to allow her the pleasure of self-pity. Literally and figuratively he had held her hand every feeble step to recovery, but had been equally ready to twist her wrist at the first sign of surrender.

Now it was she who must be the stabilizing force in his pendulum swings between rage and guilt. Assuming that the suicide had been inevitable, Mona took some comfort in the fact that she was with Bill when he discovered it and remained with him throughout the ordeal of police, ambulance, morgue, autopsy, and the cremation Richard had frequently mentioned during episodes of depression.

That first terrible night, Mona insisted on taking him home with her. 'You can't stay alone in that apartment. You can sleep in Melissa's room. She can bunk with me.' His zombie acquiescence made her feel protective and strong. In the taxi uptown, he collapsed against her in abject exhaustion. She soothed his hair, as she had her children's when they were bereft.

'I'm so sorry, Bill. So sorry, darling.'

'He didn't have to do it. The new medication was working. The doctor said so.'

A fine fury rose in her. 'Those bastards in Washington! They can put a man on the moon, but they can't spend the money on AIDS!'

'AIDS?' He sat up and took her by the shoulders, swinging her around to face him. 'You're just like the rest! Why do you automatically assume he had AIDS? Just because Richard was gay? What if he was straight? Like, what if he was your friend Nick Albert or that ex-husband of yours? What if *they* jumped out the window, would you think, "Poor things, they must have AIDS. That's why they jumped"?'

She was mortified. Prejudiced while believing she didn't have a prejudiced bone in her body, AIDS had indeed been her conclusion. 'I'm sorry, Bill. I'm so sorry. You're right. Forgive me. Please . . .'

He slumped against his corner of the back seat and closed his eyes. 'Forgive *me*. I know you're not into gay-bashing; you've been to enough fund-raisers with me. It's just that Richard had a bad enough time without people thinking he had AIDS, too.'

He had met the handsome young set designer the week he arrived in New York from London. They had been together ever since, happily for years until Richard was stricken with fits of depression. Therapy and medication would help for a while. But then he would retrogress into a near comatose black gloom. To make matters worse, he suffered increasingly from agoraphobia, too terrified to leave the apartment even when it meant canceling appointments with doctor and therapist.

Ironically, Bill had just found a therapist who would come to the apartment. 'It was starting to help. He was definitely coming out of it. Only yesterday he told me he wanted to start seeing people. "Mona," he said. He prayed for you, you know. He loved hearing about the early days in London. He loved it when we watched the telly and one of your commercials came on and I said you were the talking muffin.'

'Or the talking toilet!'

'He was a little jealous of you, you know. "Mona this, Mona that!" '

'Oh, Bill. It's all my fault!'

He was instantly contrite. 'Don't be a bloody fool. Of course not. I didn't mean that. No. In fact he asked me repeatedly to invite you over. The first visitor in five years. The therapist warned me it was too soon. I should have listened but Richard was so happy, so full of plans for having tea on the terrace. I couldn't let him down, could I?'

'Of course you couldn't.'

'And then . . . when I rang up to say, "Put the kettle on, we're on our way," he sounded so up. So ready. I shouldn't have let him talk me into it. He *wasn't* ready.'

In the weeks that followed, helping Bill helped Mona to help herself. For each of them, individually and in their manager-client relationship, work was the Great Healer. Bill's days began with seven A.M. power breakfasts at the Regency or the Sherry Netherland, and continued at breakneck speed through meetings with casting directors, TV packagers, film agents, and Broadway producers. It became routine for him to dine with Mona and children at the apartment. He and she discussed the day's events – even when they'd spent part of the day together. His casual offers to help the children with their homework soon became part of the routine. Afterwards, he might have some further business commitments. More often he and Mona settled down for a quiet evening of television, all cosy and nice.

Just like an old married couple or what she had always thought an old married couple should be, comfortable and considerate. No sniping. No sarcasm. No punishing silences. Her marriage to Brent hadn't lasted long enough to find out if that's what ultimately evolves. Bill preferred not to talk about Richard. As the months went by, it felt to Mona as if she and Bill had been together for years.

Not totally together, she reminded herself. There was still the small matter of sex. For the time being she could live without it. For the time being, she was happier without it. For the time being, Bill's affectionate presence was all she needed or wanted. The bungled nose job and the months of recovery made her protective of her body, her face in particular. Put simply, she was afraid of banging her nose. In careening cabs she held her hand up to her face, ready to cup it over her nose in case of a collision. There was no way she could make love with this fear of her nose falling off. She could just see herself in the throes of passion shrieking, 'Watch out for my nose!'

But Nature provides. Her sexometer registered warm and cozy, not hot and crazed as it had that last night with Nick Albert. For the time being she was comfortable with the status quo, a sturdy foundation for building the next stage of her life.

As Dr. Minkow had predicted, her nose slowly settled into a reasonably acceptable shape – nothing to arouse jealousy in Candice Bergen or Michelle Pfeiffer, but passable. Cancel the sour cream: the blintz was gone. Reluctantly she agreed to forget about further plastic surgery. She was convinced the risk was too great, the potential gain too minimal. She could never go through that torture again. To make sure she was never tempted to change her mind, she dug out the illustrated booklet that had helped her quit smoking. The photograph in horrendous color of a woman whose nose had been eaten away by cancer would be all she would ever need as a reminder to leave well enough alone.

When she bought the camcorder to tape Greg's birthday party, Bill said, 'Why didn't we think of this before?'

Still an actor and director at heart, he spent the next weeks taping Mona in a variety of hairstyles, makeup, and wardrobe, indoors and out, on the busy Manhattan streets and in Central Park. One day they rode the Staten Island ferry, where he taped her on the top deck, her hair flying in the wind, the Statue of Liberty in the background.

Later, at Bill's office, he said, 'This is a military operation. We're going to review these tapes as if the Mona you see is a stranger. We're going to study her from every angle until we figure out exactly how to package her for on-camera.'

'I can't look!' She turned her back, trembling with emotion as she flashed back to her early days in television, when audition tapes had been a nightmare of embarrassed casting directors praising her voice while blaming her visual inadequacy on harsh lighting or the wrong makeup. Professionally she had pretended it didn't matter, the luck of the draw and thank God for her voice, there were millions of starving actresses, right?

Even though it was just the two of them alone in Bill's office conference room, she couldn't bear the humiliation of seeing herself on tape and knowing how disappointed he was going to be.

He swung her around and gripped her shoulders, as he had that day in the cab when she'd thought Richard had killed himself because he had AIDS. There was no affection in Bill's eyes. 'This cuts it, Mona! I've spent weeks taping you, and now you're behaving like a spoilt brat! If you can't work with me to make you marketable, then –'

'*Marketable?* What am I, a product?'

'Yes – exactly! You are a product.'

'Damn you to hell! I'm an actress!'

'Sure you are, Miss Redgrave darling. I've seen every one of your films!'

'Bastard! I'll quit the business! I'll get a job in Bloomingdale's!'

'They wouldn't hire you. You can't add.'

'I can't stand another minute of this!'

'Yes, you can! You *must*! And if you don't, I'm dropping you! You can jolly well find yourself another manager!'

'You're making a bundle off my commercials, aren't you?'

'You can take your bundle somewhere else!'

Last night they had rented *The Man Who Came To Dinner*, with Monty Woolley as Sheridan Whiteside. To demonstrate her change of heart and effect the reconciliation, she stroked an imaginary Monty Woolley beard and intoned his famous line, 'I may vomit.'

'Good girl! It's going to be all right. You'll see.' He turned on the tape. 'I'm going to make you a star.'

After the initial shock of seeing her face fill the screen in closeup, she was able to look at herself dispassionately. The straight black hair she had endured so many chemical treatments to achieve was all wrong. The bouncy wig that resembled her own naturally curly hair looked best.

'You see, love? You can forget about that hair-straightening lark. I know you secretly want to look like Jane Seymour, with her straight hair down to her ass, but you don't.'

'I know I don't,' she said regretfully.

'Idiot! What I mean is, you look like Mona Davidson. You look like *you*, your own person! Trust me. You'll see I'm right.'

It turned out he *was* right. Her natural hair gave surprising definition to her eyes and magically minimized her nose. A darker, more apricot foundation, a brighter, more cranberry lip color enhanced her cheekbones and jawline.

'Apricot and cranberry? I feel like a fruit salad.'

He nibbled her fingers. 'You look absolutely edible.'

'I'll try not to let you down.'

'You won't.'

She didn't. With Bill Neal choreographing her every step of the way, Mona danced confidently into a rewarding new phase of her career, where one break led to another and another and another and suddenly, she was hot. She emerged from the voice-over to the on-camera face in a series of low-fat salad dressing commercials in which she played several different women demanding to know the secret formula.

From there she played 'your average traveler' looking for a vacation to make her feel more than average, a billionaire business executive forced to cook dinner when her household staff quit, and the mother of the bride trying to keep the silver wedding gifts for herself.

By the following year, Bill's adroit handling had landed her small but juicy roles on popular television dramas. A deranged Mrs. Danvers-type psychopath straight out of *Rebecca* on *Murder, She Wrote,* a nymphomaniacal widow on *L.A. Law,* and Dr. Fleishman's Save the Seals activist cousin from Brooklyn, who disappears from her Alaskan cruise ship in order to drop in on *Northern Exposure.*

Before each appearance Bill had her write personal notes to the top critics, asking them to watch. He hired the most prestigious publicity agency, with offices on both coasts and several places in between, to plant items and suggest interviews.

The children basked in her growing celebrity. Fellow students saw her on TV and requested her autograph. The children's marks improved, and they were more affectionate and obedient than she had ever thought possible. When Amy phoned from Washington to congratulate her, she said she had news of her own. Lou was moving them all to Gainesville, Florida, as head of a brand-new department at the university. She didn't sound all that happy.

'What's wrong, Amy? Tell me. I'm your friend, remember?'

'It's nothing. Just having to pack up everything, sell the house. I feel like an Army wife.'

'I thought you loved Georgetown.'

'I do love Georgetown.'

'And getting involved with the cultural life, right? Whatever happened with your house tour? The "Jackie tour," wasn't it? How did it go?'

'Fine, I guess.' Her voice sounded as if it were coming from her shoes.

'Why do you "guess"? Something's bugging you, Amy. For God's sake, tell me.'

'Lou said the whole thing was ridiculous, a bunch of stupid women taking other stupid women on a tour of rich people's homes in order to raise money for people who have no homes at all.'

Lou Humphries was a pompous asshole. Georgina had said exactly the same thing after the Humphries' visit to London. Georgina had phoned Mona to say hello and confide her worries about Amy. 'She's a scared rabbit. The man calls the tune and she jumps. She's still the sweetest human being in the entire world,

Mona. But she's beaten down. She's lost interest in her appearance. She let her hair go gray, but I fixed that. I hustled her and that Lolita daughter of hers over to Sassoon's.

'Two hours later? A sensational blonde. The way she looked when we first met! That pig of a husband never even noticed. She gave me her word that she would keep it up. And, oh, yes. Must have forgotten to tell you. Guess who she ran into in the South of France?'

Mona knew who it was from the tone of Georgina's voice, the flippancy masking the old tender wound named Nick Albert. 'I can't imagine. Who?'

'Nick Albert and his lady wife!'

'Holy shit. *That's* a name from the past. How is he, anyhow?'

'Can't really say. She sent me a postcard from Monaco, and that's all it said. That they'd run into Nick and Roxanne.'

'Ah, well . . .' Mona brushed the news aside as if of only marginal interest. Over a year had elapsed since her last meeting with Nick, the night before her ill-fated nose job. Bill had subsequently told her of Nick's frequent phone calls while she was in danger, and of his relief at being told everything was going to be fine. She had not heard from him since and had decided she no longer cared.

'What did you think of Sandi?'

'A little shocker, that one. I don't envy Amy.'

Neither did Mona. Nor could she bring herself to speak frankly with her old friend. She had never told Amy all that had happened the weekend Sandi came to New York. Sneaking out of the apartment in the middle of the night had been bad enough. She could have been mugged, raped, or killed for the clothes on her back. What Mona had elected to ignore was the effect on her own daughter of what Sandi had told her about oral sex. Melissa was so upset she refused to attend dances, or come to the phone when any of the boys from school called. Only recently, over hamburgers and chili at Clarke's, just the two of them, had Mona been able to cajole her into talking about it. The discussion seemed to lift a great weight off her daughter's shoulders. 'Will I have to do that when I get married?'

'Not if you don't want to,' Mona assured her.

'Is that why you dumped Daddy?'

She chose to avoid the subject for now. Melissa was still too young. 'I didn't dump Daddy. It was a mutual decision to split.'

'That's not what he says. He says you got too big for your britches and started to make tons of money and that's why you gave him the old heave-ho, so you wouldn't have to give him any, and that's why you're living with your fag manager.'

'Melissa! How dare you use that word about Bill.'

'I didn't say it. Dad said it. I'm just telling you what Dad said. I love Bill.'

'So do I.'

On balance, Mona had never been happier. She thought about last Saturday night with amusement, serious amusement. The kids had been out. She and Bill had ordered enough Japanese take-out to feed the emperor and his entire family. Miso soup, assorted tempura, pork shogayaki, negihamachi rolls, and a quart of chocolate and vanilla hard ice cream from Carvel.

Bill had heard rumors of a remake of *Casablanca*, and rented a videotape of the original classic. 'I want to see it again before I put you up for the part.'

'What part? Rick?' He couldn't be thinking of Ilsa. Ingrid Bergman would rise from her grave and make Swedish meatballs out of her.

'If you insist on denigrating yourself, let's drop the whole subject.'

'Right, as usual. I'm sorry. You really think I could play Miss Ilsa?'

'Not an Ingrid Bergman Miss Ilsa. A more up-to-date Ilsa. An American woman trapped in Paris by the Nazi juggernaut. A woman with an unsavory past, as tough or even tougher than Rick until . . . ta-ta!'

'Until she falls in love with him, right?'

'That's what the producer says.'

'But who needs me? Why wouldn't they hire a major name?'

'Because my sweet, the Rick story is the focal point. They're paying major megabucks for Rick, a Michael Douglas, a Harrison Ford, somebody like that, so that means the Ilsa part has to come in bottom-line cheap.'

'Cheap? That's me, kiddo.' She swung an imaginary handbag, streetwalker style. 'Everyone says it. Mona Davidson is cheap.'

As was their TV-watching custom, they piled large fat pillows on Mona's king-size bed and relaxed against them pasha-style with the containers of food between them. Mona cried, as always, at Rick's speech when he sends Ilsa away with Paul Henreid. Turning to Bill, she saw that he had fallen asleep.

Poor baby, he was exhausted. She gently removed the tray and dimmed the lights. Let him sleep for a while. Looking at him, a wave of tenderness rolled over her. She lay down beside him with her back against him. As sleep engulfed her she thought about how compatible they were, how deeply involved in each other's lives and careers, partners in the best sense of the word.

Not a bad arrangement except for sex. *Love Without Sex,* a new kind of relationship starring Mona Davidson and William Neal. She wondered if all the medication of the past two years had deadened her libido. As a test she turned her memory dial to Nick Albert, replaying her inner tape of their more erotic moments. She was half-disappointed and half-relieved to discover that thoughts of him no longer caused so much as a tingle.

The last thing she felt was Bill turning over and fitting himself to her, spoon-style. Nice. That was how Melissa found them the next morning, when she waltzed into Mona's bedroom with the Sunday papers – two fully grown adults, fully clothed, sleeping like babes in the woods.

Was Melissa Brent's source for his nasty remarks? Mona knew her daughter. There wasn't a mean bone in her body. But she was still a little chatterbox, and when she had met her father last Sunday afternoon, she probably spilled the beans without meaning to. Not that Mona gave a damn what Brent thought or said. She and Bill had a good thing going, such a good thing that she planned to seriously think about their future together while he was in Australia.

He had not been back home for years, not since he had left Melbourne to become an actor in London. His father had died, his mother was ill. Apart from family matters, there were production possibilities he wanted to explore, since financing was available for Australian producers. He was Australian right enough. There was no reason he couldn't become a producer, too.

During the six weeks he was gone, she thought long and hard about their future and the possibilities for a companionate marriage. Richard was Bill's one true love. He had vowed never to take another lover ever again. Show business was full of marriages between heterosexual actresses and gay or bisexual men. They worked professionally and socially with mutual affection and respect for each other's privacy. The recent disclosure that Laurence Olivier and Danny Kaye had been lovers came as a shock but no surprise, Bill said.

When, on the very night before Bill's return, Nick Albert phoned wanting *desperately* to see her, she had not the slightest desire to see him. His voice over the phone, and the body that went with it, no longer made her hot or even lukewarm. What's more, she wanted to avoid any chance of his muddying the waters. Tomorrow night she planned to welcome Bill Neal home with a proposal that they formalize their relationship by getting married.

Once upon a time, the fact that Nick was in Washington and wanted to buzz up to New York to take her to dinner would have excited her. Not now. Not after two years. She was not the same old Mona. She was the new improved Mona, with no time for fun and games. Impatient to see Bill, she decided to meet his plane with a hired limo.

'Bill! Over here!'

'Mona darling! How kind!' Close behind him was a stocky young man wearing an Anzac hat and carrying a guitar. 'Come and meet James! I've persuaded him to stay with me for the next hundred and fifty years!'

On the drive back to Manhattan, Bill had further good news. A syndicate of Australian and American impresarios was developing a chain of dinner theaters in major areas of Australia and the United States. The idea was to package touring companies in famous plays with a single set and small cast.

'They've asked me to do *Streetcar* off-Broadway, and once it's a hit bring it straight to Australia. And do you know who's going to play Blanche?'

Seated between Bill and his new love, sipping the iced champagne with which she had planned to toast her forthcoming marriage, Mona could but barely comprehend his triumphant, 'Mona Davidson!'

As she was dropping him and James off in Greenwich Village, Bill said, 'I almost forgot. We're having dinner tonight with one of the backers. An American called Sidney something or other. We'll pick you up in a hour, love.' He sent a coy glance toward James. 'Doesn't give us much time. Wear something black and sassy, Mona darling. This Sidney bloke, he's loaded.'

The limo was inching into the traffic when Bill pounded on the window. She pressed the button to roll it down. 'Yes, Bill?' *Please,*

God, don't let him ask me what I think of his new lover.

'Mona, love. I just want you to know how smashing you look. Trust me, your Blanche Dubois is going to take New York – the world – by storm.'

24

Amy

Gainesville, Florida, 1988

She got up earlier than usual so as to give herself plenty of time for her preparations. After only six months in Gainesville, she had found a slew of new friends among the University of Florida wives. Having been asked to join the Literacy Group, today was her turn to have the chairperson and the other six members to lunch.

Nothing fancy, they had insisted. *Why do women always say that?* Just a ham sandwich and an iced tea. She could just see their faces if she were to take them seriously. The question was, how to show off without showing off? When was 'nothing fancy' an insult? To make matters worse, she didn't know who was a vegetarian, who didn't eat salt or sugar or milk or butter or cheese. Or who preferred decaf or herb tea or mineral waters carbonated or flat.

For her own part, her all-time favorite lunch was tuna salad made with chopped onion, celery, and plenty of Hellman's mayo, real not light, on whole wheat toast with a side of cole slaw and a chocolate malted with two scoops of coffee ice cream.

As a way of solving her problem, she decided to serve salad bar-style, with a choice of things attractively presented on platters. Tuna salad. Egg salad. A spicy cold pasta. Two green salads, Boston lettuce and Belgian endive, with a choice of dressings. Guacamole she'd made the night before. Sliced tomatoes. A basket of bread and rolls she would pick up fresh in the mid-morning. A melange of fresh fruits, cut and arranged on crushed ice just before her guests arrived. Hot and cold drinks of every denomination. And some homemade brownies they could take or leave alone. It was up to them.

She missed her Georgetown group. Despite Lou's sneers, the Jackie Tour had been a huge success and had been repeated since she'd left. She hoped her involvement with literacy would prove just as rewarding and lead to new friendships. She had tried to involve Sandi.

'Forget it, Mom.' Her daughter was too busy with graduation and planning her summer before starting college in the fall. Amy idly wondered why Sandi hadn't staggered into the kitchen as she usually did, her eyes sealed shut with unfinished sleep, groping her way to the refrigerator like a desert rat in an old Western movie and gulping down half a container of OJ without taking a breath.

She must be worn out from all the parties, the prom, the barbecue that lasted till dawn, and all the emotional good-byes, Amy decided. You'd have thought Sandi had lived in Gainesville all her life. After this short time at school she knew everybody, went everywhere, and was voted Most Popular Girl in the senior class.

At the sound of Lou's footsteps, Amy poured his juice and switched on the coffee. He liked his OJ ice-cold and his coffee fresh and strong. 'Morning, dear!'

'You've done it again.'

Done what? Put the toilet roll in upside down? *Control yourself.* 'What's wrong, dear?' Humour the man. He was upset because his hairline was receding. According to an article she'd read, a wife is supposed to show great understanding when a husband begins to go bald.

'Sandi!'

'She's sleeping, dear. No more classes, remember?'

He addressed her in loud, slowly articulated words, as if she were deaf. '*She-is-not-sleep-ing! She-is-gone! Her-bed-has-not-been-slept-in!*'

'What are you getting so excited about? She's probably at one of her girlfriends.'

He thrust a note at her. 'Your daughter has eloped!'

Her daughter? What had happened to *his* daughter? *Their* daughter?

'You're right as usual, Lou. Sandi has eloped.' She felt as matter-of-fact as she sounded. Sandi was bright and pretty and had a mind of her own. Nobody was going to stop her from doing exactly what she wanted to do. Amy had realized this about her daughter starting at about age twelve. She had talked herself into believing that Sandi could take care of herself. To protect herself against pregnancy and sexually transmitted disease, she was using both the Pill and condoms! Or at least that's what she told her mother. Amy had no way of knowing if it was the truth or adolescent boasting.

Lou waved Sandi's note in Amy's face. 'She doesn't say who she eloped with! Don't you know? What kind of mother are you?' Her husband approached the tiled counter where she was beginning her preparations for lunch. 'What the hell is all this?' He slapped at the assembled foodstuffs with the back of his hand.

'I told you last night. My literacy committee is coming to lunch.'

'Wine, too, I suppose! What's got into you lately? You think we're made of money?'

Not *we*, she. *She* was the one with the money, a subject he talked about more and more as her fortieth birthday loomed on the not-too-distant horizon. 'I thought we were talking about Sandi. Do you want me to call the police?'

'Are you nuts? Have the police swarming all over the place? What would people think?'

She poured herself a cup of extra-strong coffee and dunked one of her double-chocolate brownies into it. 'They'd think we were concerned about the whereabouts of our daughter.'

'Are you nuts? We know where she is! She eloped with some guy!'

'All right, then. We'll just wait until we hear from her.'

'It's all your fault, Amy!'

She had wondered when he would get around to that. 'You mean St. Augustine, of course.'

Three weekends ago, she and two of the faculty wives had driven to the historic town, the oldest Spanish settlement in North America. She had accepted the invitation only because Sandi and some of her friends were going to a rock concert in Jacksonville and Lou was running a weekend seminar. That Sandi and her friends were stranded in Jacksonville when their car broke down was, as usual, Amy's fault, by her husband's logic.

'You should have been home to answer the phone!' he stormed.

'Sandi managed just fine,' she had reminded him on her return from St. Augustine. Sandi had used her mother's credit card often enough to remember the number, and she convinced the nice man at the garage to let her charge the necessary repairs.

'You'll let me know the minute you hear anything.'

'Of course.'

He surveyed the kitchen. 'You're not going ahead with this luncheon, are you?'

'Why not? You're going ahead with your classes, aren't you? What would be the point of canceling? Besides, it may come as a surprise, but I *can* serve lunch and answer the phone at the same time!'

'What's got into you, Amy? You've been acting funny for weeks!'

Not weeks. Months. Having Nick Albert make love to her showed her precisely what had been missing from her marriage. Clearly her daughter knew more about sex than she did. Or had, until Nick's sudden appearance in Washington. Sandi wore her philosophy of life on her chest; her favorite T-shirt said USE IT OR YOU'LL LOSE IT! Sandi seemed to have been born knowing how to take care of herself.

With respect to her own sexual education, Amy was a Special Ed student in need of one-on-one remedial instruction. Nick Albert had proved to be an inspired teacher, she an apt and responsive pupil.

'How super to see you, Baby Bird. How divine of you to let me call!' He was really something. The black turtleneck and white linen pants that might have looked plain on others looked magazine-cover sensational on him. Pausing for effect in the doorway, he teased, 'Are you going to ask me in?'

He kissed the tip of his index finger and touched it to the tip of her nose, the old and cherished gesture. 'Little one.'

Neither flinching nor retreating, she stood her ground. 'I am not your little one. I'm a married woman with a grown daughter, in case you haven't noticed.'

'I've noticed.'

'My daughter –'

'I noticed you, as you damn well know, that day in St. Paul. Why do you I think we left Monte Carlo so early that morning? I couldn't trust myself to be good.'

He was lying through his teeth. Or was it flirting? She didn't know how to flirt. She didn't have the instinct for it like Sandi. Sandi had known how to flirt from the cradle. Amy tried to respond in kind. 'And now you *can* trust yourself?'

'Touché. Baby bird has grown up.' He poured champagne for each of them. 'Magnificently, I might add. I hope your husband appreciates you.'

'I'll have to ask him when he gets back.'

'And when will that be?'
'Sometime late tomorrow. And when do Roxanne and her father return from Virginia?'
'Sometime late tomorrow.'
The gift of fate was hers to accept or reject. The fantasy was all very well. Making it reality would be up to her.
'Well, then, we'll have plenty of time.'
He did not rush her. 'Plenty of time . . .'
'Would you like to take a walk? Georgetown reminds me of Chelsea.'
Secure in the knowledge that they did have plenty of time, they strolled hand-in-hand through the Saturday streets. She told him about the Jackie Tour, and showed him the various houses the group would visit. 'Clever girl. Tell me more.'
Soon they were walking with their arms around each other's waists, as she had seen lovers walk in Paris and along the Croisette in Nice. She felt joined at the hip to him. She felt his hand slip from her shoulder to the spot under her arm, where his fingers touched the tender side of her breast. She yearned to stop and hurl herself into his arms, to kiss him full on the lips right there on the Georgetown street in broad daylight. But she was beginning to understand the nuances of seduction and the excitement of suspense.
Back at the house Nick asked, 'Tell me, quite seriously, is there anything you've always wanted to do but never have?'
'You mean like shoplifting?' Sandi stole eye makeup from department stores, on the theory that they were crooks to ask eight dollars for a stupid eyebrow pencil. Her anger with her daughter was mixed with a certain subliminal envy. Even as a teenager she had never had the nerve to steal anything. She prayed to heaven Sandi would grow out of it before she got caught.
He put his arms around her, his face almost touching hers. 'You know I don't mean shoplifting. I mean something wild or silly, something that would surprise Lou.'
'Well . . .' She could feel herself blushing and tried to break free.
'Tell me!'
'You'll laugh.'
The long-delayed kiss enveloped her, the hours of talking and walking and sipping champagne ending at last in a quiet implosion.
'Tell me,' he whispered.

She'd seen it in movies, people taking a shower with their clothes on, and had thought it a bad example for the audience. Her New England frugality always reminded her that clothes were expensive, shoes especially. It was as wrong as jumping in swimming pools at jet set parties. The idea was so reckless, yet so enticing.

This was her day to be reckless. Nick listened and roared with delight. He took her by one hand and snagged the bottle of champagne with the other and danced them up the stairs. Although the bathroom was old, with art deco tiles, the enclosed shower was new, installed by Amy as a birthday present for Lou.

'In you go, miss.' The water was hot and steamy, gushing from the top and from the customized spigots at varying heights on three sides of the enclosure.

'My watch!' She grappled with the strap.

'Who cares!'

His arms tight around her, he pulled her under the shower with him, watch and all.

'Nick!' she shrieked as the water cascaded through her hair and over her face, drenching them both. 'Your clothes! You'll wreck your clothes!'

'Who cares!'

The pounding water pasted the thin cotton of her shirt and jeans to her skin like papier-mâché. She could feel every pore in her body, as if she were naked, and every part of Nick through his clothes, as they wrestled for dominance in the maelstrom of water battering them from all sides.

'No!'

'Yes.'

He stripped off her shirt and kissed her breasts.

'I'll fix you!' With a strength she hadn't known she possessed, she raked his turtleneck up and over his chest and head and hurled it over the shower door, not caring where it landed. They finished undressing each other in the spirit of combat, which changed to one of tender exultation as they washed each other with infinite care.

'Darling heart.' He was all around her, before her, behind her, beneath her, until at last he adjusted the shower head so that it emitted only a gentle, tepid spray. 'Spring rain,' he said, as he backed her tenderly into a corner of the stall and they finished what they had begun so many years ago in Chelsea.

Later he wrapped her in Lou's terrycloth robe, another birthday gift, and carried her to the bed. It seemed natural to have this naked man in her bedroom. Lou didn't approve of unnecessary nudity, even between married couples. *Screw Lou.*

Nick Albert was removing the bathrobe and arranging her naked body on the Williamsburg quilt she had bought on her tenth wedding anniversary. The blinds closed, the lights soft, she thought of Goya's *Duchess of Alba*. She and Lou had seen both paintings at the Prado, the fully clothed and the naked maja.

'Let me look at you.' That was Nick's secret. He loved women, and let them know it. Women recognized this intuitively. They wanted more from him than he could give, things like honesty and responsibility, when what he had to give was rarer than both.

He placed first one pillow then another under her and around her, pausing between each to assess the affect until he was satisfied. 'Shall I recite Eliot?'

'The Love Song of J. Alfred Prufrock' poured from his lips, unbearably sad yet powerful in its rage and loss. His hands caressed her into a strange other dimension of suspended sensibility. Her flesh a totally new country of desire. 'I have measured out my life with coffee spoons' made her tremble with compassion. 'I have seen the moment of my greatness flicker' explained so much. And when he knelt at her feet and trailed his fingers up her legs, her thighs parted in welcoming reply to his anguished 'Do I dare to eat a peach?'

By the time her husband and daughter returned it was well past Sunday midnight. Alone in the house since early evening, she had carefully removed all possible traces of her visitor. Lou had said they might be late and not to wait up. At eleven she had gotten into bed with her Jackie Tour notes. But she couldn't concentrate. She couldn't sleep. What if Lou noticed the fresh sheets on their bed. She never changed the linens on the weekend. What if he missed the old sneakers she had given Nick, because his shoes had still been wet and squeaky?

What of the unlikely possibility of her husband wanting to make love, a rare event in recent months? He would be sure to perceive some change. What, she wasn't sure, but she couldn't risk it. Her ingrained morality assailed her. She had committed adultery. Her husband and daughter, the core of her life, were on their way home, to her home, their home, the family home she had jeopardized by her wanton behavior.

Nick's departure seemed to have activated her conscience. It nagged at her like a hollow tooth. She had betrayed her principles and her marriage. She could not live with this burden on her conscience. She would have to tell Lou. Not the details; he probably wouldn't believe them anyway. But she would have to tell him about Nick's seduction.

When at last the wanderers returned, and Lou announced without so much as discussing it with her that they were moving to Gainesville, she changed her mind.

Was it her fault that Sandi had eloped? Maybe it was, but not for the reason Lou would have given. Her fault was cowardice. While other women her age chose freedom and took chances, she had chosen safety in what she thought would be the security of marriage and gave lip service to the problems of homelessness and illiteracy. Her fault lay in avoiding the experiences, the temptations, the adventures, and – oh, yes – the mistakes, the stupid, lamebrained mistakes that would have taught her truths about life and love she could have passed on to her daughter. She didn't delude herself that she and Sandi would have become bosom buddies. Teenage girls and mothers were natural enemies. But she could have told her about the time she'd gotten her first diaphragm at the Margaret Sanger clinic, and about trying to throw it away. It was her fault that she had not tried to establish some kind of a womanly connection with the little girl who was now a woman.

Amy's weekend with Nick Albert had left her, nearly two years later, with a profound sense of loss for past chances missed and an abiding hope for a future she was not yet ready to take on. If not for Nick Albert, she would never have known what she was missing or what heights and depths of passion she was capable of. If she was being honest, she was jealous of Sandi's ability to take off without a backward glance. Wherever she was, whoever she was with, Amy wished her daughter happiness.

The literacy committee loved her salad bar lunch idea. For a planned poetry reading, she volunteered to recite 'The Love Song of J. Alfred Prufrock.' Sandi did not call. After the committee had finally left, Amy cleared the table and straightened up the kitchen. Still no call. The running water, as usual, reminded her of Nick undressing her in the shower she had bought her husband for his birthday. Lou's call interrupted her reverie with a brusque, 'Any word?' and an equally rude disconnect when she said no.

She wondered what would happen if she were to tell him about her weekend with Nick Albert and announce that she had decided to go back to school to get her degree in architectural history. And that she wanted a divorce.

She spent the remainder of the afternoon reading John Betjeman's *Ghastly Good Taste*, about the rise and fall of English architecture, until it was time to start dinner. Because Lou was obviously worried sick about Sandi, she decided to prepare something really special.

25

Georgina

London, 1988

'Roberto!'

Georgina had returned unexpectedly to the house to find the Madrileno going through the drawers of the desk in the small private office behind her dressing room. He had not heard her because his Walkman was clogging his ears with one of the latest tapes and because the thick carpeting had absorbed her footsteps. Although the house was a mere skip and a hop across the mews from her business complex, she rarely went back until the end of the day.

This morning was an exception. She was meeting her bankers in the City, and had decided the jewelry she was wearing did not convey sufficient clout. With the City boys, she found she could intimidate them by dressing in one of two extremes. Once, when they had come to her at the mews, she'd had Dierdre usher them into her workout room. Togged out in a lemon yellow unitard with matching Reeboks, her red hair in a ponytail tied with a Hermès scarf, she had greeted them from atop her exercise bicycle, where she continued to pump away for the entire length of the conference. 'It keeps me fit, gentlemen. I'm sure you understand.'

Today she would be going to their territory to continue discussion of her expansion plans for the continent. Her idea was to open duty-free Junque Shops on both sides of the Channel and at the three Paris airports. In asking for three million pounds, she would need the self-confidence she always felt when she wore her emeralds. Her 'working emeralds' as one of the press girls had dubbed them in a recent Sunday feature. Not too gaudy, just small clip-on earrings, plus a leopard brooch on her lapel calculated to make the point that she meant business, important business.

Finding Roberto at home was as much of a surprise to her as it was to him. Their year together had evolved into a pleasant enough relationship. He suited her requirements for a lover and escort. He was brighter than his beauty and manner suggested. He spoke French and Italian as well as his native Spanish, his English had improved to the point of conversation, and he revealed an unexpected talent for merchandising and display.

To justify his weekly allowance, she had put him on the books as a consultant – a sticky situation, her accountant pointed out. Inland Revenue might use it as an excuse for auditing her entire operation. 'Put him to work. It doesn't matter how.'

The suggestion turned out to be inspired. She had put him into the Covent Garden branch. It was like leading a duck to water. The tourists, especially the women, adored him. He could flirt with them in four languages. Sales jumped accordingly. It amused her to think she might have stumbled onto something. Barbra Streisand's hairdresser had gone on to become a major film producer. Roberto might become a genuine asset in her plans for expansion worldwide.

He had of course asked her to marry him. Tempted for a time, a television biography of Queen Elizabeth I had changed her mind. The Virgin Queen never married because she knew it was impossible to share power. Either one had power or one didn't, it was as basic as that. She did however get Roberto a work permit.

'Roberto!' she repeated, yanking the earphones off his head. He jumped as if he'd been shot.

'Georgina!'

'What are you doing here? Why aren't you at Covent Garden where you belong?'

He was so stunned, he couldn't speak.

'What were you looking for? Don't I pay you enough? You won't find any jewelry or cash here. It's all in the safe. You know that. What's this?'

The crimson leather folder was the one prepared by her chartered accountants and marked FOR YOUR EYES ONLY. It was a comprehensive analysis of her company's holdings and structure, her debts, tax obligations, and projections for future earnings. It was privileged information. It named the names of investors and noteholders, and the amounts involved. It detailed the internal workings of her accounts systems, pointing out the weaknesses and vulnerabilities.

Nice Girls

If she were to expand throughout the new European Economic Community and to North America later on, she might want more than loans. She might want to 'go public' as one *Financial Times* pundit had suggested in print. While acclaiming her acumen, he had wittily pointed out the dangers of going public. Her Junque Shop Empire could be ambushed by Junk Bond raiders.

The contents of the crimson folder could be quite informative. 'Answer me, you swine! What are you doing with this? Who's paying you!'

Once a whore always a whore. Why was she surprised? He was for sale, wasn't he? She was paying for his services, wasn't she? The question was, who was paying more?

She got it out of him. She canceled her meeting, told Dierdre she was not to be disturbed, and then turned her considerable powers of intimidation on the man who had kissed her awake mere hours ago. 'If you don't tell me everything, and I mean *everything*, I'm ringing the police and charging you with robbery and assault – and anything else I can think of!'

It had all begun some weeks earlier. A young Frenchman had come into the shop in Covent Garden and spent over a thousand pounds. Georgina remembered hearing about that sale, a thousand pounds all in cash. In the camaraderie established by such gratifying circumstances, Henri invited Roberto to share a bottle of wine.

Several casual meetings had followed. Henri dropping by at lunchtime. Henri suggesting a place that served *tapas*. Henri saying his father was in London and had heard so much about Henri's new friend that he wanted to meet him.

'I should not have agreed!' Roberto broke into sobs. 'I thought he wanted to be my friend. Not many men want to be my friend. Can you understand that?'

In fact she never had thought of that, but as she pondered it now it made sense. Other men steered clear of gigolos. A cultural barrier separated them. Men couldn't brag about their conquests with someone who knew enough about sex to be kept in great style.

The man was a simpleton. 'Calm down, Roberto.' She poured brandies for them both. 'Tell me what happened next.'

Henri's father joined them one day, a superior old gentleman, *un grand seigneur*, and after many pleasantries, he sent Henri away. 'So Monsieur Le Baron and I could talk.'

The penny dropped. The Frog's father, the Baron D'Orsainville!

In a way, Georgina envied Roxanne. Her father would do anything for her. Apparently, abducting Nick hadn't been enough. Now, it appeared, he was out to destroy her company.

'What did he pay you?'

More tears. Nauseating.

'Tell me, or you'll rot in jail!'

'Five thousand pounds.'

'You'd sell me out for five thousand pounds?'

He threw himself at her feet. 'Please, *querida*!'

'Did you get the money?'

'Not yet,' he mumbled.

'None of it?'

'Not till I bring the documents.'

Stupider than she thought.

'Get up. Did he say *what* documents?'

'Important documents. Documents with lists of assets, with numbers, with names of banks. He asked me if I knew what a business plan is. He was not angry. He praised you, Georgina.'

'Oh, really? How very amusing.'

A grateful smile crossed Roberto's face. Sarcasm was lost on him. 'Yes. He said you are a brilliant businesswoman, and that the rumor in Paris is that you will be selling shares. He has much capital to invest, but he wants to be certain of your company so he will know how safe it is to invest when you go to the public.'

The Tampax box on the bottom shelf of her dressing room cupboard was where she kept cash, her reasoning being that no cat burglar would think to look there, especially if it were a man. Men were chary of tampons. She gave him ten fifty-pound notes. 'You will do exactly as I say. When do you meet him?'

'Tomorrow.'

'You will tell him the girls in the office are going mad, that Lady Georgina has them working like stink to prepare a very important . . . "document," he calls it? A very important *business plan* that she must present to her bankers and solicitors and other advisers next week. And you will have a copy for him as soon as it's ready.'

Roberto was bewildered. Some men should be kept barefoot and chained to the bed. 'You want me to give him the documents?'

No point in explaining her intentions. It was better that Roberto remain genuinely ignorant of her plan. She would doctor her figures, reprogram her computer printout, and write some phony

Nice Girls

letters of intent on Junque Shop letterhead. All of this was pure malice on her part. The Baron's financial power was global. She could only guess what complex machinations he could put into motion once it had been leaked to him that she planned to go public.

Her best recourse was to do nothing, say nothing, announce nothing. Her companies were owned solely and only by her, Lady Georgina Crane, Prop. Let the Baron make his nefarious plans to buy her shares and take over her companies. In due course, he would discover there was nothing for sale.

'Have you met the Baron's son-in-law?'

'Only his daughter. *Très chic.*'

'Her husband?'

'No. She telephoned him and demanded he join us for lunch.'

'And . . .?'

'She was very cross. She said she would see him at the flat!'

At least Nick had some honor. Or was it delicacy? He did not want to witness her lover's betrayal.

'The flat. Is it in London?'

'Eaton Square.'

This was too good to be true. 'I don't suppose you have the phone number?'

With any luck, Nick Albert would pick up. But as she was about to ring, a thought struck her. The parcel Nick had given her: Was it still inside the linen cupboard where she had hidden it?

'Roberto? Did the Baron or his daughter mention a package that I might have?'

While he shook his head in even deeper bewilderment, she held her breath and reached behind the sheets. It was there, the string still tied tightly around the brown paper. She picked up the phone and dialed.

'Nick? Is that you?'

She could hear him gasp against a background of voices speaking French.

'What number did you want?'

'Get over to Chelsea Mews on the double. I'll be waiting for you at the house.'

'Sorry, Madam. I'm afraid you have the wrong number.'

She sent Roberto back to work at the Covent Garden shop. 'Do exactly as I told you. If you do well, I shall put the next Junque Shop I open in your name.' If he believed that, he deserved to be disappointed. The five hundred pounds would take care of him until he found a new source of income. Perhaps Nick could introduce him to The Frog.

Suddenly ravenous for something sharp and cauterizing to appease her taste buds, she consumed most of a jar of Branston's pickles in the short time it took Nick Albert to get from Eaton Square to Chelsea Mews. He arrived in a taxi and emerged carrying a Lhaso apso wearing a diamond collar.

'Asprey's?' she asked. Nick Albert was far too rattled to appreciate the reference to their first meeting in Bond Street, or to see anything amusing in her remark.

'What is it, Georgina? I'm meant to be walking this bloody dog.'

'What do you mean, what is it? You're the one who dropped off the edge of the earth.'

'And you've been a patient Penelope waiting for me all this time? I know all about you and your Spanish toy boy.'

'It's not exactly a secret.'

He made an elaborate show of looking at his watch. 'You got me here. What's it all about?'

'Did you know your father-in-law is trying to ruin me?'

He smiled weakly. 'That sounds like a Victorian novel.'

'He has bribed Roberto to steal my private records so that when I go public, he can take over my company.'

'When did you find out?'

'This morning. Just before I rang you.'

'The lying bastard.' He shook his head slowly from side to side. 'He promised to leave you alone!'

'You discussed me with your wife's father.'

'Don't you understand? He threatened to have you killed!'

'That is not the least bit amusing.'

Tears filled his eyes. 'You're not hearing me. He's obsessed with her. Must I spell it out? *Physically*. He is *physically* obsessed with Roxanne.' He lowered his eyes, unable to meet hers as he added, 'And with me. He's obsessed with me as well.'

'What are you trying to tell me?'

'Bloody hell, Georgina! How thick can you be? The rumors are true! The Baron is my father! Roxanne is my half-sister! That's why we look so much alike! We *are* alike! We're the worst half of each other! And he's the worst of the lot!'

Any other woman might have fainted at such a confession.

Nice Girls

Georgina was not just another woman. 'When did you find this out? Or did you know it all along?'

He swore that he had not known the truth until the day before he'd turned up on her doorstep. His parents had met the D'Orsainvilles when his father was a foreign service officer stationed in Paris after the war. When Nick was two, his father was killed in a hunting accident. His mother stayed on in Paris for several years before returning to Devonshire. From earliest childhood, Nick had spent summers with the D'Orsainvilles, at their chateau on the Loire or on their yacht in the Mediterranean.

' "Two peas in a pod," they called us. Two naughty little peas in a pod. We loved each other, Georgina, with the wild passion of innocent children. Until one day, we discovered the Baron was watching us through a peephole! He sent me to my room, but he kept her with him and locked the door.

'She never told me what happened. Remember I was only eleven or twelve at the time. I chose to think he'd merely given her a severe scolding. Then he sent me packing, back to England, school, and that lot. I didn't see Roxanne again until that summer.'

'The summer you ruined my life?'

'You flatter me, Georgina.'

'You actually saved my life. If not for you I would never have taken in Mona and Amy, never become the world-famous Chelsea Junque Dealer. You left three broken hearts in Chelsea Mews.'

He took her hand. 'You're so contained, so in control of your emotions, Georgina! I know it's hard for you to understand what it's like to be caught up in a tornado of desire. Swept away in a whirlwind that came to earth here and there for food and drink . . . and money, of course, Roxanne's money, and then off again until –' He stopped short. 'Do you remember the film *The Red Shoes*?'

'Moira Shearer.'

'I felt like her. I felt that I was going to dance faster and faster and faster until I died.'

'And then?'

Then the nightmare existence really began. Roxanne told Nick about the day the Baron had found them as children, and that she and her father had been lovers ever since, and that furthermore she didn't see why their marriage should in any way interfere.

'Why didn't you leave?'

'By then? My God, Georgina, by then I was hooked!'

'The good life.'

'I mean *hooked!* The purest cocaine. The best brandies. And the sea. That's what really hooked me. Weeks at a time. Through the Mediterranean, the Greek Islands, Alexandria.' He closed his eyes to savor the memories. 'I abandoned myself totally to a life of the senses.'

There was one thing Georgina had to know. 'Were you ever in love with me?'

'I have always been in love with you.' He said it as simple fact, as if there could be no question of its truth.

'Then why didn't I hear from you?'

'You made it quite clear in Paris you never wanted to see me again. And I kept seeing your photograph with the Prime Minister and then your Spaniard.'

'What about the parcel you gave me to hold for you?'

His brow darkened. 'I was hoping you wouldn't mention it.'

'What do you mean?'

'Did you open it?'

'Of course not!'

'Get it. We'll open it together.'

Videotapes and photographs.

'I don't think I care to see them,' Georgina said.

'You've got to look at them. Then you'll understand the kind of life I've been living.'

'Are you in them?'

'No. Not these. I stole these to blackmail Roxanne into giving me a divorce. She laughed. She said she'd have a private screening.'

'Is the Baron in any of the tapes?'

'Not in these.'

'In others? Where are they?'

'Back at the flat.'

'Eaton Square? Perfect. Get them and bring them to me.'

A week later, under instructions from Georgina, Roberto arranged to meet the Baron at the Eaton Square flat. 'Tell him he must be alone.'

When the French aristocrat opened the door, Georgina said, 'I believe we met when Roxanne came to tea at Chelsea Mews. Where is the VCR?'

Instead of her 'working emeralds,' which were reserved for meetings with bankers, she wore the Duchess of Windsor pearls, for which she had outbid both the Princess of Wales and Elizabeth Taylor at auction. They gave her the necessary courage to lay out her proposition. Copies of the tapes were in a bank vault. If anything untoward happened to her, instructions had been given to release the tapes to the media.

In return for preserving both the privacy of his family life and the reputation of his family name, the Baron would arrange for a quiet divorce or annulment of Roxanne's marriage to Nick Albert. 'Whichever is most expedient.'

The Baron accepted defeat with grace, offering her a glass of wine to seal their agreement. 'Forgive me, if I wonder why a woman of your accomplishment should go to this extreme for a man of such poor character.'

She wondered, too.

26

Mona

New York, 1988

Esther Davitsky had a way with words. 'Are you *meschuggeneh*, Mona?'

The phone connection with Tel Aviv was disgustingly clear. Her mother might be nine thousand miles away driving the Israelis crazy, but she sounded as if she were home within physical nagging range.

'It's the opportunity I've been waiting for.' Why did she keep doing this to herself? There had been no reason to call Israel. She could have waited the month until Esther returned. That still would have left two months for arguments and artistic advice before the play opened.

'Some opportunity! An opportunity to be cremated by that Nazi critic! A Jewish girl from Brooklyn playing Blanche Dubois? You're asking for it, and you'll get it!'

'Mother dear, I'm an *actress*. An actress plays a part. Jessica Tandy played Blanche. She's English, Mom. Vivien Leigh? English! If they can play Blanche, I can play Blanche. Please don't give me an argument. I called to tell you the news. I thought you'd be proud of me.'

'Who says I'm not proud of you? I'm totally proud of you. Your father would be proud of you, too, may his soul rest in peace.' Talking to Esther was like teaching a pigeon to tap-dance.

'Okay, Mom. Gotta run. Don't take any wooden matzo balls.'

'Wait a minute. Talk to me. What happened to California? That part you were going to do? That big-shot manager of yours. I thought you were going to be a movie star.'

'I *am* going to be a movie star,' Mona said patiently. 'After *Streetcar*, after I show everyone what I can do.'

Claudia Crawford

'Off-off-Broadway? You're not a kid starting out, Mona. Who's going to drop everything and run over to Avenue D?'

'Bill's hiring buses for opening night.'

'So when are you two getting married? What's holding things up?' Another example of willful self-destruction: In one of those rare moments of mother-daughter devotion spent at the Lord & Taylor soup bar, she had confided her plan to join with Bill Neal as a theatrical couple, like the Lunts or Julie Andrews and Blake Edwards.

The night Bill returned from Australia with James, Mona wrote in her journal, 'Life is passing me by. Soon I will be left far behind. I am Emma Bovary when the coach speeds by without stopping. I am Scarlett O'Hara, looking at Rhett's back from the open doorway. I am Hester Prynne, with a terminal case of ring around the collar.

'I am Blanche Dubois, ever dependent on the kindness of strangers.'

The 'strangers,' in this case, were Bill's Australian money men and the American investor Sidney What's-His-Name. Bill's original grandiose plans for feature films had melted with the economy. The consortium was now committed only to backing the limited run of *Streetcar* in a theater the size of a rowboat, with a free option to tour throughout Asia and Australia and culminating in a video version for international syndication to be shot in the film studios they were building near Perth.

Unless they decided she wasn't pretty enough. Venus Envy was her problem, not Penis Envy. Women didn't want to be men; they wanted to be gorgeous. The only time she suffered from penis envy was when she was wearing tight jeans, was miles from anywhere, and desperately needed to pee.

At least one important benefit had come out of all the mess: Sidney What's-His-Name, with money to burn, a romantic desire to stand back-stage when the curtain rose on 'his' play, and hot eyes for Mona Davidson. For him it had been love at first sight. She could see it happening. Here was a man any mother would like: solid, substantial, a nice looking *boychik*, clean nails, boring shoes but polished and not rundown at the heels, shy smile, eager to please, ready to pick up tabs, hail cabs. Could this be the next Mr. Right? She reminded herself that she was also a mother. Since Bill's energies had been diverted elsewhere, there was no one to fix

Melissa's bike or empty Greg's aquarium or take them ice-skating at Rockefeller Center.

As for her personally, he watched and waited and was grateful for her smallest glance, an eager courtier alert to her majestic need for a tissue or a Milky Way. He seemed to regard her person as something sacred. Putting money in Bill's production gave him the right to call himself a producer, but he did not presume that this entitled him to the traditional gropes and tongue-in-the-ear kisses that were part of theatrical ritual. When she took his arm crossing the street, he guided her through traffic as if she were made of glass. When she allowed him to help her on with her coat, she could feel his warm breath on her neck but that was all, no darting little nips or nibbles.

The man was treating her with the reverence due to the star she wanted to be. Exciting he was not. Witty? He was entirely sincere when he said he bought *Playboy* and *Esquire* for the articles. As rehearsals began, she realized his idea of living dangerously was to order meat loaf in a coffee shop, a guarantee of instant food poisoning according to the Gospel of St. Sadie, a.k.a. his mom. Wherever they were, he called Sadie in Boca Raton every night.

The chief thing she had to guard against was his unique ability to exasperate her. The meat loaf routine, for example. If meat loaf was on the menu she knew she was in for it, that smug little naughty-boy expression when he asked the waiter, as he always did, 'Are you sure it's all right?'

The first day of blocking with the entire cast, they hit the Meat Loaf Trail at a coffee shop near the rehearsal studio. The meat loaf looked embalmed. Driven by demons, she moaned in ecstatic contentment. 'The best meat loaf I've ever tasted!' With the excuse of being too tense to eat, she forced her portion on him, heartily wishing him a lethal if not fatal attack of food poisoning.

Triumph quickly gave way to remorse. Throughout the rest of the day she watched him for signs of collapse. The man had a cast-iron stomach. 'Great meat loaf!' she overheard him commenting to Bill. 'Mona and I had it for lunch!'

Sidney embodied the worst aspects of fandom. His relentless adulation was starting to make her nuts. She couldn't discuss anything with him, the positives or negatives. Whatever she said was fine with him. He simply grinned lovingly; worse than lovingly, fatuously. If she burped, wonderful. If she farted, wonderful. If she told him to go fuck himself, which she did one afternoon when her patience bubble had burst, he grinned all the more broadly at her adorable vulgarity. 'Mona. Only you can get away with that.'

He was the extreme obverse of Brent, who disapproved of everything she did on principle, or lack of principle when she thought about it later. She had misinterpreted Brent's proprietary disapproval as concern for her well-being and future as an actress. At first he had been patient in his contempt for her clothes, hair, intelligence, talent, upbringing, and penchant for grape soda and vanilla ice cream in the middle of the night.

'Very low-class. Very ghetto.'

She sure knew how to pick them. Brent's asinine behavior with Greg and Melissa in Washington, leaving them alone in the motel while he took off with his Bimbo-of-the-Week, proved there was a screw loose somewhere.

As her early career in voice-overs took off, his scorn for her ambitions had grown in direct proportion to her earning power. 'Face it. You'll pull in the bucks, but you don't have what it takes to be a star.'

'That's not what you said when we met. You said I had real star quality.'

He had been the tall, craggy stranger, long legs, good hands, great teeth, seated beside her on the plane bringing her home from London, her poor heart in shreds because of Nick Albert, her career hopes high because of Bill Neal.

'I was trying to get into your pants.'

Which was exactly what he managed to do in the sweet darkness of night. Alone in a row of three seats, Brent had pushed up the arm rests and suggested they relax.

'You said I looked sad and needed a hug.'

'It worked, didn't it?'

'You said I glowed with a hard, gemlike flame.'

'Walter Pater. A guaranteed turn-on; worked every time, especially on girls with a liberal arts education.'

If the God of Love had abandoned her, the God of Success smiled, at least out of one side of his mouth. The peculiarity in her voice that Bill Neal had noted led miraculously to dozens of commercials for radio and television. In the exclusive world of voice-overs, Mona Davidson became the one to get. When finally she'd decided she was financially secure enough, Mona changed the locks and filed for divorce. Although she insisted she didn't need it or want it, her lawyer was equally insistent that she demand child support.

When it came to her kids, she had to admit she was damned lucky. Good kids, both of them. Good grades. Sweet dispositions. No drugs. No nutsiness, like poor old Amy's girl. It was hard to think of Amy as a grandmother. With typical New England reserve, Amy had accepted Sandi's elopement and subsequent pregnancy with aplomb. Whether she had suggested an abortion, Mona would never know. The next thing she knew she had received one of Amy's Save the Rain Forest greeting cards, with a photograph of a baby. 'Say hello to Dakota! Love, Grandma.'

In retrospect, Amy hadn't done so badly. She was the only one of The Three Mewsketeers who had an orderly life. The Professor was kind of cute. But she remembered how rotten he'd been on that day Sandi got lost in Riverside Park, blaming it on Amy when he'd been the one in charge of his daughter. 'Don't mind Lou, Mona. He was scared stiff,' Amy had apologized, the loyal, understanding wife.

'Sidney's good for you, Mona darling. Why don't you stop torturing him? Give him a chance.' Bill had finished going over his notes. He embraced her with the accumulated tenderness of all their years together. 'And, Mona . . .?'

'Yes, Bill.'

'Remember you are an actress. A fine actress. Make it your first priority.'

'Haven't I? You know I have.'

'Forget about the Nick Alberts of this world. Don't waste that precious energy on them. Give it to your craft. Your art in years to come. Your audience.'

That night she went back to Sidney's apartment. *Once more into the breeches, dear friends.* A widower for five years, his sexual experience was evidently limited. Yet he was willing. When she got tired of his fumbling, she told him exactly what she wanted him to do and how to do it. *The Schoolmarm in the Boudoir*, starring Mona Davidson and featuring Sidney, the Love Slave. He turned out to be one of those men who look better with their clothes off. He had been waiting all his life for a woman like her to take him in hand and teach him things. He thanked her passionately for loving him, and vowed eternal devotion.

'Bill says you can be one of the most important actresses of our times. I've got the money and the time to see that it happens.'

It was exactly what she needed to hear from the man who was exactly the right man for her at this stage of her life. To make Blanche her breakthrough role, she needed to be totally and utterly self-absorbed, to believe totally and utterly in her ability to make the transition from soaps and sitcoms and commercials to classical and contemporary drama. Richard Chamberlain was proof it could be done. Who'd have thunk Dr. Kildare would play *Hamlet* to the highest critical acclaim in England, the very country of Shakespeare! She would do it, too. Once Blanche knocked everyone's socks off, she would do Portia at Chichester and Celia Copplestone at the T.S. Eliot Festival and later, in a few years, Queen Gertrude incestuously grabbing her son's codpiece when he pays a condolence call. *Alas, poor Hamlet, I knew him well!*

It was all coming together. Her life was in order. Bill videotaped the rehearsals so that he and Sidney could review them with her each night. After a while she could look at the actress playing Blanche dispassionately and see her mistakes and how to correct them.

If only Grandpa Davitsky were alive to see her. How he would *kvell*! He would have been well into his nineties by now. He had died when she was five, but she remembered him standing her up on the dining room table to recite nursery rhymes with extravagant gestures. He would buy dried apricots and dates from Zabar's and they would nosh on them on his favorite bench on Riverside Drive while he repeated the familiar tales about his early days as the 'young Tomashefsky' of the Yiddish theater on the Lower East Side.

The immigrants' Lower East Side was now the gentrified East Village. The theater she'd be playing served carrot cake and cappuccino. Instead of playing a Yiddische Momma with ungrateful children or a hoydenish *kurveh* doomed to suffer for her sins, she was to be the seminal tragic heroine of twentieth-century drama.

Wardrobe was going to be the challenge. Sidney told her to spend whatever she needed, which was beside the point. The garments that would spill out of Blanche Dubois' shabby trunk had to be poignant in their faded pretensions of grandeur. In a thrift shop, she found a white peplum suit and a fluffy organdy blouse that were exactly what Tennessee described for Blanche's arrival at the Elysian Fields. The peplum did something terrific for her tush, if she did say so herself. Plastic pearls and earrings from Lamston's, a white straw hat festooned with red cherries from Thirty-eighth Street, white ankle-strap platform shoes, and she was ready for her first entrance.

Living as she was as the central figure in her own universe, the invitation to Georgina's wedding came as a body blow that sent her reeling. She had successfully exorcized Nick Albert from her consciousness and replaced him with Sidney, focusing on what pleased her and sublimating the rest. She liked the way he massaged her neck until she fell asleep, and his willingness to run out to the Carnegie Deli at any hour of the night in any kind of weather for sliced turkey sandwiches on thin seeded rye with double cole slaw and Russian dressing.

The trouble was, he was no Nick Albert. No man was, or ever would be. The thought of Georgina snagging him after all these years filled her with sickening envy, and brought back memories she thought she had purged forever. Of course she wouldn't go to the wedding. Why be an extra in someone else's movie? She had more important things to do. She was glad Amy felt the same way. Her voice on the phone had sounded tremulous. Poor kid. She'd been the baby of the group. Her crush on Nick had stuck out all over. They agreed between them that Georgina had one hell of a nerve asking them to be attendants, and offering to pay their air fares as if they were poor relations. They further agreed they would send formal regrets and appropriate gifts.

That same afternoon, when she rehearsed the big rape/seduction at the end of Scene 10, she couldn't help herself. She thought of Nick. As Stanley carried Blanche to the bed and snarled, 'We've had this date with each other from the beginning,' Mona's repressed sexual rage exploded in a frenzy of savage conflict, ending abruptly in the abject submission of the conquered.

Those watching gasped. Bill Neal yelled, 'Curtain! Good work, children.' Mona and the actor playing Stanley Kowalski lay battered and bruised, his mouth bleeding where she had bitten him. She dabbed it with a tissue. 'Sorry about that.'

This was his first experience in a stage play. 'If this is what happens in rehearsal, what are you going to do opening night?'

Think of Nick. And give the performance of her life.

27

Amy

Gainesville, Florida, 1989

Her world was crowding in on her. She felt trapped like a fly in amber, a dead fly in a beautiful setting, admired by some, envied by others, approved of by her parents far away in Rhode Island. When she dared to think about it, she knew she was a fossilized throwback to the cultural ideal of the 1950s: the wife, mother, homemaker, helpmeet; competent, generous, attractive, and utterly devoid of her own identity.

The wedding invitation had blown the sugar coating off the staleness of her existence. Georgina had done something with her life, built a business empire, taken chances, made things happen, and now she had Nick Albert, too. Mona, as well. She'd had the guts to dump Brent when her marriage went wrong, and to keep on going when the nose job went wrong, and now there she was in New York getting ready to star in *Streetcar* and telling Amy about a millionaire widower named Sidney who was in love with her.

'I hate my life!' The sound of her own voice frightened her at first. It felt good to shout. 'I hate Lou! I hate Sandi! I hate Gainesville! I hate Florida! I hate this house! I hate Nick Albert! I hate –'

Out of the corner of her eye, she saw her grandchild clutching her Hug Bear in the doorway to the kitchen, her eyes big as saucers, her little face stricken. Amy ran to her and covered her with kisses. 'Not you, darling. Not you, my precious child. Grandma loves you. Grandma loves you to pieces.'

'Juice?'

She had to laugh. The kids today said 'juice' before they learned to say 'Mama.' Pouring the juice and placing Dakota's favorite mug into her fat little hands soothed Amy, but failed to alleviate her corroding sense of loss, of chances missed and nagging regret. That summer abroad, she shouldn't have been in such a hurry to get home. She should have stayed in London, traveled around England, maybe gone to Paris. And Italy, and Greece. All the glamorous and exciting places.

She shouldn't have let Nick Albert frighten her. There would have been other men to meet, other marriage possibilities. She shouldn't have been in such a stupid hurry to marry Lou Humphries. If she had stayed abroad then, she wouldn't be a dull faculty wife in Gainesville now. She would have Europe as her backyard – skiing in Kitzbühel, weekends in Copenhagen or the Dordogne, sunbathing in –

The phone interrupted her travelogue day-dream.

'Now what?'

'Amy? Is that you?'

'Mona! Gosh, I'm sorry I bit your head off like that! Must be PMS or something.'

They had spoken only a few days ago. What was up? Was the wedding off?

'You don't sound so hot. Is everything okay?'

'Everything's fine. Just a little tired, I guess. Must be –'

'Sure, sure. PMS. I'm tired of hearing about PMS. Listen –'

'I'm listening.' Mona's aggressiveness always made Amy smile.

'I've been thinking. You're one of my oldest and dearest friends, right?'

'Right!'

'So you've got to come to New York for my opening.'

'But –'

'I know, you told me, Lou's got exams and what not. But, hey, you're a big girl now. You can cross the street by yourself, right? So come on up to New York by yourself. You'll stay with me. Sidney and I will protect you from muggers. It'll be great. You need a break, right? The family can survive without you for a few days.'

'I don't know . . .'

'Besides, I want to seat you next to my favorite critic.'

'You mean the one who wrote those awful things?'

'What I want you to do is get carried away by my performance and keep sighing, "Isn't she wonderful?"'

'Oh, Mona . . .' Her friend knew how shy she was.

'Just teasing, kiddo. So it's settled, right? You're coming to New York, right?'

'I'll think about it.'

She would do more than think about it. She would do something about it, 'it' being more than just spending a few days in New York. It was at that precise moment that Amy Dean Humphries decided to run away from home. Not for good maybe, but not just for the few days of Mona's opening either. A month or so seemed about right: enough time to change her perspective, gain new insights, maybe 'find herself' like all those self-help books recommended.

A further, more daring thought struck her. Fearful of losing her nerve, she called Mona back.

'You're coming! Good girl!'

'You said it was a limited run?'

'That's right. Two glorious weeks.'

'Well, then. The timing is perfect. Afterwards, we can fly to London for the wedding!'

'Amy, dear – you amaze me!'

'I amaze myself!' Her knees were shaking.

Mona slipped into her favorite Bogart bit: 'This is going to be the start of a beautiful friendship. Here's looking at *you*, kid. And vicey-versy!'

For the first time in her life, Amy felt the pleasure of planning something sneaky. Mona's opening was two months away. She would wait until a few days ahead of time and simply tell Lou she was going to New York for Mona's big night. That would be all the notice he and Sandi deserved. Then, just when they'd gotten plenty sick of taking care of Dakota and the house and the meals, she'd let them know she and Mona were going on to Georgina's wedding.

She tried to visualize Lou's face when he got the news. That morning she had awakened before he did, as usual. He'd been sleeping on his back, and he seemed to be dreaming. He looked smug, she realized. Even in his sleep, he looked so pleased with himself she wanted to punch him. Still, she had reminded herself that he was her husband, and she should be making every effort to save her marriage.

The morning seemed so long ago and far away. Now, having made her decision, she could hardly believe what she had done just a few hours ago. Having dreamt as she often did about the Georgetown weekend with Nick Albert, she had decided to wait until her husband took his morning shower and surprise him by getting in with him. Naked, of course. Wearing clothes and stripping down under the water would be too much.

'Want me to wash your back, hon?' she had said, opening the glass door and stepping in behind him.

'Are you crazy?' He whirled on her in a fury. 'What's got into you? More of that *Cosmo* shit?' He ejected her bodily from the shower stall, but not before she saw what looked like a bite mark on his hip. Now, having made her decision, she could also hardly believe that she had chosen to ignore her humiliation at being ejected from the shower and had prepared breakfast as if nothing had happened.

She had to face the truth. Lou was becoming more and more careless about his extramarital liaisons. A few months ago, when they were taking Sandi out to dinner for her birthday, he had suggested one of his students as a babysitter, one 'Lovey-Ann.' A campus beauty queen if ever there was one, she had arrived in an oversize sweatshirt imprinted with voluptuous lips and the legend:

> PROFESSOR HUMPHRIES
> TAUGHT ME
> EVERYTHING
> I KNOW

If Amy thought her daughter would be embarrassed, she was wrong. Sandi thought it was real cool. She and Lovey-Ann took several classes together. At the restaurant, a campus favorite, their dinner was continually interrupted by a parade of nubile coeds stopping at their table, all of them with the same breathless, insinuating 'Hi, Professor!' Some of them knew Sandi as well. None of them acknowledged Amy's presence by so much as a glance or a nod.

Sandi beamed with filial pride. 'Isn't it cool, Mom?'

Ever the good sport, the understanding wife, Amy sipped her frozen pineapple margarita and tried to make her eyes crinkle with appreciation. 'There's no denying it. Your father's the handsomest professor on campus.'

'Thanks, Grandma.' Lou kissed her cheek, but she could see his eyes wandering to another table.

That was when she had most ardently wished she had had the nerve to tell her husband and daughter about her weekend with

Nick Albert, and let them know they weren't the only sexpots in the family.

'Forgive me for not introducing you, Amy. I can't remember their names. It's embarrassing.'

Sandi hooted. Father and daughter exchanged adoring smiles. 'Mom, you'll just have to live with it. All the girls are madly, passionately in love with Dad.'

That could have been her cue to suggest he could learn a thing or three from Nick Albert. She couldn't do it. Her dignity wouldn't permit it. For similar reasons, she had never mentioned the Bill Custis kiss at the faculty picnic. She knew Lou had seen them. He had never said a word. At the time it had been enough to know that her philandering husband had discovered she was attractive to other men.

As the birthday dinner progressed, and ever more grinning girls made their worshipful obeisance, she had floundered around for some means of salvaging her battered ego.

'Isn't that Bill Custis? Over there in the corner?'

Lou and Sandi turned to look. Amy knew it wasn't Bill Custis. It was just a way of reminding Lou of the stolen kiss.

'That creep!'

'Really? He speaks so well of you!'

Bull's-eye. Jealousy, at last. 'And just when did he speak so well of me?'

'Oh, I don't know. Must have been the day he called to see if I could recommend a gardener.'

'You might as well know he's a professional womanizer. I suppose he asked you to meet him somewhere. For an espresso? I hear he's great at espresso!'

It astonished Amy to find out how easy it was to fib. 'As a matter of fact, he did mention the new Italian *pâtisserie*.'

'Well?' Lou demanded, Sandi watching intently.

'Well, what?'

'Did you meet him?'

She took the time to sip the final drop of the margarita. 'How could I, dear? I have Dakota to take care of.'

'You better believe it.'

That's what had started her thinking, and what gradually made her see the reasons behind Lou's insistence that Sandi should resume her education while Grandma stayed home with the baby.

What he really wanted to do was to keep her occupied during the day, prevent her from developing her own interests. With Dakota on her hands, good old Grandma couldn't have romantic lunches with men like Bob Custis.

In fact, Bob Custis and romantic lunches had held very little interest for her. What she did resent — although she pretended as usual that it really didn't matter — was the way Lou had squelched the boutique idea. About the time of Dakota's birth, two of the faculty wives had invited her to be their partner in a boutique they were planning to open at the new mall.

It was exactly the challenge she needed. She had the money and time to invest, and the enthusiasm and energy to make the project a success. She was prepared for hard work. She was not prepared for Lou's violent objections. How could she even consider such a waste of time and money? Who did she think she was, Lady Georgina? Did she and those other hotshots think all you had to do was put up a sign and the world would beat a path to their door? And what about him? And Sandi? And the new baby? The family was her first responsibility.

'Tell them to forget it. All they want is your money, anyhow. Let them find another sucker!'

Arguments. Quarrels. Raised voices. Sarcasm. They upset her. She had always gone out of her way, done anything to avoid them. Mostly it had meant giving in. The boutique was of course a runaway success. But even if it had failed, she would have enjoyed the challenge and the experience.

It was clear she had to break the pattern of capitulation. Her involvement with the Gainesville Women's Coalition was another target of Lou's disapproval. Taking care of Dakota was no impediment. She took the little girl with her. Dakota and the other children seemed to sense the importance of what was going on. They played quietly and kept to a minimum tantrums, while the women of all ethnic backgrounds set up workshops on drugs, AIDS, child abuse, abortion, wife-beating, rape, and illiteracy.

The coalition activities gave her an outlet for her intelligence and her Yankee tradition of service. At first Lou had tolerated her participation, while barely listening to her dinner table reports. More recently, when she had been elected to the board of directors and had gotten her picture in the paper along with the others, he had blown his top. He didn't offer the congratulations she had expected. 'Those women have nothing better to do. They're all divorced, or dykes or something.' The old refrain: 'You have a husband, a home, and a family. We should come first.'

Sandi's position was equally peevish. 'Get real, Mom! You want me to get my degree, don't you?'

In place of carrying a baby, her daughter was now carrying a demanding eighteen credits toward an eventual degree in sociology, plus such extracurricular pursuits as the Vegan Club, Soccer, and Save the Earth.

Save-the-Amy was more like it. If anyone was going to save her it would have to be herself. Seated on a stool at the kitchen counter, Amy poured herself a cup of coffee, ice-cold and so strong from standing it could have put hair on her chest. That's the way she liked it, and that's the way she drank it when she was alone and away from Lou's testy disapproval.

'Juice?' Dakota was at her knee, smiling up at her.

'No, darling. It's Grandma's coffee.' She took the empty mug. 'No more juice until later. You'll get a tummy ache.'

A moment later she felt the child's weight against her leg. Dakota had fallen asleep standing up, with her head resting on Amy's thigh. The poor little thing had worn herself out. Tendrils of damp hair clung to her forehead. Her eyelashes were coming in, thick and dark enough not to need mascara later on. On her tiny fingernails was Sandi's green Day-Glo nail polish that Dakota had gotten Grandma to apply. She had forgotten how small fingernails could be. And how touching.

Lou was right about one thing: She *had* thought about having another child. Her biological clock had not stopped. She still had a few fertile years ahead. But not with Lou. If she actually did leave, she could choose anyone she wanted to be the father. If Sandi could have a baby out of wedlock, so could she.

'Then *you* can babysit for *me*, you little rascal,' Amy whispered softly so as not waken Dakota. She wondered if Georgina regretted never having had children, or perhaps was planning to have a child with Nick. With Georgina anything could happen, because she made things happen. Amy could learn a lot from Georgina. She still used the blonde tint formula created for her at Sassoon's. When she and Mona got to London, she would ask both of them to advise her on the next stage of her life.

Dakota stirred but did not awaken. Her body slumped like a beanbag on Amy's knee, threatening to stop the circulation. With the greatest of care, Amy hoisted the child into her arms and carried her to the wicker rocking chair in the sun room. Rocking slowly back and forth, she began to croon, 'Ah-ahhh, babe-*bee!* Ah-ahh, babe-*bee!*'

The slumbering child burrowed into her bosom. Though weaned at six weeks, the rosebud mouth obeyed the primal compulsion to root around the thin cotton surface of her T-shirt until it found her nipple. The rhythmic sucking through the fabric brought it erect. A gossamer peace enveloped them.

The phone rang. Reluctant to disturb Dakota, she would have let it ring if not for the fact that the sun room extension was at her elbow within easy reach.

'Hello?'

Click. Wrong number, crank call, salesman selling aluminum siding, they could all jump in the lake. She didn't give a hoot. Not with this bundle of sweetness in her arms.

The phone again. Didn't they have better things to do with their time? She let it ring, assuming that whoever it was would get tired. Dakota sat up and opened her eyes before sinking back into sweet oblivion. The phone continued to ring. Jerks! There was a sleeping child in this house! Couldn't they take a hint?

'Hello?' All ice. No warmth.

'Mrs. Humphries?'

'Yes.'

'Professor Humphries' wife?'

Had something happened? An accident? Heart attack?

'Yes.'

'I thought you'd like to know your husband's a great lay!'

'Who is this?'

Click.

A great lay? Compared to whom? Not compared to Nick Albert. She felt sorry for her anonymous caller. Never to have loved Nick Albert was never to have loved at all. The suckling mouth at her breast reminded her of Nick, betting her he could make her come through sucking her nipple without touching her anywhere else. She had paid him the fifty dollars.

The house was noon-quiet. Distant hints of dogs and children, and the faint complaints of sluggish cars, drifted into the back room of her mind. How would it feel to marry Nick Albert and live with him on a daily basis? she wondered.

28

Reunion in Chelsea

'Close your eyes and think of Harrods!' Mona exulted, as the Virgin Atlantic plane prepared for takeoff from Kennedy airport. She was so juiced from the triumphant events of the last few weeks she could barely contain herself. She fastened Amy's seatbelt as well as her own and stuffed pillows behind both their heads. 'In seven hours we'll be in London, can you believe it? Tip-top, old bread, stiff upper lip, old chaps, and God save the Queen, pip, pip, three cheers, and up yours!'

Mona was always able to make Amy laugh. Now was no exception, and for good reason. They'd done it. They were on their way to London, just the two of them, two of The Three Mewsketeers, returning to the original scene of the crime, the crime of having loved Nick Albert.

'Mona! Simmer down, or you'll get circles under your eyes! Let's try to get some sleep!'

'Sleep! Who needs sleep! I may never sleep again.'

'But your press conference! You don't want to look haggard, now do you?'

'Don't worry about it. It's not till the day after the wedding. If necessary, I'll wear dark glasses, More decadent that way, right? More Blanche Dubois, right?

But Mona had to admit that Amy had a point. She couldn't sit still or shut up. She'd been on a high since opening night. If there was ever a dream come true, this was it, she was living it. The 'overnight' success, after nearly twenty years. The critics hailing her as the next, the newest, the latest and greatest tragic actress since everyone from Tandy and Leigh to Geraldine Page. Everyone but John Simon, because he – thank God! – did not cover off-off-Broadway.

In a daring act of confidence and brilliant public relations, Bill Neal had sent copies of Simon's previous massacre of Mona's earlier stage appearance to all the reviewers, with a pair of opera glasses and the message 'Go look at her now.' The ploy had worked. Simon himself had attended the second night. In the lobby after the final curtain, members of the media were waiting for bloodshed. His comment, 'Does anyone know a restaurant where they serve crow?' made all the eleven o'clock news shows and was the headline for a follow-up column.

The flight attendant offered champagne the moment the wheels had left the ground. 'No, thank you,' Amy said.

'What's wrong with you? This trip is a celebration! Starting now.'

'I read this article that said you're not supposed to drink alcohol on airplanes.'

Mona took a deep breath and managed to settle back in her seat. 'You want to know something? I don't even like champagne. I'd rather have ginger ale anytime!' It was because of her mother. The New Year's Eve that Mona was three, Esther Davitsky had promised she would wake her up at five minutes to midnight and let her toast the New Year with the rest of the family. True to her word, had Esther brought her into the living room and poured her a glass of that pale amber bubbly she'd been told was champagne. Years later, at her cousin Adelle's wedding, she'd thought they were playing a trick on her. The champagne was bitter and burned her mouth. Once a peasant, always a peasant. If Prince Charming wanted to drink from her number nine slippers, it could be champagne, but if he wanted her to share a loving cup, waiter, bring on the Schweppes.

'I'm so glad you made it to the opening, Amy. I couldn't have done it without you.'

'And I couldn't have done it without you.' Lou was not yet aware of his wife's departure for London. He had blown his top when she went to New York for Mona's opening, expecting her to be back in three or four days. Her newly discovered talent for deviousness had enabled her to delay her return for first one reason then another, until the play's limited two-week run had ended and she and Mona could shop for clothes and a wedding present before flying off. The two of them would be sipping tea in Chelsea Mews by the time Lou got the overnight express letter she had mailed from the airport.

She hoped Dakota was screaming her lungs out for Grandma, that Sandi was discovering the joys of motherhood, and that Lou had been able to draw on his devoted army of Madonna clones to babysit. As a salve to her conscience, she had prepared several dozen individual portions of beef stew, eggplant parmigiana, sweet-and-sour meat-balls, and marinated chicken breasts for the freezer. If the professor had had half a brain he would have noticed there was enough cooked food for a month. Husband and daughter shared two basic kitchen skills: They could open the refrigerator and freezer, and they could operate the microwave. Good-bye, dears, and amen. She was getting tougher, all right.

'I think I've slowed down to a hundred miles an hour, kiddo. You okay?'

'Do you realize this is the first trip I've taken alone since that summer we all met?'

'Alone? What am I –'

'Chopped liver?' the two women shrieked Mona's familiar phrase in unison.

Mention of the past, and thoughts of what awaited them at Chelsea Mews this time, enveloped them in a fog of memories. Amy had not thought of those first months home from London for many years. How Lou had defended his affair with Chloe by saying it was Amy's fault for going abroad, and by accusing her of being unfaithful, too. As she drifted into sleep, she remembered how Lou had made her eat humble pie until at last he'd forgiven her and allowed her to spend hours researching his thesis and typing his notes.

Mona's thoughts were on the next few days in London. When she and Amy had finally decided to accept the wedding invitation, the enticement was their curiosity as to how Georgina and Nick had gotten together and what it would be like to see Nick in these circumstances. Now things were decidedly different, and let Georgina take note of it, too. Through his old London connections, Bill Neal had arranged for a West End production of *Streetcar*, with an English cast except for Mona.

Taking advantage of Mona's presence in London for Georgina's wedding, his co-producers were holding a press conference to welcome America's newest sensation and to announce the London production. A publicity agency was setting up interviews based on the fact that Bill Neal had 'discovered' Mona when she was his student and had instantly recognized her tremendous gifts as an actress. A quote from Bill in one press release said, 'Theatrical scholars of the twenty-first century will record Mona Davidson's

Blanche Dubois as having been the quintessential interpretation of Tennessee Williams' most complex character.'

That's telling 'em, Bill. Hype was all. Take Helen Hayes. Much as Mona admired and respected Helen Hayes, it was a press agent who had originally called her 'The First Lady of the American Theater.' Now you never read about her or heard about her or saw her on television without that reverential 'First Lady of the American Theater' in hushed tones.

Between the press conference and the interviews and the wedding Mona would have to make the time to buy Sidney a present. He had been very upset when she'd told him in no uncertain terms that she did not want him to come to London.

'I'm coming anyway. Try and stop me.'

'If you do, I'll never speak to you again.'

'You'll have to speak to me. I'm one of your producers!'

'Sid*ney* . . .!' He knew she didn't mean '*speak*' when she said 'speak.' He knew she meant she would never *sleep* with him again.

'Is it because of what happened at Macy's?'

'Don't be silly! It's just that Amy and I are staying at Georgina's. Old home week stuff. You know, a sentimental journey, lots of reminiscing and all.'

'And I'll just get in the way?'

'Well . . . yes! Not "in the way" exactly, but I'd be worrying about you getting bored. Like going to somebody's class reunion and having to hear about a lot of people you don't know and a lot of things you didn't share. Don't you see? I'll be back before you know it, and then we can have some time together.'

'It *is* because of Macy's!' He was being punished for something that bewildered him totally.

As a matter of fact, it *was* because of what had happened at Macy's, or rather what hadn't happened. What had begun as a playful whim on Mona's part had turned into a terrible misunderstanding that got worse and worse the longer it went on.

'You know what I did the first time my mother brought me to Macy's?' she had asked, mischief sparkling in her eyes. 'I was five years old. I got away from her and I ran *up* the down escalator!'

'That's not funny.'

'I thought it was adorable.'

'It's dangerous.'

Nice Girls

'You think so?' A deserted Down escalator was just ahead. 'Come on, Sidney. I'll race you.'

'Don't be childish!'

'I am childish! All great actresses are childish!' Couldn't he see? With all the pent-up emotion of the opening, and the plaudits, and everything else, she had to do something silly or she would explode. 'Come *on*!' Why couldn't he understand?

He tried to hold her back. She broke free and galloped up the descending steps like a mountain goat in a modern ballet, nimbly skirting a lone shopper who stood transfixed as she passed.

She kept going at an exultant trot, not caring that he would spend the next hour trying to find her and that he would eventually return to her apartment exhausted and hurt. Trying to explain her actions had been like reading a book to a horse. He had nodded a lot, but just didn't get it.

Nick Albert would have gotten it. He'd have loved it. He'd have bounded up the escalator behind her, patting her ass all the way to the top, and then danced her back down like Fred with Ginger. Was that a reason to adore one man and barely tolerate another? The real reason she didn't want Sidney with her in London was that she frankly wasn't sure how she would deal with watching Nick marry Georgina.

She was sure to be depressed and jealous. If she was going to have the green-eyed abdabs, it was better to be alone. She could just picture herself in bed with Sidney the night of the wedding, turning on him like a wounded tigress. It wasn't his fault he wasn't Nick Albert. Realistically, he was better for her than Nick Albert would ever be, but in the long run, not during the next week. Poor Sidney. If she had let him accompany her to London he wouldn't have understood her moods and behavior any more than he'd understood what had happened in Macy's.

'I say, I say, I say – any of you *Ameddicans* in need of a nice place to stay?'

Happy the bride-to-be, Lady Georgina Crane was the epitome of upper-class elegance as she stood poised at the arrivals gate, her two corgis, Di and Chuck, straining at their leashes. The two Americans reacted as they had that first day in Chelsea Mews – with feelings of nervous insecurity and social clumsiness. Whatever their accomplishments and status in America, each remained in the thrall of their aristocratic friend with her glossy mane of chestnut hair, the Lagerfeld suit, Chanel slingback shoes and quilted shoulder bag, and the satin skin that could have made dermatology obsolete.

The shrieks and hugs did not totally bridge the gap between the Americans and their hostess. Once in Georgina's stick-shift Rolls and on the road back to town, conversation lagged.

Georgina rose to the silent challenge. 'I suppose you're both pissed because in all these years I never once let on about Nick. I couldn't help myself. I never stopped seeing him, you know. Very inventive. We both were. It added to the excitement. There was the inn we found on the Devonshire coast, virtually deserted in the dead of winter. And the QE II. Did you know one can book a cabin just for the overnight voyage from Le Havre to Southampton? And once, when he and The Frog were in New York at the Plaza, I flew across and booked into the Sherry Netherland across the way. A hop and a skip for our Nick. He managed to get Roxanne piss-paralyzed on Moët Chandon, pour her into bed, and be with me before midnight! We could see the Plaza from my suite. Nick put a basket of flowers in Roxanne's window. When her lights went on, Nick grabbed his boots and ran!'

But her favorite escapade had taken place at the Hotel Splendido in Portofino, when The Frog broke her shoulder water-skiing at Monte Carlo. 'She had to be in hospital; the Princess Grace Hospital, mind you. And you know what Nick did? He hired a seaplane so he could leap down to Portofino to spend the night with me!'

Aware of her passengers' speechlessness, Georgina's poise floundered. 'Sorry about that. Nattering away like a fishwife. I've never been able to tell any of this to anyone. I hoped the two of you would understand.'

They assured her they did.

'I never got him out of my system, you know.'

Mona and Amy nodded soberly, each for her own separate and private reason.

'So when do we see the charming groom?' Mona asked.

'He's absolutely longing to see you both. Teatime, I thought. That gives us masses of time to get you settled and have a girls' lunch so we can let down our hair.'

The two guest rooms were a dramatic improvement over their earlier accommodations as students. By gradually buying up the mews houses adjoining the original, Georgina had gutted the interiors while maintaining the facades, and created a luxurious compound for visitors as well as herself. Her expansion included a state-of-the-art kitchen and laundry, a billiard room and library resonant of her grandparents' era, and a bedroom suite for herself that belied her usual understated taste with its Cecil B. DeMille glamour: the bed on a platform, the ankle-deep fitted carpets, the film-star bathroom with its double tub, terrarium, and massage cubicle. And soon, what she had planned for all these years, Nick Albert.

'Wow!' was all Amy could manage to say when Georgina had left them to freshen up before 'toddling along' for lunch.

'She did say "toddle," didn't she?' Mona inquired ironically. 'I still don't believe they talk that way. I'm still convinced that when they're alone, they talk the way we do. *Brolly, telly, wellies, bickies, stickies, knickers, knackered* – and *toddle*? Amy, old bean, do you think one can *actualleh* manage to *toddle*?' While gratified by Amy's laughter, Amy still being the baby of the crowd and still looking up to her, Mona knew she'd better get a grip on herself. She was talking too much.

Alone in her bedroom, Georgina checked her private-line answering machine for messages. Finding none, she rang across the mews to the office. Dierdre's message log was crammed as usual with calls from around the world – confirmations, questions, invitations, everything Britain's New Tycoon might want to hear with one exception. Not a word from Nick. The sickening possibility was intolerable to contemplate: *He's done a flit. He's gone back to The Frog*. Annulment or not, Roxanne had a hold on him, whatever he might say.

Yesterday had proved that. As was her regular habit, Georgina had stopped by Fortnum & Mason's to see what new items they were stocking and what the tourists were buying – market research for her own shops and overseas catalogs. Tea, salmon, chocolates, the usual; nothing much changed at Fortnum's; nothing to indicate any new trends in buying patterns; nothing for her to apply to her Junque Shoppes marketing strategy.

It was a glorious day, much like the day she had met Nick in Bond Street. The forthcoming wedding heightened her feeling of sentimentality. Strolling up Piccadilly in brilliant sunshine, she had peered up Bond Street toward Asprey's, tempted to revisit the scene of the crime. But no, Nick was coming for drinks and a discussion of his plan for an offshoot Junque Tours company, offering specialized guided tours with upper-class twits like himself as guides. Harking back to what he had been doing when they'd met, he waxed lyrical about how the Americans especially adored the Royal Family and the British cinema. They would pay through the nose to see the block of flats in Kensington that Lady Di had shared with friends during her courtship with Charles, and for older tourists, particularly the women of course, Princess Margaret's secret love nest on the London docks, where she and Tony Armstrong-Jones had courted, and Clarence House, where Elizabeth and Philip had lived before she became Queen.

The cinema possibilities were even better: Castle Howard in Yorkshire, where *Brideshead Revisited* had been filmed; Lyme Regis in Dorset, for *The French Lieutenant's Woman* locations: and of course, 165 Eaton Place in Belgravia for the *Upstairs/Downstairs* exterior.

'Not too close to Eaton Square,' she had chided him. That was where the D'Orsainvilles kept a penthouse flat. Still, Nick's idea did have definite possibilities. He had a good head on his shoulders. Too bad he had wasted his talents all these years. Georgina could quite easily keep him in style, but that wasn't the point. The man had brains and imagination and personality. He wanted to work. Together they could build an exciting, productive life.

That's what she had thought until yesterday afternoon, when a Number 19 bus slowed down invitingly alongside her as she tried unsuccessfully to hail a cab. Dangerous but exhilarating, a good way to get killed, it made her feel young and carefree to hop aboard. Although she had traveled on the crimson double-deckers most of her life, her success had meant cars, and drivers when needed for convenience and to save time.

It was hard to remember the last time she had indulged her childlike passion for climbing the half-spiral of swaying steps, fingers crossed that one of the upper front seats would be free. Lucky in love, she settled into the right upper front seat with its dirigible view high above the traffic, much better than being in motor car really. A sudden break in the traffic flow allowed the bus to pick up speed. As it careened left to get around Hyde Park Corner, she saw a tall, elegant man emerge from the Hard Rock Café, way off to the right on the far side of Piccadilly. He looked exactly like Nick, and he was with a woman. Before she could dig out her spectacles for a better look, the bus veered into Knightsbridge.

Silly cow. It couldn't have been Nick. Was she so infatuated with him that she was seeing him wherever she looked? It couldn't possibly be Nick, for one simple reason. She had sent him down to Buckinghamshire to introduce himself personally to the people who made the red telephone boxes the Americans were gobbling up like boiled sweets. It was her way of getting him involved in the business, and if anyone could get them to step up production, it was Nick. He could talk the birds off the trees. Even if he had driven like a madman, he couldn't possibly have made it back to London before drink time.

Drink time came and went. There having been no sign of Nick by eight, Georgina ran the water in the double tub and poured in a generous splash of patchouli and citron oil, a combination recommended by her aroma therapist to leave her sensual and relaxed at the same time. And slippery, which was the way Nick liked her.

She lay against the plump, terrycloth-covered neck rest and closed her eyes, surrendering herself to the warm, wet fragrance that lapped and licked her skin. There was a simple explanation, of that she was certain. The wedding was three days away. Nick would not do anything to spoil their happiness now. Adrift in a zone comparable to sleep, she became aware of the distant ringing of a telephone.

Dierdre, would you please . . . Unaware of the time and of where she was, she couldn't understand why her assistant didn't pick up. Slowly she realized she had fallen asleep in the bath. The ringing phone was right beside her, on the little wicker stool at her elbow.

'Nick?' Who else would it be? 'What the hell happened to you?'

'Not Nick! It's his wife. You know, The Frog? I know that's what you call me. Nick and I find it *très amusant, chérie*!'

First thing tomorrow, Georgina would arrange for a new unlisted number. She was not about to have her privacy invaded by this stupid woman.

'You'll excuse me, Roxanne, if I don't continue this scintillating conversation.'

'I'm ringing to warn you. If you go through with this absurd mockery of a wedding, I will kill you. I told that to Nick this afternoon, and I'm telling you now.'

'This afternoon Nick Albert was in Buckinghamshire.'

'Really? I had the impression he spent a jolly afternoon with me at the Hard Rock Café – until we felt we needed more privacy and retired to my flat in Eaton Square.'

Lying bitch!

'Go to hell!' Georgina hurled the phone against the bathroom door just as it swung open. Nick Albert presented himself, naked under the silk paisley dressing gown she had given him as one of many welcome-back prezzies, allowing it to fall open to reveal his state of readiness.

'Sorry to be late, darling. I've got something truly important to tell you.'

Did she really want to know?

He dropped the dressing gown and slid into the double tub beside her. 'I've been desperate and lonely for you all day. Let me show you how much I've missed you and want you.'

Her eyes closed in the thankfulness of surrender. *Pathetic. It is pathetic, my passion for this unmitigated louse*. But she couldn't help herself. It was sick but she didn't care. With a practiced toe, she turned the hot water tap. With a praticed hand she found the pot of patchouli and replenished the bath. Her hair sopping, her nostrils flaring from the rising heat and penetrating fragrance, all she could think to say was, 'I love you, Nick. God help me. I do.'

He drew her close, to place his face in the crook of her neck. 'I love you, too, Georgina.' His slender, graceful hand glided purposefully over her breasts, then down the valley between them to her belly and beyond. 'Especially when you're slippery.'

In the first light of dawn she reached out for him, only to find him gone. 'Nick?' Where was he? 'Nick, where are you?' The bathroom? The kitchen? Making the coffee? Staggering out of bed, she saw what looked like blood on the mirrored bathroom door. It was a message from Nick, written in lipstick.

'Couldn't find a bloody pen. Unfinished biz. See you teatime. Love. N.'

It was sheer providence that the Americans were arriving this morning. Going to the airport took her mind off the hideous possibility that all her patience had been for naught. His note had said teatime. She would wait until teatime. Then, if he failed to appear, she would be forced to do something. Exactly *what* was the

Nice Girls

question. In the meantime, there was lunch with the Americans to amuse and divert her. She had to admit both of them had worn well over the years. They were in fact her only 'real' friends. She had avoided intimacy with women, to protect her secret life with Nick Albert. Professionally, she was well liked by women in fashion and politics and the media. She was good value, for she kept her word and could be counted on for charity drives. Women invited her to their dinner parties and country weekends; she reciprocated with great style in Chelsea Mews. The countryside failed to attract her. She preferred weekends in town.

She made up her mind to banish Nick Albert from her thoughts and enjoy lunching the Americans and remembering old times. They gathered in the original mews house. The old sitting room and the three small bedrooms were now one enormous sitting room, with a skylight roof and an eclectic mix of old and new furnishings put together by David Hicks.

'The Three Mewsketeers!' They clinked glasses and collapsed in laughter as the memories poured forth.

'I owe you a lot. More than you know,' Georgina told them. 'If you two hadn't pushed me I'd never have become the Junque Lady. I'd be selling knickers from a barrow in Petticoat Lane!'

They covered everything – Mona's divorce, the nose job that had nearly killed her career, and the triumph in *Streetcar* that was going to make her a star; Amy's marriage to the handsome professor, her daughter's elopement, and the birth of Dakota, 'the most beautiful child in the world.'

'Except for Greg and Melissa, of course!' Mona's pride in her own motherhood had to be defended.

As the afternoon progressed, they discussed the economy, health, George Bush, John Major, AIDS, living wills, rock and roll, Liz Taylor's husbands, and whether Princess Diana achieved orgasm. In short, they talked about everything but Nick Albert.

Mona and Amy scrupulously avoided the subject. Finally Georgina said, 'I'm sure you're longing to hear about Nick. I know you both fancied him. Who wouldn't? But that was nearly twenty years ago. You probably don't even remember what he looks like.'

Neither of the two dared to exchange glances or make small talk while Georgina fetched a recent photograph.

The Americans agreed that he hadn't changed a bit, that he was still wildly attractive.

'But when do we see him in the flesh?' Mona asked bravely.

Georgina adroitly changed the subject. 'Remember those CARE parcels Mona's mother used to send?' World War II had ended more than two decades before their summer together, but that hadn't stopped Esther Davitsky from sending chocolate bars, canned salmon, teabags, and instant coffee.

'And what was that story about your Uncle Jake?' Georgina prompted. It was the oldest Jewish story in the world, one told by every Borscht Belt comic from the beginning of time.

'You mean about Uncle Jake getting hit by a Fifth Avenue bus?' Mona asked.

That was the one.

Mona knew audiences well enough to see something was bothering Georgina. She was laughing from the nose down; her eyes were tense.

'Well, now. Uncle Jake is crossing Fifth Avenue when from out of nowhere, a bus knocks him down. People come running. A woman wipes his face with her handkerchief. A man rolls up his jacket as a pillow under Uncle Jake's head. The ambulance comes and the driver kneels down next him. "Mister, Mister, speak to me. Are you comfortable?" '

From the expectant look on their faces, Mona thought that if *Streetcar* failed she could always get a job doing stand-up.

' "Comfortable?" Uncle Jake shrugged. "I got a few dollars set aside." '

Amy blushed as fiercely as ever. 'Mona, I have a confession to make.'

'Who am I, Mother Teresa?' The wine had gone to her head.

'I remember the first time you told that story. Mona – I didn't get it!'

Gradually the laughter slowed, the talk ran out. It was after five o'clock. The question hung over them like a storm cloud. Where was Nick?

'My darlings, you must be jet-lagging like mad. I can't imagine where Nick is. Must be held up somewhere. That is the bliss of a mature romance. One needn't fret over the other's whereabouts every waking minute.'

Mona took the cue. 'I wouldn't mind having a nap.'

'Me, too,' Amy echoed.

Georgina's distress was evident to them both. They all agreed to have a little rest and decide later what to do about dinner. By then Georgina was sure to have heard.

'We forgot to give her the presents!' Amy remembered when they were back in their rooms. She and Mona had bought silly things like edible panties for a gag, and a magnificent solid silver picture frame for real.

'Maybe we should wait. Maybe there won't be a wedding.'

'I'm surprised at you, Mona Davidson. That's a rotten thing to say. Georgina wouldn't have had those expensive invitations printed if there wasn't going to be a wedding!'

29

A Wedding to Remember

It was becoming painfully obvious to the two Americans. Nick Albert had flown the coop. In the three days since their arrival in Chelsea Mews, they'd seen neither hide nor hair of him – not at teatime their first afternoon, not at the dinner party Georgina had organized in their honor the following night, not during any of the preparations leading up to tomorrow morning's ceremony at St. Columba's.

Georgina's excuses had worn decidedly thin, as she fondly apologized for his need to clear up some business affairs in Paris, see to a sudden emergency in Zurich, collect the wedding suit being made for him by his tailor in Milan. 'Such a bore, really!' Georgina blithely brushed aside his absence as nothing more sinister than thoughtless procrastination and disorganization.

The intimacy of their girls' lunch had been replaced by tension. Stiff-upper-lip in action, Mona thought. While their hostess continued to overwhelm them with hospitality, she erected a formidable invisible barrier between them and herself. The rock of Gibraltar, Amy thought.

'No more pussyfooting, Amy. We've got to make her talk to us. Something's rotten in the state of Denmark, right?'

Georgina's bedroom door was closed.

'Georgina? It's us. Mona and Amy. We've got to talk.'

'The door's open.'

She was at her dressing table, removing her makeup with huge wads of cotton wool. 'Have a pew.'

She knew why they were there, but chose to regard them with mild curiosity.

'Georgina . . .'

'Do stop dithering.'

'We're worried.'

'Whatever for?'

'Nick – has anything happened? Is there anything wrong?'

'What could be wrong? In case you've forgotten, we're getting married tomorrow.' She turned her attention to a pot of moisturizer, which she began to apply to her neck with slow, upward strokes. 'Good stuff this. Off the counter at Boot's.'

'Georgina! Stop with the small talk! We're your friends! Where is Nick?'

Georgina slowly and meticulously tissued away the residue of moisturizer, and only when she was satisfied that her neck was clean did she turn to them. 'Bless you both. I know things have been rather awkward. It's Roxanne, his ex. Threatening to disrupt the wedding. Threatening to shout the annulment's not legal, that she signed the papers under coercion. She's really gone round the bend, that one. Nick's been seeing his lawyers in Paris, and his lawyers have been seeing her family's lawyers, warning them her behavior will disgrace the family name. The Baron has paid out a fortune to keep her out of the papers. But all the British and European press will be at the church tomorrow. Even he would be powerless to stop them if she got up to anything nasty.'

Amy smiled with relief. 'Then it's okay? Then he'll be here?'

Georgina jumped to her feet and embraced both women. 'Silly-kins! Of course he's coming. How stupid of me! I was so busy with all the details, the wedding breakfast, the flowers, the press, I didn't realize for a moment you two were worried I'd be left standing at the altar. In point of fact, Nick rang up just a few minutes ago. From Paris. He's chartered a plane for first thing in the morning. He'll be at Gatwick by nine, and St. Columba's in time for the eleven o'clock ceremony.'

'Isn't he coming here to change?'

'Mona, darling. You know it's bad luck for the groom to see the bride before the ceremony!'

Mona said, when the two had returned to their rooms, 'Doesn't sound kosher to me.'

'You mean you don't think she's telling the truth?'

Georgina was telling the truth, at least as much of it as she dared. According to Nick's frantic phone calls over the last few days, the Frog had gone totally bonkers. The problem was the video-tapes. The Baron had locked them in his private safe, away from all prying

Nice Girls

eyes, while quite stupidly forgetting that Roxanne knew the combination.

Her actual threat was worse than that she would merely disrupt the wedding ceremony. She was going to give the tapes to the media. If Nick was to go through with the marriage, she didn't care what happened to her or her father or the D'Orsainville name. Privately, rumors of his sexual proclivities might amuse the Baron. But even with his multinational interests and political power, he could not risk the scandal of incest. While the tapes were too shocking for television, he knew copies would be bootlegged by the thousands to everyone with a VCR, including his enemies.

It was true that Nick had rung from Paris less than an hour ago. The Baron had threatened Roxanne with commitment to a psychiatric hospital if she didn't return the tapes. At which point she became 'meek as a child,' as Nick described her. The Baron forced open the cassettes with a letter opener and cut the tapes into pieces. The three of them watched the debris burn in the library fireplace.

'She won't be bothering us again, darling,' Nick had assured Georgina. He adored her. He longed for her. He would see her, bright-eyed and bushy-tailed, tomorrow at St. Columba's.

'Be careful, love. It may be foggy over the Channel.'

'You know what a good pilot I am. Never had an accident yet.'

The morning could not have been better or brighter. Mona and Amy awoke to a feeling of optimism and joyful activity. The caterers had arrived early to set up the vast marquee over half the mews for the buffet, bar, and bandstand, with the tables and chairs out in the open and bordered by enormous tubs of daisies and spring flowers. The army of helpers swarming everywhere with their separate tasks reminded Mona of the filming of a commercial.

It was too bad all this would be gone by tomorrow when she was having her press conference to announce the London production of *Streetcar*. Georgina would be off on her honeymoon, of course – just a few days in Jamaica, she said. 'By all means, have them here. Use the house. Anything you like. You're going to take London by storm, Mona, and I'm going to be able to tell the world it all began in Chelsea Mews!'

In honor of the occasion, Georgina had shut down the offices for the day. The entire staff had gone ahead to the church by the time the Rolls and driver appeared to collect the bride and her two attendants. Georgina emerged into the soft sunshine of the mews an exquisite vision in the palest of peach silk, breathtaking in its simplicity, her burnished hair a gleaming halo, her makeup but a subtle glorification of her alabaster complexion. Her jewelry mixed emeralds and pearls, the exception being the square cut diamond engagement ring she had bought herself to match the slender wedding band tucked in her handkerchief to give Nick at the altar.

'Going somewhere special?' Mona asked. 'You look spectacular.'

'Should do. They've been at it since dawn.' Her retinue of makeup and hair people wished her luck and headed for the church. She held out her hands to the Americans. 'Not too shabby yourselves!' Mona heaved a sigh of relief. For once in her life, she was wearing the right thing. Back in New York Esther had dropped in at the apartment to say good-bye, and had had a fit when Mona showed her what she was planning to wear. Esther had insisted the dove-gray Donna Karan suit was too plain for a fancy London wedding. Why not a cocktail dress? Something dramatic? She was an actress; she should dress like an actress.

'No, Mom. In London you dress up by dressing down. Right, Amy?'

Amy's choice reflected her New England heritage and her life as a faculty wife – a dress and jacket in a muted glen plaid, with a single strand of pearls and matching earrings. Her thick blonde hair and slender athletic grace belied her age.

'How do you like Amy-the-grandma? She still looks eighteen, right?' Mona enthused.

The Three Mewsketeers paused for a moment in a rush of remembrance. 'I'm so glad you invited us, Georgina.'

'I'm so glad' – her voice faltered – 'so *truly* glad you came. We'd best go before my mascara runs!'

As they neared the church, Mona gave Georgina the garter she had schlepped all the way from Bloomie's for the 'something blue.' Amy gave her the antique lace handkerchief she had carried at her own wedding for the 'something borrowed.' Their sweetness and generosity touched her deeply. They were her oldest friends. They had come all the way from America to stand up for her. She wondered if Nick was having her on, with his story of having bedded both of them over the years. Or was he getting back at her for her affair with Roberto? She had thought of confronting them, just to clear the air, but decided to let sleeping dogs lie. If it was true, it might be something each of them would prefer to keep secret. She would wait until they were all old and gray and in their rocking chairs. By then it wouldn't matter. Then they could all have a jolly good laugh.

Turning into Pont Street, the Rolls found itself trapped in a traffic jam of cosmic proportions. What looked like hundreds of excited people crowded the pavement in front of St. Columba's Church. Frenzied men and women with video equipment and note pads darted this way and that, shouting into portable phones. At the sight of the Rolls a great roar went up, as the mob pushed toward them and surrounded the car.

'I'm impressed! You're more famous than I thought!' Mona said.

'This must be what it's like to be royalty. Look at them! It's scary!' Amy added.

Georgina was frankly bewildered. 'I thought there'd be a few press people. Nothing like this. It's only a wedding. What can they be expecting? The Queen?'

Before the driver could get out, the passenger doors on both sides of the car had been flung open, accompanied by shouts of 'Georgina! Over here, Lady Georgina! Look this way! Tell us how you feel! When did you first meet Nick Albert? Where . . .'

'Please, everyone!' Georgina tried to extricate herself. 'After the wedding . . .'

'Georgina!' Through sheer force, a disheveled Dierdre had managed to push her way to Georgina's side, her face contorted with fear. 'There's been an accident. He's dead, Georgina! The word just came through. Nick Albert is dead!'

'No . . .' was all Georgina could say. 'No-o-o-o-o-o.' One of the more resourceful reporters had found the Constance Spry gentleman waiting inside the church with the bridal bouquet. Without so much as a 'Sorry' he snatched it and thrust it into Georgina's trembling hands. 'Bridal flowers become burial flowers!'

'Dierdre! For God's sake, help me!'

The new responsibility transformed the quiet mouse into a roaring panther. 'Get on either side of her!' Dierdre commanded the dumbstruck Americans. 'And follow me!'

Her girlhood experience as captain of field hockey had prepared Dierdre for just such an emergency. Using elbows, fists, and knees as truncheons, she formed them into a flying 'V' and battered their way through the straining, screeching mob to the church door.

Once inside, Dierdre led them to the little retiring room, where the bride was meant to wait with her attendants for the wedding ceremony to begin.

'For pity's sake, tell me what happened!'

'His plane went down in the Channel. Early this morning. A fishing smack saw it and radioed the authorities. They found the wreckage, but –'

Georgina's voice was firmly under control. 'But *what*, Dierdre? Stop dithering like an old woman!'

'But no body.'

'Then how do they know Nick was flying the plane? He'll stroll in here in a minute and have the laugh on all of you!'

'They checked the registration – the hire firm said they had rented the plane to a Nicholas Albert.' The news of the crash hit the wire services. Someone must have noticed the name and Bob's-your-uncle, the gutter press was out in force.

'Vultures! All of them!' They could hear the hubbub surrounding them inside as well as outside the church.

'Sorry, Georgina,' Mona said, having remembered the Brits always seemed to say 'Sorry' whatever the situation. ('Sorry! I spilled soup in your lap.' 'Sorry! The man you love has crashed into the sea.' 'Sorry, old beanbag. Frightfully sorry about that.')

A timid Amy tentatively asked, 'Should we go back to Chelsea Mews?'

To no one in particular the Lady Georgina announced, 'We are staying right here. We have no proof Nick's dead. He'll probably swan in here any moment full of the joys.'

It took nearly an hour for the three other women to convince Georgina of the truth. By then she had calmed herself into a state of icy acceptance. 'I suppose you're right. No point staying here – in this chamber of connubial hope. They must be wondering what's happened to us at the mews. We'll have to figure out something amazing to do with all that food and drink.'

The minister had respected Georgina's shock by guarding the door, permitting no one to enter. Mona opened the door a crack. 'We're going to try to slip out,' she whispered.

'You'll need to do more than that, I fear,' the minister responded. Nobody had left the church. The wedding guests had remained where they were, gossiping among themselves, exchanging tidbits of new information as it was filtered through to them by the increasingly rambunctious media contingent waiting outside.

Nice Girls

Mona had an idea. 'I know you're devastated, Georgina, but I think you owe them all the courtesy of a few words.' Before Georgina could protest, Mona went on. 'Listen to me. Don't get sore. Just hear me out. I think Nick would like it, too!'

Mona explained her plan and, with Georgina's consent, opened the door and stepped into the maelstrom. The years of stage training served her well. She gave herself the combined power, menace, and authority of Catherine the Great and Elizabeth I. As she entered the foyer, the clamor quieted down. The crowd parted like the Red Sea. Eye contact, that's what Bill Neal always preached. Capture their eyes, capture their hearts. The nod to the left, the nod to the right, the condescending smirk of majesty inspired by a million miles of news footage, and then she was inside the church itself, causing a tidal wave of speculation among the assemblage.

'Ladies and gentlemen!' The acoustics were wonderful. Her voice rang out mellifluously with a rich, compelling undertone. 'May I have your attention?' As if she needed to ask. Their tongues were hanging out. You could have heard a pin drop.

'My name is Mona Davidson. Like all of you good people, I came here today to this beautiful church to attend the wedding of our dear friends, Lady Georgina Crane and Nicholas Albert.' She paused to heighten the tension. Good. They were teetering on the edge of their seats. 'As all of you know, there has been a terrible accident. The groom's plane crashed into the Channel and he is presumed dead.' Another pause. 'So of course there will not be a wedding. But . . .' She permitted herself a wan smile as she made meaningful eye contact with those closest to her, prolonging the suspense as long as she dared.

'But Georgina feels that Nick wouldn't want to cheat you out of a good party. He wouldn't want you to mourn him. For Nick Albert, life was a continuous celebration. So here's what we're going to do. Instead of the wedding breakfast you were all invited to attend in Chelsea Mews, we're going to hold a memorial service for Nick tomorrow morning precisely at dawn.

'And where would be the appropriate venue for an Albert Memorial? Where else but the steps of *the* Albert Memorial, with champagne, caviar, a dance band and the brightest, gayest people in London to give him a glorious send-off!'

In a final fit of inspiration, Mona improvised a heartwarming anecdote. 'Georgina remembers Nick's passion for poetry, and how he adored reciting Christina Rossetti because her middle name was Georgina, too. His favorite lines make Lady Georgina feel he had a premonition:

> When I am dead, my dearest,
> Sing no sad songs for me;
> Plant thou no roses at my head,
> Nor shady cypress tree.'

A hushed silence, punctuated by sobs. Not a dry eye in the house. 'Remember everyone. Be at the Albert Memorial tomorrow morning well before dawn. As Nick would say, come as you are – evening dress if you're coming from Annabel's, nightdress if you're coming from bed. Bring cushions and rugs. The steps may be cold. We want to be gathered and ready, our glasses full and raised in his honor just as the sun comes up.'

'You're quite mad. How did I let you talk me into this?' Georgina lay back exhausted, as the Rolls was finally allowed to pull away from the church. A Nicholas Albert Memorial at the Albert Memorial? The ladies and gentlemen of the press were beside themselves with anticipation.

'What else would you do with all that food?'

'And what's all the codswallop about Nick and Rossetti? "Sing no sad songs for me"? When did you hear Nick say that?'

A slip. 'Oh, that! An inspiration of the moment. I thought all you English cut your teeth on Rossetti and Byron and all that crowd.'

'Clever you!' Georgina patted her arm.

Amy put in her two cents. 'We had to memorize both Rossettis for English orals.'

Georgina was quick to realize Amy felt neglected. 'And you're the cleverest of us all. An orderly life. A handsome husband. A brilliant heartbreaker of a daughter, and the most scrumptious grandchild. You must tell us the secret, Amy.'

Amy blushed with embarrassment and uncertainty.

A question had been growing larger and larger in Mona's mind. She could no longer contain it. 'Why don't you tell us *your* secret, Georgina?'

'Mine? What secret?'

'Is Nick really dead?'

'Mona! How can you ask Georgina such a thing? Can't you see how upset she is?'

'Calm down, Amy. I'm talking to Georgina. If *my* fiancé had crashed into the sea on my wedding day, I'd be off the wall.'

'As you so often say, stiff-upper lip and all that! We English hide our emotions,' replied Georgina.

'You didn't answer my question. Is Nick really dead?'

'I really won't know until they find his body or –'

'Or he shows up?'

'With amnesia, like the old Ronald Coleman movie I saw on television,' Amy said. '*Random Harvest*. So romantic.'

Back at the mews, Mona hadn't shaken the hunch that maybe Georgina knew more than she was saying. She reminded herself that Georgina hadn't been exactly up front about the relationship – not a hint of anything until the wedding invitation had arrived, after all.

But the tragic intrigue had begun to pall. What happened between Georgina and Nick had nothing to do with her, was just a waste of her time and energy. She should be concentrating on her own agenda and the more important reason for her trip to London, that reason being Mona Davidson and the forthcoming London production of *Streetcar*.

'Sidney?' He answered on the first ring. 'It's me.'

'Mona?' He sounded wary, depressed. She really had hurt him. God in heaven, what was the matter with her? This man believed in her. He loved her unconditionally. She needed him with her. She could count on him.

'You sound odd. Are you alone?' She enjoyed pretending to be jealous of nonexistent models and stewardesses she accused him of seeing.

'Of course I'm alone!' There was a hint of pleasure in his sulkiness.

'I don't know, Sidney. I can't leave you alone for five minutes! What's that perfume I smell!'

'Oh, Mona – you're too much for me. I can't take it anymore. You've got me running in circles. I give up. I'm not in your class. I know that now. You were right telling me to stay home. I'd have embarrassed you in front of your fancy friends!'

Flirting with him was like digging a hole in cement with a nail file, but so what? In this case, and with their history together, absence was making the heart grow fonder, or at the least more practical.

'Sidney, I have a question for you. Is your passport up-to-date?'

How could she ask such a question? 'Of course it is! You know how careful I am about things like that. Why?'

'I miss you, Sidney. I want you to drop everything and get your butt over here. Right away. Like first thing tomorrow morning, okay?'

With a man like Nick Albert, a woman was always the satellite. With a man like Sidney, she was the center of the universe. Maybe in the fullness of time Mona would have what Amy had, a solid marriage to a good solid man.

What she didn't know was that Amy was also making some decisions about changes in her life. Lou had made no attempt to call her. Nor had her beloved daughter. They were both probably too angry with her for having left them in the lurch. 'What else have you got to do, Amy?' The words still rankled.

Dakota was the one she missed, that squashy little bundle of sweetness. Playing grandma had reminded her how much she enjoyed motherhood. She was still young enough to have another baby, but not with Lou. He had made it clear he was against it. Sandi wouldn't like it either. There were no two ways about it: She had to make some basic changes, but nobody was going to do it for her, she had to do it herself.

She envied Mona and Georgina. They were so sure of themselves, so much in control of their lives. They went after what they wanted. She would do the same.

As for Georgina, she knew what a superior pilot Nick was. She had meant what she'd said. She would not be convinced of his death until she saw his body with her own eyes. To make time pass, she worked alongside the catering staff in the mews. The poor creatures had waited for hours to serve the wedding breakfast following the wedding that never was. They'd salvaged whatever food would keep overnight and packed it and all the champagne on ice, ready to set up at the foot of the Albert Memorial in the darkness before dawn.

30

The Albert Memorial

Hordes of people began arriving hours before dawn, experienced night people with sleeping bags and sandwiches, the same people who lined the Mall the night before royal weddings, people Georgina had never met and who didn't know her or Nick Albert.

They had heard about the memorial service on BBC News at Ten, and here they were for the show. They knew their place, however, and maintained a respectful distance between themselves and the wedding party gathering on the granite steps and adjacent grass. Most of the wedding guests were there in force. This was a not-to-be missed event that everyone would dine out on for months to come.

With mere minutes to go before dawn, the valiant members of the press showed up, eager to chronicle the aristos at play. The recent public acceptance of breakfast television brought out rival crews with remote equipment. As a pale peach glow spread slowly across the eastern sky, heralding the new day, waiters passed among the invited guests with trays of champagne.

The modulated tones of the BBC announcer could be heard, describing in meticulous detail the one hundred and sixty-nine life-size figures on the white marble frieze at the base of the memorial, the camels, the elephants, the eight bronzed angels, and the fourteen-foot statue of Queen Victoria's beloved consort, seated under a Gothic canopy strewn with white mosaic daisies.

Having set the scene, he recapitulated the tragic event of the previous day and how what was to have been a happy celebration of a wedding had become a memorial to the bridegroom. 'And now for a word with Lady Georgina, who organized this tribute to *her* beloved Albert – Nick Albert. Lady Georgina, may I say how very beautiful – albeit sad – you look on this beautiful and sad occasion?'

Georgina accepted his homage with a brave sigh.

He slithered in snake-like for the kill. 'But don't you feel some might think it presumptuous to compare your loss with that of the Queen of England?'

Mona would have knee'd him in the crotch. Amy would have died on the spot. Georgina didn't miss a beat. She looked at him, and then directly into the camera, with grave compassion for his unmannerly abuse of her bereavement. 'I'm certain Her Majesty Queen Victoria would think of me as a woman who, like herself, has lost the man she loves.'

At that moment, the first golden rays of the sun bounced off the solitary cross one hundred and seventy-five feet above them.

'Raise your glasses everyone! To Nick Albert!' Mona cried.

'To Nick Albert! To Nick Albert!' The crowd rose to its feet as one, glasses held high, all eyes on the huge gothic monument as the sun slowly bathed it in light. Where the massive figure of the prince sat in eternal loneliness, another figure slowly emerged, a slender figure in black, the face obscured by the shadow of a crushed fedora.

'My God! It's Nick!' a woman shrieked.

'No! It's his ghost!'

'An apparition! The sun is playing tricks!'

The figure dropped gracefully from Prince Albert's lofty perch and stood poised in the enormous archway.

'He's alive! I knew it! Silly bugger!' Laughing and crying at the same time, Georgina tried valiantly to push her way through the stunned celebrants. 'Please . . . let me through . . .'

'Watch out! He's got a gun!'

'He's mad!'

'He's going to kill us all!'

The crowd froze in mid-motion, like the terrified figures of Pompeii, watching in horrified disbelief as the silvery pistol rose slowly toward them, paused, and then changed direction until it found nature's tunnel to the brain, the ear. The muffled shot hurled its victim into the air like a paper doll. It seemed to soar above them before floating downward in agonizing slow motion, until finally the law of gravity forced it to earth.

'Why, Nick? Why?' Georgina threw herself on the body, frantic to find signs of life. Why had he done it? Getting married didn't matter, as long as they were together. 'Please, someone! Call an ambulance!'

Darling! Please don't die! Pressing her fingertips to the pulse points of the wrist, she realized the hand she was holding was not Nick's. The finger-nails were crimson, a woman's exquisitely manicured nails. The fedora covered the cropped blond hair of Nick's mirror-image. Roxanne's eyes fluttered open. Seeing Georgina, she grinned in triumph. 'Did you think I'd let him go? I poured sugar in his petrol tank. I thought I could live without him, but I can't. We're the same person, the same body, the same soul.'

'Please, Roxanne . . . we've sent for an ambulance.'

She was hallucinating now. 'Fooled you, didn't I? Got the idea last night on the 10 o'clock News. *Une bonne idée, oui?* Nick would laugh like a drain, wouldn't he?' Her body collapsed like a deflated balloon, her final words a barely audible gasp. 'He's mine. Forever.'

Nick Albert was not dead, not until she saw his dead body. Georgina was more certain than ever that he was somewhere in the English Channel, clinging to a piece of wreckage. Any minute he would be found and brought home to England. Quite dispassionately, she blessed Roxanne. When Nick got back there would no longer be an obstacle of any kind. At last they would be able to marry, only next time it would be at a register office, no fuss, no bother, just the two of them together at last.

EPILOGUE

Sudden celebrity generates its own peculiar etiquette. Anyone thrust into the media limelight knows intuitively how to respond. Decades of watching film stars, politicians, royalty, mobsters, lottery winners, and victims of everything from rape, fraud, and the random absurdities of love and nature, have shown viewers how to behave when their turn comes to deal with the feeding frenzy known as the media.

In the case of the mysterious disappearance of Nick Albert on his wedding day, coupled with the flamboyant suicide of his former wife and half-sister, what the good Lord tooketh away the good Lord gaveth to those immediately involved.

For the next few days, Chelsea Mews was in a state of siege. Being a cul-de-sac, there was only one way in – and out. Because of Roxanne's wealth and notoriety on the Continent, and the presence of the two Americans including the acclaimed actress, Mona Davidson, the press contingent included *Paris Match, Oggi* and other European picture magazines, and the American supermarket tabloids, as well as the British press and several international television crews.

At Georgina's request, the Chelsea police posted a constable to prevent the hordes from stampeding into the mews itself. While a point of law could have been invoked as to the mews being a public thoroughfare, the Lady Georgina contended that an Englishwoman's home was her castle. She owned the entire mews, and therefore it was private property.

This obstacle only served to tantalize those forced to watch and wait. Each entering vehicle had to pass inspection. One delivery van containing a camera crew and poke holes devised for just such journalistic situations was inspected and turned back.

When Bill and Sidney arrived they were asked to prove they weren't journalists, and were both about to be sent on their way when Mona spotted them and went to their rescue. All three posed briefly for the cameras. Mona, somber in her demeanor, explained how shocked and saddened Lady Georgina was by what had happened, and that she would have a statement for them later in the day.

Bored and frustrated, some of the press was starting to pack up and leave when Lou Humphries pulled up in a taxi and gave them the interview they needed. Yes, he and his wife, Amy, were close friends of Lady Georgina. In fact, Lady Georgina had personally taken care of him when the family was visiting London and he fell ill. Not only that, he and Amy also knew Nick and Roxanne, had spent time with them in the south of France and in fact had been invited to cruise with them on their yacht, but were unable to do so because of previous plans.

He was heartsick over the tragedy. 'Something told me I shouldn't have let my wife come all this way alone. I should have come with her, but I didn't feel I could abandon my students. Maybe if I'd been here, I could have stopped it from happening.'

Tall, tanned, athletic-looking, the deeply concerned professor concluded his remarks with tears in his eyes and a catch in his voice, 'I have two reasons for coming. To offer my support to Lady Georgina in her hour of need, and to bring my wife home.'

For Georgina, the byword was 'dignity' in this her time of grief and despair. The circus atmosphere might swirl around her; she would remain serene at its center. If she handled herself well she would come out of it smelling like a rose, a beautiful English rose, lucky in business but unlucky in love, a strong yet vulnerable heroine who now might consider running for parliament after all.

That Nick's body had not been found fortified her conviction that he was alive, a belief she thought best not to express since it might spark speculation of a conspiracy. Better to put on a brave face and soldier on – chin up, and all that.

In time for the evening news, the Lady Georgina Crane, immaculately coiffed and looking wan yet pluckily in control of her emotions, welcomed the press into the mews. Standing on an improvised platform with her friends and staff around her, she expressed her gratitude to the press for their patience and understanding and to her friends and staff for their loving support in her time of need.

As for the double tragedy of the past two days, she swayed slightly, and then by a conscious effort regained her composure. 'What I had hoped would be one of the happiest days of my life has turned out to be the saddest. Nick Albert and I had tremendous plans for a future together, plans that included selling British goods and services abroad and doing our part for British tourism. As a woman, I am heartbroken. As a member of society, I shall pledge myself to the economic growth of Britain and to the many charities that merit all our support.

'My sincere sympathies are extended to the Baron D'Orsainville for the loss of his daughter. A divorce, however amicable, can have an unforeseen impact on a woman as sensitive as Roxanne. We shall never know what impelled such a drastic and tragic act. I shall carry the memory of her fatal beauty with me forever.'

Her words hit them like a steamroller. Touched by her show of emotion, their questions were respectful and subdued. Only when Georgina gracefully thanked them and prepared to go inside did a Fleet Street old-timer recover sufficiently to throw a spanner in the works.

'Is it true that Roxanne D'Orsainville made a dying confession to you that she had murdered her ex-husband to keep him from marrying you?'

In the stunned silence that followed, Georgina reflected that if she was indeed going to stand for parliament, this was a good test of her ability to think on her feet and deal with tough questions.

'Roxanne died in my arms, as you know. She was quite incoherent at the end. All I could make out was "Forgive me, forgive me."'

'But what about Nick's plane? Are there signs of tampering with the plane?'

Georgina stretched out her arms in a supplicating embrace of them all. 'I'm sure there'll be a report from the authorities in due course. Forgive me, but I must go in. The thought of anyone tampering with a plane makes me quite ill.'

Amy, like the others, was awestruck by Georgina's performance. Such poise, such style, just like Jackie Kennedy after the assassination. It blew Amy's mind that anyone, a woman especially, could handle a tragedy of such proportions so well.

'Why did you come?' she asked Lou point-blank.

'I'm your husband. I thought you might need me.'

'I've needed you before.'

'Look, let's not go into it now. I've come to take you home.'

'I really don't need you to take me home. I'm quite capable of getting on a plane by myself.'

'You're telling me! How do you think I felt getting a message – a *message* – saying "Guess what, I've gone to London"! What was *that* all about?'

'How's Sandi? And the baby?'

'Don't change the subject, Amy. This is serious.'

Serious? Never in her life had she been more serious. The past week had been her metamorphosis. She had gone from being an elderly girl to an emerging young woman, able to see the world as it really was rather than as portrayed by the sanitized family sitcoms of her childhood.

She remembered what Nick had said to her during that weekend in Georgetown, when in a moment of intense tenderness she'd told him how desperately she'd been in love with him in the old days in Chelsea Mews.

Her confession had angered him, or as much as Nick Albert ever showed anger. 'You weren't in love with me. You were in love with England, an England that doesn't exist now, if it ever did. The man you think I am doesn't exist!' He recalled how one of his blue-haired ladies had told him he reminded her of Leslie Howard in *The Scarlet Pimpernel*!

'You Americans have seen too many films about the compassionate bloke behind the foppish facade.' He had pulled her very close, their noses almost touching. 'Look at me, Amy. Look close, dear heart. I *am* the foppish facade. There is nothing inside. I am a Potemkin Village. I amuse the visitors. I fool them, but not myself. And from this day forward *not you*, unless you let me, and I pray you never let me.'

'I'm taking you home to Gainesville. We have things to discuss.' It was her husband speaking, but he seemed to her a stranger.

She would return with him to Gainesville, There were certainly things to discuss. For one thing, the University of Miami School of Architecture had announced an autumn course to be given by the legendary Vincent Scully, Jr. She planned to apply for admission. If accepted, she would live in Miami and commute to Gainesville on

Nice Girls

the weekends. Later, she would return to London to attend the new Institute of Architecture sponsored by Prince Charles. Her passion for British archictectural history, which had brought her to England in the first place, was as strong as ever. Hearing of the Prince of Wales's announcement, she had taken a taxi over to Regent's Park to see the two classical John Nash buildings that would house the new school.

She remembered hearing a story about the poet John Betjeman, who had been known for his irascible behavior. When he didn't like the look of a house he would literally kick it as hard as he could, with the hope of knocking it down. It was not her immediate intention to kick her house down, or to leave it forever. Rather she wanted to change the living arrangements and responsibilities of its inhabitants.

In her mind she said to Lou, 'I'm not the woman you think I am, or want me to be. I can only be the woman I am, and I need time to find out who that is.' One day very soon she would find the appropriate moment to tell him to his face.

Eventually, the press coverage of Nick and Roxanne and Georgina shifted to Mona. From playing the loyal, devoted Best Friend role in Georgina's drama, she now stepped stage center as the star of her own production. The press that had swarmed like vultures over Georgina stayed to cover Bill Neal's press conference.

'You look extraordinarily pretty, my dear. And so slim. Have you lost weight?' Sidney stood by, beaming like a proud parent, as Bill Neal whispered his sincere and heartfelt praise.

Lost weight had she? She could have said, 'Yes. I've lost one hundred and seventy-five pounds: Nick Albert.' Or she could have said, 'It's the English food, right?' Or she could have masked her pleasure with the Garbo bit she always parodied when stress made her talk too much: 'Giff me a viskey – chincher ale on the side – and don't be stingy, babee!' Not now, kiddo, save the jokes. With the cameras and reporters swarming through Chelsea Mews, she waited quietly with Bill and Sidney and the English producers in Georgina's enormous formal sitting room to welcome them.

Bill Neal introduced himself as the man who nearly twenty years earlier had found a brash young American student on the doorstep of the Royal Academy of Dramatic Arts, and who had known at once that one day that student would return to London in triumph as the star of a play that he would produce. 'Mona Davidson in

Streetcar Named Desire is a sublime example of hands-across-the-sea between Broadway and the West End. We need each other. We nourish each other,' he said.

'When *Streetcar* opened on Broadway in December, 1947, the role of Blanche Dubois was played by an Englishwoman, Jessica Tandy. Now, more than four decades later, we are proud to present it on the English stage with this outstanding American actress, Miss Mona Davidson.'

Kissing her on the cheek, he whispered, 'They love you. I can tell.'

She could tell, too. For reasons she couldn't fathom, she was the kind of American the Brits like. Whatever it was, her New York humor, her sassy Streisand style, her power to drive men mad . . . okay, okay, why try to figure it out as long as she continued to have it?

Loving her did not stop them from asking hard questions.

'Vivien Leigh played Blanche in the first London company, and of course won an Oscar for the film. What makes you believe you can replace her?'

'Nobody could ever replace Vivien Leigh!' except Joan Plowright, of course – an observation not to be made at *any* time, *ever*.

'Blanche Dubois is a faded flower of the old South. What part of the South do you come from?'

Bill and Sidney stepped toward her, as if to shield her from provocation. Waving them back, she grinned her appreciation of the jest. With the superb nuance and acutely observed inflections she brought to her voice-overs, she sighed theatrically and said in a voice straight out of Louisiana, 'The gentleman asks what part of the South I come from? Truth compels me to admit I do come from South . . . Brooklyn!'

They were hers. She could do no wrong.

Asked the name of her favorite English playwright, she said Noël Coward, then proceeded to sing with perfect Noël Coward diction, 'I'll *seize* you again . . .'

For the just-one-more photo session, she remembered to project hot sexuality by visualizing Nick Albert flicking his tongue in the corners of her mouth. It was a visualization that always worked for her in auditions and was clearly sending her message now, even as she maintained a certain decorum.

Just as their demands were becoming excessive, Bill Neal stepped forward to end the press conference.

Nice Girls

'Ladies and gentlemen. We thank you for this generous welcome. Mona – and Blanche – join me in expressing our appreciation for the great kindness shown us by Lady Georgina at her time of tragedy, and to all of you for giving us your valuable time. We expect to open in the West End in October, at a theater to be announced. For all of us, thank you and God bless.'

'Please, Mona, one more question!'

Mona was so juiced she could have gone on for hours. Bill bowed to her with exaggerated gallantry and kissed her hand, murmuring, 'Trust me, Mona. We leave while they're begging for more.'

Hands clasped at her chest, Mona curtsied in somber obeisance to her courtiers, her eyes lowered demurely until with an impish wink she concluded the conference.

The following day she and Sidney moved into a river suite at the Savoy and spent the afternoon buying gifts for Melissa and Greg. 'Don't let me forget my mother!' After the New York opening, Esther had given her ten pages of notes suggesting five hundred ways to improve her performance. To show her anger, she had not called her mother before leaving for London. She had vowed not to buy her anything. It wasn't just because of the unwanted critique: it was because Esther always returned Mona's gifts and credited them to Mona's account.

'Stop throwing away your money like a drunken sailor! Who knows, you might need it some day. Like tomorrow, maybe?'

Thanks, Mom, your confidence touches me deeply.

They found the perfect gift at Harrods, a Spode tea service for four. It would serve a dual purpose. Esther would not be able to return it. She would be able to use it to impress her weekly bridge game with her daughter-the-star's generosity, while worrying herself sick that Mona's spendthrift ways would lead inexorably to the poorhouse.

'Now it's your turn, Mona. I'd like to get you a present.' Since arriving in London, Sidney had been walking on eggshells, as if terrified of making a misstep and being banished once again. 'Something personal, I thought.'

'What, pray tell, did you have in mind?' *My God, I'm simpering like a schoolgirl!* Coy was hardly her style – she was too tall – yet suddenly it seemed amazingly appropriate. This shy, grinning man was about to ask her to marry him, and she could actually feel her eyelids fluttering in expectation.

Sidney hesitated as if striving for a precise answer. 'Oh, I don't know.' He did know, of course. He was trying to be suave. 'What about a ring of some kind?'

'What kind did you have in mind?' An engagement ring was what he was trying to say. She had never had an engagement ring. Come to think of it, she had never been engaged.

'You'll see.' With his hand tightly clasped to hers, he asked a boutonniered assistant for directions to the jewelry department.

'Sidney, darling . . .'

'Don't argue, Mona. I won't take no for an answer.'

'But, *Sidney* . . .' She forced him to a halt and pulled him around to face her. 'You haven't asked me the question!'

'What question?' he teased. 'Were you by any chance expecting me to ask you a question?' He was gazing playfully into her eyes when something behind her caught his attention. 'Come with me!' They zigzagged through a group of startled shoppers to an adjacent doorway. Beyond it loomed a bank of escalators. 'Remind you of anything?'

Macy's! He couldn't still be upset by that truly childish incident! Or could he?

'Ready, Mona?'

That of course, was the real question. Was she ready? Perhaps this moment would be a metaphor for their future life together as, with shouts of glee, they scrambled hand-in-hand up the Down escalator.

'Ready!'